I0602043

About the author

Max Cutcliffe was fortunate to grow up in Tasmania, many parts of which were yet unexplored, many mountains still untrodden. His mother christened him 'the wanderer' and wander he did, always in search of adventure or a higher mountain to climb. He climbed on five different continents, but the sixth, Antarctica, he had not considered. As a child he had learned that Antarctica was for great explorers like Scott, Amundson, Shackleton or Mawson, men of science with financial support from many wealthy sources. Antarctica sadly wasn't for him, but during a later return visit to Hobart his mother handed him a newspaper open at the 'Positions Vacant' page and remarked that there might be a suitable job there for him. He stared at one job-offering in disbelief. Impossible, he thought. An organisation called *The Australian National Antarctic Research Expeditions* had apparently built stations on the Antarctic coast and now wanted scientists and tradesmen to man them. Despite not having the qualifications asked for, Max nevertheless filled in the application and posted it immediately. Amazingly, a few weeks later, he was offered a job at Mawson Station. He later learned that he had been chosen because of his experience on high mountains and glaciers — something most Australians, at that time, knew little about. Max spent two years at Mawson Station, assisting surveyors, glaciologists, botanists and geologists, who needed support while ascending mountains or traversing unknown ice fields. For his work in Antarctica, he was later awarded the Polar Medal and had a mountain named after him.

The novel you hold was inspired by many of his experiences in the deep south.

NO TRAILS TO MAWSON

Max Cutcliffe

NO TRAILS TO MAWSON

Vanguard Press

VANGUARD PAPERBACK

© Copyright 2021
Max Cutcliffe

The right of Max Cutcliffe to be identified as author of
this work has been asserted by him in accordance with the
Copyright, Designs and Patents Act 1988.

All Rights Reserved

No reproduction, copy or transmission of this publication
may be made without written permission.
No paragraph of this publication may be reproduced,
copied or transmitted save with the written permission of the publisher, or in
accordance with the provisions
of the Copyright Act 1956 (as amended).

Any person who commits any unauthorised act in relation to
this publication may be liable to criminal
prosecution and civil claims for damages.

A CIP catalogue record for this title is
available from the British Library.

ISBN 978-1-80016-074-3

*Vanguard Press is an imprint of
Pegasus Elliot MacKenzie Publishers Ltd.*
www.pegasuspublishers.com

First Published in 2021

**Vanguard Press
Sheraton House Castle Park
Cambridge England**

Printed & Bound in Great Britain

Dedication

This book is dedicated to my many Antarctic friends.

Acknowledgements

I would like to acknowledge the dedicated assistance of my partner, Cath Morris Williams, for her help in editing and formatting this book.

CHAPTER 1

As the moon fleeted through the clouds, she saw it!

"Ice!"

Her piercing yell froze my spine, catapulted me from my bunk, forced me to leap up the companionway towards the lonely figure in the yacht's cockpit. Frantically Betty was turning to starboard.

"Where? Where?" My face flattened against the glass, eyes searching urgently the blackness ahead. Then I saw it. God! Fear shivered through my body. A mountain of ice ahead — Dead Ahead. I flung Betty from the wheel — too late to go about — strained the steering to its limit. The silver-streaked wall of peril all but grazed the bow as we swung across it into a line of angry breakers. Neither of us breathed. Waiting, waiting for the inevitable crash. But then the moonlit edge of the iceberg slid past the glass to reveal a starlit patch of sky. I bit my lip, strained even harder on the wheel. We might... we might just... Suddenly it was gone from view. We'd made it! Blood surged back into our ghostly faces. Each of us exhaled lungfuls of stale air. We'd made it! Thank God! Cleared it by centimetres!

But then came the sickening crunch of ice against the yacht's Ferro-concrete hull. I stiffened — petrified. "No! Oh, Christ, no!"

The bow shot skywards, snaked left, then right, shuddered to a halt. Our bodies hurled forwards against the glass, were flung backwards onto the floor, an avalanche of books, clothes, mugs, instruments, poured across the cabin. Amid the noise and chaos other voices were heard. Evan, Julie, stumbling up the companionway, falling, shouting, struggling to regain their feet.

Then there was silence.

My eyes opened to pitch darkness. A dream? It had all been a dream. We were safe. I sighed heavily — a horrible nightmare.

"John?" It was Julie's voice. Why was she shaking me? "What... what happened, John?"

Her voice was ghostly — compelling. What was she saying? Then she shouted. "Evan, Betty, help me, please help me, John's hurt!"

But I wasn't hurt — only dreaming — mercifully it was only a dream. "Stop it, Julie! Stop shaking me!"

"We've hit ice!" Evan shouted into my ear. "Get up, come on, John, get up."

His powerful arms locked about my waist, hauled me to my feet. My head was clearing. Hit ice? A dream? No! No! It can't be, they're joking!

"What will we do, John?" Evan's booming Australian voice demanded. "Come on, mate, you're the skipper, what'll we do?"

"Shut up, Evan! For Christ's sake shut up! Let me think. Get the lights back on — what's wrong with the bloody lights?"

"Here's a flashlight," he snapped. "Let's look at the damage. Do you think we're holed?"

The doctor's persistent voice annoyed me further. "How the hell do I know?" I took a moment to compose myself, drew in several deep breaths, then uttered a command that terrified even myself.

"Dress quickly; ready the inflatable; prepare to abandon ship!"

Anxious feet followed me through the hatchway of the enclosed cockpit and out onto the steeply tilted deck. The cold sliced though our clothes yet went unnoticed as the terrifying scene unfolded before us. I blinked my eyes, opened them immediately to the fearful massive shadow looming above — looming over us — ice poised to crash down and smear us bloodily across the deck. The restless sea smashed angrily against the iceberg's sheer face, leaping upwards like wild hounds in pursuit of their prey, thundering through blowholes, then in deluges of freezing spray rained down on the ever-restless sea and its tiny imprisoned intruder. Water eruptions whipped up by the disoriented wind danced like menacing warriors around the yacht and beat noisily against its drum-like sides.

From the uplifted bow, Evan and I flashed our lights fearfully over the hull without sighting any damage. The twelve-metre sloop had apparently slid smoothly onto the submerged spit of ice and was seemingly resting unscathed.

"I think we're OK," the doctor said quietly. "Maybe just a little paint scraped off!"

If only he was right. But I had built this vessel from scratch and knew every plank on her intimately, and wasn't so easily convinced. Was she resting too low on the ice? Or was it my imagination? No. Something was wrong; something was radically wrong!

I turned to shout to the girls, but my instructions were unnecessary; already they had furled the mainsail and stopped the flapping. Then, deep in thought, I faced Evan, staring solemnly into his dark bearded face. "All right, cobber, go and help Julie and Betty. Launch the inflatable!"

"The inflatable?" he half shouted in reply. "You're crazy, John. We're OK. There's no damage! We can rock her off the ice, we can…"

"For Christ's sake, Evan, do it! For once in your bloody life, do what you're fucking well told!"

Racing back through the cockpit and down the companionway I then traversed a mountain of debris strewn across the cabin floor, pulled myself up into the forward bunk-room, flashed my light urgently over the bow. Nothing! God Almighty, could we really have escaped such an impact? If praying would help, if holding my breath… I searched feverishly for damage that *must* never be found, yanked open the forward locker, swung the light to and fro across the shamble of spilled stores. I froze!

They were wet!

Evan called from above. "Is everything OK, John? Shouldn't we be trying to get her clear? We could… John! You've dropped your light. You OK?"

I looked up and snapped back into reality. "What? Yes of course I'm all right! I'm going below. Keep your light on me." Frantically I began tossing the spilled food stores behind me. Coils of rope and cartons of engine spares followed. Then came the sopping wet sails. For a second I hesitated. Our whole destiny lay beneath these sails! I dragged them aside as if opening a stage curtain and heard a gasp of horror from above. What I feared, what I dreaded more than anything imaginable lay before us. The entire underside of the Ferro-concrete bow had been pulverised. A two by one metre section had been completely ripped out to reveal the bare ice we were stranded upon. Around the hole, jagged chunks of concrete lay smashed and forced inwards, still bonded to twisted steel rods and torn wire mesh.

I sank onto the wet sails and wanted to vomit. There was nothing we could do. In minutes the ice would release its grip and the yacht would slide back and sink straight to the ocean floor. We were finished! How long could we survive aboard the inflatable in these temperatures? A day? Probably even less! Evan was mumbling something above my head. Gradually his voice again became discernible. I looked up. "What... what did you say?"

"You heard me. What will we do? You're supposed to be an engineer, how are we going to repair the damage?"

"Repair it?" For an instant I nearly laughed, but then anger again surged through me. "Repair that?" Now I was shouting. "You bastard, Evan, this is your fault — all your fucking fault. If it hadn't been for you and your high and mighty ideas we'd nearly be in Aussie by now. Repair it! Of course. Stick a bloody Band-Aid across it. Use a drop of iodine to stop it hurting. There's nothing to worry about, there never is with you, is there, Evan?"

"Come on, John, take it easy. We can discuss this later."

But I wasn't about to be pacified. The pent-up venom within me was now free and rampant and bursting to escape. "Admit it, Evan. You talked us into leaving the shipping lane. Everything had gone so smoothly right from Vancouver. Yet on the final leg of the voyage — a mere few weeks from Fremantle — you insisted we deviate south to collect marine specimens and do water analyses. God knows why! So you could write some bloody scientific crap and make a big name for yourself, I suppose. It's true, it's true, isn't it?" I continued without letting him reply. "The rest of us wanted to hurry to Aussie, but you harped and harped until we gave in. Nothing to worry about down there you convinced us, a bit cold, maybe, a bit rough, but icebergs? Oh, no, there were no icebergs that far north! Well, my dear Doctor Jackson, you'll never write that paper, because at any minute we're going to slip back and go straight under — straight to the bloody bottom — straight into Davey Jones' locker!"

"OK, OK. Cool it, John! That's off your chest. Now let's consider survival. What do we do next?"

I stood up, half my body above the hatch, legs still weak and trembling. Suddenly I noticed that Evan's hand was equally unsteady.

My fearless friend was as scared as I was! Somehow this realisation renewed my strength, and as I glanced into his green flashing eyes, I suddenly felt sorry for him. It was time to contemplate our next move, but then the hull shuddered, squeaked loudly, began to slide.

"OUT!" I yelled.

We snatched up our oilskins while racing through the cabin, but then, miraculously, the movement stopped. I hesitated, took a few breaths of icy air, then hurried to where the girls were holding the inflatable alongside, their heads bent low to avoid the deluge of freezing spray raking the deck. Still no trace of daylight?

"Get aboard," I said, trying to appear calm.

"But why, John?" Julie asked anxiously. "Is it so serious?"

There would be time for explanations later. "Cast off the instant the yacht moves, and then stand by to pick us up."

Neither of the girls moved; they just stared back at me.

"Get aboard, *now*!" I ordered. "Our bottom's ripped open, the yacht's going to sink!"

"Evan, get the sleeping bags, all the clothes you can find, food, water; pile everything aboard. I'll get a Mayday off — there might be a whaler nearby."

I groped my way through the debris in the cabin, raised a light to the radio transmitter — stopped dead! "Oh, Christ, no! Not that too!" The set had been wrenched from its mounting; dashed to the floor. I felt sick again. Why were we being tormented like this? If we're going to die, let's die and get it over with; spare us this pain! I thumped my fist on the bench in anger, but then uttered a brief prayer. "Give us a miracle, God, make this bloody thing work!" I composed myself as Evan rushed past with another bundle of sleeping bags, then picked up the radio, re-plugged the cables that had jerked out, nervously shoved it back into position. "Come on God, make it work!" I switched on. Hope exploded within me as the dial light glowed. A half minute to warm up — an eternity! I pressed the transmit button. "Mayday, Mayday, Mayday." My eyes glued on the signal output meter. Nothing moved! "Mayday, Mayday." I thumped the set, wriggled the cables. "Mayday, Mayday." Still nothing! In desperation I yanked the set forward in search of the trouble, and smelled something burning! Smoke began pouring from the cabinet! The dial light flickered, then failed completely!

"DEAD! Bloody DEAD! As dead as we'll soon be!"

Grabbing the navigational instruments and a few maps I hurried uneasily back onto the deck. A band of orange now washed the horizon and tinged the wave crests pink as they pranced across the still darkened ocean. I avoided another glance at the iceberg. The bitterness of the wind was now alarming. Before, from the security of our warm cabin, the decreasing outside temperature was considered somewhat of a novelty. But now it quickly coated my beard with frost and caused each of us to pull on gloves and balaclavas for protection. Evan was waiting, holding the rope that secured the bouncing inflatable.

"Did you get everything of importance?" I asked.

He stared at me for a second, wiped the ice from his face to mumble, "All we can carry."

"Radio's smashed." I mentioned it as if of little consequence, but he never replied, only the widening of his glazed eyes told me he had heard. "OK, then, let's get going."

As Evan half-heartedly hauled in the mooring rope, the yacht suddenly gave another quiver and lurched sternwards.

"She's going! Quick!" I grabbed the rope to help, pulled frantically, but then as suddenly as the sliding started, it stopped again. We stepped into the inflatable and cast off.

Betty stood up, her short ebony hair now greyed with frost, and faced us silently as she waited for an explanation. Julie, however, in her soft Canadian accent was much more vocal. "I'm freezing," she complained. "We'll all freeze to death out here. Can't we go back and warm up? Surely you can patch the hole. Then we can get off the ice and continue on our way. Everything will be all right... I know everything will be all right, but first we have to warm up..."

"No, Jules," I interrupted. "Everything won't be all right. The yacht's too badly damaged. You could walk through the hole in the hull. The moment she slips clear of the 'berg she'll go straight under." Poor Julie, I hated terrorising her with the truth. "But don't worry, honey, we'll be picked up in no time. There's lots of whalers in the area, maybe even a supply ship. Don't worry, we'll be OK, you'll see."

A rope length from the yacht our drift was halted and the inflatable swung around into the breeze to begin riding the undulating swell as it surged beneath the flimsy plastic floor. The iceberg at least afforded some shelter from the much rougher seas on the other side. The wind, however, came at us from all directions, drenching us in icy spray and swinging us to and fro at the end of our tether. We tucked the spare sail tightly around us and half cowered in the still air beneath.

Julie wriggled back into her sleeping bag and buried herself beneath a pile of clothing at the stern. Poor kid, I felt deeply sorry for her. I moved over and kissed her lightly on the forehead, forcing a smile from her pale face and at least reminding her she wasn't forgotten, that I still loved her, that I still wanted to marry her. Then I shuffled back to where Betty was sitting in the bow.

"We're going to die, aren't we, John?" She was outspoken and, as always, very courageous, yet sensitive enough to glance around to see if Julie was listening. "A few hours after leaving this sheltered area we'll either be swamped or freeze to death. Look at me. Already I'm numb all over, no feeling left in my feet, my voice is becoming slurred. First year at Oakland Nursing School taught me about hypothermia. You'll see! Sit here for an hour and you'll see what I mean. If some ship doesn't respond to your SOS and get here before nightfall then... then, it will all be over. We'll be finished. QED."

I gazed into Betty's lovely dark eyes — reading her thoughts and fears — then told her about the radio: that no Mayday call had gone out, that no ship had any idea of our latest position, that she was right, only a miracle could save us now. Her thick lips parted slightly for a second, then closed firmly. No further conversation seemed necessary. She folded her arms across her stocky body and turned away to stare back at the yacht. For a few more moments I continued to stare at my American friend's lovely olive complexion and, for a short time, remembered our London days together.

"She should have gone by now," I mumbled ten minutes later to anyone listening. "Just held by a tiny knob of ice. Any one of those waves could take her off."

"And if they don't?" A muffled male voice responded from deep inside a sleeping bag. "What if she stays firm for a couple more hours, isn't there anything we can do to save her?"

Evan's question never warranted an answer. A week on a slip wouldn't even patch her temporarily.

All conversation then died completely. I turned to gaze back at the yacht and could now read her name in the intensifying hue of purple morning light: *Evening Star*. It seemed only yesterday that Julie had broken a champagne bottle across her bow and the cheers went up from so many envious members at the Royal Vancouver Yacht Club. *May God go with her and all who sail in her*. It was at this club, I remembered, that Julie and I first met. She simply appeared in her coveralls one morning and began helping with the painting; the most beautiful blonde girl I had ever talked to. She smiled a lot, but seldom laughed like Betty, and often seemed far away in deep thought. A typical schoolteacher, I supposed. "Name your yacht after a star," she said to me at dinner one night. "And you'll never get lost at sea." Another afternoon we watched a golden sunset from Stanley Park until the last tinge of crimson vanished from the sky and the first bright star appeared. "There it is," she whispered excitedly. "There's your star — Venus — call her after Venus, call her the Evening Star."

The *Evening Star*. Three years of hard work to complete. The cold was already making me drowsy. It was so easy to dream. Down the Pacific Coast to Panama. Glorious weeks cruising the Caribbean. Across the tormented Atlantic Ocean for some wild celebrating in Capetown. Then, after five years' absence from Australia, all that remained before a great homecoming and our long-awaited marriage, was the placid Indian Ocean. Julie had contributed to a truly happy voyage — a pre-honeymoon, I suppose — and Evan and Betty were the other happy couple. Perhaps they too would marry in Australia. The last thought jolted me back to realism. There would be no marriages now. Poor Julie, if she hadn't picked up that pot of paint and got to know me, she wouldn't be here freezing to death on this godforsaken ocean. I've killed her, I've killed the only girl I really loved! In a spate of remorse, I tossed back the sail and sprang to my feet. I can't let this happen! Something... something has to be done! But what? Nothing *was* possible. The *Evening Star* was doomed. A patch? Evan had suggested a patch. A two by one metre patch? Impossible! The water pressure would blow it out in seconds. Unless... unless we had lots of stays to secure it! Again, I cast an eye back to the yacht; she hadn't budged in twenty minutes. No one was budging under the sail either. Had they already given up? Should I just let things take their course, or…

"Evan!" I called, pulling back the sail from above his head. "Are you awake?" There was a mumble of response. "We're going back. We're going back to try that patch you suggested."

He still never replied, but gradually raised himself until he was able to grasp the mooring rope and slowly haul us back to the yacht. Two other mummy-like heads appeared as we came alongside.

"Same procedure as before," I told the girls. "If the yacht begins to slide, row back quickly and pick us up."

Betty jumped to her feet. "No way, John," she called angrily. "Julie and I are not staying in this inflatable to freeze any longer, we're coming aboard too. Do you think we can't move as fast as you guys? Besides, we all need something to eat."

I shrugged. What was I trying to save them from anyway?

It was a relief to shelter again in the cabin from that piercing wind and to shed our heavy oilskins and massage our half-frozen limbs until the blood flowed freely once again. Our lighting problem was easily rectified by knocking a damaged breaker from the board and twisting the two wires together. At least this minor success proved that not everything was against us! There was no time to explain anything to Julie despite my desire to do so. I simply touched her bewildered face and forced a smile as her questioning eyes followed me back and forth as I darted from one end of the yacht to the other. I found Evan on his stomach in the forward bunk-room gazing forlornly through the storage locker trapdoor at the huge jagged hole. "Ideas?" I asked urgently.

He sighed. "If we had some plywood and lots of timber… but even then, it would take a day or…"

I interrupted. "We don't have a day, mate, maybe not even a half hour, but we do have lots of timber." After another brief survey of the damaged bow, I sprang into action with a very improbable plan. The fire axe would serve to clear some working space around the damaged section. "Stand clear, Evan." With one blow, the side of the central bunk flew to the floor and, with several more, the rest of the bunk and its underneath locker was reduced to lengths of lumber and plywood — all in a few seconds when it had taken so many days of loving care to build. Then I smashed into the locker above. Evan scrambled to stack the lumber. The girls darted forward between blows to rescue the released contents. Next, I destroyed the port-side bunk and lockers, rested a moment while the pieces were cleared away, then I hacked into the floor itself. A full half hour had passed before a large section of the Ferro-concrete hull lay bare before us.

Evan was now thinking ahead. He tossed down a waterproof tarpaulin and helped drag it over the hole. This we covered with a spare sail. Next came two mattresses from the demolished bunks which we squashed into the contours of the bow. What to hold all this down with? The cabin table! Another few blows with the axe and that was isolated and laid over the mattresses. A few more plywood pieces were fitted to cover the remaining gaps. We then started spacing solid timbers across the whole patch and nailing everything together.

Now the real work would begin. At least a dozen stays had to be cut and fitted between the cabin ceiling and the patch to hold it firmly in place and withstand the outside water pressure.

"You mark them," volunteered an unusually eager Evan. "And I'll saw…"

Everyone froze! "Hell… we're sliding again! Run! Run for your lives." But then, mercifully, the yacht stopped. We stared at each other for precious seconds, hardly daring to speak or move, but we had to. I threw up the first timber for Evan to cut.

With a frantic burst of speed, I wedged three stays into position to partly secure the table, then nailed some shorter diagonals from these to hold down the edges. Another eight or so main stays might afford some degree of hope! Evan passed the next one down, but again we froze. Once more the vessel was sliding! We dropped our tools and stood tensed: ready to run.

"She's not stopping," I called. "This time she's going!"

The ice ground like gravel beneath the hull as the yacht gained momentum. "Stop! Stop! Please stop!" But it wasn't to be. With a loud splash we crashed back into the sea and shot away from the iceberg.

Then, in gushed the water!

A dozen firemen's hoses seemed to have been turned on together, deluging the entire cabin area in walls of freezing spray. I leapt clear with the crew. "Go!" I ordered. "Abandon ship!"

We had failed! I turned to flee with the others, but stopped short of the companionway. Then, for some inexplicable reason, I returned and leapt back into the erupting water — jumped onto one side of the patch. My weight stopped one gush but started others on the other side. Already it was above my knees! Another half hour and she would be gone. There was no hope of saving her now! With a heavy heart I joined Evan and the girls at the inflatable. My saturated clothes froze instantly.

"We tried, cobber," Evan said quietly. "Are we leaving?"

My eyes glimpsed Julie standing lonely and frightened next to Betty. *God bless this ship and all who sail in her.* I shook my head in despair as memories of the launching again flashed through my mind, then stepped uneasily into the inflatable. Julie immediately moved over to wrap an arm around my waist; our eyes momentarily locked together to silently speak a million words. And she still loves me! God, how can I let her die? I can't! I pushed her arm away and scrambled back onto the yacht. We *must* do something!

A string of orders followed. "Betty, Julie, run up the jib, steer us clear of the iceberg. Evan, start the bilge pump, start the main engine pump."

Once again, I jumped back into the now waist-deep freezing water, dragged the heavy engine spares over the worst eruptions, then several cases of canned food over another. They helped a little. Further back in the bilge were other heavy cases which necessitated sinking to my neck to grip securely. The cold was sapping the strength and feeling from my body. But then the two pumps kicked into action and began sucking. For an instant I rejoiced, but then continued my frantic actions. Evan appeared. We dragged more heavy stores over the patch and hammered wedges under the stays to increase the tension. But still the water poured in. Suddenly the yacht lurched to starboard. "Christ! What now?" We braced for another impact. For a second my heart seemed to stop! But it was only the sail catching the wind; the girls were back in control. I exhaled heavily and continued the task.

The water had already filled the bilge and was now lapping over the floor into the cabin. Evan, however, seemed confident the pumps were holding their own against the inflow.

"That's not good enough," I explained. "We haven't enough fuel to keep them running indefinitely."

"Enough for a while, though," he fired back. "I'm freezing, I'm going to warm up in the cabin."

His idea sounded ecstatic. Hot coffee and food! I was shivering and barely able to stand yet, somehow, managed to follow. But then I stopped to reconsider; surely it wasn't sensible to quit at this time for even a minute. The present patch wasn't good enough without further support; we needed more stays to press down on the boxes we had dragged over it. Again, I grabbed the fire axe and this time swung into the one remaining bunk. Shit! The axe slid from my hands, crashed onto the floor behind Evan. My apologies sounded like baboon chatter. The cold had gone right through me; it was only thoughts for Julie's safety that somehow kept me working. With more care I quickly recovered six long timbers from the bunk and sunk deep into the water to bash these into place.

How much longer I worked is not clear, but sometime later Evan returned to help. The axe would no longer stay in my hands, it kept slipping away, and each time I had to submerge myself to find it. The cold no longer concerned me; in fact ,the task was becoming seemingly enjoyable. I laughed next time the axe was lost, then found it so pleasant beneath the water that I wanted to stay there.

Evan yanked me to the surface. "Come on... you 'ad 'nough," he stuttered. The girls hauled me back onto the now dry floor and sat me amongst the chaos of the upturned cabin.

Julie was crying. She was all over me. "Are you all right, darling? Is he all right, Evan?" She wrapped her arms around me and smothered me in tears and kisses.

"Corse I'm or'right." I felt gloriously drunk without a care in the world. Julie squeezed tighter.

"Stop it, Julie," interrupted Betty. "For Pete's sake stop fussing. Get his clothes off and dry him. Put him in a sleeping bag. You too, Evan, out of those wet clothes, now."

I remember the hot soup sliding exquisitely down my throat, a glow of warmth oozing through my skin, then dreams. Mountains raking the sky, meadows of Alpine flowers, emerald valleys with streams of gurgling music. Julie was trying to sleep in the warm sun when I tickled her nose with a dandelion to make her smile. But then the clouds rolled in, dark and ominous, thunder boomed, lightning streaked to earth.

I awoke with a start; sat up gazing about trying to return to reality. Evan was asleep on the floor beside me. Everything in the cabin had changed; it was clean and orderly, the kerosene heater was radiating warmth, the smell of cooking wafted down from the stove. Where were my clothes? Just then the girls dived down the companionway towards the heater.

"Ah, our good captain's awake," said Betty with a smile on her frosted face. "We thought you'd sleep for a week."

Julie gave me a longer than usual kiss and sat down at my side. "You're all right now, aren't you darling? You scared me last night?"

"Last night?" I jerked my wrist up to see the time. "Seven o'clock! You mean we slept that long?"

Julie smiled. Betty replied, "Like two snoring grizzly bears. We had to go outside for some peace!"

"Well, please bring my…" But then, I suddenly noticed an unnatural silence and sprang to my feet. "The bloody engine's stopped. Why?"

"Relax, John," Betty pushed me back down. "Everything's taken care of. We stopped the engine pump when the water level fell a foot below floor level and found that the bilge pump could handle the job on its own. It's cold and drizzling outside, the swell is moderate, no more icebergs in sight. We wanted to raise the mainsail but decided the inflatable ought to be loaded aboard first. Anything else, Jules?"

"Nothing, except we're heading due north at a mere two knots and our hotcakes and Irish stew should be ready to eat in just a moment."

I squeezed my fiancée tightly. Evan was also awake and heard the good news. It seemed that the terrible anxieties of the last twenty-four hours could now be temporarily forgotten. I devoured my meal like a hungry animal, then drifted back into the oblivion of sound restful sleep.

After the evening meal each of us were back in high spirits although I had developed a guilt complex for having neglected the yacht for so long; it was time to get back to serious thinking about our ultimate survival. I dressed warmly and stepped out into the cold grey world of the Southern Ocean. Conditions were exactly as my crew had reported; we were gliding very smoothly over a heavy swell under the foresail. The wheel had been locked in position. However, on examining the lack of wake from the stern, it seemed unlikely we were achieving the speed suggested. Possibly we were fighting a strong current and not making any forward progress at all. A navigational fix in such overcast conditions was out of the question so, with everything apparently in order about the deck, I returned to my friends in the cabin and spread the current chart across my knee. Julie moved closer and spoke softly to me:

"Everything's all right again, isn't it darling? I mean… we're not going to sink or anything dreadful like that? Perhaps we won't be too late reaching Fremantle after all!"

I ran my hand beneath her silky yellow hair and pinched an ear to make her spin around with a delightful smile. Those pale lips were irresistible. But then some moisture seeped into her tropical blue eyes and grew into tears that rolled down her thin cheeks. "I'm sorry," she whispered. "But I'm not brave like the rest of you; I pretend, but I'm still very frightened. If only I could be like you and Betty." I squeezed her cheek against mine until her shoulder-length hair flowed over both our faces and, when her smile returned, I wiped away the tears with a finger and kissed her again.

Evan and Betty moved closer as my dividers stepped out the distance from our estimated position to the nearest landfall, Heard Island, some six hundred kilometres north-east. "That will take around three days under full sail," I told them. I had already read the gasoline and diesel fuel gauges on the tanks, so added these amounts to the additional fuel stored in the engine compartment. A few simple calculations and the facts were before us. Our gasoline-driven bilge pump would cut out after fifty hours' running, or some eighty kilometres before we reached Heard Island. From then on, our main engine and pump would be started and used for up to thirty more hours. I spun around to face my friends and give them the good news. "A piece of cake, we'll make Heard Island easily. We'll even have fuel to spare."

Betty exploded with joy, throwing her arms about Evan and drawing him closer into the little group of adventurers. She planted wet kisses on each of our faces and unleashed smiles and laughter that brought joy back into our hearts. Our rather solid San Franciscan friend was a hopeless singer, but a born entertainer who soon had us remembering our favourite sea ditties and singing along with our arms about each other in the true companionship we had enjoyed before the iceberg. She was a tomboy — no doubt about that — who usually succeeded in shrugging off troubles with a smile, but whose heart was always ready to pour out love, laughter and happiness to anybody needing it. "Come on," she called exuberantly. "Let's open some bubbly and have a real celebration!"

"Better not," I replied with genuine sorrow. "We're not yet out of the woods by a long shot. Let's take a rain check on the partying. First we'd better lift the inflatable aboard and get the old *Star* back under full sail."

"And when we reach Heard Island," asked Evan. "What then? Will we improve our repair and sail on, or just wait there for assistance?"

I grinned. Evan was such a stickler for detail. Just reaching the safety of Heard Island would be sufficient for anyone else, but he would need to know the exact arrival and departure times. "That's right, cobber, we'll make a good repair, then sail on to Kerguélen Island and get a message home from the French Scientific Station. Then we can decide whether to hitch home on a supply ship or sail ourselves."

Evan nodded thoughtfully.

"All right then, let's get to it."

On deck at ten p.m. a bright ribbon of gold outlined the western horizon but, elsewhere, the grey shadowless light of day was surrendering to the gloom of dusk. There would be no more icebergs, not in reality at least, although in my mind's- eye every stretch of ocean from this day forward would harbour them for the rest of my life.

Working quickly to get finished before the cold again took its toll on cheeks and fingers, Evan and I lifted the inflatable aboard and lashed it firmly with slip knots to the deck. The girls, in the meantime, raised the mainsail, letting it snap back into life before the westerly breeze, causing the yacht to heel sharply to starboard and quickly accelerate to chop wildly through the ever-undulating sea. I adjusted the self-steering mechanism to a north-westerly course then anxiously hurried back into the enclosed cockpit to note our new speed.

At that same instant Evan sprang up the companionway and crashed into me. "Stop the boat! Stop the bloody boat!" he was shouting. "Water's pouring in! "You'll sink us!" Immediately, I realised what was happening. I leapt back to the rudder, released the lock, swung the yacht into the wind, heard the sails flap and go limp as we drifted to a stop. Inside, the crew had grouped around the hole in the floor, all peering nervously at the rising water that was about to slosh into the cabin.

"How much did we take?"

"A half metre, at least," replied Evan. "Christ, John, it just poured in. That extra speed must have put greater pressure on the patch and..."

"I know Evan, I know!"

"Well, where the hell does that leave us? You said we only have seventy hours to reach Heard Island before the fuel runs out, before the pumps stop, but we can't move. We're dead in the water. Shit man, you know what that means, don't you? You do know, don't you?"

"Shut up, Evan, for fuck sake shut up!" My head was throbbing again. Right now, I didn't need an argument. I needed time to think.

When the engine pump was again running, the water level quickly dropped a half metre below floor level, but every minute it operated precious fuel was being wasted. Betty and Evan again furled the mainsail while I paced the cabin in deep thought. Julie sat watching my every movement, wanting desperately to help; big sympathetic wet eyes, a pale worried angel's face. She couldn't do anything, could anyone? A mere half hour ago we were exuberant and ready to celebrate a victory, but now the situation seemed as bleak as ever. There was just one last thing to try. I was turning this over in my mind when Betty and Evan returned.

"What have you decided, John?" asked Evan as he threw off his anorak. "What have you decided to do?"

Sometimes I loved this guy, sometimes he made me so mad I wanted to kill him! He might be an excellent surgeon and perhaps a brilliant researcher, but his practical skills weren't much greater than a dishwasher! I turned to face this tall, well-built man as his black hair and beard exploded outward when released from the confinement of his balaclava.

"There's one thing worth trying," I suggested to the crew. "We could attempt to position a small tarpaulin over the hole from the outside so that the water pressure would hold it tightly in place against the hull and hopefully stop the leaks."

"From the *outside*?" queried Betty. "How could we do that?"

"Easy. Fix a rope to each corner of the tarp, feed it over the bow, then work it back across the hole. Come on let's do it."

When the tarp was ready, the four of us again ventured out into the cold night breeze to begin the task. The moon was now playing amongst the dense cloud pack to occasionally cast a faint, ghostly glow over the white crests of waves as they rose to rail level and seemingly peered across the deck at our late-night activities.

Julie and I took the port-side ropes, Betty and Evan the starboard. By keeping the tarp taut we carefully worked it over the bow and under the hull towards the damaged section. It seemed the job would be completed in minutes. But then, as the tarp reached the hole, unexpected problems occurred. Apparently when the yacht had slid off the ice it must have dragged pieces of concrete and reinforcing mesh with it, and now these jagged edges were snagging the tarpaulin and preventing it being slid further back into position. We tried letting it go slack in the hope it might float freely over the patch, but each time the water pressure pushed it hard against the hull making it immovable. An hour of persistent effort did nothing to rectify the problem. Our frustrations became very vocal and curses sounded across the ocean. The cold wasn't helping!

"Don't tell me I have to go over the side and pull the bloody thing across!" I remarked.

"You better not, John," advised the doctor. "You've had enough cold water; you'll end up with pneumonia."

"Well, *you* can't, Evan, you can hardly dive!"

Betty spoke. "Why the argument, guys? Don't we have a Commonwealth Games swimmer amongst us? Why not ask her?"

"Julie's not diving; the water's too cold!"

"But I could do it, John. Evan says you mustn't dive. You could tie a safety rope around me…"

I started to strip, but Julie was faster. She shed her oilskins and bared her middle to let Evan secure the rope, then threw off her remaining clothes and was over the side with a splashless dive before there was time to object.

Almost immediately she surfaced again, snorting like a seal in distress. I thought she had already had enough, but then she was gone again. This time we felt movements on the tarp as it was jostled about and pulled closer over the hole. In seconds she resurfaced. "Give it up, honey," I shouted down to her. "Come back on board." When she dived again, we all felt deeply concerned for her safety, yet the tarpaulin continued to move sternwards.

"That's it! It's in place now. Quick tie it off, she's coming back." I yanked in the rope urgently as Julie resurfaced and hung over the bow to grab her arm. She wasn't gasping or crying from the cold as expected; she was barely moving.

"The other arm, Evan, quick, she's in trouble!"

In one haul my fiancée was back on deck, a mermaid from the deep. Her eyes were wide and frightened; she was staring at me like a helpless child. Betty grabbed her legs and, in seconds, we had her back in the warm cabin where immediately she was attacked with dry towels. At last, she spoke.

"Stop… stop staring at me! You men, go away, please!"

Our concern faded, she was all right, more worried about her modesty than anything else. Poor Jules, she had always been like that; too self-conscious to even sunbathe topless while Evan was around, and now she was on display as if in a shop window! When we got her into a sleeping bag she relaxed, and her smile gradually returned.

"Thanks, honey," I whispered between kisses. "You might not be a Commonwealth Games champ any more but you'll always be a gold medallist in my eyes."

"You swim like a porpoise," added Betty. "But what's all this modesty stuff? Golly, if I had a slim lovely figure like yours, you'd never see me in clothes again!" She turned to smile provocatively at me, and whispered, "You've got it made, haven't you, mate?"

Julie spoke again. "It's all jagged under the bow, John, bits of steel and concrete sticking out all around the hole. I don't think the tarpaulin will last long; it will probably puncture and rip off."

I nodded. It was not welcome news, but what could we do about it? If it failed to survive the voyage, we would have to replace it.

Next came the crucial test!

Using the main engine pump the water level was quickly reduced to nearly a metre below floor level, then the mainsail was raised and we resumed sailing. My calculations showed that if we could average as little as five knots, we would have sufficient fuel to keep one pump running all the way to Heard Island. We couldn't ask for anything more, and we couldn't accept anything less! I taped a carpenter's rule to the hull and kept an eye glued to the water level lapping against it as we quickly gained speed.

Evan called down the readings. "Seven and a half knots."

There was a good stiff westerly blowing which heeled us well to starboard. The bilge water sloshed around inside the hull giving me the impression it was still rising, but this illusion could be roughly compensated for. We would be all right this time, I had convinced myself of that. The water, however, did appear to be gaining. Perhaps we were heeled over more than it seemed? Perhaps?

Evan joined me but remained silent with his eyes fixed on the rule. The water level had definitely risen, but perhaps this was because the tarp was still settling around the hole. Now it would stop. Now the level would stabilise.

Ten minutes passed. The water had risen considerably.

"Shit Evan! We're kidding ourselves, aren't we? The bloody water's still rising at a metre an hour. At this speed we'll go under in no time! Drop the sail. No…" I reconsidered. "Reef it in a little. I'll drain the bilge with the engine pump and we'll try again."

Things were no longer going as hoped, and again my legs were trembling with the fear of pending disaster. Christ! If we can't make five knots, we'll be back in the inflatable long before Heard Island! Probably the tarpaulin was lifting with the rushing sea, but if we tightened it any more it would rip to pieces on the jagged edges. There was nothing else we could do without taking the patch apart and making a better job; a totally impossible task at sea!

Again, Evan returned to watch. We weren't heeling over nearly as much now. Both of us kept our fingers crossed. What else could we do? Praying didn't seem to help much in these latitudes. For fifteen more minutes our eyes remained glued to the rule, and this time there seemed some certainty that the bilge pump was holding its own.

"It looks like we've won after all," I feigned confidence to Evan.

"Come on, let's look at our speed." We both knew it *had* to be at least five knots. Anything less was unacceptable; anything else would mean all our efforts had been in vain, that the likelihood of ever reaching Heard Island was very much in doubt.

Evan looked; I stood back. "Well,... what is it?"

At first, he didn't reply, just turned and stared at me, but as I moved to see the gauge for myself, he spoke, "Three... three and a half knots!"

Julie was asleep, thank God, but Betty joined the concerned group. She too was fully aware of the grave situation. "How far will we get then, John? How far before we...?"

"Before we sink? Before we freeze to death in the bloody inflatable?" Exasperation was building up within me. My voice raised. "We're right back to square one, aren't we? All that bloody work for nothing. At this speed we'll be lucky to get within four hundred kilometres of land. Even the current is working against us."

Betty sighed deeply, but this time without obvious despair. "When the time comes, we'll be better organised than at the iceberg, John. This time we'll have the inflatable stocked ready to leave, even have a small sail ready. Longer voyages have been made in Antarctic waters!"

Not in an inflatable, I was about to tell her, but didn't. Why dash all her hopes? Once hope was gone, what was left?

It was now after midnight and everyone was dead tired yet, despite this, Betty produced a steaming hot mug of coffee and generously slopped in a measure of Bacardi rum. "Not much to toast this time around, is there," she said quietly.

"How about the pumps?" I replied. "May they have a long and happy life!" But my friends weren't very appreciative of my sarcasm at this time of night and ignored me. "Well, it seems the party's over for today; you guys had better get some sleep. I'll keep watch until dawn."

On deck at one a.m. a moonlit silvered sea flowed noiselessly past the yacht, sometimes sinking low out of sight, sometimes rising to deck level, but always restless, always totally engrossed in its worldly purpose, always apathetic to the plight of those who choose to sail on it. Above the masthead hovered a single albatross, motionless; a shadowy, silent and meditative visitor that had come to share my loneliness.

The westerly breeze tugged at my hair and beard until refuge was found for it in the warmth of my balaclava. But my head remained heavy with thoughts and deep concern for the yacht and my crew. What could be done to save them? There was little doubt in my mind that if we were forced into the inflatable anywhere south of Heard Island in the fifty-degree latitudes — the *Furious Fifties* — we would not survive the cold and storms for more than a single day. Perhaps it was some consolation knowing that at least we were making more than three knots; every hour would bring us a little closer to the shipping lanes; every day would bring some possibility of a rescue ship. If hoping and praying for deliverance would help, then there was little doubt we were all doing our share, but my calculations were *not* wrong: we would definitely run out of fuel within three days. The pumps would then stop, and we would sink. No amount of hoping or praying would alter this.

"What will I do? God, what can I do?"

Returning quietly to the cabin I plunked down on a seat amongst my sleeping companions scattered across the floor. How could they sleep so soundly when in a few days they would surely face death? An endless sleep then seemed certain for everyone. I unrolled the current chart and spread it across the bench seat, then once again let my eyes wander from one corner of it to another. Nearly six hundred kilometres to Heard; a mere few steps of the dividers! Islands in between? Absolutely none. Not even an exposed rock. Again, I checked my fuel calculations; again, the answer was the same. At the very best we might get within a hundred kilometres of Heard Island before our gasoline and diesel fuels were exhausted. I marked a tiny cross south-west of the island — the *Evening Star's* watery grave. The chance of encountering another ship at a latitude so far south of the regular shipping lanes was next to nil. The chances of surviving in the inflatable at fifty-five degrees south for more than a day was also next to nil, even if this current spate of fine weather continued, which of course it wouldn't. Julie stirred. I knelt beside her, gazing forlornly into her pale troubled face, at her hand draped across her chest, at the opal engagement ring she wore so proudly, but as my eyes misted over, I rose and again hurried outside into the clear, icy air.

On deck I knocked new ice from the automatic steering mechanism, hauled in the sail slightly, peered ahead over the endless darkened ocean. Somewhere up there, ships were plying routinely between warm continents. Happy crews, lazy passengers. It seemed at least a year ago, but was merely last month, December 15, that the *Oriana* had slowed down to pass our yacht and poured flowers and gifts onto the deck. Passengers were shouting words of encouragement and cheering us on. The captain bellowed out praise on his loudhailer for our well-publicised venture and wished us God speed. Only a month ago? It might well have been a lifetime. Thoughts drifted to other adventures in the Swiss Alps. An avalanche, serious injuries, but then Evan and I only had to wait patiently for help: rescue was imminent. We'll wait patiently this time too, but when will the rescuers come? They won't. Perhaps we'll all die together in a storm; perhaps we'll go one at a time in the cold. I pray that Julie goes first, I pray that she'll just close her pretty eyes and...

Back in the cabin I plunked down again on the bench seat, staring blindly at the chart, staring *through* the chart at the drifting images of my imagination. Sometimes my eyes refocused to read such names as Crozet Island, McDonald Island, and then they followed blue arrows depicting ocean currents across the paper to the green land masses of Tasmania and New Zealand. Feint lines of latitude and longitude, a heavy black line marking the Meridian of Greenwich, a dotted line wriggling across the Southern Ocean, shades of blue showing ocean depths. How easy it was to flip from island to island, from Cape Town to Perth. How easy in one's mind: how impossible in reality!

Three more hours to dusk. My head was filled with exhaustion and lowered to the chart; tired eyes blinked shut. But a tormented mind knew no rest. Howling winds, mountainous seas, a tiny raft plunging like a roller coaster into the depths of dark angry troughs, people smothered in ice, clinging desperately to each other, fighting to stay alive, fear on every face, fear, fear, fear. I awoke with a start, trembling, sweat trickling down my skin, breathing heavily. I needed air — cold fresh air.

On deck I tried to imagine what my folks in Hobart were doing. Probably they'd be wondering why we hadn't called, wondering when we'd berth in Fremantle. But tonight, my mind couldn't focus clearly on them; it was too full of other thoughts. Of Julie, of the *Evening Star*, of the chart; why was the chart so vividly implanted in my mind? My brother would be twenty-five this week, a year younger than I: Julie and Betty's age. Evan was the oldest at twenty-eight. My brother and I were always as skinny as matches and hard to tell apart until I grew my beard and began eating properly. We were both fair, average height, and not too disappointed with our looks. That blue dotted line on the chart, what did it represent? More ocean currents? The cold had crept through my heavy sweater and oilskins and again left me shivering.

Nobody had yet stirred in the cabin despite several loud thumps on the hull as we broached a few larger than usual waves. The chart had blown to the floor, so this time I pinned it to the wall. My eyes again wandered to that blue dotted line drawn across the Southern Ocean; strange that it wasn't identified. Another ocean current, no doubt, but to appease my curiosity I pulled out the adjoining sheet and followed the line onto that. Ah, here it is in italics: *approximate limit of pack-ice*. Of course, I'd forgotten we were so near the pack-ice. Only another two hundred or so kilometres further south; how the hell did Evan talk us into coming this far down? Scott had lots of trouble pushing through the pack-ice on his way to the Antarctic continent, Mawson too. Didn't he explore the coastline south of here for Australia? And Ernest Shackleton, he had more trouble than the rest. He was beset in the ice for months until eventually his ship was crushed and sunk. Later he sailed a lifeboat to South Georgia to get help for his crew. It had been a long time since I'd read about these intrepid explorers of yesteryear.

A thought suddenly flashed through my brain. I grinned. Imagine suggesting such an idea to Evan! Yet, was it such a crazy idea? Of course it was. It would make a good joke in different circumstances. An idiotic thought. I tried to dismiss it from my mind. But why had it sent the adrenalin surging through my veins? Why was I suddenly nervous and shivering? The loneliness of the night, no doubt; the strain of the last few days. I wandered outside again expecting the icy air to sweep such ideas from my head. A slow stroll around the deck, a check on the course, once more knocking some ice from the steering mechanism, staring ahead into the blackness. An hour must have slipped by, yet that annoying thought still remained indelibly engraved on my brain. I gave up trying to fight it. Well, just how crazy is it, I reasoned? Only a miracle could save us if we continue with our present plans. The chances of us all dying in the inflatable was overwhelming. For another half hour I paced the deck, gulping in cold air to be certain my mind was functioning perfectly, that my reasoning was unimpaired, but even then, the thought remained firmly engraved. There seemed no chance of dismissing it. The idea troubled me deeply, but there was no other choice, I had to confront the crew for their reaction.

"Wake up, wake up all of you," I called, shaking each one in turn. "Come on Evan, Julie, Betty, wake up."

"Dawn already?" yawned Betty.

"Not quite."

"What do you mean, not quite?" grumbled Evan. "You said we could sleep until dawn."

Julie sat bolt upright. "What's happened, John? The patch... we're not...?"

"No, honey, relax, nothing's changed." I touched her nose with a finger hoping to make her smile, but she grabbed my hand and crushed it tightly to her face. Her tears flowed so easily since the accident.

The three were now eyeing me thoughtfully.

"Well,?" enquired Evan.

I felt uneasy. Perhaps I shouldn't have woken them. Perhaps the idea needed more thought. I hesitantly spread the chart on the floor between their sleeping bags and waited until all eyes were firmly fastened on it. "See this dotted line," I commenced. "It marks the approximate limit of the pack-ice." For a full minute nothing further was said. Surely, they understood what was on my mind, what I wanted to get across to them. But when their bewildered eyes rose from the chart to again glue themselves on mine, it was clear they remained truly puzzled.

"Don't you see," I explained. "If we change course, head south instead of north..." The three pairs of eyes glared incredulously at me; Betty's mouth gaped open, Julie's hand shot to her mouth, Evan grinned. "Well," I continued. "We could reach the pack-ice and... and be safe there awhile."

Not a word was uttered.

"Possibly we could run the yacht up on the ice and repair it."

Not a murmur. No one's gaze softened.

"Shackleton lived on the pack-ice for months after his ship was crushed, Americans have built scientific stations on it."

I felt a fool, wanted to run outside, wished I'd never mentioned such a crazy idea.

Eventually Evan withdrew his eyes from me and pulled the chart closer. At least he never laughed. I would have killed him if he'd laughed.

"Well, how thick is this pack-ice?" he asked after a long thoughtful silence.

"I don't know, Evan."

"Well, how do you know if it's thick enough to support us?"

"Large ships have been trapped in it. I suppose, sometimes it's very thick, sometimes it mightn't even exist."

"Well, if it doesn't exist, how do you…"

"I don't bloody well know, Evan, I don't know all the bloody answers, it's just an idea, we're going to sink if we continue north, probably die. Have we anything to lose? We might find thick ice, there's a good chance, isn't there? There's a chance of surviving down there, isn't there?"

Evan continued like a dreary old parson giving a sermon, recharging his pipe as he spoke. "We ran the yacht onto the ice before, didn't we? Isn't that the cause of all the trouble we're in now?" He lit up, puffed a few times. "Shackleton's ship wasn't the only one crushed in the ice and sunk, a Norwegian freighter went down a couple of years back. Hardly the place to voluntarily sail an already damaged twelve-metre yacht is it?"

Evan was talking sense, yet for some reason he infuriated me. "Shit, Evan," I blurted out. "Stop evading the question. If you won't agree to go, if none of this crew wants to go, then I won't force the issue, we'll just continue north the way we are and… and do a lot of praying. Right now, we're wasting valuable time. Give me your answer, south or north? Do you value your lives enough to take a chance, or have you already given up? Just say no and I'll forget the idea. Everyone can go back to sleep."

I rose to return outside. Their answers were a forgone conclusion. At any rate, I was somewhat relieved; after all what hope could we really expect to find in something as unknown to us as the pack-ice?

Evan spoke again. "It's the craziest idea I've ever heard, John, but you're the skipper, if you'd prefer our grave to be in the pack-ice rather than further north, then so be it. Let this be on your head, I'll do as the majority want."

He hadn't given an answer at all, but perhaps he had opened a door through which I could back down from this incredulous idea. But then Betty spoke in an almost indiscernible whisper.

"If you sincerely believe there is some hope in the ice, John, then… then we must go there." Her eyes were not seeing me, they were staring right through me into space. "If there's any hope at all…"

My vision transferred to Julie. Her eyes were wide with fear, her hand still pressed tightly to her mouth. "I love you so very much, John," she said quietly. "I do want to reach Australia as soon as possible so we can be married. Please don't ask me to give an opinion. I don't have one. I have always trusted you and done what you asked, and never regretted anything. If you say we should go south to the ice to repair the yacht, then I accept that, and we must go."

Julies few words of faith and love weighed heavily on my shoulders. If I loved her as deeply as she loved me, would I take her south into the unknown when it was so obvious that all we wanted in life was in the north? When everything was considered the decision had been left entirely to me. My feelings swayed hard against the research I had done regarding our desperate situation. A wrong decision would cost the lives of myself and all those dear to me.

I swallowed hard, pondered another minute, then gave the controversial order. "Get dressed then… we're changing course. We're going south."

CHAPTER 2

I awoke with a start. Something was wrong, I glanced around the empty cabin. Where was everyone? Christ, midday already! The sea seemed rougher than usual but why was everything so deadly quiet? Shit! Of course! The pump, the bilge pump had stopped. I leapt from my sleeping bag, bashed on the window as a lone figure moved by, threw on some clothes.

"You're deaf, you're all bloody deaf," I yelled abusively to the three as they scrambled inside. "Quick, clear everything from the floor, get the covers up." Fearing that the pump had given up hours ago and that the water level had risen dangerously high, I dived to the control panel and slammed a fist on the engine-start button. The forty-horsepower diesel kicked, spun over a few times, burst into life. "Good ol' faithful!" The main engine pump would empty the bilge in a short time but would use a lot of fuel.

"It hasn't risen much, mate, twenty centimetres at the most," Evan's initial observation eased my panic, slowed me down, induced me to work more calmly. The girls were staring at me as if I'd gone 'bonkers'. My reputation of being their cool-headed skipper had waned somewhat since the iceberg collision.

The tiny Briggs and Stratten pump that had now stopped, was mounted on the wall of the engine compartment. "Shit!" It burnt my finger as I touched it. "Christ, if it's seized…" An electrifying jolt shivered through my spine as I suddenly remembered that all the engine spares were underwater, weighing down our patch and held there by a forest of stays and wedges.

"John!" Betty spoke this time. "You should take a look outside at the weather."

"Geez Bette, can't it wait?"

"You should look now."

I sighed. The engine pump would expel the water faster than the bilge pump, but using diesel-fuel unnecessarily concerned me. We would need every drop later for manoeuvring amongst the pack-ice.

Outside, the sea was indeed disturbing. White streaks of foam snaked restlessly across the grey mountainous swell as it surged around the yacht, dropping us one minute like an elevator into the ocean's basement, then reversing to lift us onto the wave crests for a penthouse view to the horizon.

"Iceberg! Off the starboard bow! Christ Betty, haven't you seen it? Who the hell's on watch?"

Betty sighed. "We've seen it, we've logged it. Its three kilometres away. We've seen others and expect to see more. Relax, sweetie!"

"Well, we can't do anything about the swell, so what... oh, you mean that cloud bank?"

"Sure! It's as black as a Syrah grape, full of lightning, been moving like a drunken sailor across the ocean all morning. It seems to be heading this way."

"It's a squall. We can't afford to tangle with that in our present condition. Here's what you do. Get Julie to help, release the auto-steering, take over the wheel and ride the swell as gently as possible. Above all watch for icebergs; I know how much you like to nudge them, but not again, please, never again! And avoid that squall, change course if necessary."

"Got it, Capt'n. Got it, John."

Only then did I realise how close she had pressed against me. Our eyes momentarily met and locked together. Those dark overpowering laughing eyes, a whisk of a smile. I turned quickly and hurried back inside.

"Bring the light closer, Evan. Fuel line seems clear. Bearings are free enough. Can't see anything wrong. Let's kick her over and see if she'll start." To our surprise the little pump engine coughed a few times then smoothly ran up to normal speed.

"Well, why didn't you do that before? You're supposed to be an engineer. It wasn't necessary to pull up the floor and start everyone panicking. All you had to do was push the start button."

"Engine's don't just stop without a good reason, Evan."

"This one did. Perhaps you need a refresher course in mechanics?"

"Can't just X-ray it," I snapped back. "Can't just cut it open and sew it back up like you blokes do."

Evan snorted, pretending to ignore my sarcasm. But then the motor inexplicably stopped again.

"Nothing wrong, eh?" The housing was very hot again and had tripped the over-temperature safety cut-out. Was there water flowing through the cooling tubes? I disconnected the intake. "Ah... take a squiz at that, Doc — cholesterol! The pipe's blocked with ice."

Ten minutes later we had melted the blockage with a gas torch and restarted the motor. The pump purred away happily. The main engine could now be shut down to conserve fuel. Now, there would be time to consider the other problems.

Julie was on watch when I ventured out for a more thorough survey of the surroundings. She looked unwell; the yacht's motion through the heavy swell was apparently taking its toll.

"See anything new, Jules," I asked as I approached from behind.

She spun around with surprise. "John! Oh, John, it's been so long since I last saw you alone, talked to you, you've been so occupied, please hold me, hold me tight."

"You're looking pale, honey. What's the matter, sea getting to you?"

"Kiss me, John."

"Jules, Jules, don't be upset, darling, this nightmare of an adventure won't last forever. Before long we'll be back in a civilised world, find ourselves another cosy motel, lock ourselves inside for a whole week."

"A month, sweetheart, a whole year."

We kissed again passionately. "Not more than nine months, honey, please."

Already a little colour had returned to her cheeks, but sadly our personal life would have to wait as there were more important considerations at this time. "Give me the binoculars, Jules, there are more icebergs around than seem healthy."

"Five, John, all quite distant at present, except that one to starboard which Betty has just steered us around."

One iceberg in particular seemed gigantic through the glasses; many times larger, than any of the others and it had a flat sloping top that caught a glimmer of sunshine to highlight numerous parallel rows of bluish crevasses. "It must be a tabular 'berg," I said to Julie. Three more in the distance were mere shadows that merged into the grey ocean, but a closer one resembled that which we had devastatingly struck some days ago. It displayed a great leaning ice-cliff that seemed poised ready to peel off and thunder into the sea. The squall was no longer a small concentration of cloud on the horizon; it had spread alarmingly to blacken the entire western sky. Fortunately, it still remained distant. With luck we would outrun it to the south.

"Go inside, Jules, get plenty of rest, we'll all be on watch tonight."

"I'll be all right, John. Please don't favour me, I... I can stand up as well as... Betty."

I stared at her. "Why do you say that, honey?"

"Because... because I'm pretty skinny compared to her. She's strong, but... but I can do most things she can. You always ask her, you should ask me... ask me more often."

Julie's plea warranted my smile and another kiss. "Betty didn't volunteer for the underwater dive last night, did she Jules? She couldn't have done it. And her figure wouldn't have dazzled our eyes half as much as yours."

My fiancée blushed.

"Come on, the sea's clear for a while. Betty has locked the wheel, so let's go inside and warm up."

The cabin had the atmosphere of a pub with no beer; not even the ghosts of our happy, exuberant past seemed to exist here any longer. If Betty had given up her role as merrymaker, party organiser, practical joker, lover for Evan, then our future — today, tomorrow — would be faced with cold hearts as well as cold skins. If our morale was lost, what hope was there for our ultimate survival?

"Come on Bette, Jules, how about rustling up a bit of hot tucker? How about popping the cork on that bottle of Bunderberg you've both been drooling over for so long and splashing a bit in the coffee?"

Betty jerked her head up to look at me, then around the cabin at the sombre expressions on everyone's faces and caught my thoughts immediately.

"Can't," she replied. "Capt'n Long John has confined me to the wheel. Besides, Julie and I were not educated in the Antipodes like you guys and we haven't a clue what you're talking about. A bit of hot tucker, indeed! If by any remote chance that's Aboriginal for rustle up some hot grub, then right on man. You watch the wheel and we'll knock you up something that even my president wouldn't turn his nose up at! Come on Jules, let's fry 'em some easy-over eggs and French fries."

The iceberg ahead was soon within a kilometre of the yacht. I had begun altering course to give it a wide berth to the east when a thought from an almost forgotten past crept back into my mind. It had worked well on rocky coastlines, but would it work with icebergs? Perhaps it was worth a try! A few more moments of contemplation, then the decision was made.

"Take the wheel, Evan, keep us on this course. Pass the 'berg on the starboard side, pretty close in. I'll direct you."

"Like hell I will, I'm veering off now, we're not going close to anything!"

"It's important, mate, you'll see why. Try and pass within a hundred metres of it."

The girls hurried up from the cabin when they heard my instructions.

"Don't play about, John," warned a stern-faced Julie. "Keep well clear of that thing, we don't want…"

"Don't worry. I want to try something that might help us immensely. Where's our loudhailer?"

A mystified Betty handed it to me.

"When Evan brings us abreast of the 'berg I'll show you a trick an old Bella Coola fisherman once taught me. Both of you come up onto the forward deck with me."

A few minutes later we were within three hundred metres of the iceberg. I switched on the loudhailer and increased the volume until feedback to the microphone caused a piercing squeal, then I aimed the apparatus just right of the iceberg and slowly swung it left across its sheer face.

No effect. Perhaps we were still too far away?

"Don't let Evan take us any closer, John. Please, it scares me."

"Julie's right, John. Is this really necessary?"

The iceberg from this side appeared like a Disneyland castle atop a hill; vivid white, spotlighted with a ray of weak sunlight, emerald and turquoise in the shadows and crevices. A mysterious pirate-like cave at sea level was evidence of the ocean's relentless siege; the first breach in its sheer, glistening walls that would soon destroy its present majesty and eventually reduce its entire mass to part of the ocean itself. The sea thundered within the cave, and spewed out again with the force of a fire hydrant.

The yacht was now within two hundred metres of the iceberg. Time for another try. I adjusted the loudhailer until it again squealed, then guided its sound-path slowly across the majestic scene before us.

"Got it! Did you hear the difference? Listen again."

The piercing directional screech when directed over the sea was mostly swallowed up in distant space, but when aimed at the iceberg a faint reflection of sound was clearly audible. Despite the tenseness of the girls, I waited until we were even closer before demonstrating again. This time the echo was convincing.

I waved Evan away from our dreaded adversary, then scrambled back inside the enclosed cockpit with the girls to warm up.

"So, we have a radar device. Is that the idea?" asked Evan.

"Exactly! It should prove invaluable in the dark. We can't afford the time to stop, or even slow down during the night because of our fuel shortage, as long as the pump has to run, so must we. After dark one of us will sit on the bow making ninety degree sweeps with the loudhailer every two minutes; a second person will patrol the deck, watching and listening for anything amiss. Someone else will stay continuously at the wheel. The remaining crew member will attend to coffee making and keeping everyone alert. Any suspicion of danger must immediately be transmitted to the cockpit by either blasting the hailer in this direction or by thumping on the window. The person steering will then instantly swing the yacht into the wind and stop. We'll rotate our positions. It will be pretty cool outside so..."

Betty interrupted. "Pretty cool? Boy, who are you kidding? Better watch your long johns tonight, Jules, there's goin' to be a run on them. We sunny Californians aren't built for these temperatures you know!"

"Neither are we Aussies," added Evan. "I never saw snow until my first winter in England. Probably wouldn't have seen much then if I hadn't met John and persuaded him to try some Alpine climbing in Switzerland."

"Hardly needed persuading," remarked Betty. "When he first arrived in London that's all he ever talked about."

My eyes opened towards Betty.

A puzzled expression came over Julie's face.

"Come on girls," I added hastily. "That tucker you're cooking smells like it's ready to eat. What about it while the sea's clear? Then we'll have a few hours' rest before dark and the beginning of a long, hard night."

Near dusk I relieved Evan at the wheel and let him join the others for an hour's sleep. One small iceberg directly ahead forced me to veer five degrees east until it was safely passed, and then it was possible to reset a course that would remain free of danger for at least the first hour of darkness. The swell had eased off a little, making steering much easier, although with even a few icebergs around I remained constantly uneasy, and not willing to accept the known fact that there was only open sea ahead. Every ten minutes necessitated an outside survey to relieve my doubting mind. The real time for concern, however, would come with darkness. I shivered at the thought. Yet in another vein, longed for that moment when my wakened companions would again be around to relieve me of this lonely vigil.

Outside, as darkness closed around the little yacht, it turned cold, bitterly cold, the wind had increased sufficiently to pick up spray from the waves and shower it mercilessly across the decks. Reluctantly I sent my crew to their stations. Julie, bulging all over in oilskins and extra clothing, seemed willing enough to contend with the situation. She sat strapped to the base of the mast with the loudhailer slowly swinging to and fro before her, shattering the silence of the night with an eerie, monotonous squeal that searched out into the invisible distance for danger we prayed would never be found. Occasionally, our powerful flashlights were directed into the blackness, but this served no practical purpose for if ice was close enough to reflect the beams, we were most likely too close to avoid calamity. Frequently I beamed my light towards Julie, letting her know she wasn't alone on deck, that I was constantly thinking of her.

The hours slipped by without incident, although often our routine plans were changed to accommodate the desires of the crew. At one a.m. Evan requested doubling his stint with the loudhailer to an hour so as to avoid changing into outside clothing so frequently. This once again left me at the wheel, with Betty as coffee maker.

"Tired?" she asked.

"Who isn't? Four more hours to dawn."

"John... did I say something wrong today? Evan was asking some unusual questions during our earlier shift."

"So, he picked it up too, did he. I'm sure Julie did. Christ, Betty, you'll have to be more careful; you promised not to let on that you knew me in London."

"Oh, so that's it. It's about your big dark secret from your fiancée!"

"I had no reason to tell her. She thinks we met in Vancouver when you and Evan arrived to crew my yacht. No doubt Evan thinks the same."

"Sure, he does. Goddammit, John, don't blame me if my tongue occasionally slips. It's your fault, really. If you hadn't just packed up and left our little Knightsbridge flat; if you'd explained things to me before pissing off, then perhaps I might have understood your feelings and not chased after you." Betty was silent for a minute, then continued more calmly. "What really happened is that you fell for me, didn't you? Instead of just finding a girl that you could shack up with for a few months, let your hair down and have a good time, you fell in love. I suppose later, over a couple of beers with your mates, you found you weren't ready for the altar and decided to skip. When I came home from work you were gone."

Betty's hand covered her mouth for an instant, then wiped quickly across her eyes.

"Well, John, I was in London for a good time too, but your sudden disappearance hurt. Maybe I'm more human than either of us think!"

It was difficult finding words of explanation for Betty. What I did was very irresponsible, yet in those carefree days most things could be shrugged off and forgotten so easily. We sipped our coffee, listened to the muffled scream of the loudhailer, peered through the glass into the blackness until the desire again came to talk.

"You're right, Bette, it was rotten of me to skip off like that, and yes, it's true I just wanted a good time in London, but, well, our relationship did get out of hand, didn't it? How did you meet Evan at any rate? You never told me."

44

"Oh… I probably decided that you had become too much a part of me to let go so easily, so I made up my mind to try and find you again. You had often spoken about this Australian doctor friend of yours in London, so it was simply a matter of thumbing through the medical directories until a guy by the name of Evan turned up. His accent over the telephone convinced me he was the right guy."

Suddenly long dormant memories fell into place. "Betty Conway? Is there any connection? Evan often wrote about this American nurse he was dating; her name was Betty Conway."

"Betty Conway Knight. I got to know Evan quite well, but didn't want you to find out, so… so I guess my surname somehow got left off."

"You bet it did, and later when Evan was invited to come to Vancouver to help crew my yacht on the voyage to Aussie, you decided to tag along, right!"

"Not exactly. Evan had several girlfriends. I found out he wanted to take one along with him on the voyage as… well, his companion. I missed you so very much, John, so much in fact that… that I decided to make certain I would be Evan's selection… at almost any cost."

"He wrote a lot about this Betty Conway, the girl with the big boobs. His latest flatmate, the girl who could…"

"Stop it, John! Evan was a bit kinky, you knew that, and I found out very quickly; but don't you see, his other girlfriends wanted to join him on the voyage as well. If I was to persuade him to take me, instead of one of them, it was necessary to… well… go a bit further than the other girls."

"A *bit* further! Boy, from what he told me, you were way out front, in more ways than one."

"Don't be smart! I like Evan — so do you — he's a bit weird sometimes, a bit of a pervert, but a fine doctor and a very knowledgeable man. He once told me he sees naked women almost every day and sometimes becomes very frustrated at not being able to… well you know. I suppose he needed a few girlfriends as some sort of a safety valve. It's unlikely he will ever fall sincerely in love; maybe that's why we get along so well together."

"We should have talked before, Bette. We had a good time together in England, but that's all behind us now. I'm engaged to Julie. I love her very much, you know."

"If I'd known that before, I certainly wouldn't have followed you to Vancouver. You never told Evan. You were so damned secretive about your personal life, so damned…"

The door opened. Julie and Evan burst in from the cold, shaking spray from their oilskins, plunking their gloved hands on the heater until they smoked, shivering uncontrollably. I pushed back Julie's hood and yanked off her frost-coated balaclava. Her lips were tightly compressed and pale. I kissed them, watched a trace of a smile return.

The remainder of the night was the coldest anyone aboard had ever experienced. I sat alone on the bow as the yacht surged through the heavy swell and icy spray into the coffin-like blackness of the seemingly never-ending night. Every two minutes I swung the improvised radar device before me, its agonising scream piercing the imperceptible void ahead. Undesirable thoughts and nightmarish dreams persistently flooded my mind during this long vigil; all depicting the besieged crew of the *Evening Star* tossing mercilessly about in the inflatable on the coldest, cruellest ocean on earth. When the time came to return to the warm cockpit at dawn, my shivering was not solely from the cold; I was frightened and prayed in my heart that in reality we'd never have to abandon the yacht in these waters.

Evan and Betty retired to their sleeping bags as soon as the way ahead became visible through the pale light of another damp overcast morning. There were now twenty icebergs in view, causing Julie and I to shiver at the thought of how close we might have sailed to one during the night, although at present, only one gigantic castle-berg directly ahead called for a slight variation in course. Julie was completely exhausted and dozed on a seat until it was necessary to call her for wheel duty. Then I was able to make a more detailed survey of our dismal surroundings from the deck.

The black, stormy sky of yesterday had not dispersed as previously thought but was now following us from the north. Hopefully we could outrun it. Christ, it must contain enough sleet and war-like elements to threaten even an ocean liner! To the east was a small break in the cloud cover — a break from where a glimpse of the sun and a navigational fix might soon be possible. I raced inside and grabbed the sextant. How far into the *Fifties* had we really sailed? Are we now near the pack-ice? A few seconds of visible sun would provide all the answers. "Come on sun, come on beautiful sun, please shine for just one minute!" Already our last drum of gasoline was being devoured by the never silent bilge pump.

There it is! Now! A shaft of yellow sunlight suddenly beamed like a searchlight turning the sombre sky to silver and bringing alive a strip of ocean stretching to the horizon. I aimed the sextant, waited patiently. Then it appeared, the golden disk itself, a now alien sun without its life-giving warmth. Quickly I sighted the topmost arc and snatched a reading but, to be absolutely certain of its accuracy, took another with considerably more care, then excitedly hurried inside to read the chronometer and thumb through the azimuth tables. The line my pencil drew across the chart told the whole story.

"I got a reading, Jules! Here, take a look at this! We're nearly there, fifty-eight degrees south. Nearly to the pack-ice! We might even make it today!"

Julie looked over, then turned away just as quickly without commenting; her face was tense, lips tightly closed, eyes straight ahead; tearful eyes. The excitement of the moment instantly died within me. I went to her, held her tight beside me. "It will be all right, Jules, believe me, we'll repair the yacht in the pack-ice, then head for home. We have a wedding to attend, remember?" This time she looked into my eyes and smiled nervously, trying desperately to contain her fears.

Whenever the danger from icebergs was minimal, Julie was able to doze for fifteen-minute periods prior to each of my observations on deck, then after a full hour we would alternate positions, allowing me my time of rest. To close one's eyes for even a minute was morphine to the mind, utter bliss, but much longer allowed my disturbing dreams to return, and our struggles for survival on an unrelenting sea would continue to play across the screen of my mind.

"What was that?" I leapt from the couch moments after closing my eyes. "What was that thump? Ice?"

"Probably only a wave," replied Julie. "Don't worry, go back to sleep."

Probably? Probably, wasn't good enough any more. In seconds I was back on deck darting from bow to stern in search of possible trouble, but then I stopped and grinned as the source of the disturbance suddenly became apparent.

"Lock the wheel, honey," I called. "Come on deck, come out here and look."

"Whales! A pod of at least five, see them playing around the yacht? I bet one of them purposely nudged the hull to bring someone on deck." As we watched, they rolled, spouted, broached and dived like the restless sea itself; huge rounded backs, shining black islands of life on the loneliest sea on earth.

"They're orcas, or if you like, killer whales," explained Julie. "The same species as old Skana at the Stanley Park Aquarium. Poor animal, she died of a broken heart in a tiny concrete pool when she should have been roaming the oceans, free and wild, like her friends here."

"Look at their eyes gazing up at us, Jules; they're as curious about us as we of them. Intelligent, thoughtful eyes; wiser than man to the ocean's intricacies. If only they could talk — understand."

"What would you say to them, John?"

"I would say: hi, you're beautiful, we love you, and... and would you mind taking my mum a message!"

"And what questions might *they* ask?"

"Naturally, they'd want to know who the gorgeous blonde was beside me."

Seeing Julie's eyes sparkle and her pearly teeth part in a smile so rarely seen since our accident, brought joy to my heart.

"They're going now, John, off to the north, maybe to Australia or America... or even home to Vancouver. I wonder where? Why can't we go with them, why can't... John... what's the matter, John?"

"Those black clouds astern; they were quite distant a short time ago, but now they seem to be catching up. Pass me the binoculars, Jules."

It was a squall all right. Beneath the canopy of storm clouds a war was raging; wind, rain, lightning all mercilessly tormenting the sea below until it erupted like the disturbed waters beneath a free-falling waterfall. It was following an erratic course, swinging dramatically from east to west even as we watched, and most definitely approaching closer to our yacht. God, I hope it veers away; our makeshift patch surely couldn't survive such violence. I had heard of squalls in tropical climates severely damaging even large shipping, so what havoc would one effect down here on a vessel the size of the *Evening Star*? It wasn't something to think about! For several more minutes we watched it uneasily, plotting in our minds the resultant of its zig-zag course across the ocean. There was little doubt that we faced imminent danger. We couldn't outrun it any longer!

"Get back to the wheel, Jules, wake the others, tell them to get on deck, quick."

If it doesn't swing away within the next ten minutes, I thought, we're in serious trouble. Come on, Evan, hurry, please hurry. The squall was bearing down on us like an approaching tidal wave, rapidly expanding in size to now blot out the entire northern sky. Evan and Betty arrived on deck.

"Drop the mainsail, Evan, secure it. Betty, find some more rope; double the tie-downs on the inflatable, stow everything loose inside. Both of you get back inside as quickly as possible."

The engine started first try, thank God, and soon the main pump had taken over from the bilge pump. I engaged the prop and swung the *Evening Star* to port until we lay stern on to the approaching squall. Julie anxiously stood by. Five minutes later Evan and Betty burst in.

"It's our only hope. We'll take the brunt of the impact on our stern, try to protect the patch from as much turbulence as possible."

Evan nodded. "What can we do?"

"Nothing more at this time. Go down into the cabin. Just hang tight and be ready for any emergencies. A few prayers wouldn't hurt!"

The first wave from the squall lifted the stern high and then surged gently past, letting us slip back into a deep trough from where we were showered with spray from the seas above.

But then the storm struck.

The yacht shuddered, rolled drunkenly left and right, shot skywards into a deluge of hail and sleet. The cockpit windows instantly darkened; someone turned on the lights, but seconds later the glass was washed clear again by a wall of sea that spun us broadside across the wind and tilted us violently until everyone in the cabin was flung hard against the wall. I fought with the wheel to hold from capsizing, got the yacht back into position, tightened the security rope around my waist, kept an eye on the compass; every direction now seemed the same.

The vessel spun a complete circle, dipped the port rail below water, then the starboard one. From behind came an unnerving crash. Down the companionway I glimpsed Evan being flung against a cupboard; its contents disgorged around his feet, cans of food surged to and fro across the floor like the sea itself. Betty gave a muffled cry. Julie clung like a possum to a wall cupboard. Thunder deafened our ears, lightning blinded our eyes, hail hammered on the roof like a thousand pecking crows.

We won't make it, I told myself. The patch can't hold against such a buffeting. Any second now it will blow; any minute now we'll go under. Can't anything be done? I've failed my crew. Am I so bloody useless that everyone has to die? Any minute now! Turning stern on hadn't helped much — impossible to hold her there. Maybe if we could... but that was a desperate thought, it could take us to the bottom even faster! But... but we had to do something!

Without any warning to my companions, I restarted the bilge pump, pushed the engine throttle hard forward, watched the revs surge to maximum, then swung the wheel hard to port. We now had steerage. The yacht rolled alarmingly as it broached the tormented seas and shuddered around to reverse its direction. Course: due north, directly into the storm. Immediately we submerged beneath a wall of water, fought to resurface, climbed a mountainous wave, dived into the black trough behind. Go, boat, go! The extra speed gave us stability but would be inserting considerably more pressure on the patch. The sea must already be pouring into the bilge!

Five minutes passed. Still the sea raged about the yacht, tossing us in every direction like an empty bottle. My companions remained absolutely silent; perhaps they understood what I was hoping to achieve, or perhaps they were mute from fright! How much time was left before the patch gave way completely and the incoming water caused us to founder? Five more minutes passed. The vessel was much heavier now, our speed was falling rapidly, but... but surely the sea was less tempestuous, surely the sky a little lighter ahead?

Amazing! Suddenly it was light again. Even a ray of sunshine hit the glass. The sea reverted back to a mere heavy swell. We'd made it! We'd survived the squall! But at what price? I throttled back and all but stopped.

"Take the wheel, Betty," I yelled. Then dived down the companionway into ankle deep water in the cabin.

"Christ, John," muttered Evan. "Another few minutes and we'd have gone under!"

"We still might," I replied nervously. "If the patch hasn't settled back after that impact, we're going to sink."

The three of us stood gazing into the hole I'd hacked in the floor. Both pumps were working; we'd know our fate within minutes. Breaths were held. Then we knew. Evan held out his hand. "Good work, mate, you brought us through. I thought we'd seen our last hour." The water level fell below floor level as we watched.

"Everything's OK," I called up to Betty. "Bring us back on course, due south. Put some coffee on, Jules, and don't be miserable with the rum. We all deserve a pick-me-up after that little escapade! Help me raise some sail, Evan."

The cockpit hatch was stuck closed. We shook it, kicked at it, then together pushed until the mass of sleet outside fell away allowing us to squeeze through. "Geez," exclaimed my doctor friend. "It's like Christmas in Europe! Ice everywhere! Look at the railing, thick as a log of wood!" A quarter metre of slush had smoothed the yacht's superstructure into something very streamlined and futuristic; the mast, however, looked more like the summit cross on the Matterhorn. With all this additional weight it was little wonder we had sunk so low in the water.

But then I gave a yell and dived back inside, shoved Betty rudely from the wheel and spun it to starboard. "Iceberg! Straight ahead! But don't worry, we're not going to hit. Better go and scrape the windows, Bette, it might help if we could see something!" Julie hurried out also, and for the next ten minutes the sound of brooms and shovels drowned out the steady beat of the engine. Soon the iceberg was far behind; a grey mountainous shadow floating on a grey ocean beneath a grey leaden sky. Then the wind caught the sail, tilting the yacht to port. Seconds later in raced my shivering crew.

"All clear now, Capt'n. No more wandering ice-ships to get in our way for a while… we hope!" Betty was again trying to put some cheer back into our souls even though she, like the rest of us, was still shaking from our ordeals. No doubt other adventures awaited us before this voyage was through.

When the water level fell a half metre below the cabin floor, I shut down the engine, leaving the bilge pump to once again maintain a safe level. We were now desperately low on both diesel and gasoline fuels, but were once more making three knots under sail towards the pack-ice, which, by my reckoning, should have already been sighted.

"You and Julie had better turn in, John," suggested Evan. "Betty and I will stand watch for the next few hours."

"Not likely! We must be approaching the pack; we could be there any time now."

"No sign of it yet. We'll call you. You haven't slept properly for thirty-six hours."

I wasn't tired. At any rate how could anyone sleep with such an abundance of thoughts and concerns darting through their minds? Nevertheless, an hour curled up on the floor in a warm sleeping bag would give my legs a rest. Julie snuggled close in her bag. Cosy, . so very cosy…

The squeal of the loudhailer awoke me a few moments later. What was the point of trying to sleep? I turned over and tried to erase the day's events from my mind. Then it squealed again! Shit! What the hell were they playing at in the middle of the afternoon? I sat up. Hell! The cabin was as black as night; another storm? I dived from my bag, raced up the companionway to Evan at the wheel.

"Why didn't you wake me? Where's it coming from?"

"Where's what coming from?"

"The bloody storm. It's darker than…"

Evan switched on the light and stared at me. "You need a sedative, John, there's no storm, it's dark because it's ten o'clock. You've been snoring your head off for six hours."

Ten o'clock? Six hours? Maybe I was still dreaming. "Well… why didn't you call us? It takes a full crew to navigate these waters at night, you know that. We mustn't take more risks than absolutely necessary."

"Relax for a moment will you, John. To start with, the sky cleared early, so it wasn't really dark until you woke, and as we're presently on an iceberg-free course there's nothing you can do for another half hour."

"But the pack-ice? We should have reached the pack-ice long before this!"

"Well, we haven't. You'd better check your calculations. Maybe there isn't any!"

"No pack-ice? Christ, Evan, if there's no pack-ice we're finished! The gasoline tank is nearly empty!"

"Weren't there any traces of sea-ice — any sign of floating ice at all?"

"Only icebergs, scores of them. The only thing that seemed different was the bright southern sky just before sunset."

"Oh!" I paced the floor. Didn't that mean something? Hadn't I read something about such skies in Polar regions? Perhaps there was something in the dictionary. I thumbed quickly through our Oxford. Iceberg, ice-flow, icicle, ice-blink. "That's it, Evan, ice-blink: the reflection of ice from clouds. You, beauty! It's ahead, cobber, it's ahead! And another thing, the reason why the sea has suddenly become so calm is because of the ice pressing on it! The weight of ice is suppressing the ocean's movement."

"Makes sense," he murmured. "But what will this pack-ice look like? Do we just sail up to a wall of ice? Does it start gradually and get thicker, what?"

I shrugged. "We'll find out very soon."

"In the dark?"

"Well, we can't stop, can we?"

Around one a.m. the shriek from the loudhailer suddenly echoed back as I swung it across the blackness before me. My heart gave a leap! Quickly I backtracked. There it was again! Iceberg! It *had* to be an iceberg — dead ahead! Immediately I turned the instrument towards Betty in the cockpit and blasted an unmistakable warning. Almost as quickly the yacht swung into the wind and stopped dead with the mainsail flapping violently. Our long patient perseverance with an improvised device had finally paid off. Evan started the engine and reversed, took a wide berth to port, then continued south as if all this was mere routine. To be certain, however, I tracked the 'berg alongside until it was well clear of the vessel.

The intense cold of night quickly quelled the sense of personal satisfaction accrued within, allowing me to settle down comfortably for the final tedious hour of shift. But my hopes were dashed! Something banged noisily along the length of the hull: a fragment of ice? Then there was a grinding sound as if the hull was scraping a gravel bottom. Julie rushed forward with a flashlight but was too late. Whatever it was, had passed. I handed her the hailer and began patrolling the deck. It *must* have been ice! We *must* be on the fringe of the pack-ice! What now? What happens next?

At two a.m. the eastern sky was already awakening to cast a faint silver light over the yacht as it skimmed silently through an ocean so black and smooth it might well have been oil. Around us, gradually catching the morning light, was again the now familiar vista of dozens of icebergs, all grey in the misty dawn like a fleet of battleships awaiting orders to sail. Ahead, however, was something new. A sight we'd never seen before: a thin white line drawn across the horizon. Without doubt this was the beginning of the pack-ice! Is that what brought us so far south? Is that the sanctuary in which we have entrusted our lives? Will it really be our salvation?

With a coffee mug warming my frozen fingers and the hot liquid spelling joy to my innards, I stood alone on the aft deck watching as the pink glow of dawn gradually spread across the eastern sky. Soon after, the hue on the horizon intensified to a strip of bright orange, and then exploded like torched gasoline to flare red across the sea. Yellow and crimson shafts of light beamed skywards to ominously paint the thin cloud cover and spread with intensifying splendour until the whole sky was radiant and ready to welcome the first brilliant sliver of sun as it made its debut above the cold south. Within minutes the dazzling sphere had cleared the earth and a new day was born.

Peripheral ice crystals around several eastern icebergs soon caught the sun's rays, and glowed brilliantly as though a festoon of halogen lamps had just been switched on, while the icebergs to the west became bathed in yellow morning light which placidly reflected their might in the dark mirrored sea.

The line of pack-ice ahead was deceptive. From a distance it appeared an unnavigable barrier but, when more closely approached, proved to be merely a thin layer of brash-ice that in no way impeded the cautiously moving *Evening Star*. This was followed by more open water, surprisingly bare of even a trace of ice. The scene of alternating brash-ice, then open water was repeated so many times that our guard against anticipated dangers became somewhat relaxed. But then, a half-metre-thick unbroken step of ice suddenly appeared ahead, jolting us rudely back to reality. I swung the yacht into the wind and stopped.

"Lower the sail," I ordered. "From here on we'll use the motor. Let's hope our fuel holds out! Bette, you take first shift as navigator in the crow's nest."

"Crow's nest? Navigator?"

"Sure! Grab a cushion and make yourself comfortable on the top spreader. You'll be able to see any open leads from up there and can direct us along the widest of them."

She looked up the mast and shrugged. "It's nice that you think a cushion's necessary! How do I get up there anyway, block and tackle?"

"If that's what it takes! Evan will stay at the wheel with the hatch open so he can hear your instructions. Julie and I will remain up front with the boat hooks to protect the patch and ease us through any tight spots."

After only a few minutes motoring along the ice front, Betty, from her lofty perch, sighted the first sizable lead. "Can you see it?" she called down. "Turn left, turn left now."

Evan throttled back and then swung the yacht into a wide channel of glassy water that led us a full kilometre into what appeared to be more open sea but was, in reality, a very large lake. Our navigator remained silent for the next fifteen minutes until she was able to plot a course with the prismatic compass that would hopefully guide us to the entrance of a continuing lead on the far side of the lake. "One-sixty degrees," she finally called down.

From the deck all we could see was an unbroken white line across the horizon, but surprisingly, on approaching closer, the sought-after lead suddenly appeared ahead. Good girl, Bette! At long last our luck seemed to be improving.

The ice-floes all around were constantly growing thicker and larger. "Bear left again," she called. The lead we were following split into several channels. "This one winds like a snake. Lots of submerged ice.

Keep in the middle. Sharp bend right coming up."

Any finer course adjustments were left to my hand signals and were so well implemented by Evan that the boat hooks were as yet unnecessary. We rounded a corner piled high with pressure ice, then continued a zig-zag course through a dazzling maze of shattered ice for another exciting hour. Suddenly Evan shouted urgently from the cockpit and cut the engine. Something was very wrong! The patch? Was the patch failing? I ran to him.

"The bilge pump's stopped again," he cried. "Pipe's probably frozen! Get your gas torch!"

Shit! I'd forgotten about our tireless little pump during this new adventure. It should have been turned off when the engine pump was started. A quick examination of the fuel gauge confirmed my suspicion. I sighed. "No, it's not a blockage this time, mate. It simply died of thirst. We're out of gasoline!"

He stared at me for a moment. "Then we're also running out of time, aren't we? If we can't find a place to beach in an hour or so, we'll be out of diesel. We'll go under!" Without further comment he promptly restarted the engine and slowly moved forward.

From the masthead during my shift, the scene in every direction was of lonely desolation, yet there was also extraordinary beauty here, if only time and circumstances would allow for its appreciation. Black oil-like channels spidered through the white expanse of flat glaring pack-ice to join up with placid irregularly shaped lakes of varying sizes. Hillocks of broken pressure-ice stood high above the ice like cairns marking a tortuous route to nowhere.

Trapped amongst the pack were several huge icebergs that had probably only recently calved from an Antarctic glacier and hadn't yet eroded sufficiently beneath to cause them to topple over and expose the characteristic cathedral-like shapes we were becoming accustomed to. These were perfectly flat, up to a half kilometre long, and displayed on their tops a maze of crevasses that would exactly match the glacier from which they had calved, somewhere along the southern coast.

During the afternoon the leads shrunk in width to such an extent that sometimes we scraped paint from both sides of the hull at the same time, but with a large lake visible a kilometre ahead we were determined not to be stopped. Closer to the lake, however, our lead became clogged with small ice-floes that threatened the patch and further progress, but by nudging them gently with the undamaged part of the bow and giving full power, it was possible to dislodge one floe at a time which was then pushed astern with the boat hooks. Eventually our perseverance was rewarded and, after an eventful hour, the yacht broke through into the open water of the lake.

"Is this it, then?" asked Evan. "Is this where we try and beach the yacht?"

"Our fuel's too low to go much further," I replied. "We're about six kilometres from the open sea, so that should give us enough protection from ocean storms. Yes, mate, somewhere here will be our 'Tranquillity base'."

But, before making a decision on an exact location, we motored around the kilometre-long lake observing ice thicknesses and wind direction, and then decided on an area of smooth terrain near the north-west end. Evan brought us alongside the half-metre high ice-edge, where everyone, without hesitation, slid down the mooring rope and gathered together on the ice.

"'Tranquillity base', eh!" repeated Betty as she surveyed the bleak surroundings. "Very appropriate. I think Neil Armstrong would feel quite at home here, although his moon base turned out to be a lot more stable than this appears to be!"

"It feels great to me," said Julie. "You know, we haven't been off the yacht in over a month. It will take quite a while to regain our land legs."

"Hopefully we won't stay that long, honey. With lots of luck and hard work, we should be able to make our repairs and get underway again within a week. We mustn't keep the padre in Hobart waiting, you know."

"Well, let's get on with it, John," interrupted Evan. "Our fuel's very low, remember? How the hell do you propose getting the yacht up onto the ice at any rate? If we sail full bore into this edge, we'll pulverise the hull completely and she'll go straight to the bottom!"

"I've given that lots of thought, cobber. First, we'll cut a large Y-shaped section out of the ice. Then we'll sail at top speed into the V end of the Y and, as this narrows, we should ride up onto the ice and stop somewhere along the narrow channel at the Y's base. Hopefully this will make a satisfactory slip from where we can work on both sides of the damaged hull at the same time."

Evan sighed. "You're the engineer, John!"

"Well, at least nobody's been complaining about the cold lately," Betty reminded us. "We must be acclimatising like Eskimos? Maybe soon we'll be taking morning dips?"

For the first time in a week an attempt at laughter left our lips. It was music to my ears. Dare we now hope that some resemblance of our previous happy days aboard ship would return; that our morale would improve? Perhaps. Although none of us were naive enough to believe that the way ahead would be without its hazards.

"We have an axe, a spade, a bow-saw, and a few other labouring tools," I told the crew. "Find them while I mark out the cut. It's now seven p.m.; we can expect to log at least three hours' work before dark."

Betty screwed up her face. "Dunno about that, Gov. Don't see nuffin' about diggin' ruddy 'oles in me seaman's papers; besides, you ain't the boss no more when we're land lubber'n."

"Good observation, Seaman Knight, but please bear in mind that you can also be discharged at any port of call."

"Blimey! Call this a port of call?" She threw up her arms in front of Julie and danced around until drawing the smiles and giggles she sought. "Mutiny, Seaman Jules, that's what we'll do, mutiny!"

The surface ice was harder to cut than anticipated, although this was countered by the mushy, eroded ice beneath the waterline which usually broke off in sizable chunks when hit with our tools. Evan worked on one side of the V with the axe, while I sawed away patiently at the other. Betty found the spade useful for breaking off chunks we had partially cut, and Julie worked full time with the broom, sweeping the floating chunks out of our way into the lake. Everyone was working very industriously and keeping mostly with private thoughts in a world of their own when, suddenly, Julie let out a shriek that startled us all. She was pointing urgently into the lake and shouting.

"Sharks! Sharks! Stand back! Stand back all of you! There's dozens of them!"

Sharks? But even as we leapt clear, the water began erupting with activity as numerous sinister shapes hurtled towards us. But then we relaxed and laughed.

Betty was in her element. "Sharks, eh, Jules! Cutest little sharks I've ever seen. Adélie penguins would be more like it. Boy, see them come. Let's hope they're friendly!"

The small, half-metre-high Adélies never hesitated when they reached the ice, but shot from the water like flying fish to land amongst us, then waddled a few metres away to form a line from where they could observe our activities. They were, at first, extremely vocal birds emitting accordion-like squawks while swinging their heads drunkenly from side to side. We were mesmerised. They would stare at us for minutes at a time and then turn to their kind as if discussing the strange new sights, the sea had washed in.

"Well, what do we do?" asked Evan. "Give them gifts, shake their flippers — what?" He stretched an arm to touch one, but it objected noisily and threw back its head to warn him off, yet the bird firmly held its ground.

"Brave little guys," remarked Julie. "Charming too; like stuffy old native dignitaries in black dinner jackets and white tuxedos lined up to meet the Queen."

"The Queen?" exclaimed Betty. "Wow, if only she was here! Maybe we could hitch a ride home on the *Britannia*!"

"It seems more likely these little fellows are part of some managerial staff sent to supervise the job," I suggested. "So we'd better press on before someone gets fired!"

As we worked, the curious little penguins wandered quietly amongst us examining every mark our tools made and watching intently every chunk of dislodged ice as it floated away. Sometimes one would stare directly into my face as if wanting to somehow converse. Others swam energetically around our little bay as it grew in size, causing some concern when they came dangerously near the swinging axe. Julie would beat the water vigorously with her broom to keep them away and constantly shouted at them.

"Scram! Go on, get away. We don't want to be unsociable, but we don't want any amputated heads either!"

"Maybe that's not such a bad idea," suggested Evan as he stood up for a rest. "Some baked penguin on the dinner table would probably go down well."

Julie spun around. She was a staunch conservationist and animal lover and knew from earlier arguments with Evan that he was probably quite serious. Her reply was predictably cool. "This is *their* home, Evan. We have no right to come here and threaten them even if our situation is grave. I would rather starve than harm a single one of them."

The doctor, intent on pursuing the argument, continued. "That's easy to say while your stomach is full, but people change when they begin to starve, sometimes they even eat each other! All their angelic preaching and modernistic ideas go down the drain. We're carnivorous beings, Julie, animals are part of our food chain!"

"Not wild animals, Evan, not..."

Betty interrupted. "Hey, you two! That argument was put to rest in the Caribbean. Cut it out, eh! We've enough food aboard for a month at least, we won't be eating penguins."

Evan continued his work, unabashed, but Julie would smoulder over their ongoing argument for hours to come.

With darkness, came a cold so intense that it soaked right through our clothing into our very bones and encouraged us not to linger at the job a moment longer than necessary. We left our tools and hurried back aboard the yacht, then relit the heater and stove in readiness for a quick meal and a short night's rest. The engine had been turned off when it was found that the patch was quite efficient while the yacht was stationary and had only allowed a slight rise in the water level during the hours we were working. This was good news, for our fuel supply was now critical.

Betty pulled off her anorak and gloves. "Spaghetti and beans. That's all they'll get tonight, Jules, I'm pooped!"

"Aren't we all?" I replied. "Yet we made good progress. If we start again at first light, about three a.m., we might possibly finish by midday and get the yacht onto the ice with a few litres of diesel to spare."

"We should off-load the remaining supplies and essentials before trying this hair-brained scheme of yours, John," suggested Evan. "If we whack the ice too hard and split open, everything, including the boat, will go to the bottom in minutes. This way we'll at least have some vegetables to supplement our penguin diet until the ice breaks up. What do we do then? Start swimming?"

I glared at Evan. He was sometimes the most tactless bastard alive. Just when morale was rebuilding, he has to remind the girls of all the potential dangers that surely are best forgotten for the time being. "All right," I replied. "If we do that, it will also lighten the vessel and help her rise up on the ice more easily. But that's tomorrow's concern. Let's eat now and get some sleep."

There was no 'Hi ho, hi ho, it's off to work we go' song from Betty to cheer us on our way the following, frigid morning as hoped, in fact we all felt and probably looked like Siberian prisoners marching to work in the salt mines. Our boots remained wet from yesterday and consequently froze within minutes, our balaclavas and gloves turned white with frost in even less time, and our limbs were still stiff from the previous few hours of non-customary work. However, soon after the strenuous cutting task was resumed, our difficulties with the cold were quickly forgotten and zippers began opening, headgear came off, and conversation gradually returned to stimulate our thoughts.

"Anyone see the seal swimming around the yacht?" asked Evan. "Looked pretty big. Only its eyes and nostrils were showing above the water; it was snorting like a…"

"Seal?" interrupted Betty. "Why must we always make comparisons? It had the most beautiful long whiskers like my old pussycat back in…" she sighed,"… dear ol' Frisco."

Julie's affection for animals brought her quickly into the circle of idle gossip. "My cat was called, Socks," she told us while leaning on her broom for a minute's rest. "He sometimes followed me to school and became a real hit with my third-year pupils, but when it snowed — he hated snow — he would wait at the door, meowing, until I picked him up and carried him home. I think cats must have extrasensory perception, because poor old Socks disappeared the very day we decided to bring him aboard as the ship's mascot. Possibly he foresaw all this snow?"

The Adélies returned later in the morning and continued to humour everyone by lining up along the edge of the cutting and pursuing what seemed a lively discussion about the job we were doing. Whenever one got too close to my saw, I would gently nudge it into the water only to see it rebound seconds later squawking aggressively and stirring up loud protests from its kind, yet despite my harassment, none would leave the site until they were good and ready. Then they would all suddenly disappear together.

By midday our work seemed complete. The three of us stood back from the narrow cutting and waited while Julie swept the last ice chunks into the lake.

"Is that it, then?" asked Betty. "We're really finished?"

"That's it." I looked critically at our creation but, for some reason, no longer felt as confident about my plan as before. The thought of now having to put it to the test was suddenly frightening and caused a nervous shiver to shoot up my spine. What if the boat doesn't ride up as predicted? What if we lose her like Evan suggested? Even though we had so far avoided broaching the subject, the reality was, our very lives depended on this so called 'hair-brained' scheme of mine working. What were my crewmates thinking right now? But then Julie slipped a hand beneath my arm and I knew she at least shared my concerns.

Pumping out the bilge and offloading the stores took longer than anticipated, and this pleased me. Another cup of coffee would delay the moment of truth even longer. Unfortunately, Evan soon woke up to my procrastination.

"There will be plenty of time for coffee drinking later, John," he advised. "If this crazy scheme of yours works, that is; if it doesn't, we'll have little else to do except drink coffee. Hopefully plenty went ashore with the other gear!"

"It did," confirmed Julie. "But we'll have it all back aboard before evening. Everything is going to work as planned, Evan. It is, isn't it, John?"

I nodded, breathed deeply. "Come on then… let's do it! We have a south-westerly breeze, so we'll simply run to the far end of the lake, go about, pick up speed until directly opposite of our cutting, then tack again for the final run in. We'll also use the motor, but the real speed essential for success will come from our sailing skills, so let's make this a real race. Let's make this our finest feat of sailing, ever."

"Amen," whispered Betty.

I collected three yellow oilskins and took them ashore to mark each side of the V and the central point at the far end of the Y. Then we cast off. Betty hurried to raise the jib, Evan and Julie the mainsail.

"Take in the slack," I shouted from the cockpit. "Enjoy the cruise." My three companions limbered up in the frosty air; running on the spot, swinging arms vigorously, rubbing their hands together, but then, as we approached the eastern shore, they pulled on their gloves and anoraks and settled down for a race we hoped to remember for years to come.

I called to Evan with last minute instructions. "The moment the sails are set on the final run, take over the wheel. I'll guide you in from the bow."

He nodded. It was imperative we hit the V dead centre.

"NOW!" I shouted to the crew, swinging the yacht to port, watching them move quickly into action, sails swinging across the deck. Then we caught the wind and the wake began to foam. Where were the cheering crowds of a Hobart regatta? The ice-edge flew past the windows; we raced down the lake in no time at all. Our second and final tack was coming up:

Five, four, three, two. Christ! What the hell are we doing?

"NOW!" I shouted again, swinging the wheel urgently, engaging the prop, revving the engine to maximum. We came about perfectly. Sails flapped, billowed, snapped taut; we heeled heavily to starboard. Go yacht, go! Go, *Evening Star*!

"Ready, John?" It was Evan. I ran from the cockpit across the forward deck calling final warnings to the girls as I passed.

"Brace yourself, Julie! Hold tight, Betty!"

The yellow markers were already clearly visible. I waved Evan slightly to starboard. A little more. The end marker became centred. We were dead in line. Hold her there, Evan, hold her right there! The ice-edge was hurtling towards us. Hell! We're bloody crazy! The edge suddenly seemed huge! Stop, Evan… for Christ's sake… Too late! I closed my eyes — froze.

A loud thump! The hull shivered, snow blasted into the air, the bow shot skywards, rolled left, right, dived, the mast whipped forward, backward, there was a horrifying shudder, I was flung to the deck. Christ, what was happening? Were we sinking?

Then we stopped. There was absolute silence.

For a second I gasped for breath, swung my head wildly left and right in a semi daze. Ice! Ice all around! We were on an even keel. The hull must be smashed to pieces! A rope, I found a rope and slid down onto the ice, found my feet, hurried around the hull. The yacht stood high on an ice pedestal. The tarpaulin covering the patch was ripped to shreds. Our patch was smashed in. Other damage? Suddenly my friends appeared beside me, silent, open mouthed, apprehensive. Searching the hull, touching, peering through the hole. Then we turned to each other; wide eyes searching wide eyes; gaping mouths turning slowly to smiles. Someone whispered. "We've done it!"

"WE'VE DONE IT! WE'VE DONE IT!" The cry swept amongst us. Betty's arm shot around my neck; she kissed with a heart full of relief. My arms embraced Julie, squeezed her tight, we kissed. Evan hugged one and all, slapping backs, shaking hands, tremendously relieved. For minutes we stood happily in a tiny circle oblivious to the rest of the world; arms entwined, heads pressed together, laughing, fighting back the tears, friends forever.

"The penguins are watching," croaked Julie, her tears already rivers of ice. "They'll think we humans are a pretty weird lot!"

"They'd be right." Betty pulled away wiping her eyes.

It wasn't usual for Evan to suggest any revelry, but on this occasion, he was first. "We all need a good stiff drink. We deserve one, and I bloody well want one. So how about it?"

"And I bloody well want one too," added Betty using her most unlikely Aussie accent.

"And Jules and I bloody well do too, so what the hell are we bloody well waiting for?"

With the engine stopped, the silence of the yacht at first left us with a sensation of uneasiness. Somehow the constant throbbing of pistons had helped allay the lonely feeling of isolation. Now we would need to rely more on each other to keep from withdrawing into ourselves.

"Bundaberg rum?" quipped Betty. "Isn't that that queer Down Under stuff you loaded aboard in Vancouver? Gosh, Jules, that doesn't say much for Canadian boozers!"

Julie giggled. "John threw out my bottle of Bacardi the same week we met. He said…" she hesitated. "He said, Bundaberg would put hair on my chest."

"Ah, so this cold tea looking stuff is partly responsible for that lovely opal on your finger."

"Not really." Julie smiled coyly and squeezed my hand softly.

Evan raised his glass. "We should drink to the *Evening Star* for serving us so well, but this time let's drink to our skipper for keeping us afloat. To John."

Coming from Evan this was indeed an unexpected compliment!

With our meal of canned sausages and vegetables, we drank a bottle of white Grenache, then settled ourselves around the heater on the cabin floor to continue with the Bundaberg.

"If my 'ol guitar hadn't got in the way of the skipper's axe a million icebergs ago," remarked Betty with a rosy glow on her cheeks. "You guys would be in for a Carnegie Hall performance."

"Well, I'm sorry, but at *that* time you didn't seem interested in playing it, so it probably ended up as packing for the patch!"

"Packing! Struth, cobber, ya could'a used me boots, or… or Evan's pipe, but fair dinkum, mate, that music box was sold to me by a very famous Soho hippy."

We laughed a lot. Julie's face was against mine, her long blonde hair in both our eyes, my arms holding her tight against me. Evan, showing the first signs of affection for Betty since Cape Town, drew her close in front of him and rested his chin on her head. We sang a few sailors' ditties, spun a few yarns, joked and laughed a lot until Evan and I agreed that the remainder of the night had other potential.

"We'll use the cockpit," he whispered to me.

"It'll be pretty cold up there, mate, you had better start the other heater."

Evan grinned, then stretched out his arms in a mock yawn. "What do you say, Bette, must be time for some shut-eye don't you think?"

Betty looked at him suspiciously for a moment, then shrugged and took his outstretched hand. "Goodnight, all, sleep well… have fun."

"They won't come back tonight will they, John? I mean…"

"You mean, will they catch us if we play around a bit! No, honey, Evan's sights are aimed at a long night with Betty, just as mine are with you."

"We haven't really been alone since the iceberg, have we?"

"No, sweetheart, except in thought. I often remember our night at the Sheridan Plaza. Such a beautiful, comfy bed."

Julie smiled. "You would have been just as happy on the floor like we are now on top of a few sleeping bags. You had naughty intentions that night. I was a bit apprehensive when you asked me to come for a drink. After all I'd only known you two weeks."

"It cost me two Martinis, and a Bundaberg and Coke to convince you that the view over Coal Harbour from room one, one, zero, eight was worth seeing."

"And by a strange coincidence the room was vacant and someone had left a bottle of Seppelt's champagne in the fridge. Did you really think I was so naive not to know what you had in mind?"

As soon as my fiancée had removed her heavy sweater, I wrapped an arm around her waist and kissed her long and eagerly while my other hand fumbled with the buttons on her blouse. She pulled away gasping for air.

"Let me, darling, I've more to do tomorrow than sew back buttons, you're much better with bra clips, aren't you?"

Once naked and entwined together on top of our sleeping bags I desperately wanted to make love, but Julie held off. She first liked to be excited by letting me tickle her nipples with my tongue, but to really thrill her I would try sucking most of one breast into my mouth.

She laughed. "You'd enjoy doing that with Betty, wouldn't you?"

I pulled back, my eyes staring into hers. "What… what do you mean, Jules?"

She giggled. "Hers are so much bigger than mine. Do you think Evan is trying right now?"

"No doubt he's trying lots of things we've never heard of, honey. Poor old Bette, she'll be like a pranged skier in the morning."

"John, where did you first meet Betty?"

Oh, oh! So she *had* remembered Betty implying that we had known each other in London. I kissed her again, run my hand down her silky trim body to her knees and up again to cup a soft pointed breast. "She seems to think we might have met at a friend's party in London, Jules, but why, what does it matter?"

"It doesn't. It's just that, well, maybe I'm still a bit jealous of your previous girlfriends. I was a virgin before the Sheridan Plaza, you know, and… and, it would be nice to think you were too."

"Then think it! I promise to never tell you otherwise."

The atmosphere had chilled somewhat, to both our sorrow. She pulled me tight to her breasts, kissed me lovingly and fought hard to bring back that radiant smile. She then whispered, "You know, darling, I haven't taken my pills since…"

"Since the iceberg? Since that bloody iceberg! It's become a time marker for us, hasn't it? Not BC, or AD, but if you please, STI! On the sixth day STI, Julie Cane became pregnant because she forgot to take her pills!"

We both laughed. It was wonderful to laugh again. "Never mind, honey, in these emergencies we still have the old 'French letter' to fall back on. When we get to Australia, we'll not use anything for a while."

"Oh, darling, I do long for that day. Having your babies will make me so happy."

"Babies?"

"If they all have beautiful Robert Redford faces like you, sweetheart, I'll never want to stop having them."

While we talked and joked, her hand slid down and touched me where she had never had courage to explore before. "Will I… put it on for you, John? Girls seem to do it for their boyfriends these days and… and I want you to have every pleasure possible."

I kissed her graceful long neck, her cherry-stone nipples, her soft sensual lips. "There's no time for lessons, Jules, no time for anything else, we need each other right now."

The first we saw of the new morning was when Betty pushed two steaming hot cups of coffee beneath our noses and relit the heater. She looked at us with a cheeky grin and wryly remarked. "You poor dears; are we so short of sleeping bags that you both have to cram into one? I bet there's not even room for pyjamas!"

Julie reached for a boot to throw, but Betty scampered up the companionway to safety.

At breakfast our guilty contented faces hid little of the night's pleasures that we now chose not to talk about, although Betty continued to tread gleefully around the subject. "Jules and I will do all the heavy lifting today," she joked, rolling her eyes and drooping her mouth. "You guys will probably want to rest your aching backs!"

Evan grinned. "What's today's programme at any rate, John?"

"A busy one; sorry to say. We need to remove all the old stays and packing from the bilge, dry off the bow, clean all the ragged edges around the hole, then get started on a good solid repair."

"How will we do that, mate?"

"Well, first of all it'll be necessary to fit some wooden ribs into the hole, then we'll glue and nail a heavy patch of plywood sheeting to the hull. Something similar will need doing on the inside. Fortunately, we still have lots of epoxy glue and sealing compound which will be useful in bonding and waterproofing all the joints. Finally, it would be a good idea to fix some buffer timbers across the outside of the patch to give it added protection until we clear the pack-ice."

"Then on to Australia! Is that still plausible or just a dream?" asked Julie.

"You bet it's plausible, honey — unless we sit here forever talking about it. Come on, Bette, blow the whistle, let's get cracking."

Finding room to stack the numerous stays we knocked down was our initial problem, but as soon as the packing was cleared away and the sodden mattresses reached and pushed out through the ruptured section they had covered, the clean-up process became easier. Everything was then tossed through the hole and left for the girls to tidy up when they had time. The sudden glare of a sunny day flooded into the bilge as the hole was uncovered prompting a scramble for sunglasses.

Later, Julie brought around some coffee and sat nearby to talk.

"Will you be able to repair the damage permanently in Australia?" she asked rather thoughtfully.

"Of course, Jules, we'll have the old *Evening Star* like new in no time."

"And then… probably you'll want to sell her?"

"Sell her? No, of course not! We still have lots of sailing to do. We'll want to sail back to Vancouver one day, and maybe visit Tahiti or Hawaii?"

"But we'll have a family to bring up, darling! Where will all the money come from? You would have to go back to engineering. Perhaps start your own company and have a little office in Hobart."

I put down my coffee and glared at Julie. "A little office... me? Work in a stuffy office after all this?" At first, the idea was nauseating, yet apparently Julie had given a lot of thought to this and was probably right; married life would entail many new responsibilities that I had so far neglected to consider. Perhaps leading such an active life in previous years had caused some remiss, but... Betty's voice from the past suddenly returned to mock me.

"After a couple of beers, you probably found you weren't the marrying kind and decided to skip!" It seemed that patching the yacht wasn't my only concern any more.

By day's end I had only fitted one timber along the keel line of the hole, but this seemed very secure and would form a solid base for the intended eight ribs to follow. There now seemed little reason to rush the job. Far better to make a good repair that would allow us to continue the voyage safely and confidently. I had just began measuring for the first rib when a welcome call for supper came which would rescue me from the cold of evening that was already creeping through my clothes. The brilliant sun that hovered high above the horizon even at this late hour, provided us with light, but no longer radiated the warmth we so much desired.

"Well, what did you other builders get done?" I asked Evan at the dinner table.

"Are you blind?" he uttered. "You're sitting at a table again, aren't you? And we rebuilt two of the bunks and a couple of shelves. Not bad for a couple of medics and a school ma'am!"

"Great! It's a pity there's only room for one at a time to work on the patch, but later, when it comes to sheeting, there'll be jobs for all."

"What he *really* means," remarked Betty. "Is that he isn't about to let us amateurs screw up his job!"

I grinned. She was right.

"There are other useful things we can do," suggested Evan. Like collecting blood and feather samples from the penguins. That should make interesting study back home. How about giving me a hand, Bette?"

She shook her head vigorously. "I'm sorry, Doc, but this nurse is off-duty right now. Perhaps I have the same beliefs as Julie, perhaps it's wrong to violate their centuries-old lifestyle by interfering with them."

"Have it your way. No use asking Julie, either. I'll manage quite well on my own, thank you."

Julie had other ideas. "Tomorrow, let's go for a stroll, Bette, stretch our legs and explore the place, who knows, we might stumble on a MacDonald's or a Safeway!"

I interrupted. "Hold it girls! In my opinion it wouldn't be safe for anyone to go wandering away from camp." Visions of someone getting lost on this seemingly endless waste of ice was un-nerving. "Not unless you stay within sight of the yacht."

"But we will, Daddy, that's a promise. Jules and I will take a ball of string if you like!"

Two days later the eight ribs were completely installed and the inside patches of plywood sheet cut and fixed firmly into position. This had been a very productive time without anybody around the yacht to interrupt my labour, although the weather wasn't always conducive to work. Each morning a strong, bitterly cold wind blew in from the south, stirring up loose snow around the hull and blasting it through the yet unsealed hole into my face. This soon melted and stuck my beard and balaclava firmly together and caused long icicles to hang uncomfortably from my moustache. Frequently I went into the cabin to warm up and grab some coffee, and it was only then in the empty cabin that a feeling of loneliness returned. The girls were always visible; strolling aimlessly a few hundred metres from the yacht. Evan, however, tended to wander further afield amongst a group of penguins near the lake's edge.

During the morning of January 22, the wind quite suddenly increased in intensity and began lifting the snow from the pack-ice and blowing it in long streams across the surface like smoke from a fanned grass fire. At first this merely buried my boots when I lingered too long in one spot but, by midday, the drift was strong enough to prevent me completing the installation of the outside plywood patch. Soon the lake was completely obscured. I hammered in a few more nails, grabbed my tools, then fled inside for shelter.

The others weren't back yet! Shit, where were they? From the deck, however, I sighted them wading back through the waist-deep drift, looking as though they were crossing a foaming river. On went the coffee pot; they would be ready for some internal warming when this new experience was behind them.

The expected thump came on the door. "Sorry," I called back. "You'll have to wait, we're closed for cleaning."

"Like hell we will!" Two snowmen barged inside and dived for the heater. Betty tore off her ice-encrusted balaclava, wiped an arm across her face, let a torrent of words stream from her lips. "God, there was no warning. We were watching some seals... suddenly the wind knocked us to the ground, then the drift picked up... it was like salt streaming around us... got into my hair, down my neck, cold, talk about bloody cold!"

"And we couldn't even see the surface," continued Julie. "We might have stepped into a lead or... or broken a leg in a tide crack. Boy! Something for the diary. Sure, nice to be back."

The door was opened again for Evan, but when only a deluge of driving snow gushed inside, I quickly slammed it shut again and looked urgently at the girls.

"Where is he? Wasn't Evan with you?

"No! Isn't he here? We saw him heading back."

"He's not here." There was a moment's deliberation from each of us. "Where did you last see him? How far away?"

"Over... well, just east of us. He was amongst some penguins near the lake. We saw him starting back when the drift began."

I pulled on my anorak and pushed outside into an angry world of gale-force winds and swirling snow. Visibility was down to a few metres. The starboard side of the deck was already smothered in drift, yet the port side, being scoured by the wind, remained clear. I pulled myself quickly along the railing, shouting into the increasing whine. Where the hell was he? Christ, if he'd been blown into a lead it would be impossible to search for him — impossible even to leave the yacht. I spun around as someone touched my shoulder. "Evan?" It was Betty, with the loud hailer. Good thinking! With the volume turned high I called anxiously.

"Evan! Evan! Evan! This way! This way!" The distorted message seemed to immediately be absorbed by the elements and probably never travelled far. For five more minutes I called, then in desperation increased the volume even louder until our iceberg detecting screech blared out to pierce the area where he was last seen. Left to right, right to left, I swung the hailer, feeling so helpless just standing there. Perhaps his tracks could be followed? No, not any longer. What then? Nothing! There was absolutely nothing we could do!

"Evan! Evan! Evan! Over here! Over here! This way!" Where could he be? He couldn't be more than a few minutes away! He was experienced in mountain storms; his sense of direction was always good. If he was near the lake, he only had to follow… Julie suddenly appeared; started pulling on my arm, shouting something. I pushed the hailer into Betty's hand and followed her inside.

"What is it, Jules? Can't it wait, we have to…"

"Listen!" She pulled me into the cabin. "Damn, it's stopped. Wait, John, don't go, please wait!"

"Julie, I'm needed on deck!"

"There it is! Hear it, hear that tapping?"

"It's only a flapping wire, Jules, a loose shackle or something hitting the hull." But then we heard it again more clearly: three rapid taps, three slow taps, three rapid taps.

"Christ, it's Evan! He's safe! Thank god, he's safe!"

I leapt outside, was thrown against the rail by a vicious gust, forced my way towards the landing ladder. Everything had changed, nothing was recognisable any longer; snow had piled up everywhere, the ladder was completely buried. Here goes then! I swung over the rail onto a steep snowdrift, slid and waded in waist-deep snow to the bottom, and suddenly found shelter from the direct blast of wind. Breathing was difficult here; a back-swirl of suspended snow crystals floated so thickly in the air that they became drawn into my nostrils and mouth. More waist-deep snow retarded my efforts to reach the yacht's bow. Once there I fell clear of the snow onto firm ice that had been scoured smooth by the continuing blast of driving snow. On this windward side my body was driven hard against the hull, became almost airborne by tremendous uplifts, then in absolute contrast, a few seconds of eery stillness ensued. My feet stumbled over something propped against the keel. Evan!

I shook him, brushed snow from his chalky face; saw his eyes open to stare distressfully up at me, then he moved in a futile attempt to rise. I wrapped his limp arm around my neck, hauled him upright, then staggered, stumbled, rising, falling, until we rounded the bow, back onto the sheltered soft snow. Now the going would get really tough! We floundered about getting nowhere, becoming more and more exhausted; the steep slope up to the deck lay before us. Together, it would be impossible to climb! I prepared to dump Evan and break a trail. Suddenly two other silhouettes appeared from nowhere with a rope. The task was stolen from me.

The girls fastened the rope around both of us; someone pulled, someone trod down the soft snow, the climb took an eternity but then Evan dropped from my arms onto the deck. A hand grabbed my arm, yanked me forward, pushed me through the doorway onto the cockpit floor, dragged me down the companionway into the heated cabin.

I sat propped against a wall in the corner; everything now appeared under control. Two figures were darting about, snow was melting on the floor, my balaclava and face felt like one ball of ice. Julie came over to help. My voice seemed distant, croaky. "I'm… OK. Attend… Evan." But she persisted. "Evan!" I snapped rudely, pushing her hands away. She obeyed, eyes full of concern, lips quivering.

Betty quickly pulled Evan's gloves and balaclava off, letting his black tangled hair burst free to cover his face. He was fully conscious now, but not intent on moving. "Get his boots off, Julie, massage his feet, I've got the kettle on." She then attacked his face with a dry towel.

As the girls attended Evan, they occasionally glanced towards me, but my ailments were merely a little pain in the fingers as the flesh re-warmed. Just sitting and watching a skilled nurse go about her business was therapy in itself. Minutes later, Evan was dressed in pyjamas and inside his sleeping bag with a mug of hot cocoa being pressed to his lips. He reached out to take it.

"I… can manage…"

"Shut up, Evan," Betty snapped. "You can talk later."

She then examined my fingers, cast an eye over my face, handed me a cup of cocoa. "You're all right aren't you, John?"

I nodded and forced a grin.

She then flopped down on the seat and, in a much more relaxed mode, cast her eyes around the cabin and spoke softly to Julie. "Well, look at them now, Jules; not the big romping muscle men of a few nights ago, eh? Just a couple of babies we have to put to bed!"

Julie never answered. She sat quietly at my side with her hand tightly clasping mine.

I then spoke to Evan. "What went wrong, cobber, we thought we'd lost you?"

The doctor turned, his dark eyes at first staring right through me, he coughed, blew his nose, moistened his lips, spoke very slowly. "It happened so quickly. I was photographing the Adélies; getting some unusual shots as the drift swept amongst them, but, when it was time to start back, only the mast of the yacht remained visible. Finding my way around some leads proved very difficult. The drift obscured everything. Then the wind suddenly increased to real violence, snow began blasting into my face, somehow, I missed the yacht, but reached the lake, then groped my way around the edge searching for it. When you called, it dawned on me I was heading in the wrong direction. It seemed an endless struggle back. After a while my mind no longer seemed to function properly, my strength deserted me completely, sleep was my only real desire. When, finally, the yacht's hull was above me I was too exhausted to climb aboard, could only tap on the side with a knife and hope you'd hear. Thanks for coming."

I grinned. He should have had enough sense to return earlier with the girls, but there was no point pressing the issue. No doubt we would all remember the power of Antarctic storms long into the future.

The wind showed no sign of slackening its assault, in fact its intensity seemed to be increasing. Gusts could be heard approaching from the distance like the ghostly whistle of a steam train; louder and louder, until suddenly it seemed right inside amongst us, rattling everything, shaking the entire yacht, scaring us, then whining away into the distance as we braced for the next onslaught.

"Thank God we're here and not at sea," exclaimed Betty meditatively. "Especially with all those icebergs drifting menacingly around."

Evan mumbled, "We're only safe here while the ice remains firm."

"That won't move!" added Julie quickly as she spun around to gaze at me. "It's half a metre thick. We're safe here... we're quite safe here, aren't we, John?"

Perhaps my nod wasn't very reassuring. If the pack-ice *did* break up our unfinished patch would most likely be pushed in within minutes. Julie *had* to be right. We were firmly moored and hopefully not about to go anywhere until the repair was complete.

At nine p.m. it was already pitch dark and the blizzard still showed no signs of abating. We tried reading to while away the hours but found ourselves turning pages without having absorbed a single word. Drinking endless cups of coffee seemed a better time consumer. It was unlikely that anyone was contemplating sleep. At any moment it felt as though the cockpit would be sucked from the hull and bowled mercilessly across the ice. Impossible! I had to console myself. By morning the day would again be calm and we would continue our work as if nothing had happened.

"WHAT WAS THAT?" Everyone leapt to their feet, heads swung to face me. A terrific shudder had occurred *before* the expected gust. The yacht seemed to heel over slightly, something scraped the hull, but then we stabilised and nothing further happened. Each of us breathed deeply; probably we were getting too edgy. It must have been the wind. Another hour dragged by.

The storm was now howling through the rigging as though a pack of wolves were prowling outside. The hull shook fearfully every few seconds, then quivered; a long lingering quiver that forced our teeth together, made our skin prickle. The pack-ice *would* disperse. I knew it now. Did the others know? Eyes were wide and anxious, glued to each other, seeing nothing… except perhaps the pending disaster ahead!

Another shudder, far greater than before! I grabbed Julie. The stern of the vessel dropped in short, jarring spasms.

"WE'RE GOING!" I called, leaping up the companionway to the wheel, peering through the window into the blackness. "This time we're going!" The bow crashed down, everyone was flung to the floor, the yacht rolled, levelled, dropped again. Water sprayed over the windows. We were adrift. God help us now!

Chapter 3

Evan shouted at me, "Start the engine! Head into the wind!"

"No!" I called back. "I'm letting her drift."

"Drift? Don't be so bloody stupid, you'll swamp us!"

There was no time to argue. Ice was grinding noisily along each side of the hull, chunks crashed into us, the wind blew us wherever it chose, spinning the yacht in circles, heeling it dangerously left and right. The cabin was a merry-go-round, its occupants clutching for anything stable, stomachs sickening to the motion. I released the security of the wheel, groped my way down the companionway, was flung across the table, moved a little further until I could shine a light on the patch. Thank God it was holding!

On my return Evan was even angrier. "Why won't you start the bloody engine — stabilise us? We can't take this motion much longer; you'll kill us!"

Julie was clinging to the chart desk; her face ashen, already vomiting into a towel. Betty was just holding back. "Get your pills, Evan, you're the bloody doctor, *you* try doing something! I'm not starting the engine, not risking the prop. Better to drift with the ice than fight against it."

An hour passed. Miraculously the yacht stayed afloat. Had the wind died off a little? We had absolutely no idea what was happening outside and possessed no intention of trying to find out in the darkness. Betty finally succumbed to sea sickness and joined Julie in vomiting across the floor. The stench would make me vomit next. If the ice churning around us had broken into small enough floes it might be possible to continue drifting harmlessly amongst it, but if at any time the yacht sandwiched between larger floes we would be crushed in seconds. If there was a time for praying it was now; little else seemed possible!

Evan eventually found his sickness capsules. I swallowed two but promptly spewed them up again: a stinking mess across the table. Julie was sobbing quietly. Betty was about to vomit again. Christ! Another loud thump! The yacht shuddered like a harpooned whale.

"WATER!" We could hear it pouring in. I dived down the steps, lurched forward towards the patch, turned on a light. "NO! Not again!" Water was spraying across the bilge in all directions. I jumped down, was soaked in seconds, diverted the gushing water with my hands to see the damage: two ribs smashed, a football-sized hole punched through the plywood.

I sat in the hole and pushed my entire weight into it. Much of the flow stopped, the rest sprayed around me, over me, freezing water. I shouted up to Evan. "Bring the rubber mat and a cushion. Bring plywood, nails, hammer. Hurry, for Christ's sake, hurry!"

He seemed away forever. My body was already stiff and numb from the cold. Soon he could nail me to the hull! But then the materials started falling around me as the doctor reappeared.

I could not stop shivering, could do little more to help, and stammered uncontrollably. "When... when I move... throw mat and cushion over hole... push hard." Evan nodded; he too was already soaked. He helped me stand; water again showered the bilge. The moment the materials were in place I sat on them to hold them firm, pressed very hard until the water slowed to a trickle. He then slid plywood beneath me and bashed in a few nails to hold it in place. When my body pressure was again removed water continued to gush in from beneath the mat. More nails helped a little. We again needed the old stays and wedges. I tried climbing from the bilge but was unable to control my legs, my whole body was frozen and practically lifeless. "Get timbers... wedges, Evan." He too was reacting sluggishly. It took fully an hour before he had collected and nailed enough stays into position to almost stop the leak.

Then he tried pulling me from the bilge, but by this time his strength had also waned. Our clothes had turned to ice. The girls were waiting to help, grabbed my arms, tried to drag me as far as the table. I felt grossly drunk, didn't want to go any further, just wanted to lay on the floor and sleep. The walls were moving, the ceiling spinning, I vomited again. Someone kept pulling at my clothes, a distant voice made no sense.

"Crawl then, John, we can't lift you, come on, crawl."

"Crawl, crawl, crawl!" The words made music.

Someone slapped my face. "Come on, John, move, please move."

The bitch, the rotten bitch, she was pulling my hair. I slid forward to escape the pain. She kept pulling. I'd kill her, kill the bitch!

The cabin seemed stifling hot. The stench of vomit made me spew again. Was my head really spinning or was the yacht still dancing to the tune of the storm? Another saturated figure lay sprawled on the floor. I collapsed beside it. Wonderful, now I would sleep forever!

Light streaming through the windows woke me. I was still freezing. In a daze I managed to shed my icy clothes, was sick again, slid into a sleeping bag. Were all the others dead? Who cares? Sleep, wonderful sleep.

Someone was shaking me. It was a dream; a bearded warrior forced something into my mouth, poured in water. It was dark, my dream changed to the inflatable riding a stormy sea.

When next I awoke my thoughts were slightly more rational. I sat up in the half light of morning — or was it evening — —gazed about the cabin at the motionless forms strewn across the floor. The yacht was no longer tossing violently, the grinding of ice against the hull had completely stopped. I wriggled closer to the form lying beside me and pulled back the sleeping bag hood. It was Betty. Her eyes opened slightly, rolled up to look up at me, she said nothing; her ashen face was smeared with dried vomit. A few feet away a tangled mess of yellow hair spilled from another bag. I crawled over and whispered.

"Julie. Julie, love, are you, all right?" I pulled the hood from her face and kissed a deathly pale cheek. Her eyes flashed open, head shot forward, she stifled a scream.

"Easy, honey, easy now, everything's all right."

The doctor suddenly sat up.

"For Christ's sake, Evan, can't you do something to help these kids? They're ill, they're bloody ill!"

"Already have. For you too, but you were too far gone to appreciate it. We'll need to clean up this stinking mess before any of us even begin to recover."

Then the patch and storm episode again flashed vividly across my mind. Urgently I pulled on dry clothes and stood a few moments sick and unsteady beside the heater, then climbed up into the cockpit and pushed open the door to let in a gust of sweet cold air. On deck the grey mysterious morning seemed unreal. Through the dense, drizzly mist a light swell was rising and falling rhythmically around the vessel as it continued its drift before a stiff southerly breeze. No icebergs or pack-ice were visible, yet the rekindled thought of their threat sent pangs of fear shivering through my soul. I brushed a few handfuls of sleet from the windows and hurried back inside.

"What's out there?" asked Evan. "Have you any idea where we are?"

"Not a clue. But by some miracle we've survived the blizzard and ice-floes, so let's regain some control over the yacht before we hit another iceberg! I'll raise the jib, you hold her steady."

It was a satisfying moment to once again feel the sail catch the wind and suddenly bring the craft back to life. We would raise the mainsail as soon as everyone recovered and hopefully again make seven or more knots on a direct course to Heard Island. Our patch should hold now that we were clear of the pack-ice.

I took the wheel while Evan dressed himself and examined the girls. A north-west course would suffice until a definite sun fix was procured to compute our exact position. I glanced at the compass, then stared at it! What the hell was going on? The wind was directly behind us; we must be heading roughly north, yet the compass showed the opposite. Due south? Impossible! A one-hundred-and-eighty-degree compass error? It must have been damaged in the storm! I grabbed the prismatic from the drawer to determine the exact error, stared at it, shook it and felt another shiver of fear streak up my spine. Both compasses agreed. Something was incredibly wrong!

The girls were dressed now. It wouldn't be long before the cabin was washed clean, and fresh air again breathed.

After ten minutes of further thought, the compass dilemma at last became perfectly clear in my mind, although even then it was extremely difficult to accept the reality of the situation. *We were actually heading due south before a rare northerly wind,* not north as assumed! Where the hell were we, then?

I swung the yacht into the wind and stopped.

"What's the matter now?" asked a queasy-looking nurse.

Julie staggered over. She was pale and drawn, but at least could stand firmly on her feet. I put an arm around her. "Why have we stopped,

John?" she asked with deep concern.

"Because I don't know where we are, honey. We could have drifted a considerable distance off course."

"So what's unusual about that?" Evan remarked sarcastically. "Just head north-west until you can get a fix. The sky has to clear sooner or later."

"If everything was as bloody simple as you make out," I shot back. "We'd have been home ages ago."

He stared at me. "Well, what's wrong then?"

"This wind, it's not the prevailing wind, it's from the north. For some undetermined time, it's been blowing us south, not north as assumed."

The implication of my statement took time for the crew to comprehend. I then added the punchline while they were still silent in thought: "We could now be on the *southern* side of the pack-ice. Not in open seas to the north as anticipated."

Evan's mouth gaped open as he stared at me. *"South of the pack-ice?* You must be joking?"

"You... mean," Julie stuttered. "You mean that we might have to push back through the pack-ice to get home?"

"Seems possible, Jules, if it hasn't dispersed altogether."

Evan sat down clutching his head between his hands. "I don't believe it," he muttered. "I can't believe it. Why is everything so stacked against us? What brought me on this jinxed voyage at any rate?"

Betty closed her eyes and turned her head upwards. "Then God help us. We came through the pack once but could never do it in reverse. We're stuck here, aren't we; this is our Alcatraz. All our struggles have been in vain!"

During this moment of gloom, the cabin suddenly brightened. "The sun!" I dived for the sextant and raced outside to await a glimpse of the life-giving disc as it played hide-and-seek amongst the clouds. "Come on, come on, sun!" Where was my patience? Then, to our joy, the silver ball slipped across a patch of watery sky allowing ample time to obtain the shot that could well spell our destiny.

It took only a few extra minutes to compute our latitude. Christ! We were no longer even on the current chart! We never possessed any nautical charts of seas this far south, so I pulled out a large-scale map of the southern Indian Ocean that showed an outline of the Antarctic coast, then transferred our approximate longitude onto this. Next, I drew a line of latitude bisecting the first. Unbelievable! We were considerably further south than any of us could possibly have imagined. We were actually within fifty kilometres of the Antarctic mainland!

"Then we're well inside the pack-ice," remarked Betty, shaking her head incredulously.

"I'm afraid so, Bette. We'll just have to push back through. Perhaps the ice has broken up a bit after the storm. Perhaps..." Something else on the map suddenly caught my attention. I meditated over it for a full minute before bringing it to the crew's attention. "Take a look at this, everyone. What do you make of this?"

"What, John?"

"Mawson!"

"Mawson?" Evan pushed in for a look. "I know about Mawson. One time they were advertising for medics to go there. I nearly applied. It's an Australian research station. Don't know what they do there."

I laid a rule across the blue printed ocean to the black spot on the map. "About two hundred kilometres, south-west!"

"At seven knots that's only fifteen hours away!"

"Fifteen hours? We could be there by tomorrow!"

We all stared at each other in disbelief. For weeks we had looked north for security and salvation, but now, perhaps it lay right under our noses — right here in the south — a mere day's sailing away!

"That's not an old map is it, John?" Julie asked. "I mean, this Mawson place is still there... it's not abandoned... it hasn't been shifted or anything like that?"

"It's there all right, Jules. I read somewhere recently that the new Antarctic headquarters had been transferred to Hobart, and that all polar relief ships would now sail from there."

Betty was also suspicious of the new plan we were conceiving. "I don't know, John; I believe you when you say we're only two hundred kilometres from this station, but two hundred kilometres, or... or even twenty kilometres through thick ice would be an impossible task for our damaged yacht. What makes you think there's open water all the way to

Mawson?"

Her argument made sense. Nothing was certain down here. "Maybe, no one knows for sure, Bette, I only know what I've read in old books on exploration: that the coastal sea-ice breaks up in summer and drifts outward. Perhaps Evan knows more?"

He shrugged and shook his head. "Betty's most likely right when a few things are considered. Probably we couldn't make it. Somehow it... well, it just seems too simple to be possible. Look at our record so far. Nothing has gone according to plan! We've had setback after setback! It's a miracle we're still alive. At least we know what to expect up north so why not forget this Mawson mirage and head straight home."

"Are you guys kidding?" I blurted out. "Shit, what a doom and gloom pessimistic lot you're turning out to be! Setback after setback, you say! Loads of bloody good luck would be more to the point! Christ, Evan, the iceberg could have terminated us in ten minutes, yet here we are still, warm, well fed and definitely afloat. You're now saying you'd rather renegotiate the pack-ice, sail some sixteen hundred kilometres to Heard Island, then try and get home from there? All in a severely damaged craft? If that's your preference rather than trying to reach the safety of Mawson, a mere day or so away... then..."

The three stared at me.

Evan remarked: "You're the captain. Why don't you decide?"

"I *have* decided. Now I want everyone's consent!

"OK, OK," replied Betty, grabbing a deep breath. "We try for Mawson. If we don't smash the yacht up any more, we can always change course later on and head north."

"Julie?"

"If you think we can reach this Mawson place, John, then... then of course we should try."

Evan jerked his head towards me and barked out his reply. "You've got your bloody majority, haven't you? Your lovers haven't let you down. Come on then, get some sail up, let's get on with this Cook's Tour. Who needs to go to Australia anyway?"

At eight p.m. that evening I estimated we were within fifteen kilometres of the Antarctic continent. We intended not to attempt a direct course to Mawson, but instead would first sight the coastline, then sail close alongside it. This would add slightly to the distance, but with land always within reach we would feel immeasurably more secure. Again, there were numerous icebergs around, but the sea had calmed to a mirrored surface that reflected a pale, icy sun from a misty sky. I raised the binoculars again to scan the horizon.

"Anything yet?" asked Betty, who was sitting with Julie and I on the cabin roof.

"No! It's very strange. Something should be visible from this distance. Perhaps the coast is ice and not rock, making it harder to define."

Julie took the binoculars and stared ahead for several more minutes before lowering them. "Only a distant bank of cloud. I hope it's not building up into another storm."

Twice I rechecked our position. The situation was becoming more and more disconcerting. The binoculars seldom left my eyes. There should at least be an island, a rock or... "Jules."

She moved closer. "Do you see something, John?"

For another minute I remained silent, uncertain, drawing pictures in my mind of other coastlines, but then, gradually, indeterminately, a totally unsuspected image evolved before my eyes. Julie again snatched up the glasses as I spoke. "That cloud of yours, honey, look at it again, look more closely. That's not cloud, that's ice, a thousand metres of ice! It's the Polar Plateau, you can see glaciers on it... crevasses... crevasses everywhere!"

Betty grabbed for the binoculars, but Julie held fast.

"It is! It is!" She was exuberant for a moment, but then contained herself and whispered. "It *is* ice... so much ice!"

Betty then looked. "Is it real? A whole continent of ice? Makes you feel kind'a empty inside, doesn't it?"

"I'll take the wheel and let Evan have a look. We're going about now at any rate; no way are we approaching any closer to that coast."

Within minutes the yacht was on a westerly course, heading into a sky tinged with orange. Two tabular icebergs directly ahead seemed harmless enough on such a calm sea, but because there could be numerous other dangers along such an inhospitable shoreline, we would shortly set a sea anchor and await morning before continuing. A good night's rest would boost our morale considerably.

When we awoke, the morning sun shone feebly from a pale blue sky to bring alive the surrounding icebergs, and cast a yellowish glow over the massive Polar Plateau. The sea remained black, and heavy like oil. Our thermometer had dropped to minus ten during the night and the wind had swung back to southerly, allowing the yacht to skim the mirrored surface at near seven knots. Hopes continued to rise. Mawson now seemed easily within our grasp. The dominant Polar Plateau changed again to a dazzling white sheet of ice and lay mysteriously off the port side. Our deepest thoughts and imagination explored every metre of the coastline. Smiles and jokes once again flourished in the cabin.

"Naturally, Doctor Jackson and myself will be wearing formal attire as guests in Mawsonville, tomorrow. Dare we ask what our two beautiful ladies will be wearing."

Betty gave her clowning smile. "Two beautiful ladies, eh? You must be talking about Julie and Julie. I'm just one of the guys!"

Julie accepted my compliment with a shrug. "Perhaps I'll wear a cocktail frock, or my long white gown," she quipped. "Provided of course it fits over my long johns, jeans, and a couple of sweaters. Maybe I should also wear a placard reading: 'Lady'."

"No need, honey. If the people down there are at all normal, they'll figure that out very quickly. Mawson is probably an all-male base."

"A shower's what I'll go for first," added Evan. "My last real wash was in Cape Town."

"Showers?" Betty threw up her arms in glee. "Oh boy, oh boy. And with all those handsome guys to scrub our backs! Wow, Jules, it sounds like fun!"

Evan pressed a finger on the window. "There's more brash-ice coming up ahead, John."

"I see it. I'll swing around."

Julie sprang up to look. "There's more to the right, John, lots of it!"

"Too late, we're going through. Don't worry, a little brash-ice won't worry…"

The ice didn't swish past like previous patches we had negotiated, it crashed heavily against the yacht, then scoured noisily along the full length of the hull. Immediately, I swung into the wind to stop, but in the intervening seconds continued to collide with bobbing ice chunks of various sizes.

"Shit!" I turned the yacht slightly to catch a wisp of wind that would take us through into open water. "That was no brash-ice, that stuff must have peeled from the coastal ice-cliffs. From now on we'll keep a deck watch, Betty, you take…"

"WATER! I hear water coming in!"

My skin electrified. I dived down the companionway, ran forward to our patch. "Christ!" Water was gushing in like a burst fire hydrant.

Evan leapt with me into the turbulence and diverted the freezing flow with our bodies. We discovered a huge chunk of ice wedged firmly in the ruptured patch. The water was rising fast.

I yelled to the girls. "Start the engine, start the pump, steer us towards shore. We've got to get this ice out, Evan — got to reseal the hole!"

Together we jumped on the block, hacked at it with the axe, tried desperately to prize it out, but to no avail. The flood was already above our knees.

"The spare sails; help me jam them around the ice." We kicked the fabric into the jagged gaps, tried to wedge it firmly, but just as quickly it blew out again.

"Let's weight it down with … with anything. These boxes, tools! Hammer in some stays!" Soon the water reached our waists.

There was nothing left to drag over the inflow; too many eruptions to stop. For a second, we stood back, gazing open-mouthed at our fruitless attempt, then into each other's eyes.

"It's beaten us, mate, our only hope is to get ashore!"

We hurried back into the cockpit.

Julie was steering. She was frantic. "There's nothing but ice-cliffs ahead, John, we can't land there, we'd be smashed to pieces, no islands, nothing!"

"Then tack again, we'll follow them, find a bay or… something!"

Again, on a westerly course, we stared fearfully at the forty-metre-high ice-cliffs and the ocean surging wildly against them for as far as the eye could see.

"Change into dry clothes, Evan," I muttered without shifting my eyes from the frightening scene gliding past the port window. "Everyone, dress as warmly as possible then launch the inflatable and keep it in tow; throw in all the supplies and emergency equipment we can carry."

I hadn't the courage to look into the cabin again but knew that when the water overflowed into the engine compartment and stopped the pump, we had only minutes left afloat.

While the crew rushed to and fro loading the raft, I ventured briefly outside to examine more closely the pale blue cliffs and the glacial ice immediately above them. As mountaineers with proper equipment, we might be able to scale them, but from where would we start? Our inflatable would be ripped to shreds the moment it hit shore. In any event there seemed little point in reaching the plateau without hauling up sufficient food and survival gear for an overland attempt to reach Mawson: a seemingly impossible task!

Soon the work was complete and everyone regrouped in the cockpit to stare out the port window. In silence we let our eyes search the ever-changing scene of coastal ice; everyone's thoughts were the same. I wrapped an arm around Julie's waist and drew her close against me, feeling her soft hair against my face as she leaned her head on my shoulder.

"Warm enough, honey?" I asked.

"Yes."

Then the engine spluttered and stopped.

Julie tensed. The end was near!

We turned a small headland. Hopes suddenly flared again!

"Rock!" We all saw it together. A huge brown monolith of rock two kilometres ahead. The yacht would never make it, but maybe in the inflatable? God, if only we could get the yacht there!

"There's one chance," I called. "We'll bail — bail like hell — bail like a dozen pumps!"

We started immediately with all our buckets and pots. Fruitless! Almost immediately we knew our efforts would be in vain. Too far to carry out the water. Another idea hit me! I grabbed the axe, raced on deck, hacked into the cabin wall. In seconds I broke through, enlarged the hole with several more, heavy blows until my companions were visible inside. The first bucket was passed through and the water hurled over the side.

Julie took the wheel.

"Keep them coming," I urged. "Faster if you can. Come on, faster!"

Soon we were too hot. Off came our anoraks and sweaters.

The distant rock slowly evolved into a towering monolith of brown granite. I described it with growing disappointment to those inside. "It's sheer to the water like the ice-cliffs, no sign of any beach yet, the sea is smashing hard against it. Perhaps the other side will be better?"

Evan called back. "Water's gaining fast. We can't keep up with it… we'll go under any minute now!"

"Speed it up then, two buckets at a time, come on, give it everything!"

We passed the monolith; it remained impossible to land. The ice-cliffs commenced again on the other side. A second, even steeper monolith rose from the ice ahead. Was it worthwhile continuing? "Keep them coming," I called again. "We're approaching another rock, could be better!"

My mind was cluttered with final desperate thoughts. The rock, or the ice? Which will it be? Which will be the faster?

Evan called again. "We're coming out. Water's too high to continue!"

As the pair joined me on deck the yacht sluggishly crept around the second sheer rock face allowing us to look into a small bay with foaming breakers crashing onto a short crescent of low rocks.

"Tack!" I ordered immediately, then raced back to relieve Julie at the wheel. I swung the vessel to port until we were heading directly into the bay.

Even and Betty hurried back to join us. The next and final orders were not easy to give. "Into the inflatable, everyone… we're about to sink. Hold the mooring line until she goes under."

"You too, John, come on, hurry!"

"I'm staying. Might be able to get closer in!"

Julie pleaded. "Come with us, John. You can't do any more. Please come!"

"Go! For Christ's sake go!"

Alone, it was easier to stay calm. I hurried to the yacht's bow and studied the line of breakers ahead where they surged onto a flat shelf of low rock. There was no beach. If it were possible to get closer in, we might later salvage the supplies. Back at the wheel the surf was already perceivable. Some darker water ahead appeared deeper, so I swung slightly to port, then straightened up for the final sluggish run towards the shore.

The yacht's bow lowered into the green waves, lifted slightly to ride a crest for a few more metres, then dropped again. There was a thud, a loud spine-chilling thud, then the sickening sound of rock tearing open the hull. Again, the vessel lifted sluggishly on a wave, freeing it momentarily from its agonies, then again it crashed mercilessly down on the unforgiving bottom, heeled to port, smashed down yet again. The mast whipped forward, sails went berserk, rigging snapped, water surged over the bow. I clung desperately to the rail of the tilted deck. Agonising death shivers vibrated from stem to stern. The hull was being pulverised. Dark rocks appeared all around. We went under. Surfaced again. Where was the inflatable?

On the next wave I leapt overboard; was swirled against some rocks by a strong current, swam clear, was sucked under, then spat back to the surface. The undertow was intense, dragged me to the bottom, I fought back, gulped for air. More rocks. Desperately my hands clawed at anything, fingers becoming dead with cold, clothes heavy about me. Again, I went under, was swept along the seabed, bashed against rocks, tangled in seaweed. It seemed useless to struggle. Easier to submit. The sea bottom was beautiful. I floated like a jellyfish; I was weightless, free at last, making peace with the environment. Streamers of flickering light waved from above to dance across the rocks. I drifted effortlessly amongst them. Julie appeared, arms outstretched, her golden hair flowing freely about her in the gentle current. Hand in hand we strolled the rocks to the lush green meadows, laughing now, feeling the warm sun on our faces, stopping to gaze into a blue mountain pool, watching the pika store its food, approaching a day-old fawn, drinking from a jewelled stream. The world was delightful. "Julie, I do love you. Julie I..."

"Don't talk any more, darling, rest now, just rest. Evan says you'll be all right. You must get your strength back."

"Julie?"

"Yes, John."

"The sun's gone, it's turning cold. We should go back."

"Please rest, darling. You're safe ashore, we've got a sail pitched over us. Betty and Evan are here. Everything will be all right."

"Ashore? Betty and Evan? A sail?"

When next I awoke, my back ached, my bed was hard. I sat up with a start. "Julie, where are you, Julie?"

Immediately Betty pulled back the sail and came inside.

"Hi!" she said, beaming an anxious smile. "Welcome back, we missed you. Julie's with Evan picking up wreckage from the yacht. I'm the duty nurse for the next half hour. Any requests?"

"Everyone's all right then... aren't they, Betty? Nobody got hurt getting ashore?"

"We're all fine! Everything's just hunky dor..." Betty hesitated, the smile on her face faded, her eyes moistened. "John, we thought you were dead! We searched with the inflatable, waded up and down the rocks, but you... you didn't appear. We were frantic! Julie dived and dived, we had to drag her away when... when there seemed no longer any hope. Evan and I had written you off! But Julie went back; we couldn't stop her. She wouldn't leave the water. We feared she would freeze to death, but then she found you washed against some rocks. God, John, I love you, you know that, but Julie... that kid would have died for you. She saved your life."

"I'll go to her."

"No, John, please. Wait until they return. Evan's had you heavily sedated for the last twelve hours; you'll be groggy for a time. It's morning; a clear sky and low tide. Part of the yacht is well above water. We might be able to salvage some supplies."

"Then let me see outside. Pull back the sail."

When this was done, I found myself staring across at a peaceful little bay of placid blue water that washed gently over the flat, water-scoured rocks we were camped upon. The high monolith we had sailed around yesterday, rose sheer from the eastern shore and joined a slightly lower rock ridge that diminished in height as it curled around this bay to create a barrier between the ice and sea.

Betty spoke. "Here comes 'Crusoe' and his girl 'Friday', now."

I stood, staggered a bit for balance, then Julie was in my arms. Neither of us found words worthy of the moment, yet by holding each other tightly everything within our hearts flowed effortlessly between us.

Evan looked me over professionally for a moment and seemed satisfied with his patient's recovery. "You got the yacht well in, cobber; at low tide the stern's high above water so we might be able to salvage some of the contents."

It was elating to hear that my efforts had been worthwhile. "How about diving tomorrow?"

"You should be OK by then, Julie too."

There was a rare trace of emotion in the doctor's voice; no doubt later we'd all feel more inclined to relate our untold experiences. I asked what they had brought ashore in the inflatable.

"Only this sail and rope, our sleeping bags, some clothes, my medical kit, and about a week's food."

Betty added, "Like a good girl-scout I brought some matches ashore, but look around, what do we burn? We forgot our stove!"

"How about a stroll around the bay," I suggested. "We might find signs of previous visitors, or get some idea exactly where we are."

Julie agreed when I assured her, I was feeling all right. "But pull on plenty of warm clothes, it's freezing in the wind."

We ambled slowly like kids holidaying on a beach, gazing one second into the clear sea, the next at water-worn crevices in the rocks, then upwards to the steep boulder-strewn ridge towering above. Our attention was drawn to the sky above the monolith which seemed to be speckled with a large number of soaring birds.

"There are birds ahead, too," said Betty, pointing with excitement. "Adélie penguins; there must be scores of them! Maybe they have a rookery on that slope, ahead."

Julie's eyes widened as she hurried towards them. "Scores, you say? More like thousands! Look, the rookery fills all the next gully and continues halfway up the ridge."

But on arrival we were somewhat disappointed. The rookery was not packed with penguins, as first thought, only with their abandoned nests: little rings of white, excrement-stained stones surrounded by the mummified corpses of numerous downy chicks that obviously hadn't survived the bitter cold. The twenty or so remaining penguins that wandered aimlessly around were possibly immature males that had been unable to mate during the season.

Our route around the bay became increasingly more difficult as we approached closer to the monolith. Here, steep cliffs came right down to the water's edge, forcing us to scramble cautiously along narrow connecting ledges until a tiny sheltered cove was reached where a dozen large seals had hauled out onto some flat rocks. They lay on their sides, panting and snorting, and occasionally wriggling with great effort to find more comfortable positions, but none of them seemed at all agitated by our presence.

"Are you thinking the same as I?" asked Evan when the girls were out of hearing. "This could be our food supply for as long as we're stuck here."

"How would we kill them?" I asked, somewhat horrified at the thought.

"With the fire axe, if we can salvage it."

"Then we could do as Frank Hurley did when Shackelton's ship was crushed in the ice and sunk, make a stove and burn blubber to cook the flesh." Evan nodded, probably unaware of my historical reference.

On the return walk Julie brushed against a stick wedged tightly between the rocks and called us over. "It's a bamboo cane," she murmured, fingering it with curiosity. "Ablated severely on one side by the wind as if it's been here a very long time!"

"Long time or short," I replied. "At least we know another human has been here. Hopefully they come often?"

"Could it have been that Aussie explorer you were telling us about," suggested Evan. "You said he sailed along this coast."

"Douglas Mawson? Perhaps! That was in 1931." I remembered a photograph displayed in his book, and now easily visualised a handful of men standing on the rocks laying claim to this inhospitable coast while another man held the dinghy in readiness for a rapid retreat. "If this *is* the place, one day they might build a memorial here to commemorate it."

"They'll build one for us too," responded Betty. "If we don't get away from here pretty soon!"

Back at camp we contemplated the salvage operation scheduled for low tide next morning.

"Well, I'm not too enthusiastic," declared Julie. "That water's mighty cold. If it wasn't salt it would have frozen solid. It takes your breath away, leaves you numb all over. A few minutes immerged and your brain stops functioning altogether."

"Then we'll dive with a rope. If anyone gets into trouble, we can haul them out."

Evan also expressed concern. "Warming up quickly after a dive is most important; we really need a fire on the rocks, otherwise too much time will be wasted staving off hypothermia in our sleeping bags. After yesterday's experience of trying to transfer body heat from Betty to you, she became almost as frozen as you were and, believe me, I had no amorous urges when I was in the bag with Julie. She was pure ice!"

Betty gave a weak grin and suggested we use some timbers from the wreck to build a fire. "There's quite a lot scattered along the rocks, and when we recover the axe, we'll be able to hack some more from the deck if necessary."

My mouth dropped a little at this thought, but Betty was right; my dream yacht, the beautiful *Evening Star* that I had so proudly built, was now a total wreck and could only be treated as such.

Later I summed up our ideas. "We build a fire on the rocks. Three of us paddle out to the wreck, one dives with a rope and bag, we pull this person back into the inflatable and get ashore as quickly as possible. While this diver warms up in a sleeping bag beside the fire, the next party moves into action. Sounds OK to me."

Julie suggested one improvement. "If we unstitch the foot of a sleeping bag it could be pulled over our heads quickly and will save time struggling to get in feet first."

"You've got yourself a job then, Jules. Anything else?" There wasn't, so the rest of the afternoon was spent familiarising ourselves with the surroundings and improving the shelter, then we snuggled close together in our bags for a rare night of relaxation.

"Sardines on biscuit, sahib, memsahib?" Betty was shaking us. "Or would you prefer raw bacon for breakfast?"

I looked at my reliable old Seiko digital. Seven o'clock.

"No need for a watch any more, Capt'n, it's daylight most of the time. And boy, is it cold! My guess is minus twenty, and even colder in the wind."

Evan mumbled from deep inside his bag. "That gives us an hour before ebb-tide. We should be ready to dive by nine."

We were. Breakfast wasn't worth lingering over, so we jogged along the rocks to warm up and soon glimpsed the uplifted stern of the *Evening Star* washing in a gentle swell. I sighed, then quipped, "Maybe my insurance agents would like to inspect her before they pay out?"

"You mean, leave a warm cosy office to come to this frigid godforsaken place?" murmured Evan. "Not likely. And would anyone believe it, we're going swimming?"

In a short time, we had gathered enough combustible wreckage to prepare the fire that Betty would light the moment the rest of us reached the wreck.

As Evan rowed us out, I already found myself shivering, perhaps more from the thought of the intended dive than the actual morning temperature. The suggestion that this was just another routine dive was not at all convincing.

"Who's going first?" asked Evan.

It would have been easy to suggest he or Julie should but, because it was still my vessel, I reluctantly volunteered.

The yacht was heeled over thirty degrees with only the stern section above water. We rowed around this and saw that both the cockpit doors were still open as if inviting us back. It was possible to peer a short distance into the submerged cabin and see where some of our stores would be located.

"I'll go for the fire axe first and whatever else is handy," I told Julie. "Two jerks on the rope and you start hauling me back."

She nodded. "Be very careful, John. Don't take any risks!"

When absolutely ready, and when every move was clear in my mind, I flung off my clothes, scrambled aboard the wreck, then dived. God! Instant anaesthesia! My skin felt like leather! How easy to tear oneself on a jagged edge and not feel the wound. What a mess the cabin was in: drifting debris, portholes smashed, oil seeping up from the engine. There was the axe. I swam around the galley, opened a cupboard door, let the contents pour out into my bag. That was enough. Two jerks on the rope and Julie pulled me gently back to the surface.

It was easy to fling an arm aboard the inflatable but swinging an entire body over its side in the usual manner now seemed impossible. No feeling at all remained! My two companions assisted; they dragged me over the gunwale onto the canvas floor. Evan quickly began rowing ashore. Julie attacked me with a towel.

"Move your limbs, darling," she advised with innermost concern. "Don't just lay there, swing your arms, move about!"

I wasn't inclined to move anything. I couldn't in fact. Nothing would respond to my mental commands. In another minute, however, we were ashore. A warmed sleeping bag was tossed over my head; I was half carried to the glorious heat of a life-giving fire.

"How did he go?" asked Betty. "He's as blue as my undies!"

Julie replied, "He recovered the axe and filled a bag with canned food. Everything went well, although the water now seems even colder than on the day of the wreck."

"Go… now." I stuttered. "I'm… I'm OK."

"I'll dive next," said Julie. "If…" she then whispered to Betty. "If you'll dry me."

"Of course, honey, Evan won't get his big paws on you again."

While the diving party was away, I toasted my back, my front, then turned twice more around like a beast on a spit. In five minutes, my body was as warm as on a tropical beach. I quickly got dressed, threw a few more pieces of wood on the fire, then turned to watch the return of the inflatable.

Julie lay naked in the bow with Betty vigorously drying and massaging her limbs. She wasn't moving about either! I pulled her to her feet, threw the sleeping bag over her, and carried her to the warmth of the fire.

"Great work, honey." I gave her a fleeting kiss. "Just toast yourself and get dressed, we'll be right back."

Betty made the next dive. She came up snorting like a seal with a bag full of food in one hand and a bottle of Bundaberg in the other. Good ol' Bette! We yanked her aboard where, to my surprise, Evan again picked up the oars and began rowing ashore, leaving me with the not unpleasant task of drying and massaging her shapely body. This was no time for embarrassment! "Swing your arms," I said to the shivering, goose-pimply form lying helpless before me, knowing full well she couldn't.

Evan was a poor diver, but somehow brought up a can of kerosene that would fuel our camp stove, and also one of the rucksacks containing more clothing and our nylon climbing rope. After this, each of us in turn made a second dive and managed to salvage almost everything that would be of importance to us in the coming days. I even released some of the timbers and wedges we had previously used on the patch and let them wash ashore for later recovery.

"That's the lot then," said Betty, standing in the circle of toasting bodies before the blazing fire and again gleefully conjuring up another of her subtle jokes. "You know, Jules, I do hope our menfolk recover from all that freezing water; they were beginning to look like little boys again, don't you think?"

Julie blushed and changed the subject. "We'll never have to visit the poor old *Evening Star* again, will we, John?"

"Not unless it's to hack up the deck for more firewood," I replied sarcastically.

"We won't need any more," added Evan. "If we're less than two hundred kilometres from Mawson, we should build a sledge and get underway before the next blizzard."

I agreed. We could begin preparations this afternoon. He and the girls could sort out the necessary food and essentials while I would use my old skis as runners and put together a sledge that would suffice for the overland journey. With luck we could reach Mawson in three or four days but, in case of bad weather, we would carry emergency supplies for a few extra days.

"We shouldn't be in too much hurry to leave, though," I suggested. "That ridge above intrigues me. Who knows, there might be a hut or something on top: something really worth finding!"

"A hut full of supplies and... and maybe a radio!" murmured Julie, her hopes suddenly rekindled. "One of those emergency shelters!"

"Don't dream, Julie," Evan said coldly. "This is Antarctica, not Canada. These rocks are probably not even on the map."

"We'll go for a hike in the morning at any rate," I suggested. "A little exercise before starting out for Mawson won't do any harm."

With morning came a bitterly cold wind that flowed down from the plateau and stirred yesterday's calm sea into a frenzy. Everyone was reluctant to leave their warm sleeping bags and, in fact, there was no urgency to do so. Already our sledge was completed and the supplies sorted and ready for the journey. The only task remaining was to carry everything over the low end of the ridge to the beginning of the ice, then load up and get underway.

At ten a.m. the wind died away as suddenly as if a giant fan had switched off. We dressed, ate a quick breakfast, and were away within half an hour on our proposed hike up the steep ridge beneath the monolith.

As we climbed, vast expanses of blue sea and dazzling ice appeared around us. The west captured most of this attention, yet little we saw was particularly encouraging as far as a route to Mawson was concerned. Over the first few kilometres several large glaciers of broken and pulverised ice flowed into the sea where huge sections of it calved off to form icebergs. Crevasses were so numerous that a direct traverse around the coast would obviously be impossible, although, further inland, where the plateau snows covered the glaciers, a more feasible route was perhaps possible.

The dark blue water of our little bay opened out to merge with the paler expanse of ocean now studded with numerous tabular icebergs and extensive areas of closely packed brash-ice. A thin ribbon of white across the horizon was recognisable as the inner edge of the pack-ice.

"Look out! Duck!" Julie shouted as we neared the crest of the ridge.

Too late! Something smacked the top of my head knocking me to my knees. I threw my hands over my face for protection. Two large birds were making a similar attack on Evan.

"Watch them," I warned. "They might have poisonous spurs!"

We hurried on, but the attack became even more intense. A metre of brown and black wing, a menacing curved beak, and two extended webbed feet swooping towards one's head was a threat not to be taken lightly.

"Here's the cause of the trouble," called Julie. "Two chicks; two little grey bundles of down. Their parents are trying to steer us away from them."

The chicks, half the size of footballs, were found motionless in the centre of a patch of fine gravel, probably relying for protection solely on their aggressive parents and very effective camouflage.

"The little buggers," exclaimed Evan. "Causing so much trouble at such an early age."

Julie's wildlife knowledge spilled out. "They're probably McCormick skuas. If so, they are predators that range along the Antarctic coast living on eggs and chicks from any bird, even their own. I think they particularly like penguin eggs."

We moved onto the ridge-top to find a relatively flat area covered with man-sized boulders and wandered between these in the direction of the impressive tooth-like monolith a half kilometre further north. Eastward, could now be seen the other monolith where we had hoped to land two days earlier, and also the high coastal ice-cliffs that had blocked our way to safety during those desperate hours aboard our sinking yacht. These cliffs wound away without a break into the distant grey haze. Inland stretched a vast panorama of blue and white ice that rose gently in altitude to the vast Polar Plateau which eventually smothered the entire Antarctic continent. Even a half kilometre inland the ice was higher than the monoliths themselves.

There appeared to be no scientific huts or man-made objects anywhere, yet each of us still remained hopeful that something eventually would turn up.

Further along the ridge many more nesting chicks were discovered. These were much smaller than the skua's offspring, and had dark brown heads and backs, and a lighter under-plumage. Julie thought they were probably cape petrels. The chicks seemed unflustered when approached, yet watched our movements curiously with silent darting eyes. Their nests were shallow depressions in the gravel, sheltered from the elements by overhanging rock ledges and boulders.

"There are more nests over here," Evan called from ahead. "But most are empty."

Julie was fascinated with these discoveries. "These birds are only fledglings," she explained. "That's why so many nests are empty. As soon as they can fly, they're off with their parents to feed at sea and probably won't return here until late in the evening."

As we continued our exploration, it became clear that we were only yet on the fringe of the rookery, for soon we were amongst numerous other nests that probably stretched as far as the monolith itself. Julie sighted more colonies of birds and nests on the steep slopes below, but these were yet another species with silver-grey wings and bodies. "Possibly Antarctic petrels. It would take years to count them all," she sighed. "There are thousands of them. I wish I could tell the Audubon Society. I wish... I wish I could tell anyone!"

Near the foot of the monolith the ridge abruptly terminated above a deep rift that separated us from the steep smooth walls leading up to the summit. Continuing further would involve difficult climbing, so we turned and retraced our steps back through the boulders until directly above our camp, but then, in the hope of finding an easier route down, followed along the ridge towards the beginning of the ice slopes.

"Hey!" A movement ahead startled me. But then I shouted, "Stop! Stop! Wait for us!"

Betty saw him too. "It's a man! God, it's a man! Why the hell's he running? Stop! Wait! He's gone behind those rocks!"

"After him! Run!" I sprinted ahead in pursuit. It *was* a man? Why was he hiding? What the hell's wrong with him? My thoughts were in turmoil.

In seconds we were amongst a group of larger boulders where the figure had disappeared. We fanned out and searched, shouting loudly in all directions, climbing onto the high rocks to search again, but it all seemed to no avail. The four of us regrouped with bewilderment written across our faces.

"We *did* see someone, didn't we?" queried Julie. "I mean, I wasn't dreaming, was I?"

I caught her blank gaze. "Of course, you saw him, we all saw him: in a yellow anorak. You saw him, didn't you Evan?"

"Of course! He appeared on the ridge right here, seemed startled, then turned and fled. Why would he run? I can't believe it."

But Betty was already beginning to doubt her eyes. "Could it have been a reflection from the ice, or... or a flock of birds taking off, or..."

"Or what? Or bloody what? That was a man all right, a person anyway! I'm absolutely certain of that!" Yet if it had been, where was he now? Why wasn't he talking to us? Why would he run off and hide? God, this is Antarctica, there's no one else this side of Mawson!

In vain we searched for footprints or other signs, but then, more mystified than ever, began shrugging off our experience and finding explanations for the vision we thought everyone had seen. The descent continued in the silence of our own thoughts. If our eyes hadn't deceived us, we might now be safe and once again in the company of friends.

During the afternoon several portages were made with our sledge and supplies over the rocks to the foot of the ice slope from where we intended starting our haul to Mawson first thing the next morning. Here we loaded the sledge and attached two short and two longer hauling ropes, then pulled the load a short distance to be certain it was manageable. With everything looking good, the party returned to camp for a meal, giving me the opportunity to again speak with Evan about the figure we thought we'd seen.

"Of course, I saw it," he confirmed. "We all saw it, or at least we saw something. Possibly it could have been an illusion caused by ice flare or some other circumstance peculiar to these regions. Perhaps…"

I interrupted. "What you saw *was* real, cobber! You saw a *real* person. I actually glimpsed his face. Don't ask me why he ran, though. Let's you and I go and search the other side of the ridge and find this bashful bastard."

"Suits me. He might have a shelter there somewhere."

"Invite him around for coffee," suggested Betty, grinning broadly. Both she and Julie had now utterly convinced themselves the figure was an illusion. "But if he, turns out to be a *she*, tell her no thanks, we can manage OK!"

We all laughed. We could laugh now despite the cold, for it seemed certain that in a mere few days we would all stroll into the safety of Mawson Station.

A short time later Evan and I were again atop the ridge, peering down the eastern slope into a maze of broken ice between the two monoliths. There was no sign of human life. We agreed to search a flat area lower down near the glacier, and descended towards this by winding through large rounded boulders interspersed with frozen gravel to a steeper area of small rock bluffs that dropped away precipitously to the ice below. Cautiously we walked along exposed granite ledges, dropping to lower levels whenever possible.

"No camp fires, no huts, nothing," said Evan quietly. "I doubt if anyone's ever been here before."

Reluctantly I agreed. "But if we continue to the end of the slope at this level, we'll be certain."

We scrambled across a steep gully covered with more nests to where the slope became far too steep for any human habitation, then stopped to scan the rocks near and far.

"Well, now we can relax," said Evan. "There's no one here, and in my revised opinion there never was. What we saw was some inexplicable figment of our imagination."

We turned to retreat, and immediately glimpsed a pin-prick of light reflecting from something lower down beneath one of the bluffs. Evan was sceptical. "It's probably only ice. No shortage of that around here!"

"But there's none between the rocks, mate, only right down near the glacier. Anyhow, let's check it out while we're here."

By obliquely descending the slope it was possible to keep the reflection in view, but it wasn't until we approached within twenty metres of the source that we started to feel uneasy and began to realise it might not be ice after all. Our voices quietened as we crept nearer.

"Christ, Evan, it's some sort of shelter! That reflection's coming from a window!"

"All stone; it blends into the cliff. Who the hell could be living here?"

"An old hermit, maybe? A shipwrecked sailor like us. Must have gone a bit 'bonkers' over the years and doesn't want visitors."

Evan nodded. We crept to the front of the shelter and found a door behind a windbreak of rocks.

I looked at my companion. "Well, what do we do now... just knock?"

He never hesitated and knocked very loudly.

There was a scuffle inside, then silence; a bearded face flashed behind the window, then the door burst open. We were staring into the barrel of a sub-machine gun!

"Whoa! Take it easy, chum, we're friends, we're shipwrecked too. Name's John Watkins. This is my friend, Doctor Evan Jackson, we're...

The weapon pushed into my ribs; a second bearded person appeared with a rifle and held it to Evan's head. These weren't shipwrecked sailors, these were evil people up to no good, Greek or Spanish, long yellowy faces, drooping moustaches, oily skins, both in their forties.

"Eenside," one ordered, with a deep rasping voice, jabbing his gun deeper into my ribs.

"Stand 'ere. Up 'ands!"

We faced a bare rock wall stuffed with paper to reduce the drafts. They searched us for weapons.

"Now seet 'ere."

We slithered to a floor of rough planks at our captor's feet, glimpsing the rude furnishings: a pot-bellied oil stove, kerosene lamp, a small table with packing case seats, a corner stacked with picks and shovels.

I tried again. "We're friends. We mean no harm. Our yacht was wrecked here. Tomorrow we'll be leaving for Mawson."

A reply was not forthcoming. Two pairs of yellowish eyes continued to blaze uneasily at us. But then the door opened again.

"What the... Who are you? Where... Luis, Miguel, put down those guns. Put them down immediately!"

"Thank Christ someone's sane around here," I said, breathing more easily without the guns threatening us. "I'm John."

The ginger bearded man in yellow wind proofs interrupted me. "So, I never fooled you on the ridge; you didn't mistake me for another of your party? We haven't heard any choppers, in fact, we thought your relief ship sailed last week. You are Australians, aren't you? How many...?"

"Please! Can we have one question at a time. Frankly, I don't know what you're talking about. We're Australians all right, but we didn't come by helicopter; we were shipwrecked here. We have nothing to do with any Mawson expedition."

"You mean you just sailed in here and were shipwrecked? Who else knows you're here?"

I briefly explained our dilemma to the young, pleasant faced man, and watched him relax. Then it was our turn to ask questions.

"You're an Aussie too, aren't you, and your friends are Spanish, perhaps? What are you doing here?"

"These men are Portuguese. They speak little English. My name is Ralph, from Queens Terrace, Adelaide. We are here… er, on a geological expedition." …

"But surely Mawson knows you're here?" suggested Evan. "They'll be returning to pick you up, won't they?"

"No. We'll be picked up next summer by a Portuguese ship. No one else knows we're here."

"Well, why the guns?" I continued. "Why did you hide from us this morning? Why all the mystery?"

Ralph looked at us briefly, then over at his colleagues as if uncertain whether or not to answer our questions, but then he smiled nervously and apologised. "We shouldn't be treating people in distress like this. You deserve all the help it's possible to give. The truth is that your sudden arrival here is the last thing we anticipated and it's caught us completely off guard. You see we, er… we don't exactly have permission to be here, and… and are somewhat concerned that you will inform on us. This is an especially sensitive area because of the rookery, so…"

The two Portuguese suddenly urged Ralph outside. A torrent of incomprehensible words followed, growing in intensity to angry shouts. I looked at Evan. "We haven't been told half the story yet, mate. Why the guns? Why aren't we welcome?"

Evan had a hunch. "Judging by all those digging tools in the corner, it seems to me they're after something of value; gold, maybe?"

"And because of the Antarctic Treaty, no mineral exploitation is permitted. Perhaps that's why they're unhappy about being discovered."

Outside, the angry confrontation continued. The man with the automatic weapon was waving it dangerously in front of Ralph. Then they all stormed back inside.

"You must go now," said Ralph. "My friends are very upset with your presence. Go now and I'll visit you later. Go quickly!"

The Portuguese barred the doorway as we tried to leave but Ralph shoved us through, arguing fiercely in fragments of each language, then blocking the way to stop them following.

It was a relief to be free again. Without stopping, we hurried to the ridge top, glanced back to be sure no one was following, then dived down the other side to our camp.

"Did you find our elusive yellow pimpernel," joked Betty. "You were supposed to bring him around for coffee."

But when she noticed the strained expressions on our faces, her humour stopped. She handed each of us a mug of hot tea and settled back with Julie to hear our bizarre story.

"They must be crooks of some kind," she determined. "No ordinary people down here would carry guns. The sooner we get away from here the better."

"They wouldn't harm us, surely," surmised Julie. "Perhaps they're short of supplies and don't want us intruding!" I shook my head.

"Whatever's the true story, we're not going to wait around to hear it. I no longer feel safe with those Portuguese and their guns roaming about. We'll get a good night's sleep and start out for Mawson first thing in the morning."

Our sleep, however, was interrupted. At two a.m., just after dawn, a loud slap on our shelter woke us with a start. A voice called:

"It's I, Ralph." He threw back the sail and stood over us. "You must leave now," he warned. "The Portuguese are planning to kill you!"

CHAPTER 4

"Kill us?" I lurched forward in my sleeping bag. "Kill us? What are you talking about, Ralph?"

"The Portuguese talked last night; they decided you'd tell the Australians about our visit when they fly in next summer. We'll still be here then. Our ship is not due until after the pack-ice disperses. I argued with them for hours. I told them I'd speak with you, get assurances that you wouldn't say anything, but they were impossible to convince; they said they couldn't take the risk, couldn't trust you. The only certain way was to get rid of you!"

"But Ralph — Christ man, we've only been here two days, we don't know what you're up to. Why would they want to kill us?"

He looked at the four of us staring open mouthed up at him, relaxed a little, then sat down at our feet. "They don't know I'm here. They won't be looking for you yet. All right… I'll tell you my story and help you get to Mawson if you'll assure me you won't mention our presence to anyone."

"Go on then, Ralph, tell us why you're here."

"Well, two years ago I was stationed at Mawson as a biologist. During that summer while our helicopters were operating, a party of us flew here to Scullin Monolith to study incubating chicks at the rookery. It's one of the world's largest, some ten million Antarctic petrels, more than eight thousand other birds. But, because of poor flying conditions, the choppers were unable to return for a couple of days to pick us up, so I filled in time by collecting rock samples for a lapidary friend of mine. While fossicking around the lower slopes of the ridge I discovered some interesting white translucent stones mixed with the gravel. These were bagged with many other specimens and stored away for a year until I found time to show them to my friend in Adelaide. He was immediately impressed with the translucent stones and suggested I let a jeweller look at them as he thought they may be some form of native diamond. And sure enough, they were. The jeweller later gave me a sizable cheque for the handful I brought back."

Evan gave a quiet whistle. The story was becoming so intriguing that the urgency of Ralph's visit was temporarily forgotten.

"Go on, Ralph, what then?"

"Well, it was difficult deciding what to do about my discovery. If I told the Antarctic Division, I'd be in trouble for taking the stones without permission. But more importantly, because of the Antarctic Treaty, exploitation of all mineral resources down here is forbidden. That means the source of the diamonds would be recorded, but their recovery prohibited. Yet, when news of the discovery inevitably leaked out it would most certainly attract unscrupulous fortune hunters who would literally tear this unique and fragile rookery to pieces searching for other deposits. As a dedicated biologist, this was unacceptable. On the other hand, if I kept quiet about my discovery, sooner or later the find would be rediscovered and the rookery would face the same destruction."

Ralph paused a moment as if expecting questions, but everyone remained silent. He continued.

"So I decided the best thing to do was to find a ship that would return me to Scullin Monolith to collect the remaining visible diamonds, then close the book on them forever. However, finding a suitable ship for a reasonable price wasn't easy until I went to Hong Kong and discovered this Portuguese captain who seemed the most trustworthy of a bad lot. Unfortunately, this man was suspicious of my request right from the start and insisted on hearing the full story before agreeing to take me. He swore to secrecy, so reluctantly I told him everything. He would drop me at Scullin after a voyage to Cape Town and guaranteed to collect me the following summer after the pack-ice dispersed. There was of course one condition: that he received one half of the remaining diamonds. And to assure him I wouldn't disappear with the lot aboard an Aussie chopper, he insisted on leaving two men to *assist* me.

"We arrived here a few weeks before you and collected a single seam of diamonds worth perhaps half a million dollars. Later, we searched the surrounding areas without finding any further traces, so are now quite confident that no more, exist. Had you people not disturbed us, the plan would have gone well, but now, the Portuguese fear their share is at risk, and it seems they are quite prepared to kill to protect it."

"You stand to lose a small fortune as well, Ralph," remarked Evan. "So why are you telling us all this? Why don't you support your murderous friends?"

"Because I'm just an ordinary biologist, not a criminal, I never expected this project to turn sour like this. My only interest is protecting the rookery... not killing anyone! My share of the earnings will probably go towards protecting wildlife."

"You said you would help us escape. What do you have in mind?" I asked.

"Well, as shipwrecked sailors, no doubt you intended pushing on to Mawson, so I'm prepared to help you with supplies and maps. But first, you should be warned that this journey has never been done before overland, although in 1967 a party from Mawson, in vehicles, reached the Gustav Bull Mountains, only twenty kilometres inland from here and one hundred and sixty kilometres from Mawson. Their route is marked on the map I'll give you."

"Thanks, Ralph. We won't say anything about your visit. We intended leaving today at any rate."

"Good, but you'll need better footwear and a blizzard-proof tent. Get dressed, I'll show you something that will help."

Soon after, Ralph walked with us to our sledge and examined briefly our supplies and equipment. "The journey won't be easy," he explained. "In good weather you might make Mawson in six days, but in blizzard conditions... well, you know Scott's story, don't you? You should leave all this canned food here; it would take too much cooking fuel to thaw it out. You can leave your sail and boots here also."

We looked at Ralph, inquiringly.

"Come, follow me up the ridge." He led us quickly to a flat area only a short distance from where we first glimpsed him yesterday, and then to a large yellow circle painted on a flat rock. "It's a helicopter pad. But over here is what will interest you most."

Our eyes followed Ralph to a stack of cloth-bound packages beside a large red box.

"Ration packs, emergency supplies and equipment for use in situations like yours. Each pack will feed twelve men for one day, or in your case, the four of you for three days. I suggest you take all four packs.

106

In this red box are other items you'll need." He spread the contents before us.

"Mukluks!" Julie grabbed the smallest pair and began trying them on. "Just like the ones I wore back home."

"They're made in Canada. Take a pair each, and a couple of pairs of long socks. And this tent, it's designed for three, but sleeps four with a squeeze. Take one stove and twenty litres of kerosene. Remember Scott again: take plenty of fuel! Wind proof anoraks and pants; they're an early issue but very effective. And gloves, take two pairs each. There's only two ice-axes. You already have a rope. And here's the map I promised you."

Ralph helped us carry our newly acquired stores down the slope to the sledge and watched while we lashed them securely aboard. "Now you must go," he said. "You'll scare hell out of the Mawson boys when you knock on their door, but they'll make you welcome. Just head due south for a few kilometres and you'll sight the mountains to the south-west, then your knowledge of navigation will take you from there. Goodbye! Remember your promise. Good luck!"

Each of us shook Ralph's hand gratefully, then donned our rope loops and started pulling.

A stop for breath came on the steep slope only minutes later. Ralph had already disappeared. The view back over the blue, serene bay and brown monoliths impressed us with its lonely beauty; it was almost as though we were looking down on a small coastal village from the edge of a white sandy desert. This thought, however, was dispelled by a speckling of icebergs drifting aimlessly across the smooth expanse of pale blue sea. Behind them, almost obscured in the distant haze, was the edge of the pack-ice, stretching like a white ribbon across the horizon into the distant unknown.

The girls on the shorter ropes were talking. "It just doesn't make sense," said Julie. "That there are people down there who actually wanted us killed! I must have dreamed it."

"Because it all looks so peaceful and beautiful?" asked Betty. "Well, the ocean looked placid and lovely too, but remember, it also tried several times to finish us!"

"But that's different; nature is unpredictable, it isn't evil like those

107

Portuguese, they…"

"OK, time to move," I called. "From now on let's forget Ralph and his cut-throat crew and concentrate on Mawson and those hot showers!"

By keeping the sledge on roadways of clear ice, and walking on the less slippery snow beside it, excellent progress was made up the slope, but after an hour the way flattened a little, and ice hillocks appeared behind, to soon block out the view to the coast. A dramatically different world of ice had been entered. Here were gentle rolling hills with frozen melt streams meandering through the valleys to flow into milky-blue ice lakes. There was no dominating feature in any direction to absorb our interest. More than ever before, the chilling feeling of isolation closed around us.

Betty momentarily returned us all from our innermost thoughts with one of her spontaneous outbursts. "Plant a bit of grass here and there," she quipped. "Toss in a few grizzlies, and bingo, we have another Alaska. On second thoughts, maybe some chipmunks would suffice!"

She aroused a few fleeting smiles, but then lost us again. It was getting colder. Every metre we climbed above sea level would lower the temperature a fraction more, particularly now that the warming effect of the rocks and sea breeze had been lost. Tonight, would be like camping in a refrigerator, the largest refrigerator on earth! During the early afternoon the terrain again changed; we had reached the head of a valley and before us lay a very steep slope leading up to what we hoped was the beginning of the Polar Plateau. We toiled up this, slipping frequently on blue ice, sometimes pulling, sometimes pushing, occasionally jamming something beneath the runners, to brake the sledge while we rested and nibbled dry biscuits.

"Only one more pull," I told my friends to encourage them. "And we should sight the mountains."

We pushed on; but only now were we realizing that a different scale of proportions existed here to what we had previously been accustomed to. A slope we anticipated climbing in ten minutes, usually took thirty; a hill that appeared to be a kilometre away was often three or more. Antarctica's vastness would take time adjusting to.

Eventually, however, the slope began to level out, making hauling easier and faster, then, what looked like a small rounded rock appeared on the skyline. This gradually grew in size as we progressed until a full mountain eventually appeared before us, rising starkly from the plateau ice some ten kilometres to the south-west. "The Gustav Bull Mountains at last! When we reach them," I joked, "it's downhill all the way to Mawson."

Betty always went one better. "If there's a freeway, Jules and I will be hitching a ride on a Safeway truck right through to this Mawsonville resort."

"Safeway?" mused Julie. "No chance of them stopping unless we're wearing shorts, and perhaps that's not very appropriate today!"

Apart from these spontaneous outbursts of frivolity, our thoughtful silence persisted on the journey to the mountains even though the sledge was now much easier to haul across the flat terrain. This seemed an ideal time to be alone with one's thoughts. The snow surface, however, wasn't always smooth; often it was scoured by *sastrugi* — wind sculptured snow resembling tank traps of the war era — which frequently caused one runner to ride up over it and overturn the sledge. The haulers would then be jerked to a standstill and snapped back into conversation.

"Which side of the mountains are we heading for, John?" asked Evan.

"The west, I suppose, that's the way the Mawson party came. We might spot a cairn or something left by them. Another hour should do it."

"Another hour and I'll be pooped," admitted Betty. "Let's look for an early camp and examine our new tent and provisions."

Our eyes stayed glued to the mountains as we crept alongside in search of a safe camping site amongst the shelter of the steep bluffs. And at last, one was sighted. We swung the sledge inwards, bursting into a slow jog as thoughts of rest and a hot meal became foremost in our minds.

"STOP! STOP!" I shouted, yanking back on the sledge ropes. "Don't go a step further!"

The astonished trio froze, searching about them for danger.

Evan at last spoke. "We won't find a better site than that. Why... what's wrong?"

It was still uncertain whether or not I'd sounded a false alarm. "Have any of you read about wind-scours?" I asked. "Because it's possible there's one just ahead!"

With an ice-axe from the sledge I walked cautiously in front of the group, prodding the gently rising slope with every step. Suddenly it became clear I was right, the surface we were crossing abruptly ended; my feet balanced on the brink of a fearful void. Fifty metres below were rocks that had fallen from the mountain, yet from a few metres back all this had been completely invisible; the snow had appeared unbroken right to the rocks.

"Come up and look," I suggested. "But carefully, one at a time!" Evan was first; he appeared shocked. The girls saw the gigantic wind-scour and retreated quickly to the rear of the sledge.

"Another few steps and…" Julie's eyes were owl-like. "We would have gone right over, we would have all been killed!"

"What warned you, John?" Evan asked soberly.

"A bird… a skua probably. I was watching it soar overhead when suddenly it dived — straight into the snow — or so it seemed. The expected thud never came! That was my warning! Something I'd read about wind-scours flashed through my mind; it seemed possible that this bird had flown into one. Apparently, they form on the windward side of mountains where swirling winds scour out the snow."

"A skua, eh!" said Betty thoughtfully. "From now on they have my greatest respect. Can we go now, I no longer feel safe around here!"

A kilometre further on, firm snow was found on the leeward side of a protruding rock ridge, allowing an easy approach to a level snow patch beside a huge rounded boulder. This would make an ideal campsite.

Our tent was found to be made from a heavy, closely woven material, and was supported with steel A-frame poles and a steel ridge pole, and was designed to be anchored down with pegs of sharpened angle aluminium which drove easily into the hard snow. When erected, the yellow shelter felt very stable, but was barely large enough for four people despite a long sleeve extending from one end which would be useful for storing food and excess gear. We shovelled snow onto an outer flap of the tent to weight it down for even greater stability against the wind.

"You guys stay up that end," ordered Betty when Evan and I finally entered to warm up. "We chefs are about to serve your 'tucker'."

"And boy, is it special!" added Julie enthusiastically. "Soup *de jour*, Knorr's, of course, followed by HF6, some mysterious form of concentrated meat, plus Canadian freeze-dried vegetables. We mixed everything together with powdered spud to make a thick stew. And for follow-ups there are freeze-dried strawberries, navy biscuits, canned butter, honey, cheese, chocolate. Not bad, eh?"

It also 'wasn't bad' the way the little tent trapped the heat from the tiny pressure stove and held in the aroma from the cooking pot. We smacked our lips in anticipation. At this rate our hike to Mawson could even be enjoyable!

The night went well also. Very little cold seeped through the insulated floor mats Ralph had given us and, with our bodies packed so closely together, everyone remained warm throughout the allotted eight hours of sleeping time.

The sun was already high in the sky when we stirred at four a.m., although outside the air remained bitterly cold. Little time was wasted repacking the sledge and moving off.

"We'll head due west from here," I told my companions. "There should be no problem navigating while we're within sight of the mountains, but afterwards the route won't be so straightforward."

"Why not?" remarked Evan. "You're supposed to be an experienced navigator. We have the sea only twenty kilometres to the north, and according to the map there's a Mount Henderson and a Masson Range on the outskirts of Mawson to guide us in."

"True enough, mate, but polar navigation has its complications. The magnetic compass, for instance, is no longer reliable."

The first few hours over hard smooth snow was easy, but then the *sastrugi* reappeared in distressing heights, causing us to either make time wasting deviations, or to pull excessively hard over these problem areas. A heavily crevassed dome directly ahead also forced a long detour. The mountains quickly disappeared behind snow ridges as we descended into shallow valleys that led us blindly through a fantasy of glaring blue and white ice hills. Often it seemed we were dreaming. Whatever happened to the warm sunny ocean we were supposed to be enjoying?

A shriek pierced our ears! Evan and I swung around.

"CREVASSE!"

"Hold on, Julie," I shouted, leaping across the broken snow cover to seize her arms as she clung desperately to a sledge runner. Her body was swinging freely over a gaping blue hole. "Where's Betty, where?"

"God, she's gone!"

We whisked Julie to safety, lay on our stomachs to peer into the bottomless depths of an enormous icicle shrouded cavern.

"Help me!" a voice echoed from below.

"She's alive! Thank God! Still hanging from her sledge rope."

I grabbed the climbing rope, uncoiled it, looped one end, hurled it down into the void. "Bette!" I called, subduing the panic within me. "Can you see the rope we dropped?"

Only a mumble was audible.

"Can you see the rope?" I then shouted.

"I can't move," came a pained reply. "The bloody sledge rope's cutting my arms. I'm slipping from the loop!"

"Look for the other loop, Bette, I'm shaking it."

"I see the rope. Pull it up a bit."

The climbing rope suddenly went taut. She was standing in the loop, relieving the pressure on her body, resting a moment.

"Everything OK, now?" I called down.

"Cold! Bloody scared!"

"Do exactly as I say, Bette. Take the weight again on your waist loop, then let your knee bend as I pull in the climbing rope. Good, now stand in the foot loop again."

As she did this, the sledge rope went slack and I also pulled that taut. Betty caught on quickly. By transferring her weight between ropes, she was able to climb effortlessly to the lip of the crevasse, whereas a direct pull might have jerked her from the loop.

We grabbed both arms and lifted her to safety.

For a full minute Betty knelt on the snow, breathing heavily and recomposing herself while Evan brushed snow from her hair and face. Then she got up, gave a 'Bette' grin and murmured, "That was neat; that Aussie rope trick was really neat. Maybe you guys really did go climbing in Switzerland and not chasing after *frauleins* as I suspected!"

We each gave her a hug, Evan also a kiss as he held her a little longer. Julie remained somewhat pale, but was soon ready to continue.

From then on everyone kept their waist loops tight, and Evan and I prodded every suspicious depression in the snow with the ice-axes before proceeding across them.

The ensuing few kilometres were over crevasse-riddled snow which kept progress painfully slow while criss-crossing about trying to find a practical route. But then the way suddenly became clear again, allowing us to speed up across level, *sastrugi*-free snow towards the next distant ice-hills. A misty layer of thin cloud now blotted out the sun allowing temperatures to plummet and, at the same time, a rising wind began picking up snow and blowing it like fine salt across our feet. Occasionally, fiercer gusts fired ice crystals painfully into our faces, forcing each of us to draw in the strings of our newly acquired anoraks and be thankful for the excellent protection they and the baggy yellow pants gave us.

"Another early camp would be welcome, John," suggested Evan.

"Welcome, yes, but out of the question. We must push ourselves to the limit if we're going to reach Mawson before the weather really packs up. Christ knows what other obstacles lay before us!"

"Well, killing ourselves won't help! The girls have had a rough day, they need rest."

"I know, Evan, but by the look of that gathering cloud we'll all be resting tomorrow, like it or not. Today we'll push on as far as possible."

Evan mumbled something then again went quiet. The girls' heads were bent low as they put real effort into pulling, so there seemed little sense in calling a halt until they finally complained of fatigue. The drift blowing continually from the south at least made navigation easy.

At ten p.m., after an estimated thirty kilometres of travel, it became apparent that the girls had now reached their endurance limit even though neither were prepared to admit it. They too seemed absorbed in the celestial phenomena directly ahead where an ominous red sun rested on the horizon beneath a semi-circle of three mock suns; all joined together by an arc of bright refracted light. Yellow spokes radiating from the central sun to each of the others completed a fascinating geometrical pattern.

Could such a mysterious display of splendour mean anything? It was no star of Bethlehem, yet if somehow it could remain long enough in the western sky for us to follow, it would surely guide us right into Mawson. I revered at its presence.

When next I stopped pulling, the others looked up and stared hopefully at me. "Time for some more HF6," I quipped.

"Boy, about time," replied Betty. "I could eat a horse, and that's probably what HF6 is!"

Julie sat briefly on the sledge, she was completely spent. Evan unfurled the tent, I banged in pegs, Betty pushed the poles into place. Julie then revived sufficiently to help with the guy ropes.

Inside, with the stove purring noisily to melt more snow for coffee, and hot stew being spooned into hungry mouths, we revived rapidly and relaxed to allow the girls to relate more fully their unnerving crevasse adventure.

"You guys walked straight over it," began Julie. "But when we tried, the snow just fell away."

Betty interrupted. "We flapped our arms over that ruddy gaping hole for a second while our hearts tried to jump out through our mouths, then I concluded I was no sparrow and just sank. Wow, I'd still be sinking if that rope hadn't held."

"I saw her disappear," continued Julie. "Then I spun around and grabbed the sledge. I... I didn't want to let go even when you guys grabbed me." She was smiling now though her eyes were still wide from the frightening experience.

"It was cold as a whale's belly down there. I peered up to see the sky through those great blue lips, but then began feeling my wounds as the rope cut into my armpits. I was bloody petrified! The rope kept slipping up. If you had pulled... well, there would be more room in the tent tonight!"

Evan remained quiet, his eyes glued to Betty. Perhaps his feelings for her were deeper than any of us thought; perhaps this sworn bachelor was at last experiencing the first pangs of true love!

Julie and I slid into our bags with our heads towards the sleeve entrance. "Sounds like rain on the tent," she whispered as she snuggled closer.

"I wish it were, honey, then we'd probably be camped on green grass somewhere instead of inside this refrigerator. The drift seems to be getting worse."

"Hopefully it will stop by morning. Remember, you promised us hot showers at Mawson! I'm very tired. Sleep tight, darling. Goodnight everyone."

But nobody slept. During the night the wind continued its steady increase until the tent flapped and shook like a slack sail. Snow was building up against the outside wall making it necessary to frequently push hard against it to stop its encroachment on our already cramped sleeping space but, once consolidated, the build-up of snow served as a very effective windbreak.

From time to time we dozed, but then the scream of another wind gust would snap us back to reality. Drifting snow and ice granules lashed the besieged fabric. Occasional lulls allowed brief moments of welcome respite until the fabric again exploded outwards like a rifle shot, and the onslaught recommenced with as much fury as ever.

Dawn came, but it was long after the first light had filtered through the yellow fabric that I untied the door to glimpse the desolate grey scene outside. In swirled a deluge of powder snow that instantly frosted our bags and sent heads burying deeper inside them. I reclosed it quickly. There would be no travel today.

"How is it?" a male voice asked from amongst the congestion of bodies.

"Shithouse!" I replied gruffly. "A total whiteout. No chance of moving in this."

My annoyance was ignored. Didn't anyone else give a damn whether or not we continued? But once back in the warmth of my sleeping bag the urgency of travel felt within me also quickly dwindled. Everyone had been working very hard lately, so perhaps a day's relaxation was justified after all! In fact, being so warm and snug with nothing to do except listen to the howl of the wind was therapy I had long forgotten.

My arm remained around Julie most of the day; our heads close together whispering treasured confidences we'd had so little time to consider in recent times. We spoke of our impending marriage, whom we would invite, our honeymoon at Coles Bay. Then we discussed Tasmania. Its rounded eucalypt-covered hills, its warm yellow beaches, the Central Plateau with its lakes and mountains, the beautiful and rugged south-west. She would love making her home in this tiny island state with its relaxed way of life and easy-going people.

The blizzard hammered the tent all day with a fury we'd only seen before at sea and, towards evening when we hoped it would die down, the onslaught actually increased. Shouting became necessary to be heard above the piercing scream of the unrelenting wind as it tore mercilessly at the shivering fabric until the tent verged on splitting open; its steel poles flexing like fishing rods.

"Let's hope this tent was designed for blizzards," Evan said loudly as he struggled to heat some soup over the stove. "Because if it rips open, we'll be searching for a crevasse to crawl into!"

"It won't," I replied with pseudo confidence. "The Aussies have been active down here for forty years, so their gear ought to be perfected by now." Perhaps this statement consoled Julie somewhat, but not Evan or Betty, for surely the constant vibration and pounding must eventually weaken the fabric. What then? Were we really any safer here than aboard the storm-tossed *Evening Star*? If the tent ripped open, we would be spewed out into the elements with nowhere to shelter. An hour outside, or an hour in the inflatable; what was the difference? The results would be the same!

Someone banging on the tent disturbed my doze. It was Julie trying to get back inside after her nature call. "Help me, John, please help me!" she called.

I whipped open the sleeve, grabbed at a struggling snowball, yanked it inside. She was weeping softly.

"I can't see, John. My eyes, my face, my hands, all frozen. The wind is cruel, it's…"

I draped a towel over her head and rubbed vigorously to clear away the ice as she continued her frenzied story. "The wind tosses you around like paper, snow swirls into your eyes, up your nose. I let go the guy-rope for a second, only a second, stood up and couldn't find it again. I swung my arms in all directions, never touched anything; everywhere looked the same: grey, swirling clouds of snow. I was lost, scared. So terribly scared! I ran about, left, right, yelling, then tripped over a peg. Oh, John…"

She fell into my arms, pressed her face against mine. Betty moved down to massage her frozen fingers. "Relax, honey, relax, it's over now, you'll be all right, come on, back into your bag."

Day turned to night, night back to day. We were losing track of time. Betty produced yet another evening meal and sounded more distressed than ever. "Already four days of blizzard without even a minute's break. How much bloody longer? This waiting and sleeping and thinking and eating is driving me up the god-dammed wall!"

But no one was interested in her wit. "It can't last much longer," I said encouragingly. "If it clears tomorrow, those hot showers will only be days away."

Evan spoke gruffly. "We'll need a third ration pack tomorrow, and three days later we'll start on our last. What if the blizzard continues? Our twelve days' rations will be gone before we're even halfway!"

His argument made sense, but was no morale booster. "Maybe we'll find another depot like the one at Scullin. If not, a little food conservation should get us through."

"Less food? Christ, John, you're a dreamer. If we're to pull sixteen hours a day, we need *more* than normal rations; and as for finding a grocery store out here — bullshit!"

"Well, what do you bloody well want to do, Evan, run back to your mates, Luis and Miguel and ask them for food? They might give you some too, before they slit your throat! Do you want to go back? is that what you're suggesting?"

He never replied or said anything more that evening; neither did anyone else. If the weather didn't get better soon tempers were unlikely to improve! The rest of the night was spent tossing restlessly in our bags without any hope of more sleep. A few good novels at this time might be worth more than Ralph's diamonds!

On the fifth day of blizzard Evan pulled on his wind proofs for his daily venture outside. "Grab another ration pack while you're out," I asked, but he never replied as he clambered over Julie to squeeze out through the sleeve entrance. I pulled the sleeping bag tighter around my face and again let my eyes close. The tent was now almost completely covered with snow, muffling the sound of the storm, letting the fabric rest.

It was easy to dream, reclining on a hot Queensland beach with the waves gently washing my feet, a partly read novel in one hand, the other shading my eyes from the brilliant sun. Julie was there; she placed a cold beer on my chest and tried to wake me. "John!" Her voice seemed deeper than usual. "Wake up, John, wake up!"

My eyes opened to find Betty leaning over me.

"I'm worried," she said quickly. "Evan's been gone a long time. He should be back by now!"

My watch showed he had only been gone ten minutes. "He's probably digging out the sledge, Bette, everything would be iced up."

She sank back in her bag but, like me, remained tense and alert. Anxious minutes crept by. Whenever the tent shook more violently than normal, we jerked our heads towards the entrance in expectation of Evan's return, but it was never him. Twenty minutes passed. Then we reacted together: both pulling on wind proofs and mukluks and struggling to get out through the iced-up entrance.

Christ! Outside was another world; a wind tunnel of blasting ice crystals and swirling drift. Visibility was zero. We grabbed each other as the wind spun us about and tossed us to the ground. Ice cut our faces; snow filled our eyes and mouths. Desperately we struggled to pull on goggles then turned our heads until the full blast of the elements was absorbed by our hoods.

"Evan! Evan!" It was hopeless shouting into the screaming gale.

"Evan! Where are you Evan?" Betty's shout hardly reached me. She then yelled into my ear. "He's in trouble! What can we do?"

"Go back inside; heat up some soup. I'll see if he's at the sledge."

Betty was reluctant to obey so I shoved her rudely through the entrance then turned to face into the blizzard. God, merely releasing my grip on the security of the tent filled me with fear. I dropped to my knees, hands on the snow, and wriggled forward each time the wind drew a breath. I caught my own as it again howled around me. Only eight or so paces to the sledge; it might well be eighty! Shit, where was it? Where am I? Only metres from my friends, yet seemingly on another planet! A grey, turbulent world where every direction looked alike.

Still no sledge? Had I missed it? My searching arms touched nothing. A deluge of drift smothered my body, stole my air. I fought against panic; I breathed deeply, calmed myself, wriggled forward. It must be here, God, it must be here. I touched wood and hugged the sledge. I cried out with relief! But why was I here? My now leaden brain reacted slowly. A ration pack? No. Evan. Where was Evan? He wasn't here, he must have gone back. I turned to return also, but then paused, and staggered back to the sledge. A ration pack was missing. Evan *had* been here!

The wind blew me from the sledge. I couldn't see, my goggles were now useless blobs of ice. I shoved them up; icicles formed between my eyelids and blinking became impossible. I scrubbed at them with gloved hands leaving ice crystals dangling like rows of glass beads. Breath turned my balaclava to an ice mask that stuck firmly to my face. I was blown to the snow, bowled along until stopped by a mound of *sastrugi*; cowered a moment, then dived again for the tent. Another fierce gust, I crouched on my knees and waited. The next dash covered several metres; hands outstretched to stop barging into the tent. But where was it? Fear returned. This time I ran faster; dived to the snow before the next gust blew me there. Still no tent? Where the hell was it? The wind was now laughing at me, mocking me! Another deep breath, another run.

I knelt with my back to the smothering drift and tried to reason out my error. There must be no panic, no more rushing aimlessly about. Think carefully. Had I followed the wind too closely? Shouldn't I have veered slightly to the left? Have I come too far? I must retrace a little, go further left.

Rather than again face the blast of drift, I pushed backwards for a minute, then side-stepped several metres. Now the tent would certainly be within reach, my searching arms *must* now touch it, just a little more left, a little further ahead. Christ, where the hell is it? I shouted and called loudly for my friends. I hardly heard my own voice, but they would hear; they're right next to me! Why don't they come? Again, I ran a few steps ahead, a few more to the right, waving my arms in every direction. Nothing! It was all a bad dream. Tears of fear and exhaustion turned to ice. Let me wake up! Enough of this stupid nightmare.

I was staggering now; just wandering about looking for something that was probably here somewhere! My head throbbed. The blizzard raged on. Frequently I was on my knees, sometimes sobbing like a lost child, sometimes wondering. I was then back on my feet for another search. It all seemed so fruitless, such a waste of energy; how much easier to just lay on the snow and become covered in a warm blanket of drift. My friends would wake me later. It was nice to dream a little. Such lovely greenery, lovely lakes, warm beaches...

Something attacked! An animal? I kicked at it, punched it; it leapt on me, pinned me down, clawed at my face.

"Help me, Julie, help me, I've found Evan!"

I was being dragged away — had to play dead!

Something burning touched my face. My clothes were being torn off!

"It's not Evan, it's John. John darling, are you, all right?"

"Then where's Evan? For God's sake, where's Evan?"

The warm water soon cleared my iced-up face, but then pain, excruciating pain, erupted from the flesh. I smothered my head in frozen hands until the torture spread to my fingers. I pushed Julie away; tensed my whole body and fought the urge to scream. But then the pain slowly subsided and it seemed I was sweating in a steaming sauna.

"Drink this tea, darling, you'll soon be all right; get back into your bag." Julie's eyes, wide and lovely, were medicine in themselves.

Betty spoke more urgently. "John. Did you see Evan? Did you see any sign of him?"

"Evan?" My mouth gaped open, I raised onto an elbow to look around. "Isn't he here? No... no, I couldn't find him. He was at the sledge... took a ration pack."

"Then he must have missed the tent coming back. He's probably down wind of us. Come, Julie, hold the rope, I'm going to look again."

Rope? The climbing rope. Why hadn't I thought of that? Betty disappeared through the tent entrance. Thoughts of the raging blizzard outside rekindled. She mustn't go! I dived to stop her!

"It's all right, John," said Julie. "I've got her, she's quite safe. You must rest. Please get into your bag and rest."

My feet were now thawing and wracking my legs with pain. I tried to watch Julie. She was playing out the rope as if fishing, but then my eyes closed to relieve the torture in my limbs. I dozed a little, then snapped back to reality to see Julie hurriedly jerking in the snow-covered rope.

She was coming back at last. She had been away over ten minutes. A thud hit the tent shaking it wildly; in fell a snow enshrouded figure. It lay across us sobbing. Julie turned her over, wiped her frozen face with a towel, held her tightly in her arms. When the ice melted, her balaclava was peeled off.

"I couldn't find him, Julie. It's horrible out there. The air is full of ice, screaming, flying, swirling ice. It tosses you around like… Julie, you must try, please go out and look."

"Of course, Bette, of course I'll look, but… but, would he still be… all right? It's been so long…"

"Of course, he's alive. Go now. Search downwind to the left. Be careful!"

My eyes remained glued to Betty as she played out the rope, but my thoughts remained with Julie. Poor kid would be petrified. The blizzard would show her no mercy; every direction would look the same. A grey howling deluge of freezing snow. She would be sobbing, praying, ice would be plastering her face. Her legs trembling, she would be tripping, falling, shouting, crying. Then she will come back. Then we'll know Evan's fate!

When Julie returned after seven minutes, she was unrecognisable. A geisha-girl face; a ghost-like figure. A mere bundle of snow. Betty scrubbed the ice from her face to reveal dulled eyes staring into space. She urged Julie to talk, to tell her if she had seen anything. A trance-like voice responded. "Evan? Evan's dead. He died in the snow… he won't…"

"Shut up, Julie!" Betty snapped. She glanced over at me. "You're all right now, John? You must help. Take the rope, I'll try upwind."

"No, Bette, it's no…" I hesitated, then without properly collecting my thoughts, untied the rope from Julie and fastened it around my waist. "I'll go, Bette."

Julie sprang back to life and pleaded with me. "Don't go, John, please don't go, you're not well enough. It's too late now — Evan must be dead."

I kissed her and scrambled outside. God, the blizzard had become even worse! This time I crawled a few paces into the wind, searched to each side, hid my face from the blast of drift, ran my hands over every mound of *sastrugi* my feet stumbled over. "Evan!" I shouted whenever the wind quietened for an instant. But there was never an answer. It was difficult concentrating. Where was I? What was I doing out here alone? Was there really someone holding the other end of the rope? Evan. Keep searching for Evan! Was he dead? After all we'd been through together, was he really dead? God! The thought isolated me from the blizzard, froze even my spine. I continued blindly forward, dragging the rope, falling, lying bewildered in the snow, sometimes sobbing, rising again to stagger further into the merciless storm.

My feet kicked something! It wasn't snow! An electrifying surge shivered through my body. "Evan? Is that you, Evan?" I dropped to my knees, dug frantically at the snow with my hands. Damn! Only a ration pack! "Evan! Evan!" My shouts became lost in the turbulence. There would be no reply. Evan was dead. With a sorrow-filled heart I followed the rope back to the tent and collapsed inside.

The girls were waiting with warm water and towels. Betty's eyes widened when I mumbled something about the ration pack. "He probably hung on to it until things got really bad. Perhaps he's nearby?"

Betty never hesitated. "Take the rope, Julie, I'm going again."

"Drink some coffee first, honey," Julie replied nervously. "We'll all have a drink and search again when the storm eases."

"Take the rope *now*!" Betty exploded. "I'll search *now*!"

While she was away, I pulled some sleeping bags around me and closed my eyes. Sleep, glorious sleep. But then I awoke with a start. A frightening thought swept through my mind: she might cast off the rope! In her grief she might… I sprang over to Julie. "How long's she been gone?"

"Ten minutes."

"Pull in the rope; pull her back!"

Julie's eyes caught mine and seemed to understand. She tugged urgently at the rope, tugged again and again. "She won't come! She's not moving!"

I yanked on my gloves, dived for the entrance, met Betty head on. "Thank God!" We both fell back into the tent.

Betty tried to speak but her ice-encrusted face imprisoned the flow of words. She burst into tears, flung her arms around me.

"There, there, honey," I murmured softly, holding her tightly while Julie melted the ice and dried her tears.

"Evan… I've found… Evan!" She stuttered. "Follow the rope!"

Julie and I stared at each other. Was she imagining things? Or had she really found his body? She was unable to control her emotions; crying hysterically, saying little more that made sense.

"Fill the pot, make plenty of water," I instructed Julie, then hurriedly left the tent — back into the tormented world we now dreaded so much. The rope ran freely through my hands. Evan on the other end? Unlikely. Poor kid was delirious; but then I tripped and fell. "Evan"? Good God, it *was* Evan!

Instantly, the howling blizzard was forgotten. I rolled my friend over to glimpse his face, summoned my remaining strength, pulled him clear of his snow coffin, wrapped the rope beneath his arms, started pulling back to the tent.

"Help me, Julie," I called. "It *is* Evan; help me get him inside."

Betty appeared instantly. She grabbed Evan's lifeless legs and drew him into the warmth. She remained silent with fear.

"He's dead, isn't he?" Julie said coldly as she closed the tent. I grabbed a knife, cut the drawstring securing his hood, wrenched it from his head. Betty was ready with a hot towel, smothered his face in it, thawed his balaclava and ripped it off. I was shoved aside; she was again the nurse in charge. She started to blow into his lungs, stopped, then dived for a pulse.

"Quick, John, help me undress him, get him into a sleeping bag. "Julie, get stripped, you're going in with him."

Evan was difficult to manipulate, but soon we succeeded. Betty then turned to Julie. She hadn't moved. "Goddammit, girl, I told you to strip. Strip *now*, get in here with Evan — *now!*"

Julie was scared. "But he's dead; I'm not going…"

"He's not dead. He will be if you don't hurry."

While I yanked off Julie's mukluks and pants, Betty helped with her upper garments. She grimaced as we slid her in beside Evan, his icy body against her warm skin.

I packed the remaining sleeping bags around the pair and massaged Evan's feet through the down filling; Betty continued with warm compresses to the head. His breathing was deepening; his pulse getting stronger. Betty gave her unconscious friend an uneasy smile and whispered, "What next, my good doctor, are we doing right?" She then turned to me. "There's a box of morphine ampoules and a syringe in the medical kit. Get them. If he revives without anaesthetic, the pain and shock might be too much."

Later, we gave Julie some hot soup to replenish her own body warmth. She had noticed some movement in his body and a little colouring returning to his face.

Betty's eyes seldom left the still form. She occasionally kissed him, making me wonder if this was true affection or just sympathy for an injured comrade. She reported warmth in his lips. Then suddenly she withdrew! "Quick, John, the syringe; his eyes are fluttering!" Betty snapped the tip from an ampoule and drew up the clear liquid; waited until his head started rolling, then squeezed the morphine slowly into his arm. "I'll also give him a sedative; keep him asleep until morning." She then turned her attention to Julie and saw that she was pale and shivering. "Sorry, honey," she said with a fleeting smile. "John should have taken a turn, but now I'll hop in myself, besides, I've got lots more meat on me!"

Julie pulled on some clothes and slid into another sleeping bag. I curled up beside her. Outside, the blizzard raged on. Most of the tent was buried, muffling the scream of the wind as it continued its spree across the icy wastes. How much longer would it last? Would Evan recover enough to continue? Would the food hold out? But then all was forgotten in the miracle of sleep.

Perhaps it was the silence that finally awakened me. It was uncanny, like being in a grave! Were we so deeply buried that all sound was excluded? No, a trace of sunlight brightened the protruding apex of the tent; the rest remained dark and frozen. I pulled on my mukluks and wind proofs and untied the frozen entrance to find a wall of snow imprisoning us, then quickly punched a hole through the top of this, enlarged it, and squeezed out into a glaring white world. My legs were weak and trembling; an uneasy feeling returned to my stomach.

The sky was still mostly cloud covered, but rays of cold light from a speckling of blue apertures spotlit some of the distant ice hills, while, closer at hand, wisps of fine powder snow flumed up from the wind-patterned surface like puffs of smoke from a dying grass fire. The yellow tent apex contrasted vividly with the bleak surroundings; it represented warmth, security and life itself for those inside.

Julie joined me, gave a sad smile and slipped a hand beneath my arm.

"There's the sledge, honey," I said quietly, pointing to a nearby mound of snow. "Only a few steps away. Incredible! Yesterday it was an endless nightmare away. And that other little mound is the ration pack… almost at our front door!"

Julie remained silent. I felt her trembling; knew what she was thinking. "Grab an ice-axe, honey, start digging out the tent while I see if there's really a sledge beneath that snow."

An hour later we were reborn people: warm from digging, hungry, and again fluent in conversation. Julie pointed with her ice-axe. "Look at the mess we've made, John. Nature made such a perfect job of covering our intrusion, but now it seems like a bomb has just burst!"

I grinned. "These are not fragile Alpine meadows that take years to recover, Jules. Another blizzard and our sojourn here will be erased forever."

"Then, let's hope that doesn't happen until we reach Mawson. Can we leave today?"

"That depends on Evan; let's see if he's awake."

Inside, Betty had lit the stove and was melting snow for breakfast. Evan's eyes were open, but he remained motionless on his back. "How is he, Bette?" I asked.

"Colour's good, pulse about normal, but before he awoke, he was moaning as if he has substantial pain. His toes are frostbitten. You can talk to him."

"Hi, cobber," I began, feigning cheerfulness. "How's our good doctor this morning? Feel like a jog up the local mountain?" Evan turned his head and stared at me. There was something frightening in his distant expression. I tried again more seriously. "Tell us exactly how you feel, mate. Any inside problems?"

After a minute's contemplation, he struggled to answer. "Some pain. Feet mainly. Feel very tired. I remember the storm… got lost again,

125

didn't I?" His face contorted as if to cry, but he contained his emotions and continued. "It was terrifying; I searched and…"

"We know, cobber, we all know what you went through. Tell us more about how you feel."

"Shock, most likely, a bit groggy, still scared. Betty's working on me. Hot food, rest. Give me a few hours… I'll be all right."

After the meal we examined Evan's feet and found that most of his toes had been afflicted by the cold, but only two were badly discoloured and, according to the doctor, should heal without complications. Betty tenderly tucked cotton wool between each toe before replacing his socks. "You'll be back on deck in no time, 'Big Boy'," she said amiably. "Now get some rest. If you're still awake in an hour you'll get another needle."

He wasn't. Within ten minutes he was oblivious to the world. I then flung the question concerning our plight to his nurse: "How long, Bette? How long before he can walk again; before we can continue?"

She shrugged. "In hospital, he'd be confined for a week. Let him sleep, we'll see tomorrow."

"But he *must* walk tomorrow. By then we'll be down to five days' food. Even then we'll need to average twenty-six kilometres a day right through to Mawson."

"And if we get another five-day blizzard?"

I sighed. "We'll move tomorrow even if we have to carry him on the sledge."

"He's too heavy. We can't possibly…"

"Can't? Look Bette, there's no longer any *can'ts* or *maybes*. We *must* move tomorrow — we *must* move under any circumstances!"

She shrugged again. "I guess we're all pretty tired. The rest of the day in the sack won't hurt any of us."

Once more the map came out in the hope it could produce some fresh ideas. Perhaps we had overlooked something? Were we absolutely certain there were no rock outcrops along the coast where we could hunt penguins or seals if the situation became desperate? But no, there was nothing! Ice-cliffs all the way from Scullin Monolith. If a route to Mawson really existed, we were on it!

The morning was not welcomed. Betty was right, we needed lots more rest. Outside we found a completely overcast sky and long snakes of drift weaving eerily across the hard snow to disappear amongst the ice hillocks. A steady breeze amplified the cold. No one showed any enthusiasm to move.

Evan advised that he was feeling a little better, although his pale face still bore the worried expression of an old man. Probably he had made a few mental calculations and knew that there could be no further delays. We helped him into his mukluks, then outside onto the snow where he stood grimacing as if unable to step from a bed of hot coals that tortured his feet.

I urged him to try. "Come on… 'one small step for man'!"

Gingerly he shuffled a foot forward, gradually lowered his weight onto it, but then gave an agonizing shriek and collapsed into our arms.

"Steady, mate, take it slowly. Try again."

"He can't, John," pleaded Betty. "You mustn't force him."

"I can," determined Evan. "I *must!*"

He tried again. His weight eased to his forward foot, his mouth gaped open, he drew rapid breaths. I too sensed the pain he was enduring. With half his weight transferred, he began dragging the rear foot alongside. Sweat beaded his face; tears of suffering flowed. Then again, he cried out in sheer agony. We leapt forward to catch him. He was sobbing like a child.

I tried to console him. "You tried, mate, no one could do more, no one is asking for more. For the rest of the day, you must ride on the sledge."

When the tent was packed and the sledge rearranged to seat Evan, we took our places in the loops and, with a powerful heave, moved forward. Immediately I knew we couldn't do it! But I also knew we *had* to. We began puffing profusely after only ten minutes. We rested, then tried again. On hard areas of snow there were no problems, but since the blizzard, drifts had built up in every depression, often bogging us altogether until the way ahead could be trampled down. At length, the crest of a slight rise was reached and our hopes soared as several kilometres of decline lay ahead. The sledge followed with ease. We *would* make it! But then my leg sank to the thigh. Crevasse! Christ, not another field of crevasses! I became angry rather than scared and snatched up an ice-axe from the sledge and recklessly prodded the snow ahead, continuing along the edge of the tell-tale depression to a safe crossing far off our intended course.

The next crevasse appeared minutes later. It was also a mere depression in the snow but was clearly distinguishable after our previous experience. In the Swiss Alps we had crossed hundreds of them, but there it had been easy and enjoyable to wind amongst them, jumping whenever possible. Here we hadn't the time or the energy to make deviations, and with a heavy sledge trailing behind, jumping was impossible.

We struggled on. The only complaints came from Evan. He could no longer tolerate being chauffeured by his companions as if they were beasts of burden. He tried kneeling on the sledge and pushing with his better foot, but even that effort hunched him up in pain. When crossing snow drifts, however, he helped considerably by leaving the sledge altogether and following through on his hands and knees.

In eight hours, we had won six kilometres and were now totally exhausted. I stopped. The girls flopped down on the sledge like tired animals; their heads bent low, faces and clothes white with frost. We rested five minutes. When I got up, the girls also got up, not a whimper from either of them. God, I admired their guts!

"We're not going on!" I told them.

They simply stared at me. Evan stared at me. "It's not because of you, cobber, it's the crevasses. Without them we might have made it. Ralph never told us the whole story and we never considered it, but when the Aussie expedition came this way they came in vehicles — tracked vehicles — which would have rolled effortlessly over these crevasses. We tried. On a firm surface we might have succeeded. But on this — never!"

No one queried my statement or volunteered other ideas until after we had pitched the tent and eaten a good meal. Then Julie nervously broached the thoughts plaguing each of our minds. "Where then? We can't go back to Scullin Monolith. So where…?"

The same question was foremost on my mind. We knew now that we would perish if we persisted in trying to reach Mawson. We knew also that the Portuguese would kill us if we returned to Scullin. We had all studied the map and knew there were no other places along the coast where we might survive on wildlife until the Aussie helicopters began flying again next year.

Evan spoke. "Our friend Ralph seemed a reasonable bloke, but he must have known the dangers of this route? He didn't want us murdered at Scullin, but no doubt he would sleep easier if we disappeared somewhere along the way."

Evan was possibly right. "In that case Ralph would be reluctant to help us if we sneaked back without his partners knowing."

"Nevertheless…" Evan started to speak but then went silent for a full minute before continuing. "Nevertheless, that's what we must do, isn't it, mate? We must go back, there's no other alternative is there?"

I nodded slowly. "I'm afraid not, cobber. We'll have to hide from them somewhere, until…"

"Until next summer?" interrupted Betty. "Eleven months? Eleven months on that tiny hunk of rock with two cut-throats wandering around prospecting. There's no chance of evading them that long! Sooner or later, they'll find us and… and bump us off!"

I looked into her troubled eyes and replied: "We have to return, Bette. There's no alternative."

CHAPTER 5

Scullin Monolith from our viewpoint high up on the ice-slope appeared exactly the same as when we looked back at it nearly two weeks ago. Yet at three a.m., with sleep still in our eyes, it seemed a safe haven — a stable land mass between the unpredictable sea and the treacherous Polar Plateau where we could again stand without fear of crevasses gaping open beneath our feet. A stiff, cold wind from behind urged leaden clouds forward to the coast where they broke formation and plunged low to crown the monolith summit and swirl between the icebergs sailing nonchalantly across a green restless sea.

"If it wasn't for those Portuguese monsters," remarked Betty, as she relaxed on the sledge with the rest of us. "We could look on Scullin as some kind of a desert island — a place where we might find food and shelter until a passing galleon picks us up."

I glanced at her without replying. The Portuguese at this moment were my uttermost concern. It was imperative that we descend to the rocks and hide before they venture from their hut.

Evan had talked little about his frostbitten feet on the return, but as he had walked most of the way without complaint, we assumed they were healing well, although this morning he again seemed to be limping badly. I spoke to him. "Another half hour to our old camp, cobber. Can you make it OK?"

He nodded somewhat despondently and mumbled a reply. "I'm all right. When my feet warm up, I'll feel better."

I turned to Julie. "Everything OK, honey?" She peered out through her tightly closed hood and gave only an inkling of a smile. Both she and Betty had performed admirably on the return journey. "Time to move then. Keep the sledge on the ice to avoid tracks, and let's go very quietly."

The sledge grated noisily over the granular ice and began nudging into the backs of our legs as the decline steepened. I moved the girls to a braking position at the rear, asked Evan to climb aboard, then broke into a jog as we picked up speed and careered down the avenues of blue ice. My thirty-minute estimate was halved. A steep short haul over soft snow brought us to the rocks where we had discarded the yacht's supplies before departure. Nothing had been disturbed.

"We'll hide our sledge here and carry everything else down to the old campsite," I told my companions. "We can't stay there, but we need to know if the rest of our gear is still intact."

Once at the old site, again everything appeared to be exactly as we had left it except that the recent storm had snowed over the few cans of food and fuel we had discarded. I found my old rucksack and emptied the contents onto the rocks: unwanted clothing, the yacht's logbook, some water ruined cameras, the binoculars. I picked up the binoculars and unscrewed the lenses to wipe out the ice, then dried the prisms roughly with an old shirt. The result was pleasing. Now we could spy on our neighbours from a safe distance!

Evan shook the kerosene can. "It's empty," he exclaimed. "It was half full when we left. Those bastards must be short of fuel even if they do have lots of food."

"But why empty it? Why not take the can as well?"

"Hey! Look at this, John." Julie had opened the log and pushed it before my eyes. "You told us you had forgotten to make a final entry before leaving for Mawson."

"That's right, honey. When Ralph paid us that dramatic visit, my only thought was to leave as quickly as possible."

"But look, John!"

I glanced at the last entry, then grabbed the book. "I didn't write this! What the hell's going on?"

February 3. Leaving today for Mawson via the Plateau. We have taken nine ration packs and other gear from the depot.

"Ralph must have written this — but why?"

"Pretty obvious," replied Evan. "He expected us to disappear forever on the plateau; he also knew the *Evening Star* wreck would be sighted next summer and investigators would want to know what happened to its crew. Ralph certainly wouldn't want a tribe of people searching Scullin

Monolith while he and his cronies were still hiding there."

"Then, that's why nothing has been disturbed; no clues to give him away. There must have been nine ration packs originally at the depot, so to disguise his theft he insinuated that we took them all."

"It's nearly five a.m.," Julie reminded us. "We can't stand here any longer; we must hide away somewhere."

"Right, Jules. The three of you had better find an inconspicuous place amongst the rocks further around the bay, then get the gear over. You might even be able to pitch the tent."

"And you, John?"

"I'm going back up the ridge to spy on our neighbours with the binoculars. With luck, I'll be able to establish their pattern of activities so we'll know where and when to avoid them."

Julie looked at me with concern in her eyes. "You'll be very careful, John. Remember, they want us killed!"

After nearly two weeks of sledging, it felt good to once again stride out over the rocks to the ridge top, but once there it was necessary to change my movements drastically and bow low to creep down the other side amongst the boulders. In a short time, I was atop a small cliff a mere hundred metres from the stone hut from where a sweeping view of the surrounding rock slope was available. My binoculars focussed on the shelter. There was no movement. It was still very early so I settled back to munch a biscuit and enjoy a rare, few minutes of relaxation.

At eight o'clock there was still no movement outside the hut. To keep warm and fill in time I strolled for short distances between the boulders to other vantage points, and sometimes even fossicked amongst exposed rock seams for signs of the diamonds that were causing all this trouble.

At nine o'clock two figures emerged from the hut and headed down the slope towards the glacier. I focussed the binoculars quickly. One person appeared to be Ralph in his yellow anorak and red balaclava; the other, the greasy bastard who had pushed his gun into my face. But then I looked again. Was it really Ralph? This man seemed shorter. When finally, his head turned, the man's face clearly displayed another walrus moustache; it was the other gun-slinger dressed in Ralph's clothes. Then where was Ralph? The pair carried their weapons with them and never stopped walking until within a few metres of the ice. One man then grabbed a pick, the other a miner's pan and began work. Were they still finding diamonds?

After another hour's waiting, and still no appearance by Ralph, I decided to walk along the ridge towards the monolith in the hope of finding a site for a hide-away shelter similar to what our antagonists had built. As I strolled amongst the vacated nests of the rookery the biologist's words were remembered: "Ten million Antarctic petrels!" What a spectacular sight that must be during the breeding season! My binoculars revealed several groups of Adélie penguins on the coastal rocks, and a few seals hauled up near the mysterious bamboo cane.

Soon I was standing on the edge of the steep cleft we had visited two weeks earlier, looking up at the impressive tooth-like monolith. Its west face plunged almost vertically into the sea, while the east, equally as sheer, fell to the glacier. The smooth southern face, directly in front of me, was scarred by a single vertical crack that might render it vulnerable. What was up there? If we could climb it and find a place for a shelter, then, surely, we would be absolutely safe from the Portuguese. The idea fascinated me, although to attempt the ascent alone would be foolhardy; I would need Evan's help and the climbing rope. After checking that the men were still working, I hurried back to our new camp to suggest the idea to my friends.

Evan was enthusiastic. "None of us fancy staying here," he told me. "We're too vulnerable. We nearly had heart failures when we heard your footsteps."

"Then let's try. Can you make it with your sore foot?"

Betty answered for him. "He's got two very black toes, John. They don't look good."

"But climbing will help my circulation. I may be slow, but would like to try."

"Good. You girls can expect us back in a few hours."

Betty had other ideas. "A few hours? Not likely, cobbers. We're coming too. Come on, Jules, time for our first climbing lesson."

On the way along the ridge, I detoured to collect the other climbing rope from the emergency depot, then caught the others up at the top of the cleft. We descended into this by scrambling down a steep boulder-strewn gully then up the other side to the foot of the vertical crack that I had previously studied. We stood gazing up at this obstacle.

"Maybe a grade VI climb," Evan said knowingly. "Not too bad. You had better lead."

I turned to the girls. "Wait here, we'll be back for you shortly. Keep an eye out for our 'friends'!"

The first ten metres was a steep scramble up a rock-strewn gully which ended abruptly in a sheer wall, but a careful manoeuvre along a short connecting ledge brought us into the crack, which was in fact a shallow chimney cutting vertically up the face. Here we roped up and the real climb began. I led by jamming part of my back against one side of the chimney and a knee against the other, and edging up in short calculated movements until a boulder, wedged above, blocked my way. There was too little space to squeeze beneath it, so it became necessary to ease out of the chimney onto the face, spider-climb a few steps up the smooth slab, then work back onto the top of the boulder. From here I continued the chimney climb to a safe stance a short distance from the top of the monolith.

Evan joined me a few minutes later. "A bit like the chockstone on the *Zinal Rothorn*," he said, catching his breath. "The good old days, eh!"

I grinned. Those happy climbs in the Alps seemed so distant now. We left the rope and strolled to the flat summit area and peered out through fleeting clouds to the green expanse of iceberg studded ocean.

"It would be hell up here in a blizzard," I told my friend. "But if we can find a cave or overhang for the tent, and wall it up with rocks, it should make our stay tolerable."

"There are plenty of snow drifts for water and cooking. It'll be a hassle moving everything up, but if it protects us from those Portuguese bastards it will be well worthwhile. We'd better bring up the girls."

I tied both climbing ropes to a firm belay, tossed the ends over the chimney, then abseiled down one to join the waiting pair.

"We have a penthouse vacancy," I told them. "But unfortunately, the elevator has broken down. However, if you ladies would care to take a look…"

"Betty and I are a bit scared of heights, John."

At the beginning of the ledge, Betty waited while I led Julie across the ledge to the foot of the chimney and tied her to the rope. "All you have to do, Jules, is to haul yourself up on this fixed rope. Evan will safeguard you with the other — you can't fall. If you get stuck crossing that boulder, he'll ease you over."

Julie never replied. The tension on her face showed her anxiety. Evan took up the slack and began pulling. In seconds she had reached the chockstone and was half dragged over it before getting a chance to look back down and see the vertical drop below. Whenever she hesitated, Evan pulled harder. In minutes she was there.

Betty's ascent was a little less elegant, but after much puffing and frequent face contortions she stood beside Julie waiting for me to join them for the stroll to the picturesque summit. They too loved the outlook, but after a quick look around, the search for a suitable shelter away from the prevailing winds was commenced. And almost immediately we found one. A huge flake of granite just below the eastern corner of the summit had fallen away from the main rock to form a two-metre-wide cavern. This would easily accommodate the tent and provide excellent protection from most winds. Numerous rocks laying nearby would serve as material to wall up the opening and make some sort of a blizzard-proof entrance.

"Oh, boy," mused Betty. "Let's hope none of us start sleep walking. It's a hell of a drop to the ocean!"

"But what a view!" Julie tightened her hood against a stiff breeze. "We'll think we're back on the *Evening Star* with so much water around. I'll be watching for icebergs again!"

"Let them come," replied Evan. "We've got a pretty sturdy hull this time!"

On a flat slab beside our proposed shelter, we all sat and planned our next move. "We'll still need to be on the lookout for the Portuguese," I warned. "From here we can see their hut and where they are working, so let's station a guard to watch them while the rest of us lug up our supplies. Later we'll need to consider harvesting some seal meat."

Julie's nose screwed up as expected. "There's not enough kerosene to cook seal meat, John, and none of us will eat it raw; so why talk about such gruesome things?"

"Frank Hurley, an Aussie on Shackleton's ill-fated expedition, made a stove from an old drum. He burnt seal blubber to cook the meat. We could do the same."

Evan volunteered to remain on the monolith as guard and would monitor our activities and those of the Portuguese. He would wave his yellow anorak to warn of any danger.

Once back at the camp we rolled up the tent and tied the sleeping bags together to make one load, then filled both rucksacks with food and gear to make the other two. Slowly we struggled with these burdens back onto the ridge and across the rookery to the foot of the monolith.

Evan was waving his anorak!

"Get down!" I said urgently. "Something's wrong!" We huddled between two boulders, hardly daring to peer about for fear of being seen by our enemies. Evan stopped waving. I waited a moment, then stood up where he could see me. He began waving again! Obviously, our signal arrangement was inadequate. In another few minutes I tried again, and this time was not waved down, so we hurried to the fixed rope and let him haul up the gear before following.

"Sorry," Evan said at once. "But those bastards decided to move just as you approached. I wanted to see them inside their hut again before giving the all clear."

The remainder of the afternoon was spent grubbing out rocks beneath the granite slab to make a flat gravel base for the tent. Once it was pitched, the tent immediately made us feel more secure, and when our sleeping mats and bags were spread inside, we felt we had a comfortable home. It looked so good, in fact, that we quit work for the day and retired inside.

During the ensuing few days the remainder of our gear was brought to the monolith and a stone windbreak constructed in front of the tent for protection against the predicted storms of an approaching winter. Now it was necessary to plan our food supply so that only small quantities of the remaining enriched provisions from the yacht and ration packs would be used daily to supplement our intended diet of seal meat. That unsavoury task now had to be faced.

"There's no use burying your head whenever we discuss it, Julie," Evan said firmly. "You may be an animal lover, but the truth is we won't live if they don't die. You don't object to eating beef or mutton!"

"That's different, Evan; the meat we eat is grown commercially for that purpose, but seals and penguins and other wild animals are part of nature — part of our heritage — they're beautiful. Do we have any more right to come here and kill them than… than the Portuguese have to kill us?"

"Maybe not," conceded Evan. "But primitive man didn't grow his own meat. He killed native animals. We're primitive people now, Julie, and we have to do the same."

"I know, I know," replied Julie, some red creeping into her usually pale cheeks. "All I'm saying is that I hate the idea. I hate being a human being sometimes."

"We'll see what seals are available after lunch," I told Evan. "Ralph's men will be back at work; the girls can remain here on guard."

Betty was pleased with that decision. "I'll eat them," she told Julie. "But no way will I watch the killing."

"Do you think it's a job any of us relish?" I snapped at her. "Do you think we'll enjoy killing these animals?"

Before we left, Julie spread the sail on a rock above the chimney to display our new all-clear signal. A yellow static marker in its place meant danger, stay put, while a yellow waving marker meant extreme danger, get away quickly. We slithered down the fixed rope and waited while Julie pulled it up after us, then headed back along the ridge with the fire axe and two empty rucksacks. Evan still limped badly, but kept up a steady pace to the water's edge and around the rocks to where four large seals had previously been sighted.

"Will you do it?" asked Evan, offering me the axe.

"No," I replied bluntly. "I couldn't do it! You're a doctor; a little blood shouldn't affect you."

He glared at me. "Well, it will, John. I'm going to hate this as much as anyone."

We walked over to the largest animal laying seemingly helpless on its side and watched its watery eyes following us intently as we moved slowly around it. It snorted frequently and occasionally yawned to display a row of large yellowish teeth. The seal's body resembled a three-metre-long slug, but its head with beautiful long whiskers, looked more like a curious old tom-cat that had lost its ears.

"He must weigh half a tonne," I remarked. But Evan never replied. He beckoned me to stand in front of the animal to capture its attention. This wasn't easy, for the seal knew there were two figures and tried to keep both in view at the same time. At last, however, by waving my hands vigorously, it concentrated solely on me.

Evan raised the axe. My eyes closed as it struck. When I reopened them, the animal was washed in blood but far from dead. It raised to our height, lunged its body towards each of us in turn, snorting, swaying, moving forward, attacking, retreating. The axe fell again. Blood spurted into the air; poured over the rocks. Again, and again, Evan struck, yet the animal held its proud stance, snorting pathetically, eyes blazing with bewilderment and pain. I vomited. Would it never end? Gruesome beyond imagination! When it was over, I wanted to cry like a child. Evan plunked down beside me and vomited over the rocks. Finally, we composed ourselves. "Not nice was it?" was all I could find to say.

"It was horrible, horrible!" he murmured, shaking his head in disbelief at what we had just done.

After recovering sufficiently, we used our knives to slit open the carcase and drag out the entrails, then Evan again swung the axe to hew the flesh into meal-sized pieces before it froze and became unmanageable. The finger length blubber beneath the leathery skin was trimmed off and kept separately. When the grizzly task was finally completed and the meat stacked neatly away from the pool of blood, we realised that one seal would not be nearly enough. More would have to die to sustain us through the long winter.

By the time I got around to constructing the blubber stove, the temperature on the monolith had dropped dramatically and the sea was changing from pale green to grey. A sky-full of dark, sombre clouds rolled down from the plateau to hover only metres above our heads. I began by cutting the top from a twenty litre round fuel drum with the axe, then punching a row of air holes around its base. A shelf salvaged from the yacht's oven made an excellent grill plate. Small stones were then used to line the bottom of the drum. When this was finished, I laid a few slivers of frozen blubber over the stones, then puzzled over how to ignite it.

After wasting too many precious matches, I found that a piece of kerosene-soaked rag did the job perfectly. When lit, it thawed and ignited a small corner of the blubber, which in turn fired the other pieces. It was a slow process, but with time the flames leapt high to sizzle a seal steak placed on the grill, and this in turn produced an appetizing aroma which wafted through the tent to draw my companions outside.

"Smells pretty good to me," volunteered Betty. "Like a good hunk of Californian beef on the barby."

Julie seemed more interested in the fire than the smell. She pulled off her gloves, toasted her fingers, lowered her face to the flames with absolute bliss. "I feel like Sam McGee in the furnace of the *Alice May*," she said cheerfully.

It's the first time I've been warm since I left Plumtree, down in Tennessee.

We laughed and went on to recite other verses from Robert Service's famous *Tales of the Yukon*.

Betty was getting hungry. "Surely, it's cooked by now, John. Don't burn the first one whatever you do."

Evan stabbed his knife into the meat and watched a trickle of blood ooze out. "Give it another five minutes. The fire's a bit hot; it's burning the outside but leaving the middle raw."

Julie giggled again. "What, no thermostat, John. And I thought I was marrying an engineer!"

"Come on you critics," I joked. "Bugger off. Go cook your own steak; this one's mine."

"Now, now, John," returned Betty. "This isn't a wallaby you've just clobbered with your boomerang; it's seal meat. You need expert advice from us seal meat connoisseurs!"

I sliced four small morsels from the steak and handed them around, then waited for an opinion from these self-proclaimed gourmets.

Evan spoke first. "A bit oily. Strong like venison or kangaroo. Would be vastly improved with a little seasoning, or tomato sauce. But not bad, not bad at all."

"Well, I wouldn't bother ordering it at the Savoy," mused Betty.

"But… well, it's quite palatable. Probably the hungrier we get the more we'll enjoy it. Definitely should be served with French fries and Tabasco sauce!"

"What do you think, Jules?"

She looked up at me. "You know what I think, John. But besides that, it seems quite edible."

The remaining piece was cut into four and chewed slowly by each of us, as we reminisced about other barbecues we had shared with friends, in what now seemed another world.

With caution and good sense, it now appeared we could survive the winter. Our only real concern was the Portuguese, for as yet it remained uncertain whether any of them had climbing skills that would allow them to lay siege to our camp. Until this was determined it would be necessary to watch them at all times and, if necessary, defend our fortress by hurling down rocks. Soon they would discover our gear missing from the old camp and come searching for us.

The days drifted by. One morning while sitting on 'Lookout Rock' with Julie wondering why only two people went to the mine each day, Betty called me over to the tent. There was an unfamiliar tone in her voice that alerted me that something was wrong. Inside, Evan was sitting with a towel covering his left foot; he spoke the moment I sat down.

"John, I've asked Betty to help me amputate two of my toes!"

"What!" I stared first at him, then at Betty, but when he withdrew the towel there was little need for further explanations. Two were black, rotten and stank. Poor Evan, he had bravely kept his secret for so long.

"Don't worry," he said calmly. "Two toes won't hinder me much; others get around without legs."

"But this is not a hospital, cobber, this is just a tent — a tent in Antarctica — and you're the only doctor! You can't operate on yourself. You could get an infection!"

"That's why they must come off now, *before* there's an infection." He watched my every reaction. "There are sterilised surgical instruments in my box and the necessary anaesthetic. I've instructed Betty; she can do it."

Rather fearfully, I turned to Betty.

"I've attended numerous operations, John, a few amputations."

"But can *you* perform one, Bette?"

"Yes." Her voice was confident but there was fear in her eyes. "I'd rather not, but in this case there's no choice."

Betty then took over completely. "I've boiled some water. Wash your hands well, then sit on Evan's right. Come on 'Big-Boy', stretch out, keep your sleeping bag over you. Call Julie, John, she can keep our patient occupied and recite 'Sam McGee', or something."

Julie was also shocked to learn what was happening, but rallied quickly and took her place beside Evan. She talked to him briefly about the operation, then claimed his interest by asking questions about parts of Australia that he knew and liked so much.

Our nurse painted half of Evan's foot with a brown antiseptic, then explained precisely my part. "When I ask for the scalpel, carefully tear open the handle end of the package so I can grab it without touching the paper. You *must* never touch any instrument or sterile dressing. OK?"

I nodded.

Betty then broke open a glass ampoule and drew the liquid slowly into a syringe. "This is Xylocain," she explained calmly. "A good local anaesthetic." She then injected it into Evan's foot in three places above the toe line. After several minutes she began pricking his toes with a needle.

"Feel anything, darling," she asked quietly.

My eyebrows raised. 'Darling'?

"No, Bette. Go ahead."

"Gloves, John."

I tore open the sterile package. She withdrew the surgical gloves and pulled them on.

"Scalpel."

My hand shook a little as I passed it over. Hers remained perfectly steady. She sliced through the top joint of one toe as if it were a sausage, then, because it hadn't bled too much, sliced off the other just as quickly.

"Swab, John." While this was held briefly over the stubs, she called for a dressing, and moments later some adhesive, and finally his sock. The whole operation took ten minutes. Betty instructed me to clean up, and then quickly left the tent. When she returned minutes later, she was pale, and I could clearly see where the tears had been wiped away.

Immediately she wrapped her arms around Evan and kissed him, then looked up at Julie and I with a coy smile. "Evan and I are now engaged," she announced. "We're going to be married and live in Australia." Then the tears again welled up in her soft dark eyes. "So you're never going to get rid of us." She was sobbing now. "We're going to be your neighbours for the rest of our lives."

Evan improved quickly after the operation and became a less lonely and more amiable person with Betty so frequently at his side. One day I found her alone at the lookout and broached the subject of her fiancé. "He was always the confirmed bachelor, Bette, what made him change? And you once said you weren't interested in him beyond companionship."

She smiled. "Things change, I guess. Maybe it's been happening gradually since the shipwreck without either of us realising it. On the yacht we were all such close friends; never time to be lonely. Evan had me in the sack twice a week." She looked at me and smiled. "But ashore everything was different. It was too damn cold for that kind of fooling around, and there always seemed lots of urgent things to do that kept us apart; so perhaps he found a need for a closer kind of relationship."

"But what about you, Bette. Do you love him?"

She put the binoculars to her eyes and gazed for a moment at the miners before continuing. "When we left Vancouver, I wasn't sure whether you and Julie really loved each other. She is very beautiful, but not the adventurous type it seemed you needed in your life. You want to go climbing in the Himalayas, sailing around the world, exploring darkest Africa. But all she really wants is to have babies. Probably I thought, hoped even, that you two would break up and... and maybe I could hop back where we left off in London." She put down the glasses and gazed intently into my eyes. "But I was wrong, wasn't I? You and Julie will always love each other."

"But I asked if you really love Evan, Bette?"

"Love? I think a great deal of him. My feelings for him are different to those I have for you. Yes... yes, I think we are genuinely in love. When we're married and living in Australia, we'll all stay friends together won't we, John?"

"You'll be our best friends, forever, Bette."

When the persistent southerly wind finally subsided, the four of us came together on our 'patio' to watch the clouds disperse and the sun bring colour and life back to all that was grey. There were fewer icebergs now, but in the evening light these caught the last dazzling rays of sunshine and shone like illuminated cruise ships drifting across an indigo ocean. The stark white edge of the pack-ice seemed much closer now and stretched to the horizon to merge into a pale blue sky.

For an hour we sat quietly watching the sun change from yellow to orange to maroon as it hovered low on the western horizon reflecting its varying shades on the surrounding ice. But then an amazing sight transpired. The sky suddenly grew dark, not from storm clouds, but from millions of birds returning to the rookery after feeding at sea. They swooped around us, below us, soared high, circled, landed to look at us, then gradually disappeared to grey the ridge below and settle into their nests for the night. Only a few birds later returned, and in the perfect stillness of late evening soared like music over the monolith in a pageantry of elegance that would forever be instilled in our minds.

"Why haven't we seen them before," Julie asked excitedly. "How come we missed such a fantastic display?"

"Possibly because they might sometimes fly low to avoid the cloud," I suggested. "Or because we've been retiring too early."

"Well, I won't any more. From now on I'll be waiting for them every night."

By the middle of March our monolith camp was a month old, yet with so many things to keep us occupied we showed few signs of boredom. Evan's foot had healed sufficiently to allow him to walk around comfortably and even help harvest the additional seal meat required to carry us through the winter, although, as yet he had declined to join the 'Scullin Soccer Club' with its rag ball and very airy playing field. He had suggested another visit to the depot to collect the candles stored there, and that afternoon when the miners returned to work after lunch seemed an appropriate time.

At two p.m. Julie announced they had gone. "Watch our signals closely," she stressed. "Don't take any risks."

I kissed her. Evan kissed Betty, then we slid down the rope and strolled along the ridge as if on a Sunday outing; glancing back frequently to confirm that the white all clear signal remained. At the depot we rummaged through both boxes but were unable to find anything else of use besides the candles.

"Let's get back," I urged. "Until we account for the whereabouts of that third person, we can't be too careful."

"Perhaps Ralph is ill in bed. Either ill… or dead!"

"Then, maybe we should take a quick look inside their hut."

"Good idea, John. We still have the all clear. The Portuguese must still be working."

Leaving the ridge-top we hurriedly descended amongst the boulders above the hut to where we could see the miners working in the distance. Stealthily we crept closer to the stone walls. Silently I peered through the tiny window. The room appeared empty.

"Let's go inside."

Evan grabbed a shovel for defence.

I slid back the latch, pushed the rough door inwards, waited a moment, then walked in. There were three bunks, two draped with sleeping bags, the other stacked with books and clothes. Evan opened a book. "English text; must be Ralphs!"

"But where is he, Evan? His gear is here; this looks like his watch, and… here's his wallet!" Inside was a girl's picture with an inscription: 'To Ralph with love from Thelma'.

Evan thumbed through a large blue book. "It's his diary, John."

"Take it and let's go. Let's go fast!"

Although the signal remained white, we jogged for a short distance, then slowed to a fast walk right to the fixed rope. At the camp both girls expressed anger at our unscheduled detour. "Why, John, why would you be so stupid?" demanded Betty. "There might have been someone inside. He might have killed you both!"

"And then what about us?" joined in Julie. "Aren't we worth considering? How would we survive without you two?"

My apologies were ignored. The reason for the detour was not accepted. But when they calmed down, we crawled into the tent to examine the stolen diary.

The entries confirmed everything Ralph had told us about his joining the ship in Cape Town: sailing to Scullin Monolith; the two Portuguese

144

helpers; prospecting for diamonds; successes and failures; and then his meeting with us in his hut.

"It seems he was quite disturbed by the angry reception given us by his so-called friends," I remarked. "His last entry refers to further arguments. Strange?"

"His last entry was also just before he warned us of the Portuguese threats," pointed out Evan. "Just before he helped us begin our disastrous Mawson journey. Something smells fishy here, John!"

"Right! But when you're dealing with a million bucks and a bunch of crooks, it wouldn't pay to be as naive as Ralph seemed to be. Probably those thugs never intended sharing the diamonds, they wanted the lot. When Ralph stood up for us and helped us escape, maybe they killed him... killed him then, rather than wait until their ship returned!"

"He could have had an accident, or simply got sick and died," suggested Betty. "Don't you think you're being a bit melodramatic?"

"Maybe, Bette, but remember, he seemed very healthy the day we left, so why would he give up writing his dairy that *very* night? I'm sorry, but I can't help thinking he was murdered!"

Next morning Evan reported a change in the miners' routine. Instead of departing for work at nine a.m., they were outside at eight a.m., heading briskly *up* the ridge!

"Something's wrong, cobber," I said, watching their every move through the binoculars. "They probably discovered someone's been in their hut. Looks like they're heading for the depot."

After a brief visit to the depot the pair descended the other side of the ridge and headed straight for our old campsite.

"They're looking for us all right; they'll most likely search the whole area until they figure out we're up here." Evan handed the glasses to Betty when the girls joined us at the lookout.

Julie strained to see the two specks, then turned to me. "Do you think they'll find us up here? Do you think we're in danger?"

"No, Jules, we're in no danger if we stay alert. We could defend this monolith against an army with only a few rocks. In a way it will be good if they do come. If we find out for certain that they can't climb the chimney, then we won't need a guard so often."

"They've separated, John," Betty announced. "They seem to be searching the rocks around the bay."

Julie stayed on watch; the rest of us returned to the tent to warm up and make tea, but the brew was scarcely ready when our guard called out a warning. "They're coming along the ridge now. Don't show yourselves, they have their guns with them!"

I took the binoculars and peered between the boulders at the approaching figures. Their faces were now recognisable, cruel ugly faces. One still wore Ralph's red balaclava as a hat. They came to the edge of the cleft and stopped.

"Shit!" cursed Evan. "We forgot to pull in the white signal; they'll see it for sure!"

The Portuguese scrutinised the monolith through binoculars, then continued across the cleft towards the foot of our climbing route.

"Now we'll see how vulnerable we are," I whispered, edging around slightly to gain a better view of the chimney.

They kept coming; up the short gully, then hesitantly across the sloping ledge. I signalled Evan to prepare to roll a rock. But then the two stopped and stood gazing up the vertical chimney. We each breathed a deep sigh, these were not climbers. The Portuguese muttered something to each other, then turned and retreated. They stopped again on the far edge of the cleft and once again searched the monolith with their eyes.

The crash of machine gun fire erupted through the silence! Shells ricocheted around us; boulders splattered and a hundred echoes thundered in our ears. But then there was calm again. The aggressors moved away.

Julie was shaking; tightly grasping my hand. "They wanted to kill us, they wanted to…"

"Easy, honey, easy. They were just telling us they know we're here. They're not Alpinists; they can't climb the chimney. We're safe here, we're absolutely safe." But then I considered more fully the situation and made certain my next remark was clearly understood by everyone. "*Nobody*, and I mean *nobody*, must ever stand on this side of the monolith without first determining the whereabouts of the Portuguese. Are we all perfectly clear on that?"

"We're not stupid!" answered Evan.

"But we forget! And one day they might be waiting with a gun for just that moment!"

To help us forget the gunfire, I lit the blubber stove and began cooking more seal steaks. It seemed that with age, the meat lost some of its strong flavour and became even more palatable. My friends responded to the irresistible aroma and joined me to share the warmth.

"You're a bit late, Captain Drake," quipped Betty. "Aren't you supposed to be barbecuing steaks *before* the Portuguese invaders approach, not after?"

I grinned. "You Yanks were never much good at English history, were you? It was Raleigh playing bowls when the Spanish armada approached. Anyway, seal steaks probably weren't gourmet tucker in those days."

Now that I knew exactly how much blubber was needed to grill two steaks, cooking became much easier. The stove, fired by the correct amount of fat, would burn out just as the steaks were ready to eat, so now I proudly boasted of a built-in timer! Julie's thermostat remained on the drawing board!

After our meal, the rest of the day was spent lazing on the rocks watching a-kilometre-long tabular iceberg slowly drift across the tranquil sea beneath us. Then followed another memorable sunset.

April arrived. The days were now noticeably shorter and colder, and fewer birds returned each evening to the rookery. Blizzards were becoming more frequent. Often, they swirled in from the south to send sheets of snow billowing across the bay below, then, as the wind increased, this drift rose like boiling milk around us until the whole monolith was overwhelmed. The sound of the wind often began like the distant howl of a wolf stirring his pack, but soon a thousand others began echoing his call. As the crescendo continued to build, it became the sound of a squadron of jet planes hurtling down from the plateau to scream around us. The tent would go berserk. We would huddle together for consolation. But then the sound would fade away over the sea and a lone wolf could once again be heard calling from the plateau.

One morning I asked Evan what he thought the Portuguese would have done with Ralph's body if they had indeed killed him.

"Well, they certainly couldn't dig a grave in this rock, and it's doubtful if they would bother lugging it down to a crevasse, so probably they just shoved it over a cliff. Why? Why do you ask?"

"Because that's also what I think. In fact, my bet is they tossed it over the cliff below their hut.

"What's on your mind, John?"

"You see, mate, if those two are picked up before us next summer, our story about diamonds and murder will be pretty hard to substantiate. Perhaps it sounds a bit macabre, but it might be a good idea to look below that cliff and see if Ralph's corpse really is there, and if it is, we have the evidence we need for the Aussies when they pick us up."

Evan thought for a moment. "It would be risky now that they know we're here."

"Not while they are prospecting their new site near the depot. We could scramble down and be back within the hour."

"OK, but… you break it to the girls."

They were hostile. They saw absolutely no justification in taking such risks. If there was a body there, it would still be there next summer. Ralph's diary was enough proof that he actually came here on a Portuguese ship. But when it became clear to the girls that we intended to search below the cliff at any rate, their attitudes softened.

"Well, please watch our signals very carefully at all possible times. Keep well away from the depot area. Promise to be back within the hour."

We promised and left as soon as the Portuguese returned to work after lunch.

By sidling along the ridge well below the depot we quickly arrived at the miners' earlier diggings, then scrambled down a narrow gully in the cliff face to a gravel moraine beside the ice of the glacier. Our signal was still visible and white. Quickly we walked along the moraine, peering carefully into every open crevasse on the glacier edge and amongst the boulders that studded our route, but we saw only empty cans and broken bottles that had been tossed down from above. Soon we were confronted with a sheer rock-face rising from a heavily crevassed part of the glacier. Progress was halted. Without hesitation we turned to go back, but then something white and conspicuous was sighted just above our heads on the cliff.

"More rubbish?" queried Evan.

But as we drew nearer, the object was recognised as waste of an entirely different nature. It was the horrible, rotting, skua-picked remains of a human being.

"Ralph?" I murmured, staring at the grizzly half skeleton.

"Must be!" Evan scrambled closer for positive identification, then quickly returned. He spat frequently and gasped for fresh air. "Same hair colouring, a gold cap on a front tooth, still wearing his wedding ring. It's Ralph all right. His ribs have been shot to pieces!"

"Then we have our evidence. The remains are not likely to move from there. Come on, let's get back to camp."

In minutes we were passing the stone hut. Our signal remained white; the Portuguese must still be working. "Let's grab a few more of Ralph's books," I suggested to Evan. "They could contain some helpful information."

We approached the door. An instinct made me stand to one side as I pushed it open. A rifle exploded! The shell thundered above my arm, spattered into a rock! For an instant we froze! But then I raced past the booby trap, threw Ralph's books into the rucksack, ran to catch up with Evan as he sped up the ridge. I glanced at the monolith. The signal was yellow: waving! We ran faster.

Another shot ricocheted from an adjacent rock and echoed around us. We flattened on the ground, sprang up again, dived behind some boulders. Other shots whined above.

"The bastards are close, Evan! No use trying to beat them to the monolith; they'd pick us off on the climb."

There was no choice! We ran across the ridge-top, dodging the hail of bullets, dodging between boulders, then down the other side towards the bay. The yellow signal continued to wave urgently. Another machine gun burst. The surrounding rocks smoked. They were right on us!

Faster progress was made along the waterfront, past the bamboo cane, past the seals, past the last little cove to the sheer headland: a dead end! We were trapped! We turned to face our executioners. They weren't yet in sight. I looked again at the headland; at the sea surging beneath it and wondered what lay further around?

"Quick, Evan, get your heavy clothes off, jam them into the rucksack, we're going to swim!"

The Portuguese came into view. We dived as more automatic fire raked the rocks and hissed around our heads. Frantically we swam with the rucksack between us. We were too slow! The surf sucked us outwards, then pushed us back towards the rocks. I braced for the first bullets to perforate my back! We were rounding the headland. A rifle cracked, a bullet slammed into the rucksack. We dived. The sea above boiled with machine gun shells. Spent lead sank to burn our skins. Then we were clear. We surfaced and gasped for air. I seized the rucksack as it washed past, grabbed a protruding rock. Christ! The cliffs here were just as sheer!

"Are you OK, Evan? Can you swim another fifty metres? Maybe it will be better around the next bluff? Maybe there'll be some flat rocks to rest on."

Holding tightly to the buoyant rucksack we struggled through the surf to the far side of the next headland. There my heart faltered; our last hope drowned in the sea. More cliffs; cliffs all the way to the monolith — sheer cliffs — cliffs as smooth as ice! We had to rest. The only place was a small outcrop barely above the water. I scrambled up and then grabbed Evan's hand. The cold was suddenly frightening!

Evan gave a mocking laugh. "So many choices: freeze, drown, or be shot!" But then spasms of shivering made me reef open the rucksack for more clothes. Most were wet, all riddled with holes. We rang out what we still wore, wiped the sea from our bodies, pulled on everything we possessed. When protected from the wind we exercised vigorously; running on the spot, touching toes, swinging arms. It helped a little, though our skins remained pure ice.

"What now?" asked Evan in an amazingly calm voice. "Do we just stand here and freeze to death, or wait and be drowned when the tide comes in?"

I searched the rock-face for the answer. There was no doubt it could be climbed by fit expert climbers with the right equipment, but by two frozen men without even a rope. Impossible!

"We *must* climb, mate, there's no other solution."

Evan sighed. "Fifty metres, sheer, without a rope or a single piton! Not much hope is there? A fall would be very messy!"

We jammed Ralph's books into the front pockets of our wind proofs and discarded the rucksack, then edged across some submerged boulders to where a rock outcrop appeared above. To reach it I used Evan's back as a ladder until I could stand on his shoulders, then fastened myself to the water-smoothed face and hung on like a limpid. Evan pulled himself up on my feet, then repeated the manoeuvre over my back until he stood on my shoulders and was able to scramble up onto the protruding rock. With his help I soon joined him. Together we edged left across a steep slab overhanging the sea to a tiny platform from where there could be no other possible movement except up: straight up! A vertical crack in the smooth rock might possess a few handholds, but they seemed far apart. Without pitons and rope, a conventional climb was out of the question! Another method had to be tried. A method I once watched on training rocks south of London and condemned it as suicidal!

"It's about thirty metres, Evan. We'll only get one crack at it. No changing minds halfway. If there's nothing at the top to support us…"

Evan nodded knowingly. "Want me to try?"

"No, cobber, this will take all ten toes, I'll go first."

I warmed up by exercising. Took several deep breaths. Paused a moment in meditation. Then threw myself at the crack. No searching for holds, pressure climbing, bobbing upwards like a gas-filled balloon, pulling, wedging, stretching, balancing. No hesitation. All or nothing! Foam covered rocks far below. I sprang onto roughened rock, bounced off, karate chopped into a crack, sprang again, grabbed for anything above, seized a protruding rock. I was there! God, I was there! Exhausted, gasping for breath, dragged my body onto a tiny platform. My eyes closed for a moment; opened again to see Evan far below — the sea and rocks beyond. God, I'd made it, but could he?

"Easy!" I called down. Pulling off my wind proofs I tied the pants to an anorak sleeve and dangled the 'rope' down the cliff. "Ready when you are!"

Evan began. He was using my technique and flying upwards. But was heavier, less agile, frightening to watch. His mukluks kicked the rock, his back bounced him forward, clutching at anything, nothing, pressure gripping, rising. I wanted to look away, couldn't. He gave a yell. Horror gripped me; he grabbed a rock, came away in his hand. "JUMP!" I yelled, "JUMP!" He sprang again, grasping for anything, grabbed my trousers. He clung desperately, gasped for breath, then slowly and nervously climbed to my stance. He exhaled like a surfaced whale, drew in another deep breath, let it out just as loudly.

"Jump?" he repeated quietly after composing himself. "You didn't say which way!"

I hugged him, thumped his back with sheer exultation.

An easier climb followed up some broken slabs to a long scree slope that actually led us into the cleft beneath the monolith. We were almost home! Our signal was out of view directly overhead, but the way seemed clear, although, we now remembered, the fixed rope would not be lowered until contact was made with the girls. We scrambled along the ridge a little to signal them, but then looked up to see the yellow anorak waving on the end of an ice-axe. We froze! It was then we heard voices from an adjacent boulder. Silently we moved away.

"The cunning bastards," I whispered to Evan. "If we'd survived their bullets and the cliff, they intended gunning us down as we climbed the chimney!"

"Then it looks like a long wait. I hope they get hungry before us."

But they didn't! After three hours of waiting, we were famished and frozen in our damp clothes. The sun had long since set. But then there was a scuffle and the sound of metal scraping rock, and we guessed the Portuguese had finally given up, no doubt confident we were now dead.

We waited until they had disappeared lower down the ridge, then stood boldly on a rock and waved. A figure appeared above; ropes were lowered. In minutes we were all huddled together in a sobbing mass outside the tent. Few questions were asked. The girls were as happy to have us back as we were to be there. But after a hot meal conversation flowed more freely until the day's venture was well aired and sleep intervened.

When next I looked at my watch it seemed to be only midnight. How strange to wake again so soon after retiring absolutely exhausted. When my brain functioned better, however, I realised it was daylight. It was not midnight, it was midday; I had slept fourteen hours straight! Julie and Betty were sitting up engrossed in the books we had brought back. Evan was awake but still reclining.

"Hi, darling!" Julie dealt out a quick kiss and returned to her reading.

"We thought you would sleep the whole day."

"What's so interesting?" I asked.

"Lots! Do you know that besides the ten million Antarctic petrels Ralph told us about, there are five thousand silver grey fulmars and about three thousand other birds here at Scullin Monolith? Also, there are a quarter million Adélie penguins. It's all here in this biology book. Pity it's full of holes! At Auster Rookery, near Mawson, there are over twenty thousand emperor penguins! Incredible, isn't it? I haven't found Auster on the map yet."

"It's mentioned in this book," advised Betty without looking up. "*Exploration_in MacRobertson Land*. Auster Island is fifty or more kilometres east of Mawson, that's about a hundred and fifty west of here. Apparently, Mawson scientists go there frequently in winter."

"In winter?" I queried.

"That's right." Julie thumbed back a few pages. "They travel over the sea-ice to visit the rookery. Apparently, most emperor penguin rookeries are on sea-ice which disperses in the summer. That means the penguins have to breed in the dark and bitter cold of winter so as to avoid skuas and other summer predators. Because there is no access to food at the rookeries at that time, the female lives on body fat until a single egg is hatched and then awaits the returning male who has been feeding at the outer edge of the pack-ice. Get this: *a hundred or more kilometres away.* He then takes over incubating the egg while the female goes off to feed. When the chick is hatched, the female returns to feed it by regurgitating sea food. Boy, do we women get it easy by comparison"

I became interested in Ralph's exploration book. Betty started another on geology. Evan joined our little library by choosing a book titled *Australia in the Antarctic*. We all read with deep interest for another hour, occasionally sharing snippets of interesting information.

"Your 'friend', Sir Douglas Mawson, really did land here in 1931," advised Betty. "So perhaps you are right, that bamboo cane might have been left by him."

"Here's some unpalatable news," added Evan. "It says *occasional* flights are made to Scullin Monolith to monitor the rookeries' population growth. That means the Mawson biologists don't come every year. They may not be here to pick us up next summer!"

Heads rose from their reading and stared at each other. Somehow, we had accepted as fact that rescue would come next summer. But what if it didn't? Christ! That was unthinkable! We couldn't hold out another year — or longer! Without commenting further, we tried to ignore his findings and returned to our reading.

An article about a Robert Dovers interested me. He was the officer in charge of the first wintering party at Mawson in 1954. Apparently, he visited Scullin Monolith in May that same year, which, on reflection seemed rather puzzling. I had read earlier that an aircraft brought down that summer on the *Kister Dan* had been taken back on the return voyage. With the sea frozen in May, he couldn't have come by boat. How then did he come? A thought entered my mind that made my heart quicken! I browsed hurriedly through the rest of the book without finding any other specific information, except one enlightening phrase:

Due to Robert Dovers' near tragic journey east of Mawson in 1954, no further permission to travel this unstable sea-ice has been granted.

So he *did* come to Scullin over the sea-ice. Such a journey *is* possible.

"Here read this, Evan," I said, pushing the book before his eyes. But before he could, everything I'd read poured from my lips.

Julie wasn't sure what I was suggesting. "Are you saying we wait until the sea freezes and simply walk around the coast to Mawson? No, John, surely that would be impossible!"

"I don't believe it would be possible either," remarked Betty. Remember the plateau route? That was going to be easy! Julie's right, let's not even think about it!"

"But it *has* been done," I insisted. "Dovers either walked here, or came with dogs or vehicles. There are no crevasses or hills on the sea-ice, so why wouldn't it be easy?"

Evan replied, "You're ignoring this *near tragic journey* bit and this sentence about 'unstable sea-ice'. It seems to me that Dovers made a very dicey journey, dangerous enough to ban sea-ice travel this way ever since."

"But we've discovered that they make regular trips as far as Auster

Island, therefore, this questionable area of sea-ice must be the one hundred and thirty kilometre stretch between here and Auster." I unrolled the map. It showed almost no islands before the Auster group. "Perhaps that was the problem? Perhaps the sea-ice broke up in a storm and they couldn't find any place to shelter?"

"What does that say?" asked Evan, pointing to some pencil scrawl on the map. But before I could read it, he drew it closer to his eyes. "'Caravan'! So, there's a caravan at Auster Rookery. That's worth knowing."

During the following week we talked a great deal about the sea-ice and the possibility of traversing it to Mawson, but finally decided to wait until it had actually formed, and we were able to walk on it before making a definite decision. One morning, however, an observation by Evan hastened our conclusion. It became *imperative* that we reach Mawson as quickly as possible.

Julie had scurvy!

CHAPTER 6

"Scurvy?" I looked at Evan with an uncertain grin. He seldom made such jokes. "Scurvy? That went out with Captain Cook, two hundred years ago... didn't it?"

"No. We learned about it two hundred years ago, and now immunise ourselves against it by eating ample vitamin C, such as in fresh fruit and vegetables, but since our shipwreck we've had very little of these. Perhaps we get some in the freeze-dried foods we eat, but almost nothing from the cans. It's not only Julie I'm concerned about, it's all of us."

I stammered for words. "Well... how will she... we, be affected? What will happen to us?"

"At this stage, John, you'll hardly notice the symptoms in Julie, but with insufficient vitamin C she'll gradually become listless, lack stamina, get aches and pains in her joints, and eventually begin to haemorrhage as body sores break out. The disease is affecting her first because she's the weakest of us."

"Christ, Evan, what can we do?"

"Increase her intake of freeze-dried fruits and vegetables. That's all we can do in our present situation."

"But if we do that — and of course we must — we'll deplete our supply in a very short time." I thought about the implications of this new shock for a few moments, then added, "We'll have to reach Mawson this winter, won't we, cobber? We'll have to journey over the sea-ice."

"As soon as it's stable, I'd say, John. She has no other hope."

Julie wasn't pleased about eating a mug full of freeze-dried food every day while the rest of us ate only a spoonful, but when her ailment was explained, she understood the importance of maintaining good body strength, and like the rest of us began taking an intense interest in the sea around us over which it now seemed lay our only chance of survival.

It was not until the last day of April, however, after a clear and unusually cold night, that we looked down on the unrippled bay and realised that a thin layer of ice had formed across the entire surface. On such a tranquil morning the bay reflected the plateau ice and rocky surrounds on its mirrored surface, and resembled a beautiful landscape painting waiting to be hung. Yet, when looking more closely through the binoculars, the scene was not entirely static. The sea still lapped gently over the rocks around the edges of the bay to maintain an intensely blue fringe of water that stubbornly resisted the opaque membrane of ice waiting patiently to overwhelm it. Two remaining skuas slipped to an ungainly landing on it, then without their usual grace tottered like novice skaters across the slippery surface.

By early afternoon, a gentle breeze rippled the newly formed surface to shatter the thin crust of ice into a multitude of plate-sized fragments which drifted about the bay with the currents, bumping into each other until their edges become rounded. As the water lapped over these ice 'pancakes', it froze and built up around their edges to form distinctive white collars.

The next morning was again serene. The 'pancakes' had drifted together and refrozen to produce a rough tessellated pattern over parts of the bay. Elsewhere more new ice had formed, intriguing us with its transformation. Always someone sought the binoculars, waiting a turn to stare down on the ever-changing scene. By mid-afternoon the wind had again broken the ice and the bay was once more awash with loose 'pancakes'. With each ensuing day these grew thicker and more numerous, until in the more sheltered parts of the bay, large expanses of ice adhered firmly together, growing in strength until the entire surface could resist the full force of the wind and the underlying ocean swells. After a week, the new surface extended far out to sea and joined with the pack-ice, although over this section dark pools of water still showed ominously through.

We had planned to test the ice as early as possible, but on the chosen day gazed down to see the Portuguese already gingerly walking across it. They crossed the bay to the foot of *our* monolith, looked up a few times, then continued beneath the cliff face until they arrived back again on flat rocks. "Those bastards are reading our thoughts and checking for footprints," I told my friends. "Because they never found our bodies, they no doubt assume we escaped their bullets and will soon make another attempt to reach Mawson. Probably they're hoping to shoot us as we leave."

"We'd be very vulnerable then," suggested Evan. "It will take time to recover our sledge and get the gear down from here and packed aboard. Even if we get away safely, we'll leave tracks for them to follow."

"They don't have a tent or sledge, mate, that means they couldn't sustain a chase beyond midday without risking freezing to death."

"And if they catch us before midday?" asked Betty.

"They won't, Bette. We'll prepare the sledge amongst the rocks, camp overnight there, and get away before daylight."

"In the dark we could easily fall through the ice," added Julie. "We don't know the coast, we don't know what…"

"We know the bay is solidly frozen, Jules. We can traverse that in the dark. And from this viewpoint it appears that the coast is well frozen for at least the first ten kilometres."

Our plan wasn't a good one — we all knew that — but what else could we do? Everything depended on eluding the Portuguese. Until our proposed departure on June 1, it would be necessary to continually monitor their movements to know exactly how intensely they were observing us, and hopefully slip away at a time when they least expected it.

Our proposed departure date came and went. In Antarctica we were learning that it was the weather that controls one's outside activities, not the calendar, and this had been particularly foul right up to the afternoon of June 3. Then there were signs of it clearing. We crawled from the tent into a cold grey world of snow and swirling cloud and peered down at the frozen sea. It appeared uniformly snow covered to the horizon without the previous dark areas of slushy water.

"We'll go now," I informed the group.

Three heads swung to stare at me.

"Now!" repeated Betty. "You mean…"

"I mean immediately. Can't you see, the eastern side of the ridge is still cloud-covered, which means the Portuguese won't yet be aware of the clearing. We'll get the gear down, pack the sledge, and be away early tomorrow morning before they come out of hibernation."

"Hopefully," muttered Evan.

On the descent from the monolith the snow on the ridge was often up to our knees, causing us to leave a line of footsteps that no one in the vicinity could possibly miss. The sledge was retrieved and carried to the rocks above our old campsite where it was packed with a good supply of cooked seal meat and the few remaining packets of freeze-dried food. Then, instead of turning in early, we elected to sit in the freezing cold on top of the ridge awaiting darkness, making absolutely certain our enemy did not venture out and discover our tracks. Only when it was again pitch black did we erect the tent and settle in for an uneasy night's sleep.

At nine a.m. it was still coal black outside, yet the four of us moved zombie-like about the sledge making last minute preparations for departure. There was still cloud overhead, but also a few patches of stars. A gusting southerly breeze cut through our clothing to freeze our bodies, but this wind would be helpful in propelling the sledge across the bay.

"Everyone ready?" I asked, breaking the complete silence. Nobody replied, yet the three shadows around me appeared to be in their waist loops waiting to move, so with a sharp jerk to free the frozen runners, the journey began.

The snow surface at first was windblown and hard, allowing us to stride out almost without noticing the light sledge trailing behind. The wind on our backs confirmed our northerly course until our eyes grew accustomed to the darkness and were able to distinguish the great mass of the monolith now partially outlined against a patch of bright stars on our right. Then we turned westward and broke into a steady jog as a faint tinge of orange appeared in the sky behind. Already our balaclavas were white with frost and fingers and toes becoming agonisingly painful as the blood began to circulate more vigorously to thaw them out. Exposed parts of the face stung with the intense cold and would quickly whiten with frostbite whenever we neglected to shield them from the piercing wind behind our anorak hoods.

As soon as the soft light of dawn spread around us, a blood-red disc of sun rose into the sky to once again preside over the cold south. Its gory rays soaked the clouds with maroon blotches and spilled crimson over the plateau and icebergs. Beneath our feet the surface was mottled with blue shadowy depressions outlined with pink borders of powder snow which plumed up when disturbed by our fast-moving feet to glow like puffs of fire-lit smoke. Our running legs cast infinitively long shadows beside us, bringing life to the ice as they criss-crossed back and forth like patterns from a Chinese lantern.

"Whoa... hold it!" shouted Betty, puffing profusely behind. "I'm not built... for speed... like you guys."

We stopped, turned to give each other a belated good morning greeting, then more urgently directed our eyes over the ice we had just travelled. Good, there was no sign of anyone following. To be certain I scanned the distance with the binoculars. No... yet there was a slight element of doubt! For an instant there seemed to be a distant speck, but with the sun in my eyes it was more likely a shadow. It seemed pointless mentioning it to my friends.

A fast-walking pace ensued that broke into jogging spurts whenever there was a need to warm up. Conversation was stimulated. Each of us chattered confidently about reaching Mawson within a few days and expressed loudly our cravings for hot showers, enormous meals, and at last a solid roof over our heads. Many of the pleasures reserved for better times were unexpectedly released and talked about.

Icebergs ahead now glowed like brightly lit yellow marquees, while those already passed became dark silhouettes rimmed with a festoon of sunlit ice crystals. We weren't expecting to cover long distances with the sun above the horizon for less than two hours a day, although by utilising every glimmer of twilight it was hoped to accomplish five or six hours of travel between camps. If the surface remained good, we should reduce the one hundred and eighty kilometres to Mawson by at least thirty kilometres a day, and reach the first island, Stevens Rock, within three days.

The weather as always was our chief concern. If the dark clouds rolling over our heads kept their height, and the wind that was presently blowing plumes of drift across the plateau never increased, there should be little concern about the fact that we were now totally isolated from the coast by many kilometres of high, sheer ice-cliffs; the same continuing cliffs that had threatened our destruction before the life-saving rocks of Scullin Monolith had been sighted. No one was ever likely to forget those desperate hours aboard the *Evening Star*, yet here was an equally precarious situation; if the sea-ice broke up, where would we run? What did Ralph's book mean by unstable areas of sea-ice now banned to travel? Surely, we were crossing these at this very moment!

The sun moved a few degrees across the horizon then set again. The pastel light that we had enjoyed for two hours vanished, leaving the world around us once again grey and foreboding. How quickly our spirits dropped and hopes of pressing on for an extra hour changed to thoughts of a warm camp and hot food. A final burst of speed, then exhaustion brought us to a halt.

"Surely we've done our thirty kilometres," gasped Julie. "We can camp now, can't we, John?"

"Yes, Jules, we've done well, but I can't say sleeping on the sea-ice enthrals me. Who knows what animals might pass beneath during the night!"

Both girls stared back at me. Obviously, they hadn't considered this. I picked up the binoculars to make certain the Portuguese weren't following, hesitated, then climbed onto the sledge for a better look.

"Anything wrong?" asked Evan.

At first, I never answered. Was it possible? But then it became clear that it was. I cried out. "The bastards are still after us; they're less than a kilometre behind!"

Evan snatched up the glasses. In seconds he confirmed my sighting. "But you said they wouldn't follow after midday; that they'd freeze to death if they kept coming without equipment!"

"So, I was wrong! These bastards are tougher than expected; maybe they're carrying sleeping bags." After a moment's further thought, however, their plan became very clear in my mind. "Most likely they're carrying flashlights and intend following our tracks after dark until they come upon our tent. No doubt they're counting on using our food and gear! We've got to keep moving. We'll continue due west on a compass bearing."

Soon it was night again, and with the darkness came intense cold. Fear of our assassins spurred us into frequent spurts of jogging, but at other times we plodded mechanically on as if in a dream, a bad dream where every direction was coal black. Where I needed to actually feel my eyes to know they were open. Where I touched my legs to know they were moving. Where an hour's run brought us seemingly nowhere, and two hours still facing the same blackness, the same nothing! Yet there could be no stopping. Someone behind let out a cry; the sledge jarred to a halt. Julie had fallen and seemed too exhausted to rise. Again, I peered through the binoculars. The two yellow specks of light were still following! Would they never give up? "Come on, honey," I urged, helping Julie to her feet. "We must keep going. We can't stop until they stop!"

After so many hours of darkness it seemed strange that it was now only six p.m., surely morning should be near! On and on we plodded into the never-ending blackness; on and on followed the two pinpoints of waving light. We stumbled, fell frequently, legs and arms deteriorating into limbs of jelly, heads becoming dulled with cold and fatigue. I no longer thought about why we were running; no longer thought about Mawson. It seemed we had become sharks that would sink if we stopped swimming so kept moving forward instinctively. Julie fell again. This time she was sobbing loudly. Evan and Betty seized the opportunity to sprawl across the sledge and rest. Again, I picked up the binoculars to sweep the blackness behind, then swept it again. Nothing! I shoved them into Evan's hands. He searched. Still nothing. We waited, looked again, but still there was no sign of the pursuing lights. Have they given up? Have we won? For tonight at least!

In minutes the tent was erected and everyone curled up inside without the strength to prepare a meal, but then the swishing sound of the ocean below our pillows became audible; perhaps only an arm's length away. Where would we run if it broke through? I lit a candle, got the stove going, warmth flooded back into the tent. I set about making a hot drink. The snow melted in the pot, rolled over and over as it diminished in size, then became a bubbling steaming joy. I tossed in the tea, waited, then poured a reviving mug full for each of us.

"Yuk!" Betty's unexpected comment surprised me. Julie's face screwed up. Evan was more vocal. "Christ, John, did you call us for this? You've put salt in it!"

I glanced quickly at the container. "It looked like sugar, tasted like sugar." But my face contorted like the others when the tea touched my tongue. Then came realisation. "Shit, of course! Sea-ice snow!" The salt had filtered through from the ocean. We should have chipped ice from an iceberg! I threw out the tea and concentrated on sleep.

Next morning at nine a.m. there was still no sign of our followers, but an hour later as we prepared to leave, their yellow lights were again glimpsed in the distance. Won't they ever give up? How much food and equipment do they have? Must we race them all the way to Mawson? We sped up our departure and were soon jogging again into the pitch darkness with only the compass as our guide. Shortly it became possible to sense the nearby ice-cliffs. They were perhaps a slightly deeper black than the plateau or the surrounding sea-ice and occasionally caught the light from a star between the heavy clouds. But gradually the dawn approached. The darkness turned to navy, then gradually pink as the sun's fire ignited the horizon and beamed orange and yellow shafts of light onto a dense blanket of leaden cloud. We trembled beneath nature's pageantry. As the sun pushed higher into the sky, we saw that the plateau was today obscured beneath a rising plume of drift that poured down the steep slopes towards the ice-cliffs and ourselves. Ahead the sky remained jet black as though the night had refused to leave.

We stopped suddenly, uncertain of our footing. A downward step placed us on a smooth, almost black surface that made us desperately aware that all was not well.

"The ice is a lot thinner here, isn't it, John?" Julie asked nervously.

"It seems so. It may have broken out recently and only just re-formed."

Evan studied the new surface for a moment, then gingerly walked across it without it cracking. "I suppose it's all right," he told us unconvincingly.

Betty had the binoculars to her eyes, scanning behind.

"Still coming?" I asked.

She sighed. "They're not gaining, but by the look of things they don't intend giving up."

A thought flashed through my mind which I decided not to share with my friends. Perhaps the Portuguese were hoping for an ice breakout such as this had been, which would halt us and bring us within range of their weapons!

The new ice without its covering of snow unexpectedly proved most welcome, for it allowed the sledge to slide more easily with almost no exertion from its haulers. This small joy, however, did little to distract our attention from the previously observed black sky ahead which was now of the utmost concern. It spread across our intended route like a face of coal.

Something moved! I gave a startled cry! Looked about me.

"What… what's the matter?" asked Evan.

"Didn't you see it? A shadow, as if a bird flew over!"

We continued. But moments later the girls shouted from behind. They too were seeing shadows!

"But it's winter, there's shouldn't be any birds!" Evan was gazing intently above, searching.

"Then look! Look!" Julie was now pointing down at the ice while eyeing the sky above.

"Christ, John, those shadows aren't *on* the ice, they're *under* it! They must be seals… or something!"

I shuddered. The girls were petrified.

"Then the ice is only… a centimetre or so thick!"

We all felt the urge to grab the sledge for security. "Keep moving," I urged. "Move quickly, but *very* gently! We'd better spread out and distribute our weight more evenly."

The next half kilometre was very stressful. No one spoke. If the ice disintegrated, there could be no escape from the freezing water. Each of us slid our feet, wanted to walk on air. Then again, I stopped abruptly. God! There was movement on the ice ahead! People?

"Penguins," corrected Evan.

"And open water," called Betty. "Look they're diving."

I remembered then. "A water sky; the reflection of water from the clouds. That's the reason for all this blackness."

"We shouldn't be here then," declared Julie. "We'll have to go back!"

"Go back? No, Jules, we can *never* go back!"

As we stood shivering and contemplating our next move, a group of stately emperor penguins waddled over. These were twice the size of the Adélies we had previously seen, and wore bright orange flashes on their necks, and a tinge of yellow on the upper part of their otherwise vivid white breasts. Their heads, backs and feet were pitch black; even their eyes were black. Without apparent concern they strutted within three metres of us and stopped in a straight line to survey their strange visitors. We stared back at them, trying to read the thoughts in their eyes. The emperors nodded and rolled their small heads and long, curved beaks in a drunken manner before us. One sounded a weird, lengthy accordion-like note that was repeated by several others to begin an unbelievable tuning up session which brought even more performers strolling over to join the concert.

"Let's continue," I said, looking fearfully over the open water ahead. "As we can't swim like these guys, we'd better head in and hope to bypass the break-out closer to the coast."

Approaching the ice-cliffs was like nearing a waterfall of drift. At first, we hurried through fine mist, but later when forced to squeeze closer to the cliffs, a deluge of ice crystals poured down to smother us. We ran along a beach of snow lapped by dark water, then swung back into clear air as we re-joined the old sea-ice. Once more we felt secure, although with a softer snow surface to pull across our lack of food and sleep began to show. We headed directly out to sea for a kilometre until firmer snow once again allowed us to swing the sledge back onto our former westerly course.

Cape Fletcher had been passed during the morning and now Stevens Rock could only be a few hours away. At least our pursuers had pushed us well ahead of our anticipated schedule. I stood high on the sledge to search for them and, as hoped, they were nowhere to be seen. The breakout and thin ice must have finally persuaded them to turn back. We continued for an hour after darkness then pitched the tent beside a small iceberg that would supply us with fresh water. What joy it was to again warm up with an appetizing hot meal! What joy to sleep again!

At four a.m. I sat up suddenly. Something had disturbed my sleep. A stiff breeze was billowing out the tent fabric, but surely that alone hadn't awakened me! I sank back into my bag. Evan too was awake.

"What was it?" he asked with concern.

"Probably only the wind."

As we lay awake it happened again. The tent and its occupants rose up like a boat crossing a wave. Both of us jumped up quickly. "It's the sea," I exclaimed loud enough to wake the girls. "There must be an ocean storm further out and the swell is reaching us beneath the ice!"

Evan showed signs of panic. "It could crack the ice! We've got to get away from here!"

"Steady on, cobber, we can't just run blindly about in the dark. It could be worse ahead!"

"What should we do then, John?" It was Julie asking this time.

"Prepare to leave. Get fully dressed but stay in your sleeping bags. We'll wait and see what happens."

The swells continued. Sometimes they were minor, raising hopes that they were abating, but then one would push up from beneath causing everyone to grab each other and pray for it to stop; pray for the ice to remain firm.

"God, John," gasped Betty. "We can't just lay here! Can't we head for Stevens Rock? You said it's only an hour away!"

"An hour in daylight, Bette, but it's so small we'd never find it at night."

For another three hours we suffered the torment of the threatening swells as they bulged up the ice beneath us, sucked us back down, then surged noisily beneath the tent to bring us to our feet in panic. At any moment it seemed certain that cracks would appear in the ice and the sea would break through to engulf us.

I struggled outside into a strong freezing wind. A new moon, thin like curved gold wire, momentarily broke clear of the racing clouds to outline the shadowy icebergs and nearby cliffs. But then... impossible! I waited a moment. There they were again!

LIGHTS!

I sprang back to the tent door and shouted a warning. "The Portuguese are here!"

In seconds everyone was out. We scooped up the tent with everything inside, threw it on the sledge, were away with Betty running alongside tying down the load.

Our pursuers had neither sensed our hurried departure nor sped up the chase to overtake us, so in a short time we held a half kilometre lead over them and were again able to concentrate on the other grave danger beneath our feet. In the dark I could only set a rough course for Stevens Rock, but surely if the ice was about to break up, the Portuguese would also be heading that way!

The sun eventually cleared the horizon and momentarily spilled blood-red across the underside of the heavy clouds, then disappeared completely to leave them sombre and ominous as they swept across the iceberg summits so close above our heads. The plateau was hidden beneath a mushroom of drift that swirled down over the ice-cliffs and reached out towards us in long searching tentacles.

Stevens Rock was sighted a half kilometre further out to sea than expected. The sky in that direction was jet black. We raced towards it over ice that rose and fell with the swell like the sea itself. But then a sheet of water sprayed up ahead as a crack broke open and wove across the ice like an awakening serpent. Spray blew over us as we leapt the gap and continued to flee northwards.

Geysers of water were soon erupting all around and spraying across the surface like rain. We zig-zagged between them. The tiny island was soon only minutes away. Constantly we leapt snakes of angry water, yanking the sledge after us. Cracks became more numerous, splitting the ice into large floes. From one to another we jumped, sometimes moving forward, sometimes doubling back to find a narrower gap. Smaller floes were encountered that tilted under our weight; water surged over our feet. The island was before us, but so was the sea! Waves crashed angrily against the rock.

We were too late!

I stopped. The four of us huddled together, sweeping our eyes over the terrifying scene around us. "We'll head back to the coast," I shouted above the increasing howl of wind. Our eyes clashed. 'Ice-cliffs'. The word was clearly written in each of them. The invading waters were rapidly closing around us, boiling and spraying from dark leads in a rebellious celebration of freedom.

We turned and sped off with the wind now in our faces. The sledge careered left and right with each blast of wind. We fought to control it, ran faster between violent gusts, playing leap-frog from floe to floe. Open water was now all around. We advanced and retreated indecisively. Sometimes a larger floe allowed us to race over it with growing hope, but then a smaller one slowed us down. The coast was getting closer. So was the sea!

Evan and I leapt a metre-wide lead, but were then dragged to a halt by taut ropes.

"Stop! Wait!" came distressed cries from behind. The girls had balked at the leap.

Evan pulled the sledge forward to slacken their ropes. "Jump! Jump now!" I shouted.

Julie screamed. "I can't. I can't!"

"Jump!" I repeated, pulling the sledge tight against their legs. "You *must* jump. Jump now!"

She glared at me, took a deep breath, leapt. Betty followed. The sledge was yanked across. Their eyes were fear itself. We ran again. Ahead was open water. We veered left, followed the edge of a water-sprayed floe, leapt onto a smaller one, off again as our weight pushed it under. A fierce gust sent us sprawling. Our sledge crashed into us. A tongue of ice suddenly appeared, its far end disappearing into a deluge of drift. Could we reach it? We dived across bobbing floes and opening cracks, sometimes hesitating, sometimes circling, flying forward at every chance; but then a ten-metre band of churning water lay laughing before us. There was no way across! Again, we had failed!

We turned back on the floe. It was now far from its neighbour; ran around its edge, then came to a halt to face reality. Any second now the floe would disintegrate. I grabbed Julie, held her close.

"We're drifting in," called Evan.

Hope again stirred. He was right; the current and wind were in opposition. We waited at the edge. Prayed we'd drift against the ice tongue. Five metres, four, three… A black streak split the ice beneath our feet. We leapt clear as the floe broke in two. Other cracks suddenly opened. Two metres! I prepared to jump. But then the gap closed with a thud throwing us heavily to the ice. We got up, ran along the ice tongue. It broke apart with our weight leaving a dotted line of tiny floes bobbing in the sea behind.

Soon we dived beneath the waterfall of drift. Soon we were face to face with the vertical ice-cliffs. Soon the sea smashed the last remnants of ice behind us.

"Where now?" murmured Julie, tossing off her sledge rope and squeezing closer to the cliff beside each of us. "We have to get up before the waves…"

"Easy, honey," I whispered.

Evan spoke We'll never climb this without pitons, John, the ice is far too sheer and smooth."

My eyes searched between breaks in the showering drift for a possible way up the face, but Evan was right, there wasn't the slightest hope. We turned to face each other. What was there to say? I pulled Julie into my arms and saw Evan do the same with Betty. When the waves grew higher, we crowded together on the sledge. Evan touched my shoulder; his hand was outstretched. I took it, held it, squeezed it firmly, then leaned to kiss Betty.

But we couldn't just stand here and die!

I kissed Julie and pushed her next to Betty, then stepped into the knee-deep water to edge cautiously around the base of the cliff. There must be a way up somewhere, I kept telling myself. Soon a huge block that had fallen from above barred my way. It was only three metres high but if we climbed onto it, it would save us for an hour or so. I called to the others: "Around here! Come around here quickly. Bring the sledge."

When they arrived, I was on the block ready to help them up.

"What's your next move, mate," asked Evan, doubtfully.

I shrugged. But we couldn't just give up! We were still alive. If only it were possible to see through the drift. "Perhaps if we could climb up a few more metres, Evan, we might..."

He gave a disheartening grin and turned back to Betty, ignoring me completely. There *had* to be a way up! Perhaps if it were possible to... I called to Julie; tried to appear calm. "Climb onto my shoulders, honey; try and get a footing on that snow above. Take your time, go very carefully." Above this were a few more snow depressions, then the face rose sheerly into the obscuring drift.

Julie hesitated, but then struggled onto my back. She got her legs around my neck, then with grim determination stood upright. Her legs were shaking like a vibrator.

"What... what now?" she stammered.

"Scoop out a place for your feet and step into it."

"But... but I can't, it's too steep!"

"Yes, you can, Jules, try."

"But I can't move... I'll fall."

Julie was in tears, yet somehow, she got onto the snow and attached herself there like a limpid.

"Kick your feet in firmly, Jules, I'm going to use them to pull myself up."

"You'll pull me off! Don't... please don't"

I grabbed her ankles, pulled straight down on them, swung and struggled to place my feet beside hers, then continued upwards over her back to stand on her shoulders. She was shaking dangerously. Quickly I scooped snow from a tiny ledge, climbed onto it, then hauled Julie up. There was no possibility of climbing higher from here.

Julie was extremely frightened. I kissed her and told her to wait while I explored along the ledge. The snow was soft, making it easy to kick bucket-sized steps to the right until it was possible to peer around the corner into a steep gully choked with snow. A few more steps took me into this. The sea was now roaring below. I continued, kicking a stairway of steps straight upwards into the misty drift until the gully connected with a wide platform. There was no time to explore further. Immediately I returned to get Julie. She was shaking like an aspen leaf from fear and cold. I took her hand, led her into the gully, pushed her ahead of me up the twenty-metre climb to the platform. Once there I hurriedly trampled down some snow for her to sit, then left to fetch the others.

"Evan, Betty," I called from a stance above their heads. "I've found a platform. We must get everything up. Toss me the climbing rope."

The pair tried to move, but too many minutes of inactivity had allowed their wet limbs to freeze.

"Come on. Move! Throw up the rope."

They slowly pulled apart and even more slowly did as requested.

"Now both of you tie on and follow me." Betty had great difficulty moving, but Evan revived slightly and pushed her before him. I climbed back to the platform and belayed them up the gully.

Julie was sitting where I left her. Betty plunked down nearby. Evan was noticeably weaker. 'Scurvy'. That word still rang through my mind.

"Sit down, cobber," I said to Evan. "Hold on to the rope, I'm going back for the gear." But before he could prepare himself, I was carefully descending the gully. Christ! Water from ever heightening waves was already pouring over the sledge. I slid down onto it, quickly grabbed the tent with last night's contents still inside and tied it firmly to the rope. "Pull up, Evan," I called. He never responded. Spray was soaking my clothes; crests of larger waves rolling in from the grey ocean sloshed over my knees. "Pull up, Evan, pull up!" Shit, I cursed, what's wrong with the bastard? "For Christ's sake, Evan, pull the tent up!"

Eventually the rope went taut. I guided the gear ahead of me into the gully, then helped lift it onto the platform.

"Come on," I called to the three. "Get up, move about. Help me pitch the tent. When the girls refused to respond I grabbed their arms, pulled them to their feet. Evan rose and began untangling the guy ropes.

As soon as the tent was up, I pushed the girls into their sleeping bags to warm up. Evan was moving like a robot but belayed me back down to the sledge for more gear. But where was it? It was gone! Oh, God, no! It had washed away! The whole block we had stood upon had disappeared into the sea. Most of our food, spare clothing, fuel. God! All gone! A plastic bag washed against my feet. I grabbed it — a few pieces of seal meat! What else? Nothing! Only the restless sea!

Sadly, I returned up the rope to my companions to see what supplies, if any, were still in the tent, but once inside this remote piece of heaven all ideas of searching the chaos for food vanished. The girls had revived sufficiently to help Evan and I out of our wet clothes and into our sleeping bags. The blissfulness of sleep came quickly.

During the long night I awoke to what seemed like rain on the tent, but then remembered it never rained in Antarctica. I could hear the roar of surf lashing the cliffs below and realised that spray from it must actually be reaching the tent. The thought of an even more violent sea was a terrifying thought. Could we find a route up the remainder of the cliffs to the plateau? And what if we could? That impossible walk to Mawson would still have to be made. I pulled my sleeping bag even tighter around me and tried to rest my concerns until morning.

When next something disturbed me, it was eleven a.m., and about as light as the day would get. In the gloom Betty was collecting and sorting the previous night's supplies that had become strewn about the tent after our hurried departure to escape the Portuguese.

"What have we got left, Bette?" I asked quietly.

She stared at me for a long time as if I was barely visible. "What have we got? Oh… not much. Three chunks of seal meat, a few packets of vegetables, a half empty stove, some odds and ends of cutlery, your compass. That's about all."

"How long will it last?"

"How long? Oh, about three days."

"Or six if we halve the rations," I suggested.

Betty's voice rose. "What the hell's it matter, John? Why not blow the lot in one decent meal. We're not going to leave this camp! Not ever! The sea-ice will never form again in our lifetime. Even if there was a way to the plateau, what good would it do? Three days' food, six days' food, what's the difference? We tried to reach Mawson with ample supplies before but couldn't make it! We were fit then. Let's not kid ourselves any longer, John; let's not concoct a batch of false hopes. We're going to die, we're going to die right here. So, let's die with dignity. I… I will be proud to die with such beautiful friends."

Julie had heard Betty's remarks yet remained calm. I lay beside her with my hand touching her soft face, trying to revive the smile that meant so much to me. Betty was right; there would be no false hopes this time.

While the fuel lasted, we made thin stews with a little seal meat and a handful of dried vegetables, but when it ran out, we sliced the meat into slivers and let it thaw in our mouths. A spoonful of dried raspberries with as much snow as ingestible was generally swallowed in the evenings. After only three days on these meagre rations, it became a major effort to stand upright, or even to crawl in and out of the tent. My brain was becoming strangely light and slow reacting.

Evan and I staggered from the tent on the fourth day into a white world of fresh snow and suspended ice crystals that drifted gently in the still air to settle on our noses and eyelids. Above, could still be heard the mournful wind blowing across the plateau, but below, the sea now seemed more subdued. At my insistence, we examined the ice-cliff left of the tent, but no sign of a possible climbing route existed. Then we tried to the right, but here too the face was smooth and sheer without a single hand-hold.

"Now are you finally satisfied?" snapped the doctor. "Now can I go back to my bag?"

I sighed. "We had to look, cobber, we…"

"What the hell do you think's up there, anyway? A bus stop? A restaurant? Give it up, mate. Leave everyone alone."

"I won't give up, Evan. There mightn't be any hope, but… but it's not right to just lay down and die. I've got to try something!"

"Like what? Learning to fly! OK, learn, but do it on your own. Leave Betty and I alone!"

My mouth tightened with annoyance. I was pleased when he went back inside. For some minutes I sat alone on the platform trying to peer through the mist, trying to visualise the scene behind the curtain drawn across the ocean. But then I gave up and returned inside.

Perhaps it was possible to cheer Julie up a little. "Hi lovely fiancée," I whispered close to her ear. "I'm tired of waiting for wedding bells. What say we get married right now?" Her eyes swiftly opened and a smile I remembered so well spread across her beautiful, pale face. She nudged her head against mine but never spoke. "Do you, John Edward Watkins, take this gorgeous blonde, Jules Cane, to be your loving wife, for better or worse, good times and bad, until… until the moon turns to cheese. Bloody oath I do. And do you, Jules Cane, take…"

"Yes. Oh, yes I do."

Her voice was choked. I raised myself on an elbow and looked deeply into the blue of her eyes. Her golden hair was a veil lying softly across her face. Gently I parted it and touched her cheeks now wet with tears. But my heart was too full of compassion, I collapsed onto her, smothered her face with kisses, my tears mixing with her tears. "I love you, Jules. I love you so very much. I'll always love you."

Several minutes passed before the next sweet whisper came from Julie's lips. She had composed herself. "Are we… are we married now, darling?"

"Yes sweetheart, we're married at long last."

"That's nice," she murmured. "That makes me very happy."

We lay in each other's arms until darkness again overwhelmed the little tent, until the dawn came twice more, until we were almost too weak to eat the remaining morsels of food. Eventually, when the effort was made to go outside, I found it very painful to stand. My legs and arms seemed alien to my body; my head felt heavy like a lump of wood. The mist still hung about the cliff-face, yet the day had a brightness about it not seen since our arrival. I rested on the edge of the platform and let memories of a lifetime drift through my brain, but then, as if waiting in a concert hall, the curtain of mist suddenly slid aside to allow the sun to present itself and shine down on a stage-set of icebergs drifting across a navy sea. They reflected the yellow rays of sunlight like a city lighting up at dusk.

A couple of kilometres westward, the old coastal ice seemed to have held fast during the storm and was now changing in colour from yellow to pink as a wisp of cloud drifted across the sun. If only we still had our inflatable! The sea was very calm. A piece of ice fell from above and clattered and bounced down the cliff to plop into the dark water below. I leaned over to see it bobbing about where it had hit, then continued to stare at it as if there was a message waiting to be read, but my mind was now too fuddled and incapable of comprehension.

I crawled back into the tent and served my companions the last of our food, then reclined again with an arm about Julie. How pleasant and easy to just lie there like the others, dreaming of faraway places, of old friends, of a hot sun filtering through a cool eucalypt forest in the land I loved so much, in the land… Why did my mind keep returning to that chunk of falling ice? Why was it plaguing my nostalgic dreams? Julie would have loved swimming from the golden beaches around Coles Bay, clambering up the red granite boulders to look out over the blue Tasman Sea, the mirrored bays, the green hills… ice! To hell with that chunk of ice! I'd better solve that irritant once and for all!

With a feeling of annoyance, I yanked on my mukluks and once again struggled outside. Why? Nothing was clear any more. I felt very drunk; my knees trembled, my head swirled, my body wanted to float away. That piece of ice remained exactly where it had fallen. Who cares? Why didn't it float away? Our tracks down the gully were now snowed over. I retrieved the climbing rope and tossed it back down, then unsteadily began remaking the steps to the sea. Frequently I stopped and wondered what was driving me on this senseless mission; wondered where I was, wondered what I was searching for. But then I was standing on the tiny ledge overlooking where once our sledge had stood. The sea from here was almost black; it washed gently against the cliff and…

could it be? I scooped up some snow and tossed it down. Good God! It spattered across the surface. Ice! A metre from the shore the sea had already refrozen. Excitement surged through my body. I heaved a chunk of ice down. It flopped through the surface into the water as easily as through wet tissue paper. My heart saddened again. Why had I become so excited over a membrane of ice that would disappear with the next breeze? At Scullin it had taken weeks before the ice was thick enough to walk on. What did it matter? A few days, a week, a year! It made no difference. I staggered back to the tent. My companions never stirred. Would they ever stir again?

CHAPTER 7

It was only after considering every possible aspect of surviving long enough to travel over the newly forming sea-ice that I eventually fell asleep, only to be awakened a few hours later by my friends wriggling closer together in an effort to get warm. The night had become unduly cold. It was a night similar to one a month ago when the sea first froze at Scullin Monolith. I remembered the view from our camp that next morning; a thin membrane of ice had formed over the bay but not against the rocks where the tidal movement delayed the formation for several more days. Did that mean something? My brain's inability to function was clearly becoming an annoyance.

But then it came to me. It meant that the ice around the edge of the bay formed later than the ice a few metres further out. Could that be the situation here? Was the ice thicker and stronger a short distance from the cliffs? If it were, would it support us? How could we get to it? Even if it were possible to swim through the thinner ice, it certainly would not be possible to climb out again when it got thicker. At any rate, all this was hypothetical; there was probably no thicker ice further out. I tried to resume my sleep, but the intense cold filtered right through my bag leaving me shivering.

When daylight eventually came, I was determined to examine the ice one last time before finally admitting defeat, but to do this would require Evan's help. I sat up and shook his shoulder.

"Evan. Are you awake, Evan?" But he never stirred. I shook him harder. "Wake up, Evan. Wake up, cobber."

His reply was not from a person just awakening: "What the hell do you want now?" he cursed.

"I want a belay down to the water, that's all."

Evan pulled his sleeping bag tight around his face and ignored me completely. I shook him again. This time he sprang up in anger. "Fuck off, John!" he yelled. "I told you to leave us alone. Do anything you want, but for Christ's sake fuck off and leave Betty and I alone!"

"Listen to me, Evan, some new ice has formed. I want to get down and test it."

"Bullshit!" he snarled. "It takes weeks."

Betty rose up on an arm. "Ice? Did you say ice, John?"

"Yes, Bette. It's only thin, but... well we should at least look at it."

She stared at me thoughtfully for what seemed minutes, then uneasily climbed from her bag.

Evan sprang up again. "You're not going, Betty! He's crazy! New ice couldn't form that quick; you know how long it took at Scullin. Ignore him! Go back to sleep."

Betty turned her eyes to her fiancé, and in a firm determined voice said, "He's still our skipper, Evan. If you won't go with him, then I must!"

Evan's face flushed, but he said nothing more. Angrily he pulled on his wind proofs and mukluks and met me outside, then seemed surprised that so little strength remained in his body. The tent poles steadied him, as I tied on the climbing rope, and led off down the gully to the ledge. Here, we both faced out over the dark silent sea, staring at the passing parade of icebergs and the line of old sea-ice so tantalizingly near.

"You can see open water in the wake of the icebergs," I told him, hoping to stimulate some conversation. "See the difference in colouring between the water and ice?" The comparison was so slight that it could hardly impress him. Probably he was right, probably I was crazy to even think about escaping over this!

"Belay me tight, mate." I swung down onto a chunk of ice adhering to the cliff from where it was possible to reach out and touch the sea-ice. I pressed firmly on it with a hand. Amazing! Last night's cruel temperature had strengthened it considerably. I placed a foot on it and slowly increased the pressure. The surface depressed a full centimetre with half my body weight before my mukluk broke through into the water. Evan continued to ignore my actions. Should I be satisfied now and give up? In a few more hours the breeze would freshen and most of this new ice would disperse. I climbed back to Evan and once more turned to look out at the edge of the old pack-ice a mere kilometre away. I paused. So near, yet so far! Suddenly the urge to survive again flared up within me. We couldn't just turn our backs on this scene and... return to the tent to die! A terrifying shiver shook my body. I knew then what had to be done, and knew an ugly death probably awaited me!

I whispered to Evan, "Keep the rope tight, cobber, play it out only as needed." Then I dropped back to the water's edge. There wasn't room to lay on the ice block, so somehow, I turned myself upside-down with my shoulders on the block and my legs stretched up the cliff. Now my lost body weight would be an advantage. I spread my arms across the new ice, pushed off very gently with my feet. The sound of splintering ice all around made me stop, take several deep breaths, then push again very cautiously until my feet were fully extended. I wasn't wet! The ice was still holding! I spoke softly to myself to help contain my terror. "Now it's time to do a little surface swimming; a little backstroke." One arm slid forward, then after an uncertain pause, the other. Next, I gently exerted pressure on both arms and drew them back against me. God, this was insane! I did it again. And again. Kept on doing it for a full minute, then three minutes, until the rope went taut. Thirty metres of rope!

"What now?" I whispered. "Turn over, get up on your knees. Easy, take it very easy!" The ice depressed alarmingly beneath the pressure. "Now stand up! Stand on your feet!" I stood there shivering. Thirty metres from the shore and shivering like a frightened child. Then I grinned, remembered again what Neil Armstrong had said on the moon: 'One small step for man'... just one small step. I did it! It was like stepping on a foam mattress, but I did it! The ice held. "Thank you, God." Had the ice broken Evan would not have been able to haul me ashore. But now came the real test! I untied the rope and felt naked. Then I grinned again. Could only God walk on water? One step forward. Pause. A second step. Gingerly I kept going. Seemingly walking across a huge plastic sheet drawn across the ocean. If it broke now, I was dead! A distant shout from Evan caused me to turn. He was waving. I waved back. Now to retrace my steps over *exactly* the same route.

My friend helped me up the ledge and grabbed me in an emotional embrace. "You've got guts, John," he said. "I'm sorry... I'm sorry for doubting you."

"Forget it, mate. Come on, back to the tent, we don't have any time to waste."

Betty was waiting at the top of the gully. "We're leaving, aren't we,

John? The ice isn't safe, but we're leaving at any rate. Is that what you came to tell us?"

"That's it exactly, Bette. Pack your sleeping bag, we'll start immediately." I entered the tent to find Julie's still form lying amongst a pile of sleeping bags. "Come on, honey, we're going to leave. We're pushing on to the caravan at Auster Island." She opened her eyes, her white face shocked me, the corners of her mouth had been bleeding. I called urgently to Evan.

"Oh, she's just tired and hungry," the doctor lied. "Come on, Julie, you'll feel better once we start moving."

She sat outside on the snow while we collapsed the tent and lowered it with our sleeping bags down to the edge of the sea-ice, then we tied her to the rope so Evan could belay us all down to the ledge. My eyes never left Julie. She was much weaker than any of us feared, and only spoke to whisper my name. Sadly, there was no time to talk to her or comfort her as I so earnestly desired.

"Watch me very carefully," I said to the group. "Watch how I launch myself onto the ice, then follow one at a time. Don't attempt to stand until you're as far out as me, and *never* approach within ten metres of another person."

This time the end of the rope was reached much faster, cast off, then pulled back for the next person to be tied on. It was Betty. Good. That would give Julie another chance to watch. She pushed off hesitantly, but once away from the cliff 'swam' desperately to reach the thicker ice. I pointed to where she must stand. Next came Julie. She was so frail that there was little chance of her fracturing the ice, yet the tension from watching her pathetically slow movements built up within me; there would be absolute terror in her heart. Betty moved further away to make room.

Evan was the heaviest and needed to be extremely careful. He tied the other end of the rope to our pile of gear and slowly launched himself. His movements were smooth and calculated. When the rope went taut, he stood up and dragged the gear out onto the thicker ice, then selected the tent for himself to carry and made off cautiously towards the old pack-ice. Betty grabbed two sleeping bags and followed. I collected the other two bags and the climbing rope, tying one end to myself and tossing the other to Julie. It would at least give her moral support, although if either of us broke through, the other dare not pull hard on the rope in case that person also broke through. I moved off slowly across this giant trampoline of ice. Sometimes it felt firm beneath our feet, other times we would pause anxiously when it seemed unduly spongy, then make a wide detour to a hopefully more stable area.

Betty and Evan drew quickly ahead. Julie stopped frequently for rests, causing me extra anxiety at a time when it was imperative to reach the old ice before the expected evening wind recommenced. Yet I hid my feelings and spoke calmly with her to urge her forward. She seldom uttered a single word in reply.

The sun soon set; the bitter cold of afternoon seeped through my clothes to seemingly coat my skin with a sheath of ice. At least Evan would have the tent up when we arrived. We would simply crawl into our bags and sleep, glorious sleep, knowing that once again we had beaten the odds and were safe, although still on the brink of starvation. I raised an eye to a maze of blue crevasses and churned up glaciers on the plateau above our cliff camp, and was now thankful no climbing route to it had been found. The rope went taut! I spun around to see Julie on her knees crying. Instinctively I dived towards her — froze — remembered the dangerously thin ice just in time.

"Just rest, honey. It's not far now. You're going well." Tears of concern built up in my eyes. I wanted so desperately to hold her, to help her, to love her. She was saying something. I strained to hear.

"I can't... go on... John. Leave me. I'm... finished!"

Oh, Christ! "No, honey, you're fine. Just rest a little more. Evan is nearly there, he'll have the tent up for us. Come on, Jules; just a little further. Try, please try."

She did. But we continued at an even slower pace. My hopes grew when two figures approached within metres of the old ice, but then another cry came from behind. Julie was down again.

"Rest awhile, Jules. You're doing fine." I tried to encourage her by talking about the luxuries we would find at Mawson. I talked about her old tom cat in Vancouver that hated snow. Reminded her of her mum and dad, her friends back home, the happiness awaiting us. "Try again, darling, come on, please keep trying!" I gave a gentle tug on the rope.

God! It came away! She had untied it! I fought the panic surging within me to go to her. "Jules! Jules!"

A whimper came back. "I love you... John. I love..." Then she got up, looked at me, turned, half ran, staggered, fell, ran again. Moving further and further away.

"Julie!" I called after her. "Don't run, you mustn't, you'll shatter the ice, you'll..." I panicked and hurried after her.

"Stay away, John. Don't come near me. Leave me. I love you... please leave me!"

My eyes were wide with terror. She couldn't! She mustn't! "I'm coming for you, Julie."

"You'll break the ice. Go back! Leave me, please leave me!"

I stopped a few metres from her and tried to speak calmly. "No, Jules, I'll never leave you. Either you continue with me or... or I'll come to you."

She hesitated. Her arms were outstretched urging me away. I tossed her the rope. She stared at it, stared at me. Then I breathed again as she tied it back on. We continued.

The other two were about to climb onto the old ice. How I envied them. Julie would make it this time, perhaps even before darkness engulfed us. If only they could have a hot meal awaiting us. Suddenly there was only one person ahead! I stopped. What had happened? The lone figure no longer walked in a direct line, it dodged about, seemed to be heading back this way; was running!

God! One of them has fallen through!

What now? Julie can't be left. Betty's shouts were urgent! We had the rope. Hell, there was no alternative! "Jules," I said as calmly as possible. "Evan needs my help. Please untie the rope so I can go to him." She did so instantly, perhaps even willingly. Our eyes locked together. "Wait for me, darling. *Please* wait for me!" With terror in my heart for what she might do, I turned and left her standing alone on the ice.

"Evan's fallen through," Betty shouted as we drew together. "Hurry, please hurry with the rope."

"Go and help Julie," I called back, but she ignored me and followed behind. It was obvious what had happened even before reaching Evan: he had not remembered the thinner ice near the edge. I tied a loop in the rope and threw it to him. As he lifted his arms to catch it, he slipped from the ice and sank, but quickly resurfaced with the rope beneath his arms. I turned to Betty. "Get ashore, 'swim' like we did at the cliffs." I led off. Would the ice support a person here? It seemed no thicker than glass. Ten metres to safety. Five metres. Impossible that it could contort so much without breaking! Then I was there.

The awaited thrill of this moment went unnoticed as I quickly dug my feet into the frozen snow and began hauling in the rope until it was tight about Evan. Then I pulled harder. He had the sense not to struggle; just spread his arms and let me slide him over the edge, then all the way until his head bumped into the old ice. Betty grabbed her soaked fiancé and helped him to safety.

Without wasting a second, I 'swam' back to the tent Evan had flung aside, tied the rope around it, called to Betty to haul it in, retrieved the rope, then was hurrying back for Julie.

She was still coming. Thank God! My greatest fears were unfounded. She could have easily disappeared in the belief she was helping us survive. I called to her, waved to her. She was so near, so near yet, untouchable. She caught the rope and tied on, then followed behind at a snail's pace. Ahead, the yellow tent blossomed into shape. Good old Bette. Julie saw it too; her pace quickened a fraction with something real ahead that would provide us with desperately needed warmth and shelter.

Once there I pulled Julie over the thinner ice with the rope; was joined by Betty who helped lift her up onto the stable ice. Evan, still wet and frozen, joined us to share this precious moment. Our arms went about each other. The darkness hid our tears.

The night was long, beautifully long, but around seven a.m. something outside disturbed me. It was probably the wind; it couldn't possibly be the Portuguese. What had happened to them? Had they perished in the break-out, or escaped, believing we had died? Either way we were unlikely to see them again. There was that sound again! My heart beat faster. No, it couldn't possibly be them, but there would be no peace of mind until I was certain. I sat up, pulled on my mukluks and crawled outside to investigate.

A new moon shone brilliantly from a clear sky casting ghostly shadows over the old ice and reflecting clearly from the new. The cold stung my face, stole the feeling from my bare fingers. God, what a lonely place; what a terrible place! I turned to re-enter the tent; a shadowy form suddenly startled me. Portuguese? A penguin! My nerves must be shattered! A beautiful stately emperor penguin that somehow endures this cruel land without an apparent care. A ghoulish thought flashed through my mind as I remembered Evan's words at Scullin: "We're primitive beings now, we have to kill to survive."

The thought sickened me. I opened my pocket knife, crept up behind the animal, grabbed it' head tightly beneath my arm, ripped open its throat. When freed, the penguin kicked itself across the ice, smearing it red, squirting hot blood into the air. Forgive me! Forgive me! When its reflexes finally stopped, I attacked it again, split it open from neck to groin, cut out the liver and heart, scooped up the blood in my hands, gulped it down, trying desperately not to vomit. Then I went inside to awaken the others.

"Jules, honey, eat this." I sat her up, pushed a piece of warm bloody liver into her mouth, watched her gulp it down. The next piece disappeared equally as fast.

"What… where did you… get this?" she asked.

"Just eat, Jules, eat all you can."

"What is it?" echoed Evan. But then he knew. "Penguin! Good work, mate."

"Use your knife, Evan, cut off some pieces, eat it while it's warm."

Julie was sick, poor kid, I shouldn't have pushed her so fast. Now that she knew it was freshly slaughtered penguin she hesitated, held the morsels a long time in her mouth before swallowing. "Shut your eyes, honey, think of it as chicken, eat some more, please eat some more."

By the time our gruesome meal was finished, and everything packed away ready to continue our journey, the first hint of dawn was at last replacing the light from the sinking moon. Julie's health had not improved during the night, although this morning she showed some enthusiasm about proceeding. Evan was limping noticeably but insisted he would improve during the day. Betty apparently had no worries of her own; she grabbed two of the sleeping bags and was first to set off across the ice, encouraging the rest of us to try and follow at her pace.

I estimated our position to be forty-five kilometres from the caravan at Auster Island. Our next landmark would be the Strahan Glacier which, according to the map, protrudes several kilometres out to sea and should be visible as soon as the light improved. Beyond this there would be several tiny islands close to the coast, and then, after thirty kilometres, the Austskjera group — the first of numerous islands along the remaining route to Mawson. After yesterday's ordeal on the thin ice, today's journey over a smooth firm surface should be much easier, provided no further breakouts were encountered.

As the dawn matured, the long-projected tongue of the Strahan Glacier gradually evolved ahead of the slowly moving party, forcing us to alter course and swing directly towards the glacier's snout much further out to sea. But as we approached closer, our route became unclear, for the actual terminal face was hidden amongst a multitude of icebergs that had previously calved from the glacier and became trapped in the winter freeze-up before they had time to escape out to sea.

Eventually we swung into the line of icebergs in the hope of finding a shortcut through, and immediately found ourselves amid a make-believe ice city of narrow streets winding below towering high-rises. Sadly, the streets were empty. Ghostly blue and white walls echoed Betty's shouts to hurry, but like exploring tourists we could not. Time seemed temporarily suspended. Then we emerged out the other side into a huge bay and continued along the northern side of a tiny brown island on a direct course towards Austskjera Island.

Before the morning departure we had stuffed our shirt pockets with chunks of penguin flesh to prevent it freezing, and now absorbed its nourishment by retrieving a piece from time to time and chewing on it as though it were toffee. In this manner we relieved our voracious appetites without becoming nauseated by a larger meal of it. Only Julie would not eat voluntarily, although she frequently accepted a piece when it was pushed into her mouth. She would hold it there for many minutes before bringing herself to swallow.

The sun set again behind a heavy blanket of cloud without any of the celestial displays of colour we had previously become accustomed to. Ahead, in the encroaching gloom, a small dark island merged into view. Our eyes glued on it. In this world of ice where we trudged ever onwards, it somehow warmed our hearts, was something solid and real that offered protection from the sea beneath our feet. It was a landmark to steer by, a crystal ball to stare at and allow our minds to wander from today's realities to wherever one's fantasies desired.

The island, however, never matched my dreams of an exotic ocean paradise. On passing, in fact, I saw only a low, inhospitable brown rock striped with ice from recent wave activity which had frozen before it could drain back off. Yet, when it passed from view, and only a long stretch of featureless ice again stretched ahead, we missed it; missed it as though it were a friend.

Julie was now staggering noticeably and frequently stumbled despite my arm around her for support. She rarely spoke, yet her face still contained the same look of determination with which she had started the day.

"We're only three kilometres from Austskjera, honey," I told her. "It's a large island where we'll be safe from the whims of the sea and all those animals swimming under our pillows."

She looked up at me and hopefully raised a smile, but it was now too dark to see. I selected a westerly star to guide us until the moon rose, then withdrew deeper inside my anorak hood as the temperature again plummeted.

With every half kilometre travelled, Julie's arm tightened a little more about mine, warning me she was on the verge of collapse. She no longer looked ahead. Her knees more frequently buckled; yet each time I lifted her back onto her feet she courageously continued her personal struggle for survival.

"Stick with it, Jules," I said softly to her. "The islands are already in sight. Only a few more minutes and you can rest for the night." She never looked up to see the moonlit islands ahead. Perhaps her eyes weren't even open; it was merely some instinct within her that kept her legs moving.

Then we were there. Betty called from ahead, beckoning us over some flat rocks to a gravel strewn patch large enough for the tent. Here I let Julie slip to the ground until we unpacked a sleeping bag and got her into it fully clothed, then I turned to Evan for the tent. But Evan wasn't there!

"He's coming," advised Betty. "He's been dropping further and further behind. His feet seem very painful."

When Evan arrived, we had the tent up within minutes and were soon inside wrapped in our sleeping bags chewing on chunks of penguin flesh. There seemed so many things to discuss before going off to sleep, but a few minutes later, even before the sound of chewing had stopped, eyes had closed, and it became clear that any talk would have to wait until morning.

It was already daylight when Julie woke me. She was tossing about in her sleeping bag muttering incoherently. "What is it, Jules?" I asked, jumping up with alarm. But she never replied. Her eyes remained tightly closed, her lips were bleeding, her brow hot with fever. I called urgently to Evan. "She seems delirious, I can't wake her. What's wrong with her?"

The doctor wriggled closer to Julie without leaving his sleeping bag, looking critically into her mouth, pressing back her eyelids to examine her eyes, then he slid his hand down to feel her knees and elbows.

"What is it, cobber?" I asked anxiously. "She's all right, isn't she? She's just worn out... just a little..."

"She's gravely ill, John," he whispered. "The scurvy is rampant in her now. That, plus general fatigue, hunger, and so much stress has taken its toll."

"But... but can't you wake her... can't you..."

"I don't even have a Band-Aid, John."

"What then? What must we do?" I braced myself for his answer.

Evan thought for a moment, ran his fingers through his straggly black hair, shook his head slowly, then asked solemnly how much further it was to the caravan.

"About fifteen kilometres. We can make it easily today. She'll be all right when we get her there; get her warm and fed."

"There might not be a caravan, John. You've been assuming there's one, but in fact it's only something pencilled on Ralph's map. Perhaps it's proposed for the future or was removed long ago. You're hoping for a small hotel, aren't you?"

"I'm praying for it, Evan. There might even be scientists there from Mawson."

Evan looked at Betty sitting at the end of the tent, then at me. "There's something else I must tell you both," he said mysteriously. "I

186

can't help you carry Julie, my feet are frozen."

"Oh, God!" I muttered. Betty stared at her fiancé but was probably already aware of his plight. "Then shouldn't we massage them, get some life back into your toes?"

"No, John. It's best to leave them frozen until it's possible to treat them properly in warm water. I can still hobble on my feet, but if we managed to thaw them it would be too painful to even stand. My circulation has remained poor since my earlier frostbite on the plateau."

Thoughts about what best to do flooded my mind. Should I go alone to search for food and help? No. Our only real hope lay in everyone reaching the caravan. Julie had to be carried there without delay.

"We'll go now," I said, when everything was clear in my mind. "To hell with the tent and rope, leave them. You bring the three sleeping bags, Bette, I'll carry Julie."

"In her bag?" she queried. "How?"

I demonstrated by ripping open the bottom of her sleeping bag and pulling it above her knees. "I'll carry her piggyback and tie her to me with a piece of climbing rope. Come on, let's move."

It was after ten a.m. when we left, and just breaking dawn. God, what a sorry procession. Evan was using two tent poles as walking sticks and hobbling slowly with great difficulty. Betty walked with her bulky load tied to her back and kept well out in front to act as pace-maker. I brought up the rear with my light, silent load bundled across my back. The surface at least remained smooth and easy to walk upon.

Once clear of the Austskjera group, our course swung to the northeast, directly away from the coast. Under normal conditions a day might be saved en route to Mawson by not detouring to the off-course Auster Islands, but now, it was clear our only hope of survival lay in finding the caravan so dubiously marked on the map. I dared not think about the consequences of another storm or break-out, but simply kept my head lowered, watching the snow pass beneath my feet. Frequently I spoke to Julie in the hope she might hear, but there was never the slightest response. Sometimes I passed Evan. This gave me a chance to sit down and rest until he caught up again.

A line of icebergs ahead stretched like the Great Wall of China for many kilometres out to sea, so rather than wind amongst them I led the group along its eastern side until noon, then swung westward amongst them to search for tiny Auster Island. It was then that the sun appeared briefly to give radiance to the icebergs and accentuate the green and blue pastel shades in their smooth, monolithic walls. It was then also that Julie broke her long silence to whisper my name.

"Oh, Jules, you spoke!" I yanked off the rope holding her, laid her gently on the snow. "You're getting better, Jules. You'll soon be walking again." I brushed the ice from her eyebrows and balaclava, pushed away a wisp of golden hair. Evan and Betty joined us. Julie's bewildered eyes rolled from one person to another without any emotional change.

She repeated only one word. "John."

I hugged her, kissed her, spoke softly of our love, kissed her again and again. "She's getting better, Evan, she'll soon be…"

Evan interrupted. "Keep going, John. Every minute is vital now."

I stared into the doctor's face, sensed his unspoken meaning, then started out again at a very brisk pace. Julie seemed weightless, but when Evan wasn't able to keep up, another frustrating wait became necessary. A huge tabular iceberg towered above like a medieval fortress. Ahead was a clipper ship with its sails billowing. On the left stood a Gothic cathedral amidst a village of tiny cottages. We wound along narrow corridors between these, climbing over small snow drifts, skating along pathways of smooth ice, finding a way through puzzles of ice-blocks that had fallen from above.

"Look! Look ahead!" Betty's call echoed through the towering ramparts as if a dozen pirates were shouting down at us. "Two emperor penguins. They look like a couple of sheriffs waiting to take us in!"

"So long as they feed us," I murmured. Then we saw a large group of penguins standing silently in a near perfect circle.

"At least there's plenty to eat if we don't find the…"

I cut Evan short. "We *must* find the caravan, mate. We left our tent behind, remember? We *must* find the caravan, and soon!"

Already we had come a kilometre into the maze of icebergs, yet there was still no sign of reaching the other side. Penguins were becoming even more numerous. Small groups of them waddled across the snow in front of us as if hurrying to a department store sale. Others stood silently aside to watch as we staggered by; still more strutted busily past with only a turn of their heads and a few eerie squawks. But then everyone stopped suddenly. Were we dreaming? Never had we anticipated such a sight!

"It's the rookery!" gasped Betty. "Auster Rookery!"

A black seething mass of emperor penguins. Thousands of them! Perhaps twenty thousand of them! All milling around a central arena amid a circle of towering icebergs as if at a Saturday market. More came into view as we moved closer. In corridors between the 'bergs; in long lines of commuters hurrying about their business as humans do in any modern-day community.

"But why here," asked Evan. "Why so far from the coast in this godforsaken place?"

"Ralph's books explain why," I replied. "They breed in the middle of winter to avoid predators; and to guard against ice break-outs they find a stable area of sea-ice protected by all these grounded icebergs."

"Grounded icebergs?

"Of course, Bette, that's why they're all in such a straight line; there must be an underwater reef. Auster Island is probably part of it."

We edged closer to the main mass of birds without distracting any of them; they seemed to be shuffling closer together to conserve body heat now that the sun had set and the afternoon cold was intensifying. From the multitude rose a steady drone of sound like the monotonous hum of a power transformer.

"Look, John!" Betty tugged at my sleeve. "On their feet under those stomach bulges, aren't they eggs? God, how can they incubate eggs in this terrible cold?"

"Eggs? Food! Grab one, Evan."

He used his pole to dislodge a baseball-sized egg from beneath a penguin's incubation flap. It protested noisily and was supported by cries from others as they shook their heads wildly in objection while emitting their weird accordion-like squawks. Yet not one of them moved to recapture the egg as it lay on the ice before them; nor was there any attempt to drive Evan away as he warily picked it up, shook it, knocked a hole in it, then tipped it to his lips.

Evan showed no sign of having just sampled a gourmet entrée when he handed the egg to Betty. She in turn took a few sips and passed it on to me. The liquid was lukewarm and slid easily down my throat but had very little taste. To drink more might have induced vomiting. I returned it to Betty hoping she could coax Julie to drink a little, but her eyes were tightly closed and she could not be roused. Again, the urgency of our journey was remembered, prompting us to hurry to the far side of the rookery.

I stopped again. Evan and Betty halted abruptly beside me. They looked left and right with growing excitement, then straight at me. Smiles spread across all our faces.

FOOTSTEPS!

"Footsteps, Jules! Human footsteps!" I set her gently on the snow. The thrill of the moment was overwhelming. "Jules, Jules, we're almost there... all this is about to end! There will be a doctor... medical supplies... we'll have you well again in no time." But my fiancée never stirred. I kissed and hugged her; became very frightened. Evan took her pulse.

"Keep going, John," he said softly. "We must try and move faster."

The line of fresh footsteps joined up with others and led us to the base of a prominent iceberg where it seemed a party of about six people had grouped together to begin their survey.

Betty called from ahead. "Dog tracks, John. They came by dog team!"

"Then there's got to be... yes, here, Bette. Two pairs of sledge tracks."

Evan hobbled to catch up and join in the excitement. "Maybe they'll be having roast lamb for dinner tonight? Hope they won't mind a few party crashers."

We pushed on immediately. The fresh, well defined sledge tracks led in a south-westerly direction along narrow corridors between the icebergs, and past other groups of penguins scurrying towards the rookery. Often these tobogganed over the snow on their breasts by pushing forward with their powerful legs, but always when they neared this strange human procession they stopped, stood boldly upright in a straight line, and watched with obvious interest as we staggered by. After we had passed, the emperors dropped back on their breasts and continued their journey.

An hour's travelling in the afternoon twilight brought us to the other side of the iceberg chain and back onto open sea-ice — but there was something else — something low and rounded silhouetted against the ice. The others saw it too. God! At long last! It *had* to be Auster Island. I fought to dispel Evan's previous thoughts from my mind. The caravan *must* be there!

"Go ahead, Bette, don't wait for us. Tell them we're here! Tell them about Julie. Get them to prepare their medical gear… get them to radio Mawson."

Betty started running. But then she stopped and turned back to look at us. "I can see it!" she shouted. "I can see a red caravan!" She turned forward again and started waving, running a few metres, stopping to wave, running again.

"Oh, Jules," I whispered. "If only you could wake up. Wake up and join in this momentous occasion. You're going to get better now. my darling, we're all going to get better. Our journey's over. Our nightmare journey is over."

Betty disappeared. Boy, what a surprise for the Mawson men! I almost laughed. Did she bother to knock? What would she say first? She's probably swigging hot coffee while they get over their shock! I tried to run. Poor Evan was left far behind.

Betty appeared again. She darted to the top of some high boulders. Something was wrong! Why weren't they coming out for Julie? Where were they? In bed… that's it, she's waiting for them to dress.

At the first rocks of the low island Betty met me with a shrug. "Nobody home!"

I stared at her in disbelief. "Nobody home?"

"Maybe they're still working somewhere," she added. "Perhaps they'll be back soon. I don't know!"

Evan caught up and walked with us to the door of the tiny fibreglass shelter. We entered. It was colder inside than out. Two porthole type windows glowed with the twilight but failed to illuminate the dark interior. Betty grabbed Julie and lifted her from my back as soon as the rope was untied. Suddenly I felt weightless, as if I'd drift away. There seemed to be four bunks: two on the side, two on the end. She laid Julie on a lower mattress and pulled a pile of sleeping bags over her. "Well, I guess we're home," she said with a strangeness in her voice.

I ran my hands over a multitude of objects on a small table in search of a flashlight or …"

"Here's a candle," said Betty. "No matches yet."

But Evan found some. I lit the candle and waited while the frozen wick spluttered, and then flamed up to spread light and shadow over the rounded walls and onto the table strewn with a score of everyday objects that we had almost forgotten about. A pressure lamp hung from the ceiling. I shook it to check for fuel, primed the bowl with methylated spirits, lit it and left it to vaporise.

Betty was cursing beside me. "There's no goddammed gas, not even a hiss."

She was trying to light the burner of a Propane stove. "Let me look." I nudged her aside, began tracing the supply pipe back along the wall. "The cylinder's outside, Bette, probably turned off."

She snatched up a flashlight and hurried out the door. I pumped up the Tilley lamp and lit the mantle. Light and warmth instantly flooded the shadows. Evan was sitting next to Julie on the bottom bunk, his head lowered in his hands. Betty rushed back inside, grabbed the matches from my hand, lit the two burners and watched them flare into life. We found two cooking pots and packed them with snow. On the floor a kerosene heater was discovered, identical to the one aboard the *Evening Star*. That too was soon radiating warmth.

Betty was now searching through the cupboards. "Look at this, John, food galore!" She pulled down a tin of cream biscuits, grabbed a handful, pushed some into Evan's and my hands. "God, what a treat!"

"What about Julie?" I asked Evan. "What can we give her?"

He turned slowly to look at her; asked for the flashlight, pushed back her eyelids, felt her pulse, listened to her breathing. "Look under the bunk, John, there should be a medical kit somewhere. Find it."

He was right: a large red box. I flung open the lid for the doctor to examine. "Good," he muttered. "We can do something now." Minutes later Julie had her first antibiotic shot. "I can probably bring her around for a short time, but first prepare some warm soup or thin stew to give her."

"Coming up, Doc," advised Betty. "Heinz vegetable soup with a block of our old staple, HF6 meat."

We were now munching plain biscuits spread thickly with concentrated butter and honey. The coffee was awaited, anxiously.

Evan then made what seemed a strange request. "Please turn off the heater, John. Consider my feet. I'll need to be under sedation when they start thawing. Probably I'll be out of action for a few days."

Betty dived to turn it off. "Sorry, mate. Too much excitement; we weren't thinking too clearly. Julie's soup is about ready, can you try waking her now?"

"Bathe her face in warm water first, Bette; I'll prop her up. John, you sit in front and talk to her as she comes around."

I started to speak softly to Julie about the discoveries we had made in the caravan, but Evan stopped me. "I said talk, talk loudly so she can understand and recognise you, and stay clear of these smelling salts, they're pretty potent. More warm water, Bette."

"Come on, honey, wake up." I gently brushed aside some hair from her pale face. "You're safe now, darling. We have lots of delicious food for you to eat, then you can sleep for as long as you want."

The salts took effect immediately. Julie reeled her head to escape the pungent vapours.

"Wake up, Jules. Wake up, honey." Her lips began to tremble, parted slightly, but no sound escaped. "Come on, darling, we're all waiting for you to join the party."

Evan gently lifted an eyelid and was encouraged when the eye focussed on him. She then opened the other eye.

"Welcome back, beautiful!" I stared into her blue eyes and in an instant remembered our whole life together. "There's three top class chefs waiting to serve you, honey. First on the menu is our house specialty: soup *de jour*." But I couldn't keep up this charade any longer. My voice began to choke, tears welled up in my eyes and I threw my arms about my fiancée, pressed my face against hers, muffled my sobs in her soft golden hair.

But it wasn't *my* tears that Evan observed flowing freely down Julie's cheeks — it was *hers*. She was reacting to my embrace; was aware of what was happening.

Betty spooned some of the rich soup to Julie's lips and forced it into her mouth. She spluttered, coughed it out again, but the next spoonful was swallowed without hesitation. I took over from Betty and continued until the bowl was almost empty, until Evan stopped me.

"No more to begin with," he insisted, letting his patient lay back and close her eyes. "Get her out of those clothes, Bette; give her a good scrub and let her get a good night's rest."

When Evan moved away to explore the cupboards, I brought the Tilley lamp closer to Julie to keep her warm while we stripped off her stale smelling garments. Betty grabbed the new cake of soap I had found and for a moment pressed it tightly to her face. She gave a deep sigh and smiled. "You're going to love this, Julie, dear. Palmolive! The Mawson boys must have expected us after all." But then she called Evan back. "Look at her knees and elbows; they're swollen. They've been bleeding."

"Yes, I know, Bette. In a few more days she would have broken out in horrible sores. We're lucky there's lots of vitamin C here: tablets, drink powder, freeze-dried carrots, fruits. I'll dress her wounds. She'll recover from the scurvy if only…"

"Only what?" I asked quickly.

"We'll see tomorrow, mate. A good night's rest should work wonders for her."

After her wash, we found a blue cotton tracksuit amongst a bag of spare clothing and dressed Julie in this, and minutes later had her snugly inside a clean sleeping bag. I kissed her again, then reluctantly turned to other concerns.

"Your feet, Evan, we should attend to them next."

"No hurry, mate, a frozen foot is like meat in a refrigerator. First let's gorge ourselves, then I want a good wash."

The moment each of us had dreamed about for so long at last eventuated. Betty's vegetable soup was champagne to our taste buds. The rich meat and vegetable stew was sheer ecstasy; a plate of sunshine. We washed it down with hot milk and coffee, then gulped down a tin of peaches before switching back to biscuits, butter, cheese and honey. By then the well-stocked cupboard was losing its appeal. Canned ham, tuna, beef, cherries, pineapple, packets of puddings, custards, rice, chocolate; things we dared not even dream about a few hours ago, were now being refused!

"Let's postpone this banquet until morning," suggested Betty. "My

194

eyes must have been bigger than my tummy, I'm pooped!"

"Me too." The desire was there to go on eating, but stomach space was limited! "When we empty the cupboards, Bette, there's still a stack of ration packs outside."

Betty ceased her jesting and turned to Evan. "You're next on the schedule, aren't you, 'Big Boy'? We've got to start work on your feet."

Evan stripped and washed and clad himself in a pair of flannel pyjamas. His feet were still lumps of ice, although not black like they had been at Scullin. I filled the dish again with warm water and relit the heater while he prepared a syringe of morphine and handed it to Betty.

"OK, Bette," said the doctor, sitting on the bunk with his legs dangling over the edge. "I'm ready. You know what to do."

She nodded, made him turn around to prod the needle into his buttock, then sat quietly until the drug took effect. We placed his feet in the warm water and changed it frequently as it cooled. Evan supervised for a short time, but after seeing everything going well, closed his eyes and leaned back to enjoy total relief. His feet were thawed for over an hour before Betty was satisfied, then she carefully dried them and separately wrapped each one in a soft woollen shirt. We helped the doctor into a sleeping bag, pushed a sleeping tablet into his mouth, and left nature to try and work its miracles.

With both patients asleep, Betty finally flopped down at the table beside me to drink another coffee. "Well," she sighed. "We're a pretty sorry bunch, aren't we?"

I nodded. "According to the visitor's book we just missed the scientific party by four hours. They left at ten a.m. for Mawson. A pity, eh!"

"A hell of a pity, John. God, we could have hitched a ride. Julie and Evan could now be receiving proper care in their hospital, if they have a hospital."

"They'll be back, Bette. So long as Julie and Evan are recovering, we can wait a little longer."

She jumped up as a pot of water boiled over on the stove. "My turn to wash. Then a *real* bed; boy, I'll sleep forever!"

As she stripped, she cursed and muttered something in disgust, but then laughed and tossed a handful of smelly penguin flesh over my shoulder onto the table. "Another world, eh, John?" she said simply.

At five a.m. it was necessary to get up and touch things around me to make certain I wasn't dreaming. But everything was real; we actually were in the Auster caravan. I then rolled over and slept again until the first light of morning shone weakly through the tiny windows; until Betty relit the heater and pushed a steaming hot cup of cocoa into my hands.

"I've been reading the visitor's book," she said quietly while leaning over my bunk. "Yesterday's visit — June 14 — was the first of the winter, but last year they came monthly between June and October with either dog teams or Skidoos."

"Each month, eh! We've got ample food to last that long, Bette, but what about Julie and Evan, will they recover properly without hospital treatment?"

She shrugged. "I'm not sure about Julie, but there certainly are specialised drugs that would speed up Evan's recovery. He'll tell us about them when he wakes."

After an hour-long breakfast, Betty and I wandered outside to avoid disturbing the sound sleep of our patients. The sun had already set again after merely rising to show a red sliver above the horizon, and it seemed likely that it would not reappear until a week or so after June 21 — midwinter's day. We strolled a short distance between large boulders protruding from patches of frozen gravel to the top of the island and gazed over the flat iceberg studded sea-ice to the now distant Polar Plateau. Emperor penguins, like lonely gentlemen, strolled regally beneath the rocks on their journeys to and from their iceberg protected rookery.

"What are you thinking, John?" Betty asked during my long silence.

I looked at her; uncertain how to answer. "So many things I suppose, Bette, but mainly about Julie. She's gravely ill, isn't she? Despite what Evan says about improvements, it frightens me to see her lying there so helpless when…"

"When there's probably a hospital only fifty kilometres away? Is that what you mean?"

I never replied. On the way back to the caravan a nearby grunting sound startled us and, on investigating, found it to be a large Weddel seal lolling about on its side as if enjoying a balmy day on the beach. Nearby a small rounded tunnel through the ice seemed to be its lifeline to the sea.

"It must have kept that hole open since the sea froze," I suggested, as we edged closer to the huge slug-like creature. "It could never have gnawed through a metre of sea-ice."

The seal watched us carefully with large tear-filled eyes and only wriggled back into its hole when I attempted to touch its mottled, hairy skin.

Evan awoke and sat up as we returned through the squeaky door, then watched as we toasted our chilled fingers over the heater. Betty kissed him. "How's my Big Boy today?" she asked with a smile.

"Hungry, but otherwise pretty fair."

"How fair?" I asked.

He took the plate of muesli Betty offered and answered between gulps. "Can't be certain, yet. Feet are naturally very tender. I don't suppose I'll be walking anywhere much for a week or so."

"Betty thinks you need special drugs, hospital care."

"Don't we all?" he replied simply.

"And Julie, have you examined her this morning?"

"Yes, John. We should wake her for another meal."

"But how is she, Evan? Is there any marked improvement?"

The doctor now understood I was pressing for realistic answers. "She's not good, John. She's a very sick girl. I can give her antibiotics, vitamin tablets, good food, but…"

"But that mightn't be enough! Is that what you're saying?"

Evan looked at me thoughtfully and nodded. "The truth is, she is unlikely to make any significant improvement without specialised treatment."

The blood drained from my face. This was news I had expected but hearing it from a doctor was scary. My mind was now made up. "Julie is going to recover quickly, Evan, because… because I'm going for help. I'm going to Mawson."

"But she can't be moved. I can't walk!"

"I'm going alone!"

Both Evan and Betty stared at me. Evan finally spoke. "You wouldn't make it, John. Its only fifty kilometres, I know, but… but we're all wise enough now to the dangers of ice break-outs, blizzards, whiteouts. You've brought us this far; you've done more than anyone expected of you. Be patient, wait it out here until the Mawson boys return."

"They may not return for a month, Evan. They may not even return this year. I can't just sit here hoping and praying they'll show up. If help doesn't come soon Julie might die, you insinuated that yourself. Well... well I won't let her die. I'm going for help. You must take care of her while I'm away, and Betty will take care of you."

"But alone, John, God!

"I'll leave first thing in the morning."

Betty had been silent throughout our discussion, but now she stood up, faced us both, and announced firmly:

"You're *not* going alone, John. I'm coming with you!"

CHAPTER 8

Evan was not pleased with Betty's decision to accompany me to Mawson, nor was I, although for different reasons. In my opinion, the risks of such a journey could well be borne by one person, and she would be more useful here as a nurse tending to the sick. Betty, however, had made up her mind, arguing she could do little of importance in the caravan, but in view of the dangers and urgency of the journey, was adamant that no person should travel alone. In the event of an accident or injury, she explained, the other person could offer aid, and in a dire situation could push on to Mawson to raise the alarm. Neither Evan nor I admitted her logic was sound, although when the situation was considered further, it would be no hardship having her along.

Two hours before daybreak, Betty helped assemble the gear for the journey. An aluminium rescue sledge hanging on the outside wall would be ideal for transporting the small amount of gear we intended taking. A single ration pack would suffice, also a small cooking stove, two sleeping bags, and a plastic tarpaulin to serve for the one overnight bivouac. Lots of luxury items tempted us, but the importance of making a fast trip with a light sledge excluded these.

At ten a.m., the dawn brightened sufficiently to allow us to get under way. One last glance at the map and it was time for our party to disband for the first time in nearly a year. Betty sank into the warm embrace of Evan's arms; I pressed my lips to the pale inert face of my fiancée. "God be with you, my darling," I whispered, pulling away to gaze thoughtfully into her lovely face as tears again moistened my eyes. Betty tugged on my arm. I turned to Evan. His eyes too were wet. "Expect us back in three days, cobber. Take care of Julie, take care of yourself."

Evan nodded; just smiled and nodded.

In the half-light filtering through a dense cover of cumulus clouds, the Mawson party's tracks were barely visible, but seemed to lead off across the open sea-ice towards the coast. We stopped moments after starting for a last look back at the tiny red caravan that had been our salvation, perched high on the little rocky island. Betty again touched my arm. "Don't worry, John, she'll be all right; Evan will take care of her."

The sledge was so light and the surface so smooth that it was easy to forget we were pulling anything, and this allowed us to alternately jog and walk at five-minute intervals to keep comfortably warm. Nevertheless, our thoughts continually returned to our friends. Not of them lying ill at Auster Island, but of happier times in a green world of warm sunshine where a forgotten ingredient called money could place almost anything in one's hands: a warm bed with soft white sheets; a steak with roast potatoes and green peas; a glass of sparkling white wine in a long-stemmed glass. My dreams obscured the concerns we should be having for the darkening clouds and freshening winds so clearly visible about us.

After two hours we again neared the coast and stopped at Macklin Island where evidence was found of an earlier camp by the Mawson party. It wasn't an inviting place to overnight, amongst low ice-sheathed boulders, although we now appreciated that any inhospitable speck of rock along this frozen coast could suddenly become a godsend to travellers in conditions of storm, like that which had recently dispersed the ice around us near Stevens Rock.

Turning west again on a direct course to Mawson raised our morale, and at the same time diverted the wind that had been blowing directly into our faces onto the sides of our anorak hoods. The wind higher up on the plateau seemed very much more active, and was stirring the snow and billowing it high into the air like smoke from a spreading grass fire; signs that encouraged us to extend our jogging times. The nearby ice-cliffs also did nothing to cheer our passing.

To allow our minds to escape these disturbing thoughts I spoke to my companion to end our long silence. "We'll make camp on one of the Paterson Islands, Bette, about another ten kilometres from here. We should sight them pretty soon."

"Oh," she muttered, looking around as if seeing me for the first time. "Ten kilometres? We won't make that before dark, will we?"

"Probably not. We'll do the last section on a compass bearing."

"John, you must have noticed the weather; it's deteriorating fast isn't it? The signs are similar to last time... when the ice broke up. We *are* going to make it, aren't we?"

We started to jog again. "We'll make it, Bette. It's scary I know, but we'll make it this time."

By the time dusk again settled over the ice, the wind was much more than an inconvenience that caused us to cover our faces. It had grown into a force that swept the drift from the plateau down over the ice-cliffs like white water over a spillway, and sometimes reached us to sting our faces with sharp ice crystals. The trailing sledge became something more than an object we could forget; it caught the wind-gusts and swung sideways across the snow, dragging us forcibly with it.

The Paterson Islands were in sight for only a short time before long tentacles of drift and the encroaching darkness obscured everything from view. We continued running in the blackness as urgently as if the clock had been turned back and we were still fleeing the Portuguese. Then we were deluged with drift. It gave body to the wind and blew into our hoods, down our necks, beneath our balaclavas until our jogging no longer produced sufficient warmth. Soon we were shivering from the cold and running so fast to gain the shelter of the islands that we forgot our nearness to them, and suddenly crashed headlong into the rocks. Quickly we regained our feet and hurried to the lee-side of the island.

It was miraculous. A few metres above the sea-ice beneath an overhanging cliff, we found complete shelter from the drift and from all but an occasional backdraft of wind. The gravel surface wasn't particularly level, but that was a minor consideration. We piled rocks upon one end of the tarpaulin and tied the other to rock nodules protruding from the overhang to form a lean-to that should give us sufficient protection for the night. Once inside, we spread the snow mats and climbed quickly into our sleeping bags to warm up before lighting the stove to prepare a much-needed meal.

The purr of the burner, the added warmth trapped beneath the cover, and the aroma of cooking stew were, to us, the nearest attainable things to absolute bliss. Betty had cheered up. "Not bad, eh, mate. We've jogged about thirty kilometres with only a ten-minute break at Macklin. That leaves twenty to go, doesn't it? You know, there's still life in my old bones yet."

In the flickering light of the stove, I saw her smiling. "Twenty is about right, Bette. Tomorrow will be our big day: walking into Mawson and knocking on someone's door."

"Quite an occasion," she agreed, raising herself on an elbow and edging a little closer. "What will we say? Excuse me, sir, could you tell me when the next ferry leaves for Hobart?"

I laughed. "If we get there early enough, maybe they'll have a fast vehicle to whiz us back to the caravan for Julie and Evan."

"Then it will be all over, won't it, John? I mean… we'll have nothing more to do except repair our damaged bodies and wait for a ship to take us home. There will be no more waking up of a morning thinking we might be dead by afternoon. No more freezing in blizzards, no more nearly starving to death, no more strugg… ling…" Emotion had crept into her voice but this time she made no attempt to hide it. She stretched an arm across my chest and buried her face in my shoulder. I held her tightly.

"You've been a great companion on this venture, Bette. Perhaps in Vancouver I wasn't keen to have you along, but since our troubles with the iceberg, you've given each of us the will and strength to survive. We all owe you more than we can ever repay."

"I'm not sorry I came, John. It's been a hell of a trip, but… well, it brought me closer to the real you. The guy I knew in that sordid little London flat wasn't the real you; I know that now. Nor was the gal you knew, the real me. We've learned a lot about each other since those days, haven't we, mate?"

"We have, Bette. Life was too fast for us in London. Maybe if…" I stopped myself abruptly.

"It's too late for maybes and ifs. You chose Julie; I settled for Evan. We both know how much you love her, and… and I guess I love you enough to want you to have only the best."

"Evan's a great person. None of my friends thought he would ever find a girl good enough for him, until you come along. You do love him, don't you, Bette?"

"Yes… I love him. I'll make him a good wife. Have his babies, if that's what he wants. But, John… is it wrong of me to say I… I never want to be far from you? Can we live close together in Australia where we can enjoy life as friends, you know, call around for coffee, go to the concerts together, have lots of barbecues on the beach."

"You and Evan will always be our most loved friends, you know that."

After eating our meal and tidying up we relaxed to listen to the wind howling amongst the rocks above our heads. Betty snuggled closer. I felt her soft breasts and steady heartbeat against my chest. "John," she whispered. "Tonight, will be the last time we'll be together... I mean, really together. Can't we turn back the clock a few years... can't we forget all our commitments and... well, imagine we're still back in London. Won't you hold me tight again, just for old time's sake?'

I put an arm around her and kissed her lightly on the forehead, but then she found my lips and pressed hers passionately to mine. I drew away.

"Don't, John," she murmured. "Stay close to me. Give me this night. You said you owed me, well pay me, pay me now! No one will see us; no one will ever know."

"We mustn't, Bette. It's not right with Julie..."

"But isn't it an old tradition, mate. Aren't the guys entitled to one last fling before tying the knot?"

My resistance was weakening, my desire for her rising. She turned around so that her silky black hair pushed into my face, then pulled my hands down across the front of her shirt and pressed them tightly to her breasts. "You used to be good with buttons," she said mischievously. "Don't tell me you've forgotten."

"But this is Antarctica! We're under a plastic cover on a tiny island in the middle of a frozen sea."

"What could be more exciting?" she giggled.

My hands lowered until they rested on bare skin at her waist. She turned her head until our lips were again together. My hands moved up beneath her shirt until each cupped the softness of a breast.

"Took you a long time to get there, didn't it, cobber? How do you like the new slimline me?"

"You've been dieting well, Bette." I gently ran my hands over her enchanting contours, squeezed her, tickled her nipples. "In London I could only handle one boob at a time."

"Then you haven't forgotten? You didn't just run out on me and forget all the good times we had together?"

"No, Bette, it wasn't possible to forget. You were right, I left because..."

"Because I got too hot for you? Is that why you brought me down here, to cool me off, to put me on ice?"

I laughed in her ear, nibbled on it, kissed her neck.

"These are pretty big sleeping bags, John. If you'll shove over, I'll pay you a visit."

"They might be big, but with all the polar 'clobber' one wears to bed, they need to be."

"Take it off, silly, we'll keep warm with what we were born with."

Her skin against mine without the heavy clothing we so seldom shed was like being again in bed between smooth silk sheets. Our arms tightly embracing each other isolated us from the loneliness of the inhospitable outside world. Her warm kisses, her soft curvaceous body, revived in me dormant passions so alien to the cruel life that had been forced upon us. We made love, and a new person seemed born within me.

Morning came too quickly. At first, I was surprised how warm we had stayed without our clothes, but on trying to move realised that snow had weighed down the tarpaulin allowing it to act as a very efficient bedspread. "Bette," I called softly to awaken her.

"Mmmm!"

"We're snowed in, Bette. Help me shake it off."

I never expected her to kiss me again, but then we wriggled and pushed with knees and elbows until the snow slid off and the cover sprang back into position.

Betty giggled. "No one will ever believe this! Not even my rough old girlfriends in 'Frisco. Who would believe I was snowed in the sack with a Mr Wonderful in the middle of Antarctica?"

At ten a.m. there was only a tinge of orange reflecting from the unrisen sun, but that was sufficient to show the weather hadn't improved at all. The wind was still howling through the rocks above.

"Hood up, Bette, the wind's still coming from the south, so keep it on your left. Are you ready?"

"Ready, John. Only twenty more kilometres to pull this ruddy sledge! Maybe we'll be there for lunch?"

Away from the shelter of the rocks, a frigid wall of drifting snow pushed heavily against our bodies tending to force us off course, so until the next landmark was sighted, I occasionally consulted the compass now tied handily around my neck. For much of the time it mattered little whether our eyes were open or closed; we simply plodded on in a semi-daze with our minds alternating between thoughts of nearby Mawson and pleasurable times we'd known before in far off lands. I frequently thought of Julie back in the caravan, and last night with Betty, but there was no feeling of guilt. As Betty said, it was a traditional last fling before wedding bells. It was now hard to believe that the bundled-up figure in yellow wind proofs struggling alongside me was the same silky skinned girl in my arms last night.

But then the full urgency of our mission was remembered: Julie's illness, Evan's feet. Their lives depended on help coming quickly. I tried to walk faster, but the battle to remain upright against the wind prevented this. Betty grabbed my arm to command attention, then pointed ahead. A slight break in the drift allowed a glimpse of several rocky outcrops that could only be the Klung Islands. My eyes then rose to the plateau where a dark pyramid of rock stood silhouetted against the horizon. I remembered every landmark around Mawson without reference to the map.

"That's Mount Henderson," I shouted into Betty's hood, hoping to be heard above the whine of wind. "It's one of the mountains just south of Mawson."

She nodded and pointed to a high distant island slightly right of our route. My heart pounded. "Welch Island! It's only four kilometres from the base."

Betty again grabbed my arm and shook it to show her excitement.

A moment later the drift streamed back over us, locking us once more in the confinement of our immediate world. We staggered on. The strength of the wind continued to increase, forcing us frequently to our knees to regain stability, yet as long as the gap between us and Mawson diminished with every step our difficulties with the weather could be tolerated. Another feeling within me, however, sounded a warning. Time was rapidly running out; we *must* move faster!

Three kilometres from Welch Island we stepped from the snow-covered surface onto clear ice and stopped abruptly as memories of treacherous thin ice were revived. But this wasn't new ice, it appeared to be ice stripped of snow by the strong winds. We continued hesitantly. The slippery surface was as difficult to walk on as a skating rink; in fact, skating across it seemed the logical way of making headway. But then a fierce gust struck from the side flinging us heavily to the ice and sending us careering in struggling heaps across the surface with the sledge acting as a sail to drag us even faster. We crashed into a ridge of snow and lay there panting until the wind abated sufficiently to allow us to get up and move on. The incident unnerved us. What would we do next time?

Next time came moments later! The wind screamed at us like an express train, softly at first in the distance, then roaring as it grew closer until we cowered in its path. We grabbed each other, braced ourselves, were again flung heavily to the ice and bowled across it with the speed of a bobsleigh. We smashed into a snow-bank and were jarred to a halt.

"Are you all right, Bette?" I called, lifting her dazed body back onto its feet.

"God, John, my bones aren't steel, I can't…"

"Come on, run; run between gusts."

It wasn't possible to run, but we slipped and skated and forced ourselves forward at a reasonable pace. At the next patch of snow, we lay across the sledge while another express train of wind thundered over us and sped off into the distance. Again, we tried to run, moving from one huge ice-rink, across a ridge of snow to the next. Welch Island seemed as far away as ever.

"Hang on!" I shouted, as yet another gust slammed into us. Again, we flung ourselves across the sledge, tried to grip the ice with our feet, accelerated, went hurtling across the mirrored surface, crashed into another snow-bank. The sledge struck us moments later and rolled painfully over our bodies. Betty screamed. I cursed. Then there was a moment's silence.

"Are you all right, Bette?" I called, alarmed that she hadn't moved, then lifted her bloodied face from the snow. She revived quickly and fought to get back onto her feet. "Easy, mate, rest a while." I blotted the red stream from her nose with a rag and held her until her legs stopped shaking; until she stopped panting and gazing about her with the eyes of a hunted animal.

"Have… have we anything to eat, John? Some chocolate…"

"I'll get some. Lay down, brace yourself." Another onslaught hurtled towards us but this time my feet held fast in the snow until it passed. I hurried to untie the frozen knots securing our load, pulled the plastic cover aside, dived into the ration pack for two chocolate bars, tore off the wrapping and gave one to Betty.

"Thanks," she murmured. "This will sure…"

The next gust was upon us. I swore, leapt back to the sledge, replaced the cover, threw myself across it. The ice seemed to tremble beneath the savage attack, snow blasted into the air, the sledge took off, bashed into my head, flew like a kite on our waist loops. Then we were sliding again, sliding across the next ice-rink, speeding across it, the sledge diving, rising, swooping on us like a madman attacking with a shovel. But then we hit the next snow drift and lay there stunned.

Unsteadily I got back on my feet, helped Betty rise, righted the sledge. "God! God, almighty. Where *is* everything?" The sledge was empty! I flung off the waist loop, one thought in mind: find the sleeping bags. I skated off. Betty shouted after me. The next gust caught up, rolled me across the ice, spun me about. I clawed the surface, picked up speed, hurtled into more snow. The stove! I grabbed it, darted about for something else, anything else, but… but there was nothing, nothing else in sight; just ice and drift and… nothing!

Then Betty was beside me. We threw our arms about each other, lay on the snow as the next onslaught tore at our clothes.

"I… I found the stove."

"Matches?"

"Matches? Shit!" I hurled the stove to the ice and kicked it into the distance. "Come on, Bette. Nothing to pull any more. There's only us now. Come on, mate, let's go… let's go to Mawson!"

We linked arms for stability. It was nearly dark again. We staggered along the ridges of snow, followed them as they zig-zagged about, hardly daring to step on the ice; but soon there was *only* ice. We lay down between gusts, no point fighting them, slid wherever we were blown, jumped up and ran whenever it was still again.

It now seemed ages since the chocolate. We were weakening, feeling the cold seep into our skins, losing our drive. Where were we? It was pitch dark. We clung tighter to each other for fear of being separated. Every time a gust sent us sliding over the ice, we closed our eyes and waited to stop, then often rested there until the next onslaught had come and gone. Sometimes I pulled Betty up, sometimes she tugged on my sleeve to start us moving. The urgency of our mission was being forgotten!

But then we slid onto some rocks!

We clutched at them to protect our ribs, struggled back to our feet.

"Welch, John? Is it Welch Island?"

"It could be. Probably is. Come on... let's look for shelter."

We felt our way around the snow-fringed island and into a small bay where we huddled together behind a tall boulder. The island was big; it *had* to be Welch!

"How are you holding up, Bette," I asked after a long silence.

She sighed heavily. "At least we're out of the wind. I've probably got a thousand bruises. I feel kind of weak; feel like a bowl of jelly. What time is it?"

"Four o'clock."

"Four. That means we have eighteen hours before daylight. God, John, we'll never make it! We won't survive without sleeping bags and shelter, will we?"

"We'll make it, mate. We're only four kilometres from Mawson. We haven't come all this way to die on their doorstep!"

"Four kilometres! Four kilometres or a million; it doesn't seem to make much difference down here, does it?

"Tonight's going to be rough, Bette. We'll need to fight every minute of it. We *must* keep awake. We *must* keep old man frost from us. Are you with me?"

"With you, cobber."

"Come on then. Every half hour we'll walk around this bay." I helped her to stand, wrapped an arm around her waist, walked. We left a circle of footprints imprinted in the soft snow. Soon these would deepen into a trail we could easily follow with our feet. Our walk took only five minutes. This wasn't long enough to rekindle any warmth, so we went again. The wind and drift were still howling through the crags above our heads.

When next we sat on a small boulder, our arms remained tightly about each other to help keep out some of the cold. "Maybe I should've brought... my old guitar," Betty stuttered. "Nothing like a good sing-song to... while away the hours."

"You don't need your guitar, Bette. Try... try without it."

"Sing? Sing here? I was... kidding."

"Try... try your favourite. You know, by Woodie Guthrie, *This land is my land*,"

She joined in quietly. "*...from California to the New York Islands.*"

Betty forced a chuckle. "We sound like two old tom cats on a wall. ... *This land was... made for you and me.*"

"Bet you'd rather be in the Redwoods now, eh, Bette?" Her face was already ice against mine.

"You'd betta... believe it. Or maybe skinny dippin' on the Sonoma coast."

"Would like ta be there with ya, mate."

"Sorry, jus' the nurses f'om work. No guys."

About every hour my friend would ask the time. Each time her words took longer to form, each time her voice become harder to understand.

"Eight o'lock." Mine wasn't any better.

"Four... teen... a go. Toes froz'n... John."

I forced myself from her arms, tugged on her frozen mukluk laces, got them off, rubbed her feet. They were like my fingers: pure ice!

"Better... now?"

"Don't know. Can't... feel anyt'ing."

I massaged until it was difficult to keep my eyes open. She was nearly asleep too. Got her mukluks back on; forced her to stand again. "Time ta wawk. Come on, time... or a liddle wawk." At first our legs buckled under us, but then we were moving, moving around on wooden stilts.

"Once 'round's 'nough."

"Twi... twice 'round, Bette." God, every circuit now seemed like ten kilometres; the last few metres like the end of a marathon. We dropped again onto our boulder. I shoved her hands beneath my shirt and mumbled to her, "Sing... mate, sing sa more. Come... 'Red 'ood fores' ta da Guf Stream…'"

"Can't sing more. Wat time?"

I struggled with my watch. "Ten 'lock."

"Ten? Should be light."

"Ten night; not ten mornin'… twelve ta go."

We gave up walking twice around the bay every half hour. Once was difficult enough. Then we decided on once an hour. Then we missed a few circuits altogether.

"Bette." I shook her. Shook her again. "Time ta wawk."

"No!"

"Wawk, mate, come on." My knees wouldn't straighten any more. My back seemed permanently curved. I pulled at her arms, both of us fell to the snow and lay there panting.

"Betta 'ere… sleep betta 'ere."

I drew her tight against me, kissed her. "Fight, Bette… fight… don't gib up!" We struggled to our feet, stood there like snow-men, collapsed again. Next attempt we held each other tighter, moved one step, moved another, another. We were still able to walk. But the circuit now seemed endless. We felt around in the pitch blackness for a halfway rock to rest upon, leaned on it for minutes, staggered on, dropped down again on the snow. Sleep. How wonderful to sleep!

I awoke. Silence! There was a deathly silence. The wind had stopped howling above. The sea-ice was creaking with the incoming tide. Our faces were frozen together. I pulled away. She awoke.

"Time?" she murmured.

I could look but, wasn't sure where my hands were, wasn't sure where any of my body was. We lay awake for a short time, then dozed off again.

Betty woke me later. "Watt time? It light!"

Her frozen lips rasped against my icy face. It was light. So what! I closed my eyes again and continued my sleep. But she refused me any peace; kept nagging me. Yes, I know it's light. Why would she want to keep telling me that? Then I half remembered, weren't we going somewhere? A picnic? No. Where then? I fought with a dulled memory until yesterday's events gradually sorted themselves out in my brain. Some things fell back into place. Mawson! Yes. We were going to

Mawson. "Gotta move… Bette… come, git up!" But how could she? No part of my body would respond in any way, so how could hers? We were frozen hunks of meat in a refrigerator! Her head bumped into my nose; my arm jerked instinctively forward. I *could* move after all! Only one limb at a time, but… but yes, I could move. I massaged my legs, my feet, tried to swing an arm, stood up. God! We weren't going anywhere; there wasn't an active muscle in my whole body!

After some minutes rubbing my face, the skin softened and became painful. I moistened the ice on my lips, moved my tongue, worked my jaws until the possibility of speech returned. "Move… Bette… move." I grabbed her arms, pulled them sideways, pumped them up and down, bent her elbows, let her cry out in pain; tried the same with her wooden legs, dragged her to her feet. We fastened ourselves together by wrapping our arms tightly about each other. "Now… step for'ard." She couldn't. I kicked her leg forward with mine. "Now… da udda. Good… agin… agin." We were moving!

A grey mist, like smoke, hung in the air to obscure the next islands. My compass was lost. Did it matter? If the breeze continued from the south, we merely had to keep it left of our faces for a south-west course direct to Mawson. "Are ya… or'right," I asked, looking briefly at her grimacing face, but she never attempted a reply. Gradually some rhythm came back to our steps. Soon we were no longer pausing after each stride to consider the next. Four kilometres! Christ! Could we make it?

After traversing a half kilometre of snowed over sea-ice, some warmth began creeping back into my body. It moved gradually to my hands and feet. Then the inevitable pain of thawing flesh commenced! I dropped Betty. Evan had insisted on morphine while defrosting his feet. I kept walking, moving faster and faster, almost running as the pain continued to increase. My feet were suddenly in a Chinese torture box; every step caused the screws to tighten more. I stopped, dropped to my knees. Agonising pain clawed its way up my legs. Sweat poured from within. My whole body began shaking. I bit my lips, held back the cries. God! God, help me! I rolled on the snow, hugged my knees, tried to extinguish the red-hot coals. Then my fingers started to thaw, my nose, ears. I writhed about like a dying animal, beating the snow, kicking the air, screaming within me, dripping with perspiration. But then the pain began to subside. I lay there wet, panting heavily, very frightened.

When eventually I struggled back to my feet, my head swirled about me. I dropped again, waited on my knees, rose once more after several more minutes. Where was Betty? I spun around. Oh God, no… not her too! She was kneeling on the ice, elbows on her knees, hands clasped over her ears, rocking to and fro, face contorted in agony. I hurried to her, grabbed her in my arms, pressed her head to my chest. "Don't hold back, Bette, cry — yell your head off." She did. Screamed, a long piercing scream. I squeezed her tighter. She struggled, fought with me, cried like an injured child, but gradually the sobs became softer, turning into rapid breaths. She pulled away, flung her arms about my neck, cried again. Sobs of relief this time. At length she drew back her head and let me gaze at her saturated face; let me mop away the tears.

"Never… never again… John. Don't ever let this happen to me again. I want to die first… wished I could have died!"

I kissed her, helped her stand, continued the journey.

Recovering from the ordeals of last night would be slow. Food was very necessary. We were both extremely weak and staggered across the snow in a semi-daze as if everything we saw around was unreal, a dream. Betty was dropping further and further behind. I wanted to wait, but it was important to press ahead in the hope of sighting the next island should the mist disperse for even a second.

Another hour passed. Why hadn't we reached the next island? As long as the wind continued from the south, I was confident of holding a straight south-west course. But what if it had changed overnight? If only I'd not lost the compass. Panic was beginning to build in my stomach when the mist ahead seemed to darken. A cloud? Open water? Rocks? It was rocks… thank God! I turned to Betty. She was more often on her knees than her feet. She struggled on slowly and determined until catching up, then arm in arm we continued to a resting place on the boulder-strewn foreshore of the island.

"How much further?" she asked quietly without looking up.

"Not… far, Bette, come on, let's… keep moving, we musn't freeze again."

"I… I'm not going well, John. I need… I need lots of rest."

"Grab my arm tightly. We'll stay together now, we'll walk into

Mawson together."

After bypassing the rocks, another higher and longer island loomed ahead in the gloom. We decided to cross it at a low point but were immediately sorry when we tried. The ten-metre climb had us puffing and gasping for breath as if it were a Himalayan peak. We wound between small boulders cemented by ice to gravel patches, then stumbled down a shallow snow gully to a tide-crack and back onto the sea-ice to regain our course. Betty's knees crumpled beneath her. I held her, pulled her back up.

"John," she mumbled. "Go on… go on without me. Get help. I'm… I'm done… no more energy left."

"No, mate, you can make it. Just keep plodding. We're more than halfway. You can make it."

"I can't … I'm…"

Betty rested for a full minute, then raised her head again. "All right… we'll go on."

My strength was also beginning to wane. Already the remaining daylight was surrendering to the encroaching gloom of evening. We were both puffing profusely as if we'd run all the way from Welch. Again, the mist parted momentarily and a long line of boulders were glimpsed ahead with a high rock-strewn hill in its centre. On top was… "Look, Bette, look mate! On top — a trig point — a metal trig point! We're nearly there! We're nearly at Mawson!"

I bent to look at my companion. Her head never raised to the sight that had thrilled me. "Bette?" I called softly. "Bette!" She collapsed onto the snow. Her eyes were open. She attempted a smile.

"Leave me … cobber… go… go for help."

"I won't leave you; I'll never leave you. Come on, please keep going." Her arms were as weak as her legs; she was pure jelly. Her head lolled around on hunched shoulders. "I won't leave you, Bette." Tears welled up in my eyes. "We'll make it together. We'll walk into Mawson together." I pulled her arm across my shoulder, fought to get back on my feet. She groaned, gave a little cry, moved her legs in a futile attempt to walk, then gave up and let me drag her across the snow.

We reached the rocks as darkness closed about us. The station huts would be near. Off again, feeling the way with my feet, keeping the darker mass to the left, continuing along the shoreline. Any minute now! "Hold on, Bette, we're nearly there; just around the next point... it will be around the next point, you'll see." I rested a moment, continued, tripped over some rocks, fell into tide cracks, moved further out to avoid them, came back in to orient myself, lost all track of the passing hours, forgot what I was doing, rested again. The snow brightened. The moon was trying to break through. I stopped suddenly, mouth agape, and dropped to my knees. TRACKS! Human tracks!

"Bette! Bette!" I called to the figure beside me. "There's footsteps, honey, I've found someone's footsteps!" Her eyes fluttered beneath my probing hand. She knew! "Just a few more minutes... just a few more metres." I yanked her back across my shoulders; tried to run but could barely move.

The tracks were very fresh. "The next point, Bette... just around the next point." Soon there would be lights... lights everywhere... warm lights, friendly lights... just around the point. Any minute now, any second now.

But behind each rocky point was another rocky point. The tracks led on and on. Frequently I dropped to my knees sobbing. Rose again, pushed on. A few more metres... we'd be there soon... hold on, Bette.

Suddenly I stopped! Stood thoughtfully gazing at a moonlit rock. The footsteps led up to it, then doubled back. Just like... just like a rock we had rested on hours ago! I looked back along our moonlit tracks, then ahead again. A horrible sensation swept through my body. "No! Oh, God, no!" I dropped to my knees, buried my head in my hands, cried like a lost child. "How long... how many hours have we been circling this island? How long have I followed my own footsteps? I pulled my friend onto a flat rock and collapsed beside her.

"We tried, mate. God, we tried!"

It was heavenly to simply lay there without the thought of ever having to rise again. So peaceful; so beautifully peaceful. Why had we struggled so long... so far? The iceberg; the storms; Scullin; the plateau; the ice-cliff. Why? Why have we fought so long against dying? Surely dying is the ointment of life. Dying is being saved; it is the end of our ordeals, the beginning of perfect peace. My eyes closed. For the first time in months, I felt truly at rest.

But it wasn't to last. Clouds swirled in my mind; formed into a Ferris wheel of lights. Every colour of the rainbow spinning before me, circus people laughing, shouting, singing. A ghostly wail pierced my ears, tormented my brain. I buried my head to drive it away, it continued on and on, then stopped. Stopped for the wolves — hundreds of wolves — howling at the moon. This was their home. They lived with the wind. Wolves and wind howling across the frozen sea. Wolves and wind preparing for their hunt.

My mind cleared. All was peaceful again. I wriggled closer to Betty, pulled her hood tighter around her face, pushed her hands beneath my shirt, wrapped my arms about her, drew her tightly against my body. She stirred, mumbled incoherently, had a smile on her face. Seemed to be dreaming happily. Her breathing quietened until it was barely audible.

My eyes closed again. Sleep came quickly. But my lips were parched, where was the water? No one could cross a desert without water. The hot sand was burning my feet, I sank to my knees in it, crawled, staggered, rolled down the dunes. There was greenery ahead, mountains, waterfalls, lakes. A fence barred my way! A high wire fence! People! Thank God! "Water, water," I called, but no sound left my lips. "Water, give me water!" Crowds gathered to stare at me, laugh at me, throw stones. "Water, water!" The more I pleaded, the more they laughed, the more they tossed rocks. But then a distant piercing sound alerted the wolves. They howled and howled and howled; frightened everyone away.

When next I awoke and wiped a sprinkling of drift from my face, a soft curtain of grey light had replaced the blackness. It was very comfortable and warm on our mattress of rock, but there was something strange about the body around me. Was it mine? There seemed to be no life in it, it was frozen like the rocks themselves. What did it matter? I didn't need it any more. My companion and I would just wait peacefully here until we drifted into oblivion; until a storm buried us in a warm blanket of snow. I thought about my yacht; about its wonderful crew and about a girl I once knew. A lovely blonde angel. What would happen to her? Would she find happiness too? And the other person? What would become of him? I brushed some snow from my companion's frozen face. She stirred.

"Whoooooooo!" Her ghostly cry startled me. "Whoooooooo!" she repeated. "Wolves! The wolves are coming! Run! Run! The wolves are coming!"

I touched a gloved finger to her lips. She stopped. Strange! My dreams were also about wolves. There were no wolves down here. Why was she having the same dreams! Perhaps it was the wind we had heard. Perhaps it was the wind howling between the rocks! How long will we have to wait? It doesn't matter. It is so pleasant just lying here thinking about all the beautiful times we've known in life. Dreaming, remembering friendly faces, wondering… There they are again! Wolves? But… but wasn't that a dream? Am I dreaming now? Surely, I'm awake! They *are* wolves! A howling pack of wolves! Betty heard them too. I rolled myself off the rock, forced my frozen head towards the sound. Just left of the wind. That sound could only be coming from Mawson. Left of the wind, beyond the mist. So near! God! Could we… is it still possible? We must! We must try again!

I fought to get back on my feet. Impossible! We've been lying here for nineteen hours. I threw my frozen arms over a boulder and dragged myself up. My legs were visible; they were still attached but were now wooden stilts. We walked on stilts at school, why not now? I tried, fell. Crawled back to the boulder, climbed up again, walked a few metres, fell again. I could do it! I could do it! We were going to Mawson.

I turned my gaze into the smoky mist that blanketed the way ahead, then stepped uneasily forward with the breeze almost full in my face. I stopped. My head felt as wooden as my legs, yet it seemed to be floating in cotton-wool clouds. Something was wrong! What had I forgotten? The girl! I tried to speak, but only thoughts emerged. "Sorry, Bette, come on, it's time to go."

My companion didn't stir. I ran a hand over her face to dislodge some ice, then shook her, but she was intent on continuing her sleep. "Come on, Bette, we've got one last journey to make." I grabbed an arm, pulled her roughly from the rock onto the snow. "One last journey." She was too heavy to carry. I cut a hole in her anorak hood, pushed my belt through, picked up the loop and heaved. She slid easily over the hard surface. "Now left of the wind; we'll beat straight across without a single tack."

The rocks of the island dissolved into the mist as we drew away, leaving us sailing on a grey mysterious sea where every direction seemed alike. I pulled my load with one hand until that tired, then changed to the other, sometimes walking backwards and pulling with both hands. Time was of no consequence. Being with my mates was all that mattered. "Wind's slackening — come on fellows, haul in those sheets. Bar's open. I'll have a Cascade draught. Boy I'm tired. Too many late nights. Take the wheel, Bette, I'm for a kip, right here in the sun; kitbag for a pillow."

When next I awoke my crew had gone; didn't need them anyhow. Got to get home. Boy, what a head! Serves me right! Could hardly stand; crawled a little, got to my feet. "Where's me bloody kit?" Staggered back for it. Heavy, Christ, it's heavy. Forget what's in it. Grabbed the strap and moved off. Left of the wind. The bloody wind's stopped, who cares, straight on. "How about a couple of songs, Bette? Come on, give us a song... you know the good ones. *From the Redwood Forest... to the Gulf Stream...*' Bit of a swell this afternoon — roughin' up a bit. *This land was made for you and me...* Better put the coffee pot on, mate; a dash of 'Bundaberg' won't harm us. Maybe we'll drop the old anchor for a couple of hours — heave-to until the breeze picks up. Might have a couple more beers; another nap."

The wind freshened. "East of the wind... that's where we're heading. Gee, Bette, I'm weary. Keep her east of the wind. Sooner we're home the better. Bloody fog. We'll never find a mooring in this. Ahoy there! Hear the echo, we're coming in now. Bring her into the wind. Good enough; drop the sheets."

I dragged my kit up the beach to a row of town houses; didn't recognise the place. Cold smooth walls, no doors, no windows, strange. "Anyone home! Anyone in the pub? Open the door will you." I kicked at it. Where the hell was everyone? I was cold, needed a rum. "Open the bloody door will you, it's early, come on, open up." Stuff 'em then, there'll be another pub. Boy, what a day! Tired, hungry, can hardly move. Up here, up this street. Gotta find a place to kip; got to lay me head somewhere. What kind of a place is this, anyhow? Nice and flat up here; a feather mattress Where's my kit, my pillow? I'll sleep forever.

Shit! A screeching siren! What a bloody racket! Cops, noisy cops. Shut up will ya! What's that? Hell! No! Wolves! A pack of wolves!

Coming for me! Howling! Everywhere! The home of the wolves! Run! Run! Snarling jaws. Snapping fangs. I tripped, jumped up, ran again. They were at my throat, kicked out, hit out, was pinned down. Got up, ran, ran, ran…

CHAPTER 9

"This bloody pemmican gets heavier every day. It's about time some other bugger took a turn at feeding the dogs." The words come from David Palmer, a young Mawson physicist who had volunteered to help look after the station's twenty huskies.

"There's no problem when the weather's fine," replied his meteorologist friend, Steward Swift. "But in a 'blizz' it's a real bastard. Still, the poor mutts have to eat."

"Fair enough, but sometimes it craps me off — say, isn't that a tent over there? Must have rolled off the Snowtrac!"

Dave broke off his discussion and strolled over to the yellow bundle lying between the rocks. He gave it a kick, then yanked one end up for a closer look.

"Probably Jovan's," Stewy called back. "He's just home from a field trip." But when the physicist did not answer, he continued with his load to the dog-lines.

"Stewy!" Dave called feebly a moment later. Then, eyes wide with astonishment, shouted after him. "Stewy! Come here — come here quick!"

The meteorologist dropped his box of pemmican and sprinted over to his friend. "Why! What's up? What have ya found?" He was mystified at Dave's unusual behaviour.

"It's... somebody! It... it's a person! He's dead! The physicist was stunned by his find and stuttered nervously. "Who... who is it? Who the hell...?"

Stewy tried brushing snow from the victim's face. "Haven't a clue! We'd better call the O.I.C. and the Doc, right away."

"Wait here, I'll go." Dave sprang up and ran at full speed over the granite slabs, jumping smaller boulders, dodging patches of ice until he reached the slope leading down to an array of shining aluminium and brightly painted huts. Without hesitation he raced past two of his companions working in Market Square and up a short walkway between box-like sleeping huts to a larger building with 'Surgery' painted across the door. He flung open the storm door and stepped into the dimly lit cold-porch, then thumped loudly on the inner door before pushing it open.

The consulting room was empty. "You there, Doc?" he called.

"In the surgery, where else?" came a cheerful reply.

Dave stepped in and confronted a greying, middle-aged man with a neatly trimmed beard and numerous smile lines etched below his sincere blue eyes.

"Well, what's all the hurry?" asked Dr Desmond Phillips with his usual broad smile.

"Bad news, Doc! We've just found a man... a man's body ... over by the dog-lines."

Dr Des' eyes widened. He knew Dave well enough not to dispute anything he said, yet the smile did not immediately leave his face. "Tell me more, Dave."

"He's dead... he looked dead, anyway. Don't know who he is. Come on, Doc, come and look!"

The physician grabbed his bag and followed Dave outside and into the quarters of the officer in charge, next door. They looked down on a well-groomed younger man sitting amongst a pile of radio telegrams.

Dave spoke first. "Come with us, Neil. Stewy and I just found a dead man over by the dog-lines."

"Oh," replied Neil Robeson with a grin. "It's not April Fool's Day. What's the gag?"

"No bloody gag, mate, he was lying amongst the rocks. I thought it was a tent or..."

"There were twenty-six of us at morning 'chompers', fifteen minutes ago," interrupted the O.I.C. "So who's this 'screwball' who races over to the dog-lines and pegs out before his fruitcake has digested?"

Dave thought for a second. Neil was right. No one was missing. "Come and look, come and see for yourself!"

The three men ran agilely in the morning gloom, back through Market Square to the Field Store, grabbed a stretcher, then continued over the rocks to where Stewy was anxiously waiting.

Neil shone a flashlight into the victim's face. "Christ! Then it *is* true.

Poor bastard. Who is it Stewy?"

"Haven't a clue! Can't get his balaclava off. He's too plastered with snow."

Dr Des knelt beside the body and pushed back an eyelid to look into an expressionless eye, then pulled off a glove to grasp a wrist.

"Bloody doctors," thought Stewy. "Anyone can see the bloke's had his chips."

But then the doctor surprised everyone. "He's got a pulse, weak, but… quick boys, get him back to the surgery."

Hardly believing what they had heard, the four tossed the frozen body onto the stretcher and ran with it back to the heated surgery where they immediately began yanking off its mukluks and wind proofs. Dr Des saturated the iced-on balaclava with warm water, then slowly peeled it from the youthful face.

"Clean shaven! Must be Ken or Graham?"

"They're both working on the new snow-melter," advised Neil. "We just passed them outside the workshop."

"He can't be one of us," concluded Stewy. "If he's stood at our bar before, I'd recognise him."

The O.I.C. was shaking his head. "Then how did he get here? Where? It's incredible!" But after considering the facts a little longer came to an obvious conclusion. "A plane! He's from a plane! There's an aircraft down somewhere, Russian I suppose. There might be other survivors!"

Dave followed Neil as he darted across the narrow board-walk between buildings and into the dining room cold-porch where he pushed the siren switch to send a piercing wail throughout the station. When the huskies on the dog-lines heard this, they began howling like a pack of marauding wolves. Neil pushed the switch twice more at five second intervals, then repeated this emergency sequence twice more until all the expedition men had had time to assemble in the rec-room. Then he addressed them:

"Fellows," he said calmly to the scruffily-dressed expeditioners in blue coveralls, yellow anoraks or tartan shirts. "What I'm about to tell you is not 'bullshit'! We've just picked up a survivor from what must be a downed aircraft, probably Russian en route to Mirny or Molodezhnaya.

There could be other survivors, so we're going to commence an immediate search of the area. Here's what we'll do…"

While Neil organised three search parties, Dave returned to the surgery where Dr Des and Stewy were still struggling with the survivor's iced-up clothing. When they got to his underclothes, the doctor became visibly alarmed with the man's bloated chest, and on removing his singlet his eyes widened and everyone's mouths gaped open with astonishment. They were staring down at the breasts of a young woman. In disbelief the doctor yanked down the pants. He then sighed, looked around at his helpers and said nonchalantly, "In case you innocents have forgotten, this is called a female. What the hell's she doing here?"

"The bath should be filled by now, Doc," advised Stewy. "Do we just dump him, her in?"

"And kill her? If we immerse her in water too warm, her circulation will increase and the cold blood nearest the skin will surge directly to the heart. We'll need to gradually raise her surface temperature, and at the same time keep her core temperature from dropping too low. So, let's increase the heat in the bathroom so that she inhales plenty of hot air, then we'll immerse her in water around forty degrees, and gradually raise it to normal blood temperature. Wrap her well and take her across, we'll get started immediately.

The only bath at the station was in Balleny Hut and had been installed solely for emergencies such as this. The girl was brought over and, on a gesture from the doctor, slid into the tepid water while he stood by with a hypodermic syringe.

"If she responds to the warmth," he said "she'll need morphine to survive the pain until she thaws out fully."

The three watched the patient carefully as she lay motionless in the water. For a short time, it seemed she might regain consciousness: there was a deepening of breathing, a flicker of eyelids, a slight opening and closing of the mouth, but beyond that there was no further recovery. The doctor was concerned. He suspected the girl was in deep shock. Her fingers seemed only superficially frost-bitten and had already regained some healthy colour, but her feet were another matter: each remained swollen and very blue right up to the ankles. Gradually the water temperature was raised and the patient let lie there to soak up the warmth for another hour. After that her feet were wrapped in cotton-wool and lightly bandaged, then she was dressed in flannel pyjamas and put to bed in the surgery.

"That's all we can do for the present," the doctor told his helpers. "She seems a strong girl; she could regain consciousness at any time."

But Stewy was concerned about the rest of the incident. "She hasn't been able to tell us anything yet, Doc. Can't you bring her around long enough to find out where the plane went down?"

"We don't understand Russian," Dave reminded him.

"But Jovan does, he could translate."

The doctor was now wanting to clear his surgery and restore some peace and quiet. "Thanks for your help, boys. I'm sure our guest will tell her story when she's able. We'll have to wait until then."

Outside, three of the station's mechanics had already left in the Skidoos to search around the islands, although, in the encroaching darkness their only real hope for success would be in sighting a light. Another group left in two Snowtracs to search the plateau area south of Mawson where the Russians had an emergency landing strip and fuel depot. Neil, with the remainder of the men, was searching the West Bay and West Arm areas, hoping to locate the survivor's tracks which might lead back to the aircraft. The entire coastal scene was now alive with pressure lamps and flashlights, bobbing about the ice like mating fireflies.

A single line of footsteps was soon discovered beneath the ice-cliffs of West Bay. Neil radioed the Skidoos and instructed his men to try and trace their origin further out to sea. The tracks indicated that the victim staggered a great deal, but Neil was particularly interested in the continuous mark left in the snow behind the prints. Something had obviously been dragged.

Carefully the men followed the tracks from the sea-ice over some rocks to the dog-lines. When the huskies caught sight of the lights, they immediately flew into a frenzy of excitement; barking and straining at their chains in an effort to greet their visitors and gain a little affection.

"Shut up you rowdy mutts," shouted Jovan.

"He must have headed straight into the dog-lines," deduced Neil. "That would be quite a shock for any stranger."

"Old Shardu must be a bit off colour tonight," suggested another voice from the dark. "He hasn't bothered to bark at anyone yet." Someone walked over to the animal, shone a flashlight — shouted with alarm! "Over here everyone, over here quick!"

Neil and Jovan raced across. Shardu was lying over the end of a long yellow bundle. "Get off boy."

The dog obeyed. Another victim was revealed!

The men crowded closer to stare down at the stranger's face. It still retained some colour but showed no signs of life.

"If he's alive," said Jovan, "he probably owes it to Shardu, the old boy's been keeping him warm." Jovan pressed his favourite huskie's head against his leg and rubbed an ear. "Good dog. Good dog, Shardu."

On a makeshift stretcher of anoraks, the second victim was rushed to the surgery. "Got another one for you, Doc," Neil called as he pushed open the door.

The M.O. glanced at the figure's bearded face, then pointed to the table. "No surprises this time; the last one turned out to be female."

"What!" exclaimed Neil. "A female down here?" But then he shrugged. "No reason why not, I suppose. The Russians have female cooks. How is she, anyway?"

"Not good." The M.O. then turned back to his helpers. "Fill the bath again, Stewy. Dave, get this man stripped. Brian, organise another bed next to the girls." As he spoke, he felt a weak pulse in the man's wrist.

Neil waited for an initial diagnosis.

"Hypothermia and probable frostbite. Same as the girl; except she's not responding as well as expected. She's still in a deep coma."

A knock sounded on the door. In hurried Ted Gillies, one of the station's radio operators. "Neil, I've got replies back from the two Russian bases, the Yanks at Amundsen-Scott, the Froggies at Dumont D'Urville, and the Japs at Syowa. All state emphatically that they have no aircraft overdue. Head Office in Hobart is still checking."

"Thanks mate." Neil watched while the last clothes were peeled from the victim. The incident was becoming more puzzling, more mysterious every hour. "Anything from the vehicles, Ted?"

"Not much. The Skidoo drivers followed the tracks to Béchervaise Island and found that they completely encircled it, but so far nothing has been picked up leading from there. Too dark, I suppose."

"Call it off then, mate. Call everyone back and we'll get a good night's rest and resume first thing after breakfast."

The second victim responded immediately to the warm water. He needed restraining to prevent further injury as he writhed about like an injured snake, but it was not until his eyes burst open to stare fearfully about the room that the doctor injected a syringe of morphine. The man stiffened, let out a chilling yell, then fought to escape the hands attempting to restrain him. Dr Des tried to comfort his patient until the man's iron grip relaxed on Dave's arm, until his eyes closed, until his body went limp and he slipped back into unconsciousness. "I'll keep him sedated overnight," the doctor informed his helpers. "He'll lose a bit of skin from his fingers and toes, but otherwise should recover without complications. Let's get him to bed and call it a day."

By two a.m. the only sound heard about the station was the steady pulsing throb from the power-house. Everyone was asleep except the night-watchman who made routine safety checks on the station's buildings, and Dave Palmer, who volunteered to monitor the two patients and watch for signs of their awakening.

The night probably slipped by too quickly for Mark McCall, the cook, for at seven a.m. it was time for him to re-enter his kitchen to start preparing breakfast. A half hour later he pushed the siren switch to arouse the rest of the men, and by so doing disturbed the huskies on the dog-lines which then began their day by howling mournfully in harmony with the wailing alarm.

There was another person awakened by the morning siren, the male patient in the surgery. He sprang from his bed, tripped over Dave resting in a chair. "Wolves! Wolves!" he shouted. "Get away! Get them away! Wolves everywhere!"

Dave dived for the telephone, called the M.O., then brought the man down with a football tackle.

CHAPTER 10

Soft, ghostly voices floated in to quell the confusion of dreams that had tormented my brain, prompting me to listen intently in an effort to grasp the flow of meaningless words. Something cold touched my eyelids. A flood of brilliant light streamed in to dazzle my eyes. A man in white leaned across my chest, gazing intently into my face. He seemed deeply concerned; but then a smile crept across his face and the wrinkles around his eyes danced into life.

"Hello!" he said softly. "I'm Doctor Des Carter. Welcome to Mawson."

I stared at him; let my eyes wander across the unfamiliar room to a younger man, then on to a figure sleeping in an adjacent bed. Was this a hospital? Did I have an accident? Perhaps it was the anaesthetic that dulled my brain and filled my head with the motion of drifting clouds.

"Can you understand English?" the doctor mouthed slowly to me. "Or Russian — Ruskie. Are you Russian?"

What had happened to me? I searched a black void in my mind for a clarifying thought. There were only the wolves! The howling and snarling of those horrible wolves. They must have torn me to pieces. "Woov... wool... wolves," I croaked in a voice that surely wasn't my own.

"Wolves?" repeated the doctor with a frown replacing his smile. "What wolves?"

Again, my eyes fastened on him. If he doesn't know about the wolves, then why am I in hospital?

"There's no wolves here my friend. You're quite safe; this is Mawson."

"Maw... son? Mawson?"

"What's your name my friend?"

"Name? My name? My name is... it's... I don't... John! My name is, John."

"How many other people on your aeroplane, John? Where did you come down?"

I smiled at the doctor and wondered why his face had turned so serious.

He then moved to the other bed and turned the face of a young woman towards me. "Your friend is still sleeping. What is her name?"

Why is he asking such strange questions? How should I know her name? Another man noisily entered the room.

"So, our patient's awake. Good. I'm Neil Robeson, Officer in Charge. Now let's hear the whole story; where did you come down? Are there any…?"

The doctor grabbed Robeson's shoulder; whispered something in his ear.

"Well, if he can't tell us, how the hell will we know? There might be a dozen people dying on the ice somewhere!" The O.I.C. spun back to me, but his words were delayed as another person entered with a steaming bowl of soup. I struggled to sit up; the doctor helped. My hands stretched towards the magnificent aroma.

"Hungry, eh?" The doctor spooned the thick liquid into my mouth. God, it was nectar! It burned my throat as I slurped it down. Why was he so slow? Would there be more?

"Bring some stew, Mark," the doctor told the cook. "This man's starving! Bring some milk and cheese and fruit."

When the stew arrived a few minutes later I grabbed the spoon and flew into it. My hand was unsteady. It frequently missed my mouth and, by the time I co-ordinated my movements, all the plates Mark brought were empty.

The doctor left my bed and went to the girl. "If this one's as hungry as he is, then I'd better start intravenous feeding."

"Who… is she?" I asked hesitantly.

No one answered until the dishes were cleared away and Neil pulled up a chair. "We don't know," he began. "You have all the answers locked up within you, and we've got to release them — perhaps to save many lives. Think, John, are there any more people left on the ice — your friends — waiting for help?"

I stared into Neil's eyes and murmured, "Ice? Friends? What… what do you mean?"

227

He sighed, slapped a hand on the blankets and seemed to want to start all over again. "You know where Mawson is, don't you?"

"Mawson! Yes, it's... it's..." The name was so familiar — yet it remained just out of grasp. I eventually shook my head. "No... no, I don't know."

"How about Antarctica?"

When I nodded, he said something about Mawson being a small research station on the coast. "We are completely surrounded by ice. There is another Australian base six hundred kilometres west, and a Russian station, seven hundred kilometres east."

There was a long pause while Neil let me think about this. He was a strange man! Perhaps his stories were supposed to cheer me up? I grinned at him. Where was I really?

The O.I.C. seemed to sense my thoughts. He stood up, strode to a door marked 'Emergency Exit', flung it open. In howled a blast of frigid air and snow that quickly coated the floor. Dr Des dived to slam it shut. He glared at Neil. Neil glared at me. "Well?" he snapped.

Oh, God. What has happened to me? What am I doing here? How... how did...? I squeezed my face between my hands; tears moistened my eyes. Who brought me to this place?

"Your accent is Australian, John, yet you're not associated with any of our expeditions, nor are you reported missing from any other base. The only possible way of getting here in winter is by aircraft. Where did you come from? Where did you come down? Where the hell is the rest of your crew? Can't you tell us any bloody thing?'

My body was now shaking, my lips trembling, tears trickled over my nose. Loudly I answered my interrogator. "No. No. I know nothing about an aeroplane. I don't know who this woman is. I don't want to be here. I want to go home!"

"Home? Where *is* your home?"

"Home?" I stared up at Neil — through him, through the walls, through the snow, through an immense distance. Home? God! I spun my face into the pillow. Something pricked my arm. My head swirled. A ghostly voice murmured something, then faded away into the distance.

That evening the doctor woke me for another meal. The only questions asked this time were by myself. He told me the girl's condition was stable, but unchanged; that there was physically nothing wrong with me, that I could get up in the morning. I began asking about Mawson itself, but Dr Des only smiled as he injected another sedative into my arm. "We'll talk tomorrow," he said simply.

When the siren sounded at seven a.m., I tried not to let the howl of animals upset me, for now it was clear they were only sledge dogs. I lowered my feet to the floor and, for a minute, clung to the bed as my legs trembled unsteadily beneath me and my head tried to float away. I groped around the room trying to co-ordinate my movements, then stopped beside the girl's bed. Her shining black hair and olive complexion contrasted with the white pillow. A warm feeling flowed through my body. My hand gently touched her cheek. "Who are you? Who are we? Please wake up and tell me."

After bathing my face in warm water from the sink, I dressed in the heavy woollen trousers and bright tartan shirt left beside the bed, then pulled on some long woollen socks and nylon mukluks.

By pushing hard on the outside door, it opened against the wind and allowed me to peer out into a dimly-lit Mawson walkway. Drifting snow as fine as salt was streaming down the hill behind the station to funnel noiselessly between the guyed-down buildings and then sweep smoothly across a high snowdrift compressed by foot traffic. A nearby electric light momentarily shone brightly, then seemingly went out behind the next surge of drift like the moon fleeting between clouds. The bitter cold stung my bare face and hands making me hesitate to go further. Instead, I let the door close again and retreated to put on the thick sweater and yellow wind proofs that previously seemed unnecessary. At that moment Dr Des burst in, shaking off the snow.

"Ah, so you're up already?" A beaming grin lit his ice-speckled face. "Let's take a look at your blood pressure and temperature, then we'll go to breakfast."

I nodded. The check-up took five minutes.

"Everything seems all right, John. Come on, you must be hungry."

There was something exciting about stepping out into the darkness and drifting snow of an Antarctic winter, but before the cold could be felt we pushed through another door into a cold-porch cluttered with cartons of canned food. Here we hung our anoraks, then continued into a large well-lit room where some twenty work-attired men were sitting around four long tables having their breakfast. Each turned to gaze at me.

"Fellows," announced the doctor. "This is our mysterious guest, John."

There was a mumble of words, some men gave a wave, some smiled, others continued to stare, but then a burly man in oil-soaked overalls pulled out a chair and motioned me into it. "Sit with the elite," he said with a grin as friendly as his dancing green eyes. "Meet 'Daddy Dieso' and 'Thatch': my mechanic mates. And if you want to risk being clobbered, call me 'Pig Pen' like everyone else."

I laughed. My face hurt as though I'd never laughed before.

Several other men shuffled across to introduce themselves and talk briefly during breakfast, but the conversation was embarrassingly one-sided, as I seemed to be looking at their faces without really hearing or seeing them. A hand grasped my shoulder causing me to look up at a tall thin man with shiny black hair down to his shoulders and a well-groomed Don Quixote type beard. He had been in the surgery with Dr Des.

"My name's Dave Palmer," he said with an affable grin. "Stewy and I found your girlfriend having a kip over at the dog-lines. Neil suggests I show you around 'Cos-Ray' and see if we can jog back your memory."

Dave helped me back into my anorak, gave me a balaclava and gloves, then turned on his flashlight to lead outside into the biting wind. Soon we were climbing a steep boulder strewn hillside with a thick rope draped down it for use as a handrail. The springy-legged physicist waited several times for me to catch up, but soon we were atop the ridge in front of a large aluminium-sheathed building. I looked back expecting to see the lights of Mawson below, but the drift had blotted everything out leaving only darkness. We hung our wind proofs in the cold-porch, then moved into the warm lab with its rows of fluorescent lights and pulsing electronic equipment.

Dave rinsed out two grimy mugs before filling them with coffee. "Never begin the day without a 'cuppa'," he said, handing one across as my eyes moved between computers and instruments to a huge box-like object mounted on a swivel base. "That's our Cosmic-Ray telescope," he explained. "It collects data from the atmosphere which is analysed in the computers and printed out on recording paper. Pretty boring stuff, I suppose, but at times we get cosmic storms that can be mighty exciting to research."

After skipping from one subject to another during the morning, Dave sat down again and gave a laugh. "Well, one thing seems certain: you're no bloody scientist, are you? You're more interested in *how* things work, rather than *why*. I bet you're a technician or engineer of some kind. Actually, science isn't my favourite occupation either; photography and the outdoors are my real love. Here, take a look at these prints. These are our six-month-old husky pups — first time in harness." He laughed heartily as he related their antics when he first drove them across the sea-ice. "The little buggers ran in every direction at once; talk about tangled traces! This picture is Joe, he's big for his age and pretends to be dumb, but actually he's very strong and smart. His brother, Bandit, is the disappointment of the Kelly Gang."

I found a growing eagerness to talk with Dave. "Would it be possible for me to run with your huskies, sometime," I asked enthusiastically. "It must be exciting visiting different places around the coast, almost… almost like sailing."

"Sailing!" Dave pondered my assertion, but then dismissed his thoughts. "Well, you didn't sail here. We can't even get our polar ships through the pack-ice during the winter." He pulled some more pictures from a drawer and spread them on the table before me. "These were taken last week at Auster Rookery — that's fifty kilometres east of here. We took two dog teams."

I looked at a dozen black and white prints of penguins tightly packed together like regiments of soldiers parading amongst an array of silver icebergs. "These would look better in colour," I suggested. "Emperors are such regal birds."

"Where did you learn about emperor penguins?" Dave asked quickly.

I looked at him, thought for a moment, shrugged. "From a book, probably."

The physicist continued to stare at me. "You sounded as if you knew about them more intimately. There are about twenty thousand emperors at Auster. Here's a picture of the caravan where we stay."

I snatched up the print, stared at it, tapped my finger on it; wondered why my heart pounded.

"What is it, mate? Remember something?"

I didn't answer. My stare seemed to penetrate the caravan walls. Into its darkness, its coldness, its warmth — something was there! My body prickled with sweat, my face screwed up as I tortured my brain to let me pass through a veil of mystery into my real world which somehow seemed hidden there. But it was to no avail. I blew out my breath, dropped my head into my hands. The door had slammed shut.

"Let it go, John. You're on the wrong track. You wouldn't know anything about Auster. Few people do. Like I said, it's fifty kilometres from here."

I nodded.

Dave peered through a tiny window behind the table. "Look, it's getting light at last. The sun won't appear again for another few days but see how the glow from it reflects off the clouds and turns the ice pink."

The scene below was pure solitude, yet strangely beautiful. The coastline was now clear, allowing us to see a multitude of dark islands and shadowy icebergs studding the frozen sea.

Dave pointed to one island in particular. "That's Béchervaise Island. You walked right around it, then you dragged your friend across the strait to those ice-cliffs at West Bay, and finally ended up at the dog-lines where you decided to quit."

"But where did we come from before that, Dave? We couldn't just walk in from... from..." I waved an arm across a vast area of inhospitable ice.

"It will come back, mate; give it time, then we'll all sleep better at night."

When the lunch siren sounded, we moved outside to gaze down at the station nestling on the inner edge of a horseshoe-shaped bay. Thirty or more huts had been erected around two main walkways that lead down through Market Square to some workshops on the foreshore. Electric lights shone from most windows and exterior fixtures to supplement the meagre contribution of light from the unrisen sun. Dave named the various scientific huts scattered across the hilltop beneath an array of high radio aerials. "You should see all this in the summer," he said "When the sun shines twenty-four hours a day and the sea is calm and blue, and the ice sparkles like a diamond mine. Mawson is then very beautiful."

As time passed, I fitted into station life very well and even became a little disappointed when told that the girl and I might soon be evacuated by helicopter when the US ice-breaker, *Eastwind,* passes along the outside of the pack-ice sometime during the next few weeks. There seemed little reason to return to Australia until my memory returned. That could be soon, though. Test results on the girl, in collaboration with medical specialists in Melbourne, indicated that it may shortly be possible to bring her out of her coma. In this event she could help me regain my identification.

There was plenty I could do to assist around the station: helping Mark in the kitchen; cutting snow-blocks to fill the melt tanks; assisting the hard-working mechanics with vehicle repairs and powerhouse maintenance; but the job I preferred most of all was feeding the lovable huskies and repairing the sledges and harnesses for the next run.

Numerous recreational activities also kept me occupied after the evening meal: movies twice a week, billiard and dart tournaments, cards, chess, photography exhibitions, riotous Saturday night parties. Or, if it was necessary to completely relax, there was a well-stocked library, a record player with the latest records, and 'Mawson Mud': the expeditioner's prided home-brew.

Near midday on June 27, I joined a gathering of men in Market Square to watch the fierce orange glow from the sun flood across the horizon and gradually increase in intensity until it flared like a rampant forest fire. Each man raised his camera and waited patiently. Rays of brilliant yellow light suddenly beamed into the sky to decorate the heavy cloud cover in a celestial celebration to announce the return of the sun to this land that needed it most of all. The horizon shone for a minute like a ladle of molten steel, then with heart-felt splendour, the first brilliant sliver of golden sun made its debut for all to see.

"Welcome back, friend," murmured Dave. "We missed you."

All the huts were now bathed in a yellow glow; windows and doors were flung open as though summer had already arrived. But then the sun seemed to hesitate, change its mind, then slowly withdrew its majesty back below the horizon.

Dave turned to me with a fresh look in his eyes. "How about that run with the dogs we talked about?"

"Great!" I exclaimed happily. "Everything's ready to go."

Ted and Stewy were also keen for some exercise. We wandered over to the two sledges parked on the sea-ice below the dog-lines and collected the webbing harnesses, then confronted the wildly excited huskies. First the lead dogs were brought down and clipped to the front of the traces; next came the more placid animals, and finally the real troublemakers who cared little about the whips we threatened them with.

"Sit boys!" shouted Dave to his team. He moved back to the brake position while I paraded amongst the raring-to-go animals in an endeavour to keep fights to a minimum.

"Ready boys!" Dave called. The dogs froze — their ears pricked for the next command.

"MUSH!"

Like Olympic sprinters they exploded forward. I grabbed the sledge and hung on tightly while it accelerated, bounced, squeaked and flew over the rough surface as it hurtled out of Horseshoe Harbour. The dogs were as overjoyed as their handlers to stretch their legs after the long spell of bad weather.

Near Entrance Island, Stewy's following team caught us up when we called a halt to allow the puffing animals to rest after their initial joyous dash, but from then on, our team settled into a steady rhythmic pace with the other dogs plodding happily along behind.

"Come up front," called Dave, as he leapt from the sledge and raced alongside to catch up with the lead dog. I joined him, running at a fast jog. It was easy to see how the men kept so fit. Old Randy pulled proudly on the lead trace, his eyes frequently cornering to catch mine in the hope of receiving a rewarding pat; he would then run with his muscle-bound little body pressing gently against my leg.

Tiny puffs of steam burst from the dogs' open mouths; their long tongues hanging loosely in contented canine smiles. Occasionally a husky would cross the main trace to run close beside his working partner or, in the case of Kossi, to give his counterpart a spiteful nip on the back leg to speed him on his way.

Soon I was hot and exhausted, no match for the other runners, and dropped back to the sledge for a rest. But instead of swinging easily aboard, I tangled my feet and fell hard to the snow.

"Whoa, boys, whoa," Dave shouted to his dogs. But it was too late to stop Stewy's following team. When they saw an opportunity of fun ahead, they leapt on me where I lay, plodding over me, licking my face, victoriously planting paws on my chest, then proudly looking back at Stewy with great healthy grins on their mischievous faces. I laughed heartily at the heavy bundles of fur that so affectionately sat on my body, but when I flung an arm around one's neck for a pull-up, another jumped on me to force me back down.

"OK, boys, OK!" Stewy called as he came to my rescue. "You've had your fun, let him up."

Riding the sledge wasn't particularly enjoyable at any rate, for the force of cold wind quickly froze my inactive body. We headed around the eastern edge of the Jocylin Islands, then past dominant Welch Island where Dave explained there was a summer rookery of half a million Adélie penguins. Suddenly we both sighted a fleck of colour ahead on the ice. Dave swung back onto the sledge and directed his team towards it.

"Whoa boys!" He gently applied the brake, then leapt off to retrieve the blue bundle. "It's a sleeping bag!" he shouted to Stewy. "Some careless clod has dropped it off a sledge!"

The other team halted in front of us, and both men strolled over to investigate another blob of colour. Soon Ted was calling for us to join them. He had found another sleeping bag caught up in a tide crack together with a quantity of packaged food. We followed along the crack adding to our find: a cooking pot, a stove, some tent pegs, a brass prismatic compass.

"Where the hell did it all come from?" asked Stewy. "I've never seen a compass like that at Mawson."

"Nobody's been out here recently except us on the Auster trip," added Dave. "And we lost nothing — certainly not all this stuff!"

I was barely hearing the men's conversation; my eyes were fixed on the compass. It was mine! I knew it was mine! Again, I fought to drive away the mists shrouding my memory — to step back into the other life I must know. The compass was from that life. Why — why, can't I return there! Suddenly I become aware of three pairs of eyes staring at me.

"It's your compass, isn't it, John?" Dave asked quietly.

"Yes... yes I think so." I fought with my memory for another minute before giving up. "But how could it be? It's impossible! It's impossible, isn't it?"

Dave attempted to assemble the jigsaw. "The sleeping bags could indicate there were only two of you; and the provisions make me think your journey might have been a long one. And somehow this doesn't seem the kind of stuff carried on an aircraft. Maybe you did come here by yacht after all; maybe you were wrecked near the ice-edge and struck out for Mawson!" He thought for a short time longer, then made another important supposition. "If my theory is anywhere near correct, it means the girl's present condition is not the result of an aircraft impact, it's more likely to be from pure hypothermia and stress. The Doc's been hesitant to try and bring her around for fear of aggravating some internal damage or concussion caused by a crash. Perhaps now he'll go ahead. Come on, let's get back and talk to him."

The next afternoon, I was called to the surgery. Neil and Dave were seated beside the girl's bed; Dr Des bent over her with his light carefully examining her eyes. Neil gestured for me to sit down.

"Don't be alarmed," the doctor said a short time later. "In view of what Dave told me yesterday I've decided to try and bring your friend out of her coma. If she comes around, she may, or may not say something of importance before going into a more normal sleep, but tomorrow, when she re-awakens, she'll be well enough to relate the whole story."

The thought of learning the truth about myself suddenly seemed very frightening. Who am I? What am I? A technician as Dave suggests, or... or an escaped convict. A murderer even!

The doctor injected some fluid into the girl's arm. "Move closer," he requested. "Listen carefully for anything she might say."

I was now shivering nervously.

With his stethoscope on the girl's chest the physician listened very carefully for any change. He turned to us, his eyes seeing no one, but then he nodded and smiled.

"She moved," whispered Neil.

I stared into the young woman's face: a lovely friendly face. What was she to me? A stranger with whom we fled some disaster? A lifelong friend? What?

The girl's head began tossing from side to side. She gasped for air and let out a mournful cry. Her eyes remained closed. The doctor steadied her head and waited. She moved her tongue, moistened her lips, fluttered her eyelids. I prayed she'd never speak!

But she did. "Ev... Evon ... Evan."

The three spun around to stare at me. The name meant nothing.

"Evan... Jul-lie... help... help."

Thank God she stopped. Her voice sounded like a broken record. Who were these people?

The doctor adjusted the girl's pillow and beckoned us into the consulting room. "Well, she responded very well. She'll be much better in the morning."

Neil had more immediate thoughts. *"Evan, Julie, help.* It's a message isn't it? It's a message she's had on her mind since arriving here. *Evan, Julie, help."* He turned to me. "Who's Evan and Julie, John?" But he never waited for a reply. "They're out there somewhere, aren't they? Frozen to death! They waited and waited for help, then died. They're both bloody well dead by now!"

A short time later Dave found me sitting with my friend Shardu at the dog-lines with the husky's head resting blissfully on my lap as I stroked his ears. When it wasn't possible to talk to anyone else, it seemed my canine friend would always listen.

"I sometimes come here too," admitted Dave as he knelt beside me and let Shardu grasp his bare hand so gently between his sharp teeth. "A husky's like a dumb woman, it will listen to you for as long as you want to talk, look at you with eyes full of sympathy, even laugh along with you. But when you leave, its only thought is for its next meal."

I grinned. "Dave, I'm scared. What Neil said must be true. There are others out there somewhere who depended on me for help. But I let them down. It's too late now, isn't it?"

He touched my shoulder. "We don't know for certain, mate. When your friend wakes up in the morning, we should be able to piece the whole story together and then decide what to do."

A distant sound caught our ears. We both raised our eyes into the darkening sky. It was the unmistakable pulsating chop of a helicopter.

"More bloody Russians," moaned Dave. "Looks like they're coming in. Last time they paid us a visit they stayed three days, until all our home-brew was gone and there wasn't a sober man left at the station. When they finally left, every Russian was wearing Aussie clothes, and every one of us, fur hats and leather jackets.

We watched them touch down on the helipad; two men jumped out, then the aircraft immediately whirred back into the sky and continued in the direction of Molodezhnaya.

"Who the hell are those two?" murmured Dave, but then he answered his own question. "A couple of Ruskie boffins wanting some of our expertise, I suppose; come to scrounge some of our data."

We bumped into 'Pig Pen' on the way back through Market Square. "What's going on?" asked Dave. "Who are the two Ruskies that just left the chopper?"

"They're not Russians," the mechanic informed us. "They're Portuguese. According to the Russian radio-op these two were picked up at Scullin Monolith where they were shipwrecked last summer. They were only spotted today when the chopper flew over."

"Shit! More trouble. We should open a guest house here."

We went directly to the rec-room where afternoon 'chompers' was being served, and glimpsed the newcomers ploughing into Mark's fruit cake and hot coffee. They already had a large audience, so I stayed back and played a hand of darts with Jovan, hoping to meet up with them soon and learn about their adventure.

But it was only a short time later that Neil called me over. "John, meet Luis and Miguel. I've just been telling them about you. It's quite a coincidence having two pairs of castaways here within a few weeks of each other."

I stretched out my hand to greet the pair, and immediately caught their piercing yellowish eyes. A shiver ran through my body. Both wore long black handle-bar moustaches and a week's stubble on their faces.

"Feeling all right?" asked the O.I.C.

"No... er, yes. Sorry... I just felt a little strange."

"Their English isn't too hot, but apparently they are biologists who last summer made a historic voyage by yacht to Scullin Monolith —

that's a couple of hundred kilometres east of here — to make observations at the rookery, but it seems bad weather forced their yacht onto the rocks and wrecked it. They've been waiting five months for rescue which only came today when the Ruskies sighted the wreck and landed to investigate. The Russians know about the *Eastwind* passing off Mawson next week, so they dropped them off here expecting they'll get a ride back to the United States."

"Ow long ya bin 'ere?" asked the man called Luis.

"About… about two weeks." I sensed something evil about these men.

"Where you come from?"

I shrugged.

"Just two of you, boss say?" The smell of tobacco from the man's stained teeth, became stronger as he pushed his face closer to mine.

"There's two of us here." My head dropped when I remembered the other names the girl had spoken. "There may be two others."

"Four? Two 'ere, two maybe dead?"

I had to get away from these people. They seemed to be sneering at me. Why were they asking so many questions?

"You no rememba good?" asked Miquel. "Woman sick, say nothin' also?"

Neil replied, "She probably will in the morning. When she wakes up, we expect an explanation for everything, and hopefully that will revive John's memory as well."

"Tomorra mornin, eh! You sure he no rememba nothin? He might rememba tomorra too!"

I drew away, left the rec-room, went to my 'donga' in Shackelton Hut and sat there to ponder why these men had upset me so much. It was almost as if we were old enemies. What a strange coincidence that they and we had arrived at Mawson within a short time of each other — both after accidents! The whole situation left me feeling very uneasy, and not at all eager to hear the girl's story in the morning.

At dinner that evening I sat as far from the Portuguese as possible, yet all the time they kept turning to stare at me.

"Rather an evil pair, aren't they?" Dave remarked as he joined me.

"Yes, they are. What are they talking to Neil about?"

239

"About you and the girl, mostly. They seem to have taken a big interest in your adventure; probably because it's a little like their own. Remember, on our dog trip I suggested that you might have been shipwrecked somewhere, and then walked into Mawson? Are you sure you don't know these men?"

"I have a strange feeling about them, Dave. Are you certain they're biologists? They don't look like scientists to me."

The physicist looked at me without replying. He was suddenly deep in thought.

Foregoing the evening movie, I retired early to bed to prepare myself for the truths I would hear and have to accept in the morning, but within minutes fell asleep with one lingering thought on my mind: the Portuguese!

A hand sliding over the dark walls of my 'donga' awakened me. "Who is it?" I asked. But then everything happened at once. Someone threw their weight across my legs, another person across my chest and arms. Fear gripped me. Before it was possible to yell, a cloth was held over my face — ether! It was impossible to struggle free; my body was pinned firmly inside the sleeping bag. Desperate cries for help never even reached my own ears. My eyes dulled, head spun like a whirlpool, relaxed, sank back into another dream.

The cold revived me quickly, but it was minutes before I realised what was happening. A sudden burst of fear shivered up my spine. I was tied to a sledge — being drawn across Horseshoe Harbour by a Skidoo. Why? I knew it was the Portuguese, but why? Why were they taking me away from Mawson? I twisted and tugged on the ropes binding my wrists, but my whole body was secured right to the ankles. Why had they abducted me? Our paths *must* have crossed somewhere before! What were they up to?

As Entrance Island slipped past in the moonlight the sound of Mawson's siren pierced the air. For a moment I thought it was an emergency alert, but no, it was merely the seven thirty a.m. wake up call. No one yet seems to have missed me! My desperate struggles with the rope brought a trickle of blood to my wrists causing me to give up and just lay there. Whatever was planned for me would happen! Nothing could be done about it!

The Skidoo stopped near the Paterson Islands. One of the men came back, shone a flashlight into my eyes, crashed his huge fist into my face. I spun my head in fear of the next blow.

"Bastard Australia!" The man spat his words at me. "You make big trouble. Good for us you forget, but not good for you! We kill you now. Woman also dead. She tell us about other two at Auster Caravan. We go kill them too. Then nobody know about diamonds, eh?"

"Let me go, you bastards, I know nothing about any diamonds. If you harmed the girl, the Mawson men will be close behind."

Wham! The fist again smashed into my face; blood trickled from my lip. "We not stupid, bastard Australia. Woman die natural; no one know we help a leetle. And no one find you or dead people in caravan. We nice people; we go back to Mawson and know nothin. We kill everybody if they make trouble; go back to Scullin and wait Portuguese ship."

The men left, but the Skidoo wasn't restarted. Were they waiting for daylight to continue? I was freezing in my flannel pyjamas and socks. Perhaps that was how they intended killing me? It was a clear morning; twilight would come earlier than usual. Were they walking to get warm? My eyes closed; this had to be another nightmare!

When the Portuguese returned it was light enough to see the ice-cliffs a kilometre away. They started the machine and drove off; but stopped again a minute later. To my surprise they untied the ropes and yanked me to my feet.

"Ride finish for bastard Australia!"

We were beneath the towering walls of an iceberg, beside a pool of green water formed by ice falling from above. They dragged me to its edge.

"You swim away from us at Scullin, you forget. Me not, now maybe you swim away agin!"

The man's sinister laugh echoed in my ears as they pushed me into the ice-studded pool. I sank but struggled straight back to the surface. The water at first seemed amazingly warm. A boot stamped on my hand as I grabbed the ice-edge, another kicked me back under the water. I shot back gasping for air. The next boot smashed into the side of my head sending me under in a daze; they were both laughing loudly when I again glimpsed their faces. Boots were attacking from both sides of the pool. It was a relief to be out of reach, but hell to return.

Below the surface was a safe haven. My limbs drifted around me like lengths of waving kelp. There seemed no sense in fighting. I waited each time until my lungs nearly burst, then surfaced to endure the next onslaught of kicking boots. I was losing consciousness — wasn't caring any longer. I floated to the top without trying to swim. A boot was placed on each shoulder; my dulled brain heard ghostly voices counting. "*Una, dos, tres.*" Then I shot back beneath the surface, deeper, deeper, into the black depths; floating weightless and free. It was pleasant here; no sense in returning above, but then I was rising. There was nothing to grab and stop myself, another boot would be waiting, the laughter would be louder...

But I never broke the surface! My head slammed into the underside of the sea-ice. My lungs were bursting. I had to breathe. My mouth opened to gulp in lungfuls of salt water. I was dead!

But I wasn't dead! Nor was I swallowing water! There was air here — air trapped in cavities eroded in the ice. I was breathing air as penguins and seals do. But what did it matter? In a short time, the cold would claim me and I would sink forever.

The minutes drifted by. It would be preferable to die here than suffer those boots again. My eyes closed. I reopened them with a start. Julie and Evan at Auster caravan! How long have I been here? Is it possible to hold on for another minute? Which way was the hole? Again, my eyes closed. My mind swirled; my body sank back beneath the water. But then I was struggling, fighting my way back to the surface. Where is the hole? Where is the air? I swam, scraping my back along the ice, lungs bursting. AIR! I sucked it in, blew it out, sucked it in. I opened my eyes to the sky, braced for the next boot.

But there weren't any — my enemies had gone!

There were lots of shattered pieces of surface ice to grab. I dragged myself from the pool. God! The air was bitterly cold — anaesthetic! It was impossible to move; I stood there like a statue — freezing into one. I yanked off my pyjamas and socks, wiped the ice sheathing from my body, wrung everything out, put them back on again, started to move: a slow walk, a jog, a sprint. In minutes I was running; in minutes the warmth began to creep back through my veins. I was puffing but kept going — kept going towards Mawson.

At nine kilometres an hour, I calculated, it would be possible to reach the station in about two hours. God! I'd be too late! Too late to summon help and save Julie and Evan from the murdering Portuguese. Betty was already dead. Betty dead? Oh, no! I stopped running. Not Betty — not after all we'd been through, not my dear friend Bette. What was the use, then? All my friends would soon be dead. I dropped to my knees. Nothing seemed worthwhile any more!

The sound of a motor caused me to look up. The Skidoo! The bastards haven't gone yet! They've seen me! I started running, running back to the iceberg. Could it be climbed; was there a place of safety somewhere — anywhere? Should I jump back into the pool and hide beneath the ice? Too late. They were gaining fast; any second now — a hail of bullets! I braced for instant death.

"John! John!"

I spun around. "Dave! 'Pig-Pen'!" I raced up to them. A Snowtrac stopped behind the Skidoo. Out sprang Neil and Dr Des. God, it was wonderful to see them!

Neil looked furious. "What the hell's going on, John. You have no right leaving the station without permission. Where are the Portuguese? Where's the other Skidoo?

Before there was time to reply, Dave asked, "Where are your clothes? Why are you wet? You'll kill yourself!"

"Quit the questions," I yelled at them. "There's too little time. We must head for the Auster caravan immediately. I'll explain as we go."

'Pig-Pen' was left to drive the Skidoo; the rest of us piled into the Snowtrac and sat on a stack of boxes and propane gas cylinders. "Flat to the boards, Neil. Two lives are in imminent danger!"

"We know. The girl told us."

"The girl? Betty? Betty told you? She's not dead — please tell me she's not dead!"

The three stared at me. Dr Des spoke. "The girl — Betty if you like, was found by the night-watchman just before seven a.m. She had somehow turned on her pillow and disconnected her oxygen supply. Poor girl nearly suffocated; it was fortunate we found her in time. Before I gave her a sedative, she muttered something about Auster caravan, and

Julie and Evan."

"Thank God! Thank God, she's alive!"

The men relinquished some of their excess clothing and gave it to me. A sleeping bag was tossed across my shoulders and a seat found in the full blast of the vehicle's heater.

"You weren't too concerned about this Betty girl before, John. Your memory, it hasn't…"

"Yes, yes, many things have come back. The cold water, the shock; all must have helped."

Before the three attacked me with obvious questions, I threw one at Neil. "Can't we go directly to Auster instead of via Macklin Island. That would save time, wouldn't it?"

"It would," he replied. "But via Macklin is the safest route, and because this vehicle is not supposed to be traversing the sea-ice at all, that's the way we'll go."

"Neil… please, we *must* go direct. Please head straight out towards Auster Island."

"Like hell I will! We need this vehicle to transport your friends; we're not taking any more unnecessary risks."

"Unnecessary risks? There's still a lot you don't know, Neil. Betty's dilemma this morning was *no* accident — the Portuguese tried to murder her!"

All eyes flashed towards me. The doctor's mouth gaped open.

"I was wet because they abducted me from my 'donga' and tried to drown me in a pool. Now they're heading for Auster to kill Julie and Evan."

"You're crazy, John," said Dr Des. "Why would they want to kill you? You only met them yesterday!"

"Wrong, Des, we met at Scullin Monolith last January. They lied about being shipwrecked. It was *my* yacht the Russians sighted. They were already there, mining… er, minding the rookery?" Christ, what an idiotic statement, but my promise to Ralph suddenly came to mind. Without telling the Mawson men about the diamonds I continued. "They were assisting an Australian biologist, and because of some disagreement with him they murdered him. When they discovered that we knew about the crime they also tried to kill us. They pursued us towards Mawson and

244

probably thought we died in an ice break-out near Stevens Rock, but when they later arrived at Mawson and found us still alive, they decided to try again."

Neil swung the Snowtrac half left directly towards Auster. "There's obviously a lot more to your story, John. My mind boggles at the adventures you and your crew must have endured, but we'll hear about them later. Right now, let's concentrate on the task ahead."

I agreed. "We must reach the caravan before the Portuguese and get Julie and Evan away without them knowing. They might then conclude that Betty was hallucinating, and that my friends died elsewhere. When they return to Mawson, they'll pretend to know nothing about my disappearance, and it would be advisable to accept that until they're confined"

During the journey Dr Des enquired about Julie and Evan's medical problems, and between long periods of thoughtful silence, asked about our other adventures in the yacht and at Scullin Monolith.

Suddenly Auster Island was in sight. I pushed open the roof hatch and peered ahead through binoculars at the tiny outcrop of brown rock. Excitement built up within me. After what seemed an eternity, I was now almost reunited with my fiancée. How would she be? She was so ill when we left two weeks ago. She would have recovered; she would be waiting; she would...

"Stop, Neil! Stop! We're too late! We're too bloody late! Those bastards are already there!"

"Don't worry, mate," said Dave. "There's five of us, we can stop them doing any…"

"Stop them!" I interrupted. "We can't stop them! They've got automatic weapons. They'll blast us to shreds if we go near!"

"Machine guns? Shit! Then, what can we do?"

"Drive to the other side of the island. Keep out of sight." Dave's question was a good one: "What *can* we do?" For certain we had to act immediately before they killed Julie and Evan. But how? A crazy plan flashed through my mind. We stopped behind the island.

"Neil," I said urgently. "You're the O.I.C. here, but this crisis is mine. Please do as I ask. Grab your medical equipment and supplies from the Snowtrac, toss it on the Skidoo sledge, then all of you drive back twenty metres and wait amongst the rocks. If... when the Portuguese leave the caravan, get in there quick and race Julie and Evan back to Mawson."

"What do you intend doing, John, what...?"

"Leave the Snowtrac here. Leave the engine running. Go immediately!"

I left them standing on the ice. If they ignored my request, we'd all be dead within minutes. If they complied — was there any hope? I ran in stockinged-feet over the rocks to the caravan. Was it too late? Julie was now within arm's reach! I flung up the latch; kicked open the door.

There was an immediate scuffle inside. The surprised Portuguese swung their weapons towards me. I dived for safety as a hail of bullets whined and ricocheted between the rocks; then raced for the Snowtrac, leapt aboard, threw it into gear; was off.

My pursuers appeared in the driving mirror a full minute later. Perhaps they had been wary of an ambush. They then vanished again only to reappear seconds later giving chase in the faster Skidoo. I put my foot down and headed east towards the icebergs. But what then? If it were possible to keep them occupied long enough the others would escape back to Mawson with Julie and Evan. But that wouldn't be the end of it. With their weapons they could easily annihilate everyone at the station then return to Scullin and still escape undetected next summer. So, whether or not they now catch me seemed of little consequence.

I left clear tracks while zig-zagging through the towering chain of icebergs — impossible to hide from them for even a moment — then I raced out the other side and headed across an open expanse of sea-ice, heading for nowhere in particular.

Desperately I fought for ideas — some sort of a plan — but nothing came to mind. The only chance of anyone surviving at Mawson was to capture or kill the Portuguese. That surely was impossible! How could a few unarmed men disarm two murderers with machine guns? They were gaining on me slowly. In a short time, the problem would be out of my hands. Jules, poor Jules — the immense joy of rescue at last — but what then? I would be dead. Would she ever see Vancouver again? Would she ever again stroke her old tom cat, Socks? I was dreaming and watching my intended assassins through the mirror when my eyes fastened on the two huge Propane gas cylinders laying on the floor of the vehicle. They started thoughts computing through my brain.

A large tabular iceberg appeared ahead like a Foreign Legion fortress in the middle of a white sandy desert.

The gauge showed the Snowtrac's gasoline tank was half full. There were four, twenty-litre jerricans of gasoline strapped outside the vehicle. Another desperate idea came to mind. Would it work? Probably not. But soon the Portuguese would be close enough to open fire. There was nothing to lose. The Snowtrac was fitted with a hand throttle; I pulled this out to its limit and felt the vehicle slow down only slightly when my foot was removed from the accelerator. Then I left my seat and clambered back into the bouncing cabin to open both valves on the Propane cylinders before returning.

Being tightly sealed against drift I assumed that very little of the gas would escape from the vehicle. The cab, in fact, should act as a larger container for the heavier than air gas. I opened the roof hatch and stood with my head outside, steering with one foot.

The iceberg was close now. I expected my pursuers to open fire before reaching it, but they held off; perhaps there was no fun in killing anyone from a distance when there was no chance of escape.

I raced along the southern side of the iceberg, swung left around its end, then seconds later turned again to head back along its northern side, searching for broken ice that had fallen from above. Some was coming up now. My pursuers hadn't turned the corner yet. I pushed the hand throttle half in, felt the vehicle slow, then quickly clambered up through the hatch, closed it tightly, waited for the right moment — jumped.

The hard ice jarred my legs, I rolled, sprang back up, ran to hide behind the ice blocks. Had they seen me?

Fifteen seconds later the Skidoo hurtled past. I breathed a sigh. They would catch the Snowtrac within seconds. Then what?

The Portuguese drew abreast of my vehicle. One man stood half up in his seat and raised his weapon. The stutter of machine-gun fire echoed around the iceberg, rumbled across the sea-ice. I almost felt the hot bullets tearing through my flesh as they were intended to.

But then, oh my God! A brilliant flash of flame. A red fireball of Propane gas exploded from the Snowtrac; a thunderclap boomed in my ears, echoed from the clouds. The fireball lifted from the ice, changed into a billowing body of black smoke; soared higher and higher into the sky like a rising hot-air balloon.

Had I won? Were the Portuguese dead?

When the smoke cleared nothing was left on the ice. I began running towards the scene, hesitating in case they might reappear but when near the explosion area I breathed more easily. All that remained was a large green pool with a blackened ice-edge. Our pursuers were finally dead. All traces of their ill-gotten diamonds would have gone with them. I felt no joy, no satisfaction; all I wanted to do was run and run and run until exhausted. But then the shock grew less, my mind cleared, I slowed down and turned to head back towards the iceberg chain.

Minutes later, a black speck appeared ahead. Another Skidoo? More men must have arrived from Mawson. Julie and Evan would be well on their way back by now. Thank God they are now safe; thank God I'll soon be reunited with them. For the first time in months my heart felt free of torment.

The Skidoo pulled up beside me. "Dave? What... why aren't you heading back to Mawson with Julie and Evan?"

He dismounted, put a hand on my shoulder, said softly, "Sorry, mate, Evan's dead."

CHAPTER 11

"Evan dead?" I clutched at the Skidoo, dropped onto the seat, locked my eyes into Dave's. Evan dead! After all this, when our troubles seemed near an end. When Mawson was only an hour's ride away. "And Julie, Dave? What about Julie? She's all right — she's all right, isn't she?"

The physicist stared back at me and replied simply, "The girl's alive, mate."

I sighed with relief. Julie was alive. We'd get her to hospital, let her rest and recover. Let her be happy again.

"What happened to Evan, Dave?"

"They smothered him. Poor man was probably too weak to resist. You arrived a minute too late to help him, but just in time to save Julie."

A minute too late! My head shook in disbelief. How many times in a lifetime have I been a minute too late and never thought anything about it?

"I saw the explosion, John. It was a hell of a shock. At first, I thought you were in the Snowtrac when it exploded. A brilliant idea. Those murdering bastards deserved all they got."

"We all lost, Dave. Every bloody one of us lost something." I stood up. "Please take me to Julie."

The return journey was cold and solemn, but the closer we got to the caravan the less I thought about Evan and the more my heart quickened for Julie. Why hadn't they taken her to Mawson? At last, we jarred to a halt outside the tiny refuge. I leapt from the vehicle, hurried on frozen stockinged feet through the open door.

"John! Thank God! We thought…"

"How's Julie, Des? Why is she still here?"

"Sit down, John, let me explain." As he poured some coffee and handed me a mugful, I stood before my fiancée. She was in the shadows of the bunk, laying close against 'Pig-Pen' for warmth. Her face was thin and white; her eyes still closed as when we left her. I kissed her cold lips, stroked her unkempt yellow hair. While Dave enlightened the others about the Portuguese, I fought with the mists clouding my eyes.

"Jules," I whispered. "You'll soon be all right again my darling, we'll soon have you well again." Then I spun around angrily to confront Neil. "Why the hell…"

The doctor stopped my intended onslaught. "We couldn't move her on a sledge, John. The journey would be too cold and rough. We've radio'd for another Snowtrac — it should be here shortly."

"But what are you doing to help her? You brought a whole stack of medical equipment. Why are you both just sitting there, drinking coffee?"

"You haven't noticed yet, but it's freezing in here. We have only a small camp stove. The IV solutions we brought have thickened and breathing cold bottled oxygen into her lungs would be worse than having none at all. As you know, we brought lots of Propane and kerosene on the Snowtrac, but it seems you found another use for it!"

Dr Des continued. "According to Dr Jackson's notes — Evan if you prefer — he had your fiancée on antibiotics and vitamin tablets, and kept her warm with his own body heat when their fuel supplies became exhausted. I've given her some medication and a taste of thin soup, but until we can warm the caravan, it is best to keep her lightly sedated."

"Here comes the Snowtrac now," announced Neil. "There's plenty of Propane and kerosene aboard. Don't worry, we'll soon have Julie warm and comfortable for the night."

"*For the night*? What do you mean? We've got to get her to the hospital immediately!"

"It will be dark in a few minutes, John."

"And then it will be another eighteen hours before it's light again. We can't wait that long — we must leave now!"

"Sorry, mate. If it were a straight run to Mawson, we might manage it in the dark, but winding between those islands and 'bergs would be very dangerous and time consuming. Much better to let Julie rest here until daylight."

I thumped my fist on the table. There *had* to be a way. But then the Snowtrac pulled up outside and everyone rose to greet Brian and Jovan. I grabbed the doctor's arm before he could join them. "Give me the truth, Des. Julie's gravely ill, isn't she?"

He nodded and placed a hand on my shoulder. "She's extremely weak. The scurvy, and her ordeal since your shipwreck, has severely taken its toll. Yes, she's gravely ill, but we'll do all we can for her."

God! At that instant I too seemed to die. "But... but if we could get her straight into your hospital, couldn't you... couldn't we, do something? Wouldn't she stand a better chance?"

"Undoubtedly. But be realistic, John. it will be dark soon. We would surely miss our way and end up in severe trouble. Believe me, we have to wait."

Then I pulled the O.I.C. aside. "How many flares have you at the station, Neil?"

"Crates of them, why?"

"And we have another Snowtrac and two more Skidoos?"

"Yes, but... what are you driving at, John."

"Just this. Julie might die if we don't get her to hospital immediately. Call up your chief mechanic, instruct him to issue flares to every man left at the station, then get everyone aboard the vehicles and sledges and head this way. Have him drop one man off every kilometre along the route. If we leave now, we'll sight their first flare soon after dark and be able to follow them back to Mawson."

Neil stared at me as though looking at a maniac. It was clear what he was thinking. All I could do now was to go to Julie and pray that she survived the night. But then the O.I.C. surprised me. He gave an order that astounded everybody. "Get the girl aboard the Snowtrac, fellows, toss in some sleeping bags, we're leaving immediately." He then dived into the Snowtrac to use the radio.

We were away in four minutes. Julie was well wrapped and placed atop two mattresses on the vehicle's floor. Neil drove, I sat on the bench seats next to the doctor. The other men rode on the Skidoo and sledge. It was a tremendous relief to be doing something at last to help Julie.

Auster Island disappeared from view as the gloom of twilight dulled the ice and merged the surrounding icebergs into the darkening sky. Neil then swung the vehicle to the south-west, reversing this morning's shorter route to the Paterson Islands.

"Hold these bottles in front of the heater," the doctor instructed me. "While I organise the rest of my gear."

It was soon warm and comfortable in the cab, allowing my hopes to climb even higher for Julie. "Hang on Jules, darling," I whispered. "We'll make it this time; this time we'll make it for sure."

When the IV solution reached room temperature, I strapped the bottle firmly to the back of the seat and watched while Dr Des uncoiled a long tube and inserted the attached needle into Julie's arm.

"Enjoy it," he murmured. "It's probably the most nourishing food you've had in months." Then the oxygen bottle was connected to her mask and the flow commenced.

When I looked ahead again it was dark. "Where are we, Neil?" I asked while scrambling into the front seat next to him.

"About five kilometres from the Patersons."

The speedometer was registering thirty kilometres an hour. We should reach the islands in ten minutes if he maintained this speed. He fumbled for a switch on the dashboard that sent a brilliant beam of yellow light flooding over the ice to make the way ahead look as smooth as a concrete freeway, but with each of us clinging to the seats as we bounced over patches of *sastrugi*, this illusion was unconvincing.

"There's no radio in the other Snowtrac," Neil explained. "We can't make contact to see where they are."

"Then switch your lights back off for a minute," I requested, as I stood up with my head through the hatch. But even in the pitch darkness there was still no sign of any flares ahead. When back inside, I checked the compass and my watch. "We should be near the Islands now, mate. You had better swing due west."

Neil switched the lights back on and turned.

For another five minutes we raced over the snow with the tension inside us continuing to build. The O.I.C. reduced speed. I prayed a little. Where was Joan of Arc with her guiding light? Were we expecting too much of the others to be here so soon after the radio call? Could we have missed them? Will we reach Mawson tonight?

Again, I poked my head up through the hatch. Neil stopped the vehicle and turned off the lights. He handed me the binoculars, but even with these there was absolutely nothing visible. In the pitch darkness it was easy to imagine this as a dream, although one glance into the dimly lit cab at the motionless bundle on the floor soon revived in my mind the urgent reality of our mission.

Neil climbed onto the roof and set off a vivid red flare that spurted fire and sparks high into the air to dazzle our eyes and colour the ice in a crimson glow. When its intensity waned, when the last brilliant spark died, I again raised the binoculars — held my breath — held it for Julie.

"There!" I called. "Over there! A green flare to the left, thank God, a half kilometre to the left!" I sank back into the seat as Neil again sped off, closed my eyes, sucked in a lungful of fresh air. Now we were certain to make it.

The distant green glow gradually brightened until suddenly it was a spluttering shower of phosphorous sparks beside us. We stopped beside Ken's Skidoo and empty sledge.

"What kept you?" the chief mechanic joked. "There's too many spooks around here to be left standing alone!"

"My lift-off rockets failed," replied Neil. "Where to now?"

"Hold this course for half a kilometre, then Graham will light up for you."

We roared away with both Skidoos following behind and, sure enough, the next green flare soon glowed ahead in the distant blackness. If only Jules could awaken and share the excitement of these moments with us.

The journey now seemed like a night flight over landmarks lit with green beacons, or when the vehicle's lights were on, like flying over a solid pack of cirrus cloud. Occasionally the shadowy form of an island sped past to confirm our whereabouts, but mostly, distance was computed by checking off a kilometre every time a man was picked up to join the convoy.

With the journey almost over, my thoughts again turned to Evan, and my heart saddened with the great loss I had barely had time to contemplate. But then my attention bounced back to Julie, allowing my spirits to again rise as I began to dream about the future we planned together, and the happiness awaiting us in a distant warm country.

Another flare was tossed to the ice as we passed yet another patiently waiting man. Only a few more remained.

"Hold it, Neil!" called Dr Des unexpectedly. "Stop! Stop will you!"

We both spun around to see what the doctor wanted. The vehicle came to a halt.

"What is it, Des?" I asked, scrambling back beside him. He never answered. A sudden fear shivered through my body, drained the blood from my face. "She's all right, Julie's all right, isn't she?"

The doctor injected something into her arm. In the dim light her face was obscured. Then unexpectedly — God! No! — he began pushing, pumping his hands up and down on Julie's chest.

"Let me help, Doc! What is it, what's the matter?"

"Neil," he called. "Resuscitation, take over, out of the way, John."

The heart massage continued. The doctor prepared another syringe and injected the fluid. I couldn't believe what was happening! Julie was having a bad turn. We're only minutes from Mawson. Come on, darling, pull out of it. God, if only Des would say something, tell me what was wrong, let me help. That bundle on the floor was Julie — *my* Julie!

I pushed nervous fingers through my hair, rubbed trembling hands across my face. Help her God! Don't let her die! Not after all this, not after all her struggles. Let her see Vancouver again. Let her walk the green hills of Manning Park, the brown Fraser Canyon, the blue Rocky Mountains. Let her love the animals again, the wildflowers, pick blueberries, doze on the meadows in the warm sun. Let me take her back to all she loved, let me make her dreams come true. I love you, Jules. I love you so very much.

The oxygen flow was increased. Dr Des took over from Neil. I prayed — prayed more sincerely than ever before. Julie would be all right. God would know how young and beautiful and loving and kind she was. God would care for her. There was nothing to worry about.

The doctor stopped, used his stethoscope again, glanced up at me.

"Don't stop, Des. Keep going. She'll be all right soon. It's just a bad turn. Don't stop — please don't stop!"

But he did stop. Julie was dead!

I leapt from the Snowtrac and walked. It didn't matter where. Just on and on and on across the ice. The cruel ice. Into the blackness. Tears soaked my face. First Evan, now Julie. My best friend, then the girl I was to marry. Why? Why, why? Why hadn't we all died together in the *Evening Star*? Why had such impending agony been delayed so long? I fell to my knees and cried. Cried out in the darkness. Cried out every tear that was ever in my heart. Cried until a mask of ice sheathed my face. Cried until I rolled over and hoped I too would die.

Dave appeared beside me. He took my arm and helped me to my feet. He never spoke. Slowly we walked back to the pin-points of yellow light.

I went to Julie. Shone a light on her lovely face. Her eyes were closed as in a light sleep. Her lips were turned up slightly in the hint of a smile. Her hair still shone like threads of gold. A beautiful goddess. On her finger was an opal ring, a ring of love given to her a million years ago by someone in another world that truly loved her. I kissed her cold lips, ran my fingers through her silky hair as she liked me to, prayed that she would be happy on her new journey.

"Goodbye my darling Jules. God go with you for ever."

Another two flares were passed before a beam of light from Mawson's searchlight was sighted, piercing the black sky. We crept around a shadowy point to see a single electric light on the hill, then, as suddenly as if a slide projector had just been turned on, the whole station appeared before us. A blaze of warm yellow light reflected from the metal buildings and spread softly among the snowdrifts and out across the ice of the harbour.

We stopped in Market Square. We were at Mawson. The four of us were at long last at Mawson! I left the Snowtrac and stood in the shadows amongst a score of busy men as they organised and carried off their loads. What now? To my 'donga', and bed?

"John?" A voice, a woman's voice called softly beside me. I spun around. Julie? It was Betty. In my grief she had been forgotten. She fell into my arms. I held her silently for a full minute before pulling away to look deeply into her saddened face. She forced a smile.

"I know about Evan, John. They radioed. You don't have to talk about it now."

"And Julie?" I whispered.

Her lips parted. She stared at me and read my heart. "Oh no! Not Julie, too! Oh God, no!"

I pulled her tight against my chest, muffled the sobs that froze every passing man's soul. Let her cry for Julie when the tears hadn't yet dried for Evan. Let her cry until the sobs become far apart, let her cry until there were no more tears left. Evan and Julie were dead. Then we again looked into each other's eyes. She smiled again. God, she had guts!

We started to walk back to the surgery when I noticed her bad limp. Her feet seemed extremely painful. "Dr Des will be mad at me," she said softly. "I shouldn't be out of bed until more skin has grown on my toes." Brian came to our aid. We half carried her across the rock slabs and back to her bed. Then I left for the solitude of my quarters.

The following day I listened to the siren on three occasions for meals, and twice more for morning and afternoon 'chompers', but only once was I obliged to leave my bed for the next-door toilet. On returning, a meal was waiting on my table. Good old Mark! I ate it and slept through until ten a.m. the next day.

During the remainder of the morning, I talked with Neil in his office, filling in the many gaps relating to our lives, and the journey we had made over so many months from Vancouver. He shook his head in disbelief when told of the iceberg that had holed us, and of the struggle for survival in the pack-ice. But when I spoke of Scullin, and our attempts to reach Mawson via the plateau he was more understanding; he knew the ice well and understood the terror of the blizzard that had finally beaten us.

"You must write your adventure story," Neil said with his usual friendly grin. But I felt such a novel had already been written; that the adventures still so vivid in my mind were extracts from the chapters within. They didn't really happen. They were figments of someone's imagination. Yet when I glanced out of the window at the glistening ice and the heavily clad men, my thoughts reeled in conflict. I was pleased to leave Neil's office without having revealed anything about Ralph's diamonds. What diamonds at any rate? We hadn't seen any diamonds! Maybe these too were mere figments of my imagination.

Betty was waiting for me in the surgery. She was sitting up with an unopened book on her lap. "About time you visited your old mate," she said with a pretence of wrath. "Dr Des says I can get up anytime I wish, provided I don't go running off with the dogs like you did. Not today at any rate!"

I sat on her bed. There seemed so much to talk about, yet there was nothing we wanted to talk about. We understood each other's thoughts.

She placed her hand over mine. "We won't forget them, John. As long as we live, we'll always love Julie and Evan, and reserve a place in our hearts for them. We're sad now, but we're alive, so we have to heal our wounds and carry on."

I was looking at a very courageous woman. "Come on then. If the Doc says you can get up, then get up. The sky is clear outside and the bright lights of Mawson are beckoning. Let me show you around."

She dressed and pulled a large pair of plastic thermal boots over her bandaged feet, then walked slowly beside me out into the early afternoon light. The cold breeze blowing on our faces for once felt fresh and invigorating. There was no longer any urgency to do anything or go anywhere; it almost felt as though life was beginning again.

We looked into the carpenter's and electrician's workshops, then the biologist's lab, but for some reason Betty showed little interest in these; her thoughts seemed far away. I asked her where she would like to go next. She hesitated. "I… I want to climb the hill behind the station. Mawson Hill, I think they call it."

"Can you make it, Bette? It's quite steep."

"You help me. I promise you won't have to carry me again."

I grinned, but her face remained serious until our eyes met. Then her lips parted in a smile I'd not seen for a long time. It warmed me and turned my thoughts to spring in faraway places.

For a time, we dragged ourselves up the blizzard line behind the surveyor's hut, but when this swung right towards Cos-Ray we left it and continued upwards between huge granite boulders and over patches of frozen gravel to where the hill flattened and joined a snow slope that climbed even higher to blue fields of glaciated ice. Here we turned and instantly it seemed the whole of Antarctica lay beneath our feet.

Betty took my hand. "I want to remember this, John. All my life I want to remember the view from Mawson Hill."

"Why, Bette?"

She never answered. We gazed down over the bleak community of half buried huts to an array of orange vehicles parked on the brown rock-slabs below, then out across frozen Horseshoe Harbour to the endless pack-ice. Small islands, like blobs of paint dripped from an artist's brush, studded the dazzling white sea. As far as the horizon icebergs lay sleeping in the ice, waiting the summer thaw when they could resume their slow drift to warmer northern seas and their eventual destruction. Ice-cliffs, sheer and blue, snaked east and west of us, while behind rose the ever-mysterious Polar Plateau with its stark gathering of serrated mountains.

"Name the islands for me, John," Betty asked, after absorbing the cold bleak scenery around us.

I turned in the direction of Auster Island and pointed to a group of dark specks in the distance. "Those are the Paterson Islands, Bette."

She stared at them for a long time, then turned to smile at me. "Our first night out from the caravan, wasn't it? Remember the snow-covered plastic sheet we had over us? Remember celebrating what we thought would be our last night on the trail to Mawson?"

"There are no trails to Mawson, Bette. We learned that the hard way." I then pointed to a high rounded hill that was Welch Island.

The smile left her face. She was seeing the same picture as I: two lost people staggering like drunkards in the bitter cold and blackness of night trying desperately to stay alive.

She pointed to a larger island closer to the station. "That's Béchervaise Island, isn't it? Where you carried me, then dragged me across to West Arm. Why, John? Why didn't you just dump me in the snow? You could have made Mawson easily on your own."

This time it was I who remained silent. The reason was only now becoming clear.

As we returned to the station, Neil bounded from his office to intercept us. "You're in luck," he called. "The *Eastwind* is going to pick you up! They refused at first, but when we told the skipper that Betty was an American citizen, they changed their minds. So, my friends, you're going home."

"When?" I asked.

"Now. Perhaps within the hour. A helicopter will come for you. You never arrived with lots of suitcases, so packing won't be any problem."

I looked at Betty, she back at me. Was it possible? Within an hour! Suddenly I felt frightened of the other world awaiting us. I didn't want to go. But that was crazy. Already it was getting dark, perhaps they would wait until morning?

Ted joined us as we walked into the rec-room for afternoon 'chompers'. He had just run down from the radio shack. "They're already on their way," he told us between pants. "They say the weather's packing up out to sea, so they need to get in and out without delay. Guess where the chopper pilot is from, Betty?"

She looked at Ted and shrugged.

"From Oakland, California. Your hometown, isn't it? You'll be back there in no time."

"Home... town?" Betty's face never lit up as Ted expected. Instead, she turned to look at me with eyes that had quickly moistened.

The expedition men approached Betty and myself in small groups to wish us well and to entrust with us a multitude of precious letters to their loved ones back home. We could only begin to thank them for all they had done for us. I promised them all that we would meet up with each other again in Australia under more happy circumstances.

Betty looked at me inquiringly when we were alone for a moment.

"John," she said hesitantly. "You said... you said we would meet up with them in Australia. What... what did you mean?"

I smiled at her and took her hands. "You know what I mean, Bette. We're part of each other now. I'll never leave you again."

We stood in the dark by the helipad. The Mawson men had gathered around in a tight circle joking and listening to the portable radio as Ted and the helicopter pilot conversed. "ETA Mawson, five minutes," drawled the American flyer. "Hope ya got lotsa lights for us."

"Roger, Eastwind," replied Ted. "Our searchlight is on. We have ringed our helipad with red flares."

I shook hands with Dr Des and Neil, hugged my good friend Dave. Betty kissed with true sincerity every man on the station, then returned to tightly grasp my hand.

"Ya searchlight's visible now, Aussie. Sorry we can't stop for a beer. Stand-by for a quick turnabout."

The flares were ignited the moment the sound of chopper blades were heard, cutting the air. They sprayed fiery jets of red phosphorous sparks high into the darkness to bathe the rocks in dancing streams of crimson light.

Flashing red and green strobe-lights appeared above. A landing light switched on and centred over the pad to dazzle our eyes with its brilliance. The jet engine screamed. The massive shadow lowered itself gently between the spluttering circle of flares. We glanced around for the last time at our newly made friends. The aircraft door opened. A man leapt out and unfolded a small ladder.

"Go now," said Neil.

We pushed through the hands that touched our shoulders, climbed the ladder with the airman following behind, heard the door slam shut. The engine screamed to regain full power. Seat belts were fastened. We were airborne.

Through the window we again glimpsed our friends already far below. A circle of red bathed the rocks, a cluster of lights marked the station, a searchlight pierced the low cloud. Then everything suddenly disappeared. There was darkness over the ice.

THE END

www.ingramcontent.com/pod-product-compliance
Lightning Source LLC
Chambersburg PA
CBHW031957120726
47898CB00002BA/558